I0763331

THE SPERLING CHRONICLES

Books by K. Adrian Zonneville:

Novels;

American Stories

Carrie Come To Me Smiling

Great Things, A Novel

To Dance Among The Stars

To Sail The Barren Seas

Biographies/Memoirs:

Z; One Family's Journey from Immigration
through Poverty to the Fulfillment
of the Promise of America

A Life in The Wings; My Sixty Year
Love Affair with Rock and Roll: A Memoir

Children's Books:

Lost Dog Found

The Sperling Chronicles

How Fate and Fame Conspired to Ruin a Good Man's Life

K. Adrian Zonneville

Mumford House Publishing

ISBN 978-1-7344332-7-2
ISBN 13-978-1-7344332-7-2

First Printing, 2023

Dedication

This book is dedicated to those who play and create the music that is the soundtrack of our lives. And for sacrificing time, love, stability, to the belief that music heals, can help solve the problems and suffering of mankind, and bring some light, love, and joy into the darkness. To my parents for gifting me the love of the written word. To David Spero for believing in me. To those who have supported my meager efforts in writing. But mostly to my wife who has supported my dreams, my endeavors, my love of writing, performing, and the road. She has been my inspiration and one true love.

Acknowledgments

Without the support of those who believe, none of this is possible. To create, to fill a blank page with words, to find the melody and lyric out of silence, to paint the world as it is and as it should be, to capture that one perfect moment in a photograph, to inspire, to find the beauty in all things, these are the people who are the future and give hope. To my children, Kathryn and Adrienne, their significant others, Rich and Michael, and my brand-new eleven-year-old granddaughter, my Lexi, this book is for you and your future.

Cover art, design, and brilliance Janet Sipl

Edited by Linda Wike Calkins

To Tom Misuraca for playing golf so I could work

This is Important

Caution!!! For those of you about embark on this journey please understand this is a work of pure fiction, it is meant to be a humorous glimpse of the music biz and fame. The concept was suggested by my friend, David Spero, as a whacky look at his participation in the rock and roll game. Any of the characters or names you think you recognize are figments of my and your imagination. This is not meant to represent anyone in any way except as I see musicians and artists in my own little peanut brain. This is not a brilliant work of fiction such as Steinbeck, Hemingway, Tolstoy, Chekhov, or Sulu. It is a B Movie you sneak in to see with a twelve pack and a few friends at the local Drive-in. None of the events chronicled in this book happened outside my cranium, though...that doesn't mean they won't!

From The Mouths of Celestials

The sun was warm on their uncovered skin. It always was this close to it. The two minor deities let the warm rays wash over their naked bodies. They heard the sun chuckle as it gazed down on perfection.

They were bored. They had been for decades. Humanity had changed and, with them, so had the gods. For millennium it only affected the major gods. Zeus, Hades, Poseidon, Aphrodite, Odin, Frigg, and Thor had all faded with mankind's evolution and the rise of the Christian god. Power came from worship, there was a power outage when the worshipping came to an end. These two beauties had clung for longer than most, but their power was waning.

Fate for centuries, millennium, controlled human destinies. She had feared when the Christian god came along, he would usurp her, yet humans immediately believed he controlled their destiny and that belief was all she needed to keep trucking along. Belief that they had no influence over their own lives was all that mattered in the scheme of things. Fate wins. No matter what religion claimed the game, she would get the fame.

Ah, Fame, fickle as ever, she had not believed anyone could take her place. Humans had worshipped her since they crawled out of the cesspool. It was what they all clamored for, either through glory in war, glory in love and sex, glory in creation and invention, glory in words, it mattered not. Mankind craved fame more than he craved air or sustenance.

Until the last half century or so where everyone, it seemed, was famous. And with the invention of this interwebby thing you didn't have to actually do anything to be famous. You didn't need talent, intelligence, courage, or strength of character or soul. In fact, it served you better to be devoid of all those qualities.

One would think that with all the fame going around Fame would be the most powerful of all the gods. She was not. She was spread too thin. Her power increased when she could concentrate it on a few. What is fame when so many possess it? Hell, she couldn't even count on a good old-fashioned war anymore. No one fought for glory, so their names would be whispered throughout the ages. Where were the Odysseus's, the Caesars, the Napoleons? Who sailed into danger and certain death so their name would live for thousands of years like Achilles or Icarus? No one. They sang silly songs or pretended they had wisdom through their tockery. They called themselves influencers. Yet all they influenced were the weak, they did not inspire. Their immortality would not be thousands of years or a century. Maybe a decade, hell, a year, month, weekend, or nanosecond. They were the blink of an eye. How could Fame survive such?

So, Fate and Fame dipped their perfect fingers into the reflecting pool and watched as mankind tried to make himself important to others yet only made himself look silly.

It was then they both noticed, at the exact same moment, one who stuck out. Not because of his extraordinary good looks, his massive strength, talent, intellect, or plenitude. It was how ordinary he appeared. Actually, it was how he seemed to not attract attention to himself. He appeared to disenchant. Here was the one human being who not only did not desire fame but seemed diametrically opposed to it. They couldn't take their eyes off him.

Their perfect fingers swirled the pool so it would concentrate just on this one human. His life, his loves, where he came from and as Fate would have it, where he was going.

There was magic. Not powerful. He would never rule the world with it, though he helped many. He had a knack for music. Had since a young teen, interesting. An accident, something terrible they couldn't make out exactly what had happened, but it was there; and it had changed his life. For the better. They should inform Apollo; he would love to know about this man. But, nah, if he was paying attention he would have known since the child was born.

Fame noted that he worked closely with the famous and ne'er-do-well yet had no desire to be one of them. Just being a friend and helping them achieve was enough for him, but it was not good enough for these two bored young, compared to other gods, minor deities.

"He seems quite happy to be standing on the side of the stage of life," remarked Fate.

"That is because he has not tasted my rewards," implied Fame.

"Maybe not all want to taste what you set on the table," Fate replied with a faraway look in her eye.

"All humans desire me, whether they realize it or not," Fame dug her heels in.

"I would tread carefully," warned Fate, "sometimes what we think others desire is not what is best for them."

"Once he has a taste he will want more, it is human nature. Others will worship him and sing his name to the stars and he will crave the love and admiration," Fame had seen it happen a million times, it would happen again and the intensity of it would feed her need for power over mankind.

Yes, this insignificant mortal would taste the sweetness of Fame and he would, in turn, worship her every day. This boy was theirs and theirs alone. They required a diversion and Ian Patrick Sperling was about to fill that bill. Unbeknownst to Ian Patrick Sperling, he was about to become their pet project.

No Innocent Act Goes Unpunished

Testing! Testing! One, two, testing! Check! Check!

The background noise of preparation. Every band in every venue, large or small, began every night the same way. Before the first note was struck mics had to be tested to prove they worked. Soundcheck would soon ensue. The man who was too old to be in this club shook his head and tried to block it out, though he could tell the mids were too prevalent and the sound would tend towards mush. And the 'sound man' was making no discernable adjustments. It was not an auspicious beginning. Somebody needed to take out their ear buds and listen to the damn room.

He sipped the last of his diet cola and held up the glass so the bartender could put his phone down and refill the glass.

"You know you only get one refill for free, after that I gotta charge you," the young barkeep's attempt to sound empathic was lost in the lack of caring. His main concern was that this ancient guy at his bar was going to suck down free sodas all night and then leave him a quarter tip.

Shit, old guy didn't belong in here in the first place. Some Alzheimer patient who got lost on the way to the Mahjong tourney at the senior center. Another old man who'd wandered into the wrong club, sitting, drinking cheap sodas all night. Then he'd bitch the whole time about the music being too loud, the kids too rowdy and 'it wasn't like this when he was young', until you know who had to throw him out.

They played music here. Loud, angry, mosh pit stuff most of the time. What did father time think? He was going to sit there all night, turn off his hearing aids and hope to see some young titties as the kids slammed into each other. There were some nights when the young kid behind the bar just wanted to close early, go home, pet his cat, watch some mindless dribble on the tube, and drink himself to sleep. Tonight, was beginning to feel like one of those nights.

"Yeah, that's OK," said the guy old enough to be the founding father of the family of any the kids coming in the door. This sombitch had to be fifty! "I'm just here to hear the band. I'll pay the tab." He laughed at a private fifty-year-old memory of Tab and Jack and lost days and nights. He could afford a few diets, even at two-fifty a pop. And he chuckled out loud at the bad pun. Junior bartender just stared at him, ah well, so much for silent humor.

Kid was dismissive just like most he ran into these days at clubs. Guess they thought music was only for the young. No one under thirty ever considered the fact that those over thirty might have limboed under that prime number at some point in their lives.

"You know the band?" Which, had grandfather Chronos replied in the affirmative, would have been weird, considering the tender himself hadn't. And he considered himself pretty hip to the local scene and all the new artists coming up. This guy had to be a relative. "What kind of shit do they do?" He raised his voice over the screech of a guitar feeding back and the drummer banging on the skins to get a level. Soundcheck was now firmly engaged. "I'm not familiar with this outfit." He admitted with a dash of respect for the elderly if this guy actually knew this band.

"Not sure. They were recommended to me by a friend of a friend, so thought I would come down and check them out while I'm in town," he sipped the diet, not really wishing for mindless conversation just a couple tunes and be on his way.

"Must be either a good friend or someone who doesn't care about your hearing," the barkeep tried to be cute or funny. He was neither.

"She had a pretty face and a nice set," ancient grinned dismissively, " and real good taste in bands."

The place was filling quickly with youth. This dive had a reputation for new bands, up and comers and the kids—yeah, old man, kids—

around here still wanted something new and about to break. So, a new act with a bit of buzz would bring them in for the novelty. If the band sucked or were some kind of tribute bullshit, the true music fans would migrate to another joint. No harm, no foul, no cover.

The young voices coming in crowded around music history—though they wouldn't have known this old man or what he'd done—and screamed their orders into his ear hoping the bartender would catch them coming out the other side. They bumped into him as others crowded the tight spot, pushing against him with only a couple of the kiddies mumbling weak apologies. Young almost men trying to buy young almost women drinks to impress them while the young almost women tried to ignore the proposals of trade.

The voices, screeches of laughter and excitement of the young women surrounding him rode frequencies only dogs and young boys could hear. And, unfortunately, one old man sitting, sipping a diet cola at the bar. If there was one thing that had kept him on the straight and narrow path of fidelity all his life, it was those piercing screams that emanated from the depths of the late teen early twenties tight bodies of women. Thank the gods, females grew out of that screech. Well, the band should start soon and if Buddha loved him, they would drown out the piercing cry of the post pubescent girls.

He had been coming to these joints for the past half century. It was the music, not the tail, that drove him in. He loved music. He breathed music. A lyric that made you want to stop the world to hear it one more time. A riff or chord change so sweet it made that lyric want to snuggle up and make love to it. A fit so perfect it brought chills to the heart. It didn't happen often but when it did, you could cum. He dreamed arrangements, horns, strings, power chords and pure vocals.

He had to laugh at how ludicrous that was. He couldn't read a note of music, write it, play any instrument—oh, a couple chords on guitar he'd learned back in the late sixties-early seventies to impress young girls— he could barely hum a tune, but he could feel it. Down to his soul and in his head. Something clicked when he heard the right combination of lyric, melody, and arrangement. The touch of finger on keyboard, the lead that just fit the song. No, he couldn't read music but he could feel it flow through his body and mind. He wasn't a guy who could take a band from the ground to the stratosphere but he could help move them a few steps closer. He could get them to the next level where someone with more juice could take them higher. He was the guy bands came to when they'd been around a while, to help them maintain the high quality that got them noticed in the first place and could keep them at the top. It was what he did, who he was.

He wasn't 'the guy' that made stars, he was 'the guy' who knew why they were stars. And he'd lucked into making a living doing what he loved because he didn't know any better. He hadn't studied business or the industry or what made things tick, he just knew. He felt it, heard it, knew it. And that ticked off many of the powerful because they thought he was holding out some secret from them. That he knew some formula, some way to mix and match sounds. They could learn it, if only he would share it.

So, they fucked with him. Oh, they'd put his bands on the big stages or tours as the second or third act like they were doing him a favor. They'd throw him an old chewed up bone and then they'd take the bulk of the gate. He made a nice living in spite of it all, and he pissed off the supposed holy music mavens to hell and back. And that made him smile. They never realized he was just too dumb, too naïve, with balls as big as his lack of knowledge, to fail. And the best part was, they needed him, he filled a niche no one else could. They didn't have the knack, that little bit of magic. That was the formula he couldn't share. It was innate, in his DNA and soul, somehow, he just knew.

He grinned. That was the great secret, there was no secret. He had no secret power, no secret recipe, no secret. He was honest. Simple. Oh, he could hear things no one else did, he never kidded himself, but he was honest to a fault. He couldn't lie to an artist. He couldn't tell them he loved a song or the production, if he didn't. He would tell them exactly what he thought. He wasn't an ass about it, he didn't beat them over the head or degrade their work. He gently told them what it needed to be better. Even if that was throwing it away and starting over. Not every song was a hit. Not every band was comprised of superstars. Not everyone wanted that. And most didn't want to hear truth. He told them the truth and let them decide what they wanted from there.

Many times, that was to go with the producer, manager or company that promised them the most. Smoke feels like silk when it is being gently blown up your ass. He didn't care. It's not that he didn't want to work with big time stars, the top of the pops, but sometimes working with a band on the way up or helping them to land gently on the way down was much more satisfying. They appreciated the kindness more than the coke.

He sipped his diet cola, the only coke he now preferred, having almost killed his career, his relationships, himself with the other. He was known for being clean and sober! Well, a little pot to take the edge off life, but that didn't really count.

He took a peek at his watch. Hmm, looked like the band was going to go on late. One of his great pet peeves in the industry was tardiness by an act. They didn't go to work until eight or ten at night, they ought to have the ability to start work on time. The crowd was here, and a crowd it was. These folks had shown up to hear someone on a rumor. If you want to impress a new crowd, start on time!

He raised his glass one more time to catch the roving eye of the innkeeper and gave the international sign of pretending to scribble for the check. The bar was getting too crowded for his comfort. He was used to being backstage. Of course, in a joint like this backstage was an alley where the band could smoke a couple joints before entering the joint to entertain.

As the bartender pretended not to see his raised glass, he caught his reflection in the mirror. A middle to late aged guy with close cropped white hair combed to the back—though it really didn't need help finding the back of his head, it was headed in that direction anyway. He'd cut the ponytail off years ago when he realized how ridiculous it looked on his ancient head. He wasn't twenty-one and should not attempt to pretend. Not overweight but a couple pounds shed wouldn't hurt, though that would mean giving up the fries and sides, not something he was willing to do just to pretend he was in shape. His wife accepted the little paunch and so should he. He liked the new glasses, they made him look learned, whatever the fuck that meant.

Then something caught his eye.

The young kid in the long, wool coat just entering the door and ignoring the doorman's attempt to catch him while others poured in. There wasn't a cover, but I.D.'s would be checked and this kid, apparently, didn't think that applied to him. But there was more, for one it was about eighty degrees out, this being Miami and all, and he was wearing a long, wool coat, and something more odd, something not right about the kid's face. His blank expression, as if he was the only one in the world. His right hand in his pocket while the left held the front of the coat together. And then he was bumped from the side and the front of the coat opened.

From somewhere next to him a woman screamed, "He's got a gun!" And people reacted badly, pushing, shoving, saving their own skin rather than attempt any kind of purposeless pluck and heroism.

The concept of herd mentality kicked in hard, every man for himself seemed to reverberate through each bone and sinew in his ancient body. It was time to make scarce. Not that he was a coward, but he wasn't a hero, that was not part of his DNA. He instantly recollected he'd never completed his self-defense courses, really never got past the white belt or cowering stage, didn't own or have knowledge of guns—though he could see the one the kid had was quite large and long and being brought up from the prone position.

Putting both hands on the bar to, hopefully, ease himself back enough to slip out behind the action, he pushed. Apparently, adrenaline is a powerful drug giving one the strength of ten, if not the courage, and he pushed with more force than he intended. The back legs of the barstool caught on a crack in the floor causing the stool to flip, complete with occupant, directly at the assumed assailant just as his finger found the trigger. One shot went into the ceiling just as Ian Patrick Sperling landed on top of the shooter in a ball of confusion.

What the fuck had just happened. Ian turned his head to look into the glazed and glassy eyes of the former implicit mass murderer. He jumped off the rumpled form inadvertently kicking the long gun—he had no idea what the hell it was—away from the unconscious fingers.

People began slapping him on the back, young girls kissed him almost everywhere they could find, crying and thanking him for such bravery. He was a Hero, they all proclaimed. And he was having trouble breathing. He was pretty sure he was having a panic attack right in front of his now adoring fans. Somebody handed him something to drink, the bartender smiled. Ian chugged and began coughing and spitting at the same time. This fuck had given an alcoholic bourbon. Didn't he know? No, of course, not, how could he? He pushed the glass up on the bar and asked for a diet cola, please.

The rest was, as they say, a complete blur. There were police everywhere. Then reporters, television, CNN, FOX—fuck them—though he did not speak the words out loud. The cops wanted to know what happened and every single idiot in the place pointed to Ian and told how he had jumped from his stool when he saw the rifle and saved hundreds of young people out for an evening. Even the fucking bartender confirmed the story. The reporters and talking heads picked up this obviously, to Ian at least, fabricated story and ran full tilt boogie with it.

Ian tried to explain he wasn't a hero; he was trying to escape with the rest of the sheep and tripped. He fell on the fucker, he didn't tackle anybody, he fell backward. He was just as big of a jellyfish and wimp as the rest. That's the true story. He had to tell the truth.

But that's not what the public wanted, they assured him. He had done something heroic; he had saved many lives. That was the story. That was the headline. He would be celebrated and loved throughout all of civilization. He had taken down a ruthless killer, a man armed to the teeth (apparently the kid had other weapons besides the rifle) all with no weapon of his own. The bravery! The courage! His fearless act would inspire the nation. He was the all-American heart throb, Captain America, if you will, exactly who he didn't want to be.

And a liar. Well, he wasn't a liar but they wanted him to be. And he could only tell truth. Though when he tried to tell the police and the reporters and the kids at the bar, they thought he was being humble, which only magnified all he was and had done. But it wasn't true. And he had to be honest or he might lose his knack, his magic, his music. And that was what he cared about.

He was the guy behind the scenes. One of the nameless, faceless folks that ran the music industry. He didn't want to be the lead singer, the blazing, brilliant guitarist, the sex symbol—OK maybe a little but he had a wife fer Christsakes! –he was happy with his life. He didn't have to appear on the front cover of Rolling Stone, he didn't even have a subscription!

Now he, literally, fell into something he loathed. Not for others just himself. Fuck! He had to put a stop to this before it got completely out of hand.

The phone in his pocket was ringing before the hotel room door closed behind him. Shit, it had been ringing all the way back but he had refused to answer. He just couldn't, the whole thing was too preposterous, too Hollywood, too not him. He glanced at the screen, damn, it was his wife. Her fourth call.

"Hello," he couldn't keep the frustration and weary out of his voice. He hadn't even tried.

"Are you out of your ever-lovin' fucking mind?" At least she didn't scream, she just sounded confused and relieved and on the edge of tears. He could almost hear her pulling at her short locks of hair. Scrubbing her head as if the lack of hair length made her head itch.

"I was trying to get out of the damn place," he said it almost by rote, he had said it so many times earlier, maybe, he couldn't remember, "I'm not a hero, I'm just a coward who fell over the wrong guy."

"Of course, you are. That's why I love you. I knew in my heart you couldn't be so stupid as to be a hero. My man would run like a scalded kitten. Screaming like a three-year-old and crying for his mother," she sighed.

"Thanks, Hon." God, he loved her. Only she could right the ship. She understood him better than anyone, she had shared his life, his dreams, his fears, his inner most weirdness for almost forty years. She knew, he didn't have to expound on his craven impulses, she knew in her heart he was no hero. Oh, she loved him, she loved his honesty, his loyalty and devotion to all those around him. She loved his love of music and his artists but mostly she loved his simplicity of soul.

"Are you alright?" Of course, she would ask that, she could hear the panic in his voice.

"Yeah, I'm at the hotel. It's quiet. I'm going to smoke a joint and try to sleep, then I'm coming home." He took a deep breath attempting to slow his heart rate and the blood racing through his terrified veins. "It's just..."

"You're afraid." She said simply and he nodded his head without realizing. "You're afraid of losing your anonymity. Your invisibility. It's fine for your artists to be bothered by fans while trying to grab a sandwich, a beer, or a young girl, but you would prefer to have peace." She knew him better than he knew himself. She was the perfect woman.

"I need the peace to think, to hear, to listen, evaluate and quantify what I've heard, not have the press and every late-night TV personality busting down my door and ringing me every five minutes. I can't have this constant sensory bombardment. Right now, I need to put something on my headsets that blows my mind, smoke a joint and ruminate," he took a tightly rolled stick out of his faux prescription bottle and opened the sliding glass patio door. This was a non-smoking hotel room and that meant it was an extremely non-joint puffing palace. He didn't mind, he enjoyed standing on the balcony of hotel rooms staring at the night sky while enjoying a few puffs. She waited on the other end of the ether, her own pipe glowing red as she inhaled.

She coughed out the nice hit as the roar of humanity screamed over the speaker of the cell, immediately followed by his cries of, "Oh shit, Oh Christ, Oh fuck, fuck, fuck!" and his own coughing out of an apparent deep inhale.

"What happened?" Fear and concern collided in a screech. He went silent. "Ian! Ian! What the fuck just happened?"

The coughing fit continued for several seconds before his voice returned. "There's a thousand assholes standing outside my window with signs, placards, and noise makers screaming they love me. One woman displayed her ample breasts so I would know how much she appreciated me. I need a higher room or a higher me in the room." He attempted a laugh but only coughed harder.

"And how much did she appreciate you?" Fear and concern now replaced by righteous indignation.

"On a scale of one to whatever, I'm guessing a thirty-eight. And either well-kept or modified," he coughed into the phone. "Shit! And that was a really good hit. What the absolute fuck? This has got to stop; I can't live like this. A man can't light up on the privacy of his own balcony without being assaulted by idiots!" His nerves were frayed by the events of the evening, his tone one of resignation, almost to the point of tears. He just did not need this shit!

"Did you explain to the police, the news people, everyone what actually happened?" She tried distraction.

"No, of course not, I embellished the whole thing with me finally standing on the perp's chest like a conquering hero so all could worship the impressive manly man." He sighed and took a toke while the crowd roared its approval. "Yes, I told the police, the newspapers, the television talking empty heads, everyone who wouldn't listen! I told them all and they didn't listen. They have their own agenda, they needed a good news story, preferably one with an unassuming, humble hero. Enter moi, and they don't give one rats ass about the truth. They make it up and you are expected to live with it," now he did weep. He had lost all hope of retrieving his life. She heard him strike a match and inhale. Apparently, he had decided if the non-smoking rule was to apply then the hotel should clear the voyeurs from the lot.

"That's going to cost you," she quietly chastised, though just.

"Fuck 'em. They can take the cash out of my hero's account."

"Do you have a hero's account?" She didn't know but thought it might be possible.

"No! I was being facetious!" Chagrin made his weeping stop and his irritation blossom.

"Well, I didn't know! Sometimes people set up accounts for people like you who save the fucking world!" OK, maybe there was a bit of irritant in the pot or the phone line.

"Look, I'm sorry, it's been a rough day. I just want to come home and hide from the world for a few decades until this passes over," the sigh that followed broke her heart. It was the saddest thing she had ever heard.

"Can you get a flight out tonight?"

"I might be able to book it but whether I can fight my way through the adoring knuckleheads below is another story. And what if there is a mass of humanity waiting for me at the airport?" Visions of the supergroup and teen heartthrobs, the Mersea Beats from back in the Sixties, fighting their way through the adoring hordes while people ripped and pulled at hair, jackets, and pants caused him to shiver.

"Well, no one is expecting you until tomorrow. maybe, just maybe, you can get some sunglasses and a hat..."

"Oh yeah, that always fools the paparazzi and the fans. Did you really think no one recognized Superman just because he put on a pair of glasses?" But he knew it was the only possible course of action. He would have to ty to come up with some kind of costume and a way to sneak out of the hotel unnoticed, then make his way over to the airport, wait to board, hunker down at the gate, and pray no one recognized him. Home was only a miracle away.

K. Adrian Zonneville

Giving The Bird With One Hand and An Ugly Shirt

He needed a disguise, something no one would imagine as him. He had never been well-known, he was the guy behind the talent not the talent, and that was the way he liked it. That had changed in the few seconds it takes to, literally, fall into a bucket of shit. Now his picture had been splashed all over every paper, television news report, and post office within fifty miles of humanity. What to do? Wasn't there a tourist shop in the lobby of the hotel?

The phone rang once, twice, four times, eight times, thirteen times before the sleepy clerk picked up the other end. "Hotel Ingringo," he slurred out the wrong name in heavily accented English, though from what Ian had seen it was exactly the right one, if by mistake.

"What time does the crap shop close in the lobby," he made his voice gruff so the guy would never know who this was.

"It's open all night, Mr. Sperling." Shit, Ian had forgotten, of course the room number would show up on the front desk phone.

"Thanks." He'd wait until around three in the morning when all the world, and especially the idiots and idol worshippers out front, were asleep. They had some tackey hats and sunglasses in the shop he'd noticed, so gaudy you couldn't miss them with your eyes closed. He'd grab one of each and no one would ever know the guy in the shitty outfit was him. He'd read in some magazine that the best way to be ignored by people was to try and force their attention on you. At three a.m. he bought a bass fishing hat made of Styrofoam and netting, it was bright orange, and green plastic framed sunglasses. That should do the trick.

Back in the room he tried to pick out clothes that wouldn't give him away, nothing that would scream music. It was surprising that he'd never noticed that every item of clothing he owned either had the name of a band or a venue boldly emblazoned on the front, back, and sleeves. Had he never bought an article of clothing in an actual store? Shit! Back down to the shit shop, there were some really ugly t-shirts down there. Christ, this escapade was going to cost him a fortune, and he probably couldn't even write it off as a legit expense.

He found three that were hideous. One, a powder blue with the state of Florida emblazoned on the front, and the back said something like, "If found return to Margaritaville!". A white, long-sleeved T with fish copulating on it. Well, that should avert the eyes of parents, and a rakish pink one with rainbows of every shape and size all over it, that should take care of the locals down here. Now, to see if he could change his flight. He would tell them there was an emergency at home and he needed the next flight out. Hell, he'd call them on the way to the airport. It would distract him during the forty-minute drive.

There was no one at the car rental kiosk just a box to drop your keys. Perfect! And he still had thirty minutes to make his flight. With no bags to check, just carry-on, and his global entry plus TSA Pre-check he should make the flight without any problem.

For it being four in the frigging morning the airport looked like rush hour in Seattle. What in the hell were all these people doing up at this time of day? They should be sleeping. Nope, they were bright eyed and bushytailed heading either home, the beach, or out to see the Mouse, there was nothing else to do in this state.

It took almost half a second before someone recognized him. Great, not only didn't the fucking disguise work but now people would think he actually dressed this way. The next thing he knew he was surrounded by adoring masses of humanity wanting to touch him. He got to the gate just as they were closing the door. At least he was in first class.

It's not that he didn't like people, they had their place, like filling seats at a concert or buying albums, but he just didn't like humanity. A few people as friends or to do business with were just fine, but when you put people with other people on top of more people, they became humanity. And seldom was humanity humane. Humanity became mobs with the drop of an innuendo or the whiff of weakness. He settled into the first-class seat, pulled the bass down over his eyes, propped the 'Do Not Disturb/No Moleste' sign he'd stolen from a hotel a decade or so back, on his lap, and tried to fall asleep to dream of his wife and peace.

The dream came in technicolor for his pleasure and enjoyment. Well, his and the other two pair of eyes that viewed from the sidelines. If he was going to dream a "This Is Your Life', Fame and Fate would not be denied a seat.

He was about fifteen going on thirty-five at a high school dance. They had a live band playing the psychedelic rock hits of the day while pubescent teens attempted to find a beat to dance to. If you were tripping this was the perfect scenario. It was awful. Not necessarily the band itself, but the sound.

They played in the school gym with the sound bouncing in every direction and the sound guy was laying on reverb he desperately needed to lose. The guitar was lost with the reverberating bass and the drums were pounding so hard he thought he might be having a heart attack.

Ian had never played in a band, studied music or attempted an instrument, to his memory. Which, truth be told, was not complete. He couldn't remember anything from twelve to last year and his formative years were puzzle pieces of bad sports, bad recitals from other members of the family, bad family vacations, and other familial gatherings best forgotten. Yet he understood music. And this was bad.

He cautiously stepped up to the sound guy and tapped him on the shoulder. The long haired, pimpled junior swung around angrily and stared Ian in the eyes, daring him to say anything. Ian didn't know that, so he said something.

"The drums are too loud and the mids are killing any dynamics. Pull down the reverb, you don't need it here, it's nothing but an echo chamber." And walked away. Sometimes all you could do was mention the problem and hope the person in charge would take care of it.

Instead, the person in charge had chased after Ian and now stood, towering over the young teen, then crouched down and screamed in Ian's face, "If you think you can do better then go ahead, otherwise leave me the fuck alone!"

Ian was inexperienced when dealing with drugged up, paranoid, delusional sound men so he sat in the vacated chair and studied the board, as it was. It was simple enough, he pulled down the mics surrounding the drums, killed the reverb, balanced the guitar with the bass and finally EQ'd the whole mess as one. It wasn't perfect but it was listenable.

Ian stood up, nodded his head, held out his hand, shook the hand of the stunned sound guy and walked away. His work was done.

Fame looked over to Fate and they both smiled. Where had this project been?

The lovely middle-aged woman pulled up to the Arrival doors and looked for his familiar slumped shape. There weren't very many people picking up this time of morning. He would see her and wave and she could pull right up to him so he could slide into the passenger seat. She heard the disturbance before she saw the scrum. Something was happening right by the exit door. And then, like the parting of the Red Sea, or a mother giving birth, he popped out of the horde almost falling on the sidewalk before he righted himself and saw her. He was completely disheveled and looked much the worse for wear. She reached across and opened the door before the car came to a complete stop, allowing him to roll into the vehicle as it accelerated away from the mob.

"Popular?" She knew she shouldn't, but sometimes you just couldn't help yourself.

He glared. "Just take me home."

"Sorry," she rubbed his leg in apology.

"People are disgusting!" he began as he sank into the passenger seat. "They attack from every direction and try to touch you, kiss you, hug you, and they all smell."

"Not a bather in the bunch?" She tried, again, to lighten the load.

"Some, but they reek of alcohol, perfumes that would make a buzzard wretch, food of every ethnicity and potency, and they slobber while they talk. I am going to have to throw everything I have on away.

And I only wore it once!" The waste of hard-earned cash was chaffing him worse than the too tight fish copulating tee.

She chanced a glance over at the ensemble and thought, 'Thank God!' She didn't know where or why he bought that horrid outfit but she would've thrown it away, maybe burned it first, whether it was soaked in the unwashed masses or not. Jeez, what was he thinking?

He saw her face, "It was supposed to be a disguise, your idea, remember?" he answered her inner horror. "I thought no one would recognize me in this. That the sheer ghastliness would make people recoil in disgust, but it drew them to me like a moth to a flame!"

"A very ugly flame," she thought, though, apparently, spoke the words aloud.

"I couldn't get through the airport, they mobbed me. I had to figure a way to get them to move away, just so I could walk," he sounded distraught and exhausted.

"Well, you made it out, what did you do?" Might as well bleed the wound until the flow was clean.

"Remember when I was touring with Joe and we had the same kind of problem getting him anywhere?"

She nodded.

"Well one time, he was so worn down from the travel and playing night after night, no sleep,"

"Well, that wasn't unusual," she chimed.

"Whatever. But he got real sick. Flulike, or heavy cold, and he was coughing and sneezing and hawking up loogies left and right. Christ, it was the most disgusting thing ever. Well, it kept every one of his fans, press, curious bystanders and, well, everyone at arm's length or, at least, out of loogie range." He giggled.

"You didn't!" she could see it clear as a bell.

"All over anyone who got close. I just kept a Kleenex in my hand and pretended to apologize. You know what I learned about sneezing, coughing and hawking shit up?" He smiled a beatific smile.

"Please do tell," knowing he was going to whether she gave him permission or not.

"It's like shooting someone when threatened by a large mob, you don't have to kill anyone in a large group of people, just wing a couple and the rest will stay away!"

He seemed so pleased with himself she had to pop this balloon before he decided this was a brilliant way to avoid humans. "You sneezed on people?" She couldn't keep the disgust out of her voice.

"Just a couple. The best was a couple kids, who had it coming anyway. You know children are germ factories put on Earth to infect as many of us as they can. They hope to kill off the elderly to make room for their grubby, sticky little selves." She could feel him giggling on her side of the car.

"You sneezed on kids." Now, she didn't even try to keep her revulsion out of the words.

"I just coughed on a few, but mostly the parents and others. I didn't loogie anybody," He said defensively. If innocence was what he endeavored to employ as his mainstay of defense, he was going to be convicted by every jury in the land.

She kept silent for the rest of the twenty-minute ride home. Yes, she loved him with all of her heart but sometimes she had to check the level to make sure she didn't need a fill-up. He was not normal, not like other men in the least, except being a four-year-old in a sixty-year-old body. She was pretty sure every man was a child when you scraped off the responsibilities. Happy wife...

The time of day and rush hour worked in their favor for once. Traffic was going into town; they were heading out. Ian slouched down in the passenger seat, Bass pulled down, and praying they made it home without incident. They were racing for the peace of home; the rest of humanity was heading to life. It was going to be photo finish to see if Ian and Maggie could reach the safety of home before the news of their arrival.

The sidewalks and tree lawn in front of their house were devoid of humanity, the entire side of the street was quiet. No walkers, no gawkers, no stalkers. Those who had to work were on their way. The welcoming committee consisted only of the sweet, lovely Rosalita, their petite terrier who could not have been happier to see her poppa and cared not a whit that he was a hero. He'd always been that to her.

And Ian could not have been happier to be greeted just for the love of the greeting. Rosalita never wanted anything from him but love, well, and snacks, cookies, and to be fed twice a day. Oh, and walks, she loved to go for walks. And belly rubs. OK, he served his purpose in this home but it was defined and he accepted his role. He was not a lifesaving, superstar hero here, just the guy that cleaned up poop.

Since it was early, early in the morning, around eight if the clocks were to be believed, they decided to go to bed and hope this all would blow over by the time they awoke. That was one thing you could count on about humanity, they had the attention span of a meth addict. Oh sure, if they were focused on the next bump, they were laser focused, but eating, bathing, paying rent or work, well, squirrel. They hoped by the time they roused themselves this afternoon all this would be behind them. The People would be focused on the newest distraction on the interweb. If mankind had shown any proclivity towards focus in the past, the invention of the web, tikkity tok, instagratification, and 'likes' had snuffed the inclination. Focus was not a modern matter.

Ian slept the sleep of the innocents. And would have continued through the day if the commotion and flashing lights had not woken him and Maggie both, before they found their way through R.E.M. They lived on a particularly sharp curve of a hill that people loved to miss and wind up wrapped around the tree on the tree lawn (now just memory, the tree not the tree lawn), the fire hydrant (number fifteen if memory served), or the fourth telephone pole, which had replaced the tree. So, seeing red and blue flashing lights reflected on the ceiling was not that uncommon.

Ian ventured a peek out the window and immediately cursed.

"What," she called drowsily from their king bed as she attempted to bury her head in the pillows.

"There have got to be a dozen of them out on the lawn!" He wanted to scream but feared drawing attention to his boxer bedecked body standing in the window.

"A dozen what," she asked, though was rapidly reaching a horrifying conclusion in her crystallizing brain.

"Cop cars," he slumped into the upholstered chair next to the window.

"Somebody hit the hydrant or the pole?" she could hope it was nothing out of the ordinary.

"Somebody plowed right into the center of my life!" He sounded so despondent she wanted to get up and just hug and rock him like a baby.

"What?" it was all she had.

"Some little fucker, whose momma didn't love him or whose girlfriend was boinking somebody else, or was told by some jock he was weird and a freak, got himself a gun, because that's what we do in America, and shot the shit out of my very happy life!" She now understood. Though he hadn't actually shot anybody or thing, Ian had fallen on him before that could happen, she could dig the metaphor.

Donning her robe, she made her way to the side of the window. Yup, there had to be a dozen cop cars, with more than twice that of cops, setting up barricades to keep the throng of humanity off their lawn. And their success rate would not make the record books. There had to be hundreds of people crowding onto the lawn, spilling over into the street, blocking traffic effectively in the downward flow. All with placards and handmade signs wishing to touch him, thank him, kiss him, have their fucking baby blessed by him, or to make a new one with him.

"Oh. My. God." Was all that squeaked out between her lips. All she could envision was a life spent hiding, running, avoiding, just to get something to eat or, god forbid, go to the bathroom. That was something she had never considered. Though Ian had worked with some of the biggest acts of the last half century, she never considered they couldn't go to the bathroom in peace. Oh. My. God, indeed! "How does anyone live like this? How do they survive? And why would you want to?" she murmured under her breath and couldn't help but think of so many of their friends who toured, played, wrote, were stars; they had to deal with this every single day.

Ian felt something else. The horror of the animal in the zoo while the masses hooted, hollered, threw peanuts and candy, and hung their children over the side of the moats for a better view. He now understood the way the ferocious would stare at the offered.

"It's simple, they aren't people anymore, they are the scrum of humanity. They have given their will over to the degradation of the mob, incited by the hysteria of the media, and now they want their ounce. They feel entitled to suck the marrow of each 'celebrity' because they went to a movie, bought a record, sat a hundred rows back from the stage at a concert." He shook his head in disgust, at them, at himself.

He had never been this way. He had never thought these thoughts. He had gone out of his way for years trying to improve some fans experience, he thought he owed it to them. Though now he was the recipient and he had no desire for the attention. "I think they just don't know what they're doing. They get caught up in the celebrity, the fame, the fantasy of being the person they love. It's like if they can just steal a piece of that person, some of his or her magic will rub off on them." He chuckled, "The funniest thing is, if they were to become famous like their idols, they would hate it. The loss of privacy, the sneaking in and out of back doors, people always trying to snap their picture at their most intimate moments. Who the fuck wants to live like that?"

"Your clients," she muttered, she thought, to herself.

"You'd be surprised how many of them are glad that aspect of their lives is gone. Now, the people who come to their shows are older, they aren't chasing anything except some memories. The fans purely want to say hi, say thank you for a life of great music, great times, and wonderful nostalgia. Memories they rest on, like a huge, comfy recliner as they while away their golden years.

"I remember years ago there was this stray cat that used to follow Jaxson to every town he played." He smiled at the recollection and his lifelong friendship with Jaxson. They had met in the very late sixties when Jax was first making noise on the music scene and Ian was the hip new kid on the hip new radio art form, FM. They had hit it off and became best friends immediately, all the while promising they would never work together, as it might end the friendship. The vow sacred and inviolate through a lifetime. He brushed away the quick retrospection returning to the story, "She was scraggly, a bean pole, her hair was mousy and, though I'm pretty sure she bathed and washed, her hair always looked like it would love to luxuriate in some shampoo. Her shoes didn't match, ever! She wore oversized second- or fourth-hand clothes and she LOVED Jaxson. She would rush the stage and I'd be waiting and gently try to throw her off. I'd block her from him—danced her off the stage one time— the next night she'd be back.

"Shit, I didn't work for Jaxson, I was just a friend acting as security for something to do while I hung around. I thought someday she'd get tired of chasing him.

"And then one day she did. She wasn't at the show in Albuquerque, nor Winslow, I thought for sure she'd be there! She was always at the western shows. Not in the Springs or Fort Collins. I guess it was close to two weeks before it really sank in. And it bothered me. Shit, she was almost part of the show. She'd come running and Jaxson would start laughing at me trying to catch her before she caught him. Keystone cops' kind of thing." He looked out the window as if half expecting her to be breaking through the police line and making a beeline for his door.

Maggie couldn't take it, fifteen, twenty seconds and the tension was killing her, "Well, what happened?" She'd wanted to scream but held her voice in control.

"It took some time but I found her outside of Chico. She'd had some bad luck, healthwise, the money she'd been traveling on, inherited from her folks, had been used up chasing Jaxson. She was living alone in a two-bedroom shanty just on the fringe of downtown. Not much, but it was paid for and she had food and some friends, other old hippies that were taking care of her. It was sad," He took a deep, steadying breath. "After years of chasing her dream and never catching it, she was alone. Saddest damn thing I ever ran across."

"What did you do?" She almost accused him without any shred of evidence, but she knew her man.

"Sent her a bouquet of flowers and with a note that said, 'sorry about your luck'," he shrugged and turned back to the window.

"Fuck you!" And she sat hard on the overstuffed chair.

He laughed, "What do you think I did. I flew out to LA, grabbed Jax out of his studio and said, 'we're going on a mission of mercy', and flew into Sacramento. We rented a car and drove up to spend the afternoon with her. Jax brought his guitar, he played some of the old songs for her, signed some stuff and gave her a kiss. It was lovely," he sighed, "She died the next year. I heard she was buried with all of his records."

She wiped the stray tear that had pushed itself over the lip of her lower eyelid.

"See, she was kinda crazy when she was in the mob, though never dangerous, some can be. But one on one she was just a kid with a crush. The most interesting thing was, she was actually quite shy. But that's what I'm talking about. Why you can't trust people!" He walked away from the window to sit on the bed where, hopefully no one could see him.

"But you work with a lot of people, are you saying you don't like them?" She was a bit on the confused side, a piece of flotsam caught in an eddy of a tumbling rapids.

"No, I love them. I know them, they are not people, they are friends. I know their kids, their kids' kids, their brothers, sisters, their closest friends, they are family. Even if in business we split up, we will always be friends. And they know that. They know I will help them even when we're not working together." He half-smiled his explanation of life.

"This though," he pointed at what should have been a beautiful, sunshine filled afternoon with them having nothing to do but kick back and enjoy each other's company, "is a horse of a different reality. And it isn't mine. We need to escape. I need someplace where I can concentrate and make some phone calls!"

The Trick is To Make Them See The Pony While You Ride The Scooter

Ian sat on the bed wracking his brain to devise a plan, to come up with the next move, any move he felt would force the world to swim around him. But as soon as a concrete idea came it would blow away like smoke in a hurricane. He couldn't seem to grasp any thought, or get a grip on reality, a problem he had suffered most of his life. This was different. His vision blurred and his head swam, his body felt like it was bloated and about to take flight. He knew Maggie was saying something to him but he couldn't quite grasp the words. Wow! Did he take too many gummies or was his blood sugar off? Or could it be he was finally having that heart attack he'd put off years ago.

He'd supposedly had a heart incident years back, as they called it then, but had narrowly avoided a major collision. That had been a close call. Too close, and all his own fault. The doctor told him not to go to Denver for a three-day outdoor concert at Red Rock but he had several acts on the bill and had to be there. Well, the thing was, he didn't 'have' have to be there, but he really wanted to be there. So, he convinced himself his presence was necessary, though someone could have easily filled in for him. Whatever.

Yeah, he'd had a little incident at an early morning meeting where he couldn't get his breath, his heart was pounding like the tolling of the bell of doom and he'd passed out. When he came to, he was in an emergency room with tubes coming in and out of every orifice of his body. Maggie was beside him. She was weeping and looked terrified, and the doctor looked concerned. He was saying something about surgery, blockages, sticking a tube up his inner thigh, and a week in the hospital. That would not do! He had shit to do. He just needed to rest for a day—he'd been pushing pretty hard for the last few weeks, he admitted reluctantly to himself—but let's not go overboard.

He promised all involved he'd take time off and get his health back as soon as the festival was over. Certainly, a three-day rock festival couldn't be that taxing. It was just hanging with friends, listening to music, and taking care of his acts. It wasn't like he was going to roadie or act as gaffer, running the truss. He was going to be backstage and relaxing. Yeah, that's what a manager does when he has a half dozen acts on a major outdoor festival, he relaxes because everything is going to be just peachy.

Well, he'd lived through it, though there were times he wasn't so sure he'd made the most intelligent decision. Ian had entered the hospital right off the plane, they had put in a stent or two, run the roto rooter through the rest and he'd been fine, just like he told them. Kind of, sort of, well not really. And now the bill was coming due.

At least he was home, on his own bed so death would be comfortable. He laughed. Imagine dying from the stress of being a goddamn hero and saving a bunch of lives, even though he didn't and wasn't. It was ludicrous. He wished Maggie would be quiet for a few seconds so he could die in peace. God, he was tired, if he could just get a fingernail, or toenail, on reality he knew he could get his shit together. What the hell was she asking, over and over? All craziness and psychedelia must cease, my wife wants to know something!

"...something," she certainly was insistent if not coherent.

"What?" not the most intelligent thing he would ever say but he was dying.

"When. Was. The. Last. Time. You. Ate?" You know, she really didn't have to speak to him like he was a three-year-old.

"Oh! Yesterday morning," he realized. He would be nicer to her if he lived through this.

"Get your coat we're going to Nick's!" She said as she grabbed him under the arm and lifted his carcass off the bed.

Nick's was a Jewish Deli just up the road from them that was their go-to place. It was a typical Jewish Deli, though larger than most, but still had the regular Jewish deli clientele. The average age was God's waiting room and the staff was loud and had been there since the beginning of time. Everybody knew everybody and it was boisterous; filled with laughter and friendship. The food was good, plentiful, and varied. Ian had been going there so long that he had three dishes named after him. They were family. And he was hungry.

"But how are we going to get the hell out of here. There's hundreds of them out there and only about a dozen cops!" In his weakened condition he knew he would only be fodder for the masses.

"I don't think they know you are actually here. I think they are expecting you on the plane you originally were supposed to come back on. They seem to be looking down the road as if expecting a sighting any minute. So, we'll go down to the garage, stuff you in the trunk so no one will see you, and I'll make the getaway!" Her evil grin did not reassure. Was she happy because she was going to outsmart the crowd or because she was going to 'stuff him in the trunk'?

"I'm not so sure about the trunk part..." he began nervously.

"Oh, c'mon, it'll be fun. Like we're in a movie and this is the part where the hero makes his getaway from the evil hordes of brain-dead zombies," again, he didn't care for the grin she wore, as if she was tricking him, not them. He had to wonder who was the evil one in this scenario. But they had been married for decades, he'd have to trust her.

"But isn't the hero supposed to fight his way through the mob with guns a-blazing, maniacally laughing while he mows them down knowing he is going to die?"

"We don't like guns, remember? That's what seems to have gotten us into this mess," She said matter-of-factly. He had to agree, though none of this was his fault, he was trying to be a good little coward and steal away into the night. It was the fucking bar stool's fault!

Maggie loved sports cars and that was what she drove. She'd picked him up the night before in his sedan but it was now in the drive, the sporty was in the garage. The trunk was going to be a very tight fit.

I was mid-afternoon as they pulled into the parking lot at Nick's. Her plan had worked flawlessly, though she'd had to sign a few autographs herself as the wife of America's newest hero, but it was painless. Now for a huge salad and diet cola.

Shit! She could see the crowd inside the door, milling about the lobby. What the absolute..."Hang on," she said closing the trunk lid, "I'll go get the birds eye lowdown on this caper." It was one of her favorite lines from Firesign Theater.

She pushed her way through the door, which, of course, the mass of humanity was crushed up against, pushed her way through the mass of humanity, and pushed her way into the restaurant proper. By the time she got through she was disheveled, had punched one groper—you can only be so antiviolence—was on the verge of tears from holding back her building indignation and wrath and just wanted to punch someone, anyone, but the first one she saw was Morrie. She couldn't punch Morrie; he was the sweetest man alive and the owner of Nick's. Don't ask. Besides he looked like he was just waiting for someone to start something so he could release what was boiling up inside him!

"The next time your husband," and Maggie had never heard Morrie refer to Ian as anything but Ian, "decides to save humanity and raise himself to Mr. Hero status tell him to call me so I can talk him out of it." He hugged her. "Or tell him to save a better class of humanity than young rock and rollers. These people got no money. They just block the people with money from giving it to me. Tap water, that's what they want. Tap water. I told them, we don't got tap water only bottled, they got to buy the bottled or get out." He sounded tired, frustrated, and broke.

"I'm so sorry, Morrie, but you know Ian didn't mean to save any -body but himself. He fell over the guy with the gun trying to save himself. He truly is a coward, not a hero, but nobody wants to hear that," she let her own exasperation carry the words.

Morrie smiled, "Now, that's my Ian. A man after my own heart. I knew, in my heart, I knew he was no hero. I said to my wife, Myrna, they got the wrong guy. I mean Ian will hold the door for old ladies and guys with walkers but he's not going to throw himself on some punk with a gun. I mean if trouble broke out here, Dave and Carmine would throw themselves on Ian to keep him safe. He is a good customer, a good man, but a hero, nah!"

"Well, right now he's a hungry coward locked in my trunk. Can we get to go?" She plead. "I could call the police while you make it, you know to clear a path." She nodded her head to the knot of human flesh blocking the paying public.

Ian had begun to protest as she closed the lid. The ride over had reinforced his forgotten claustrophobia. How in the hell had they forgotten that? It wasn't exactly a subject of everyday conversation but like all phobias it rested at the base of the brain just waiting for someone to whisper it was time to get up. This time the alarm had gone off and it had started awake, like a lightning strike immediately followed by a cacophonous thunderclap. It was awake and angry, as he bounced along the route from home to food the trunk closed in around him. Fuck!

So, when she opened the boot and he saw sunlight his mind screamed joy for freedom, only to be denied with a quick 'hang on' and some inane quote from Firesign. Shit! Even if he forgot his phobia in the insanity of their lives right now, she should have remembered. After all, when they had taken their first cruise together, they'd been given an inner cabin the size of a shoebox, size 6B, in a tight uncomfortable loafer, and he'd freaked. They were supposed to be cruising the romantic Caribbean and he was cruising a massive panic attack and about to jump ship. Certainly, she remembered that!

Now all he could do to keep his sanity was replay an outdoor concert with Joe and the band headlining a rock star studded day to over a hundred thousand. Ian standing in the wings, proud of his number one act and two supporting acts that were also his. It had been a banner day of great music, pride in his friends' accomplishments, and knowing he'd played a small role in getting them all here. The music in his head pounding on his skull kept the evil Claustrophobia away. But, for how long?

She unlocked the door, threw the bag with their salads, drinks, and accoutrements on the passenger seat before pulling the car around the back of Nick's and a hidden alley for deliveries. She popped the trunk, once again, and he jumped/fell out of the boot. She immediately realized how he had stopped the shooting at the club. He was a graceless klutz; it was one of the things that endeared him to her. And the fact he never tried to pretend to be anything more or less than what he was. He was uncoordinated, yet just so damn loveable. She helped him up and into the car. He, of course, sat on the bag with the vittles but luckily didn't crush anything essential; just his ego.

"What the fuck happened in there?" he asked as if nothing had happened in here.

"The Ian Sperling fan club was having a meeting and, though I'm quite certain they would have loved having the man of the hour pop in to say hello, I didn't think it a grand idea." She winked and smiled to take out any sting from the words. She had to try and keep his mood light. She knew his world had been turned upside down, so had hers, but for him this was disconcerting to the nth degree. She didn't need him freaking any more than he had. And she certainly didn't need him backsliding on decades of good behavior and climbing back in a bottle or a straw.

"This has gone far enough. We have to find a way to stop this and stop it now!" He took the small bag of fries out of the larger bag and began relentlessly shoving them in his mouth. Fuck the weight, he'd lose it when this was over. His cell came to life. He jumped at the sound of the ringer as it reminded him it hadn't rung all morning. An accomplishment that had not occurred in more than three decades, it usually rang every five minutes. He should have noticed the silence. It was an overseas number, England, London if his brain was operating properly. At least it would be business and might help right the ship of reality and get him out of hero and back into Ian.

"Hello, Ian Sperling," he began and was immediately cutoff.

"Ian, darling, what in all hell are you up to over there? What is it with you Americans and guns and why are you playing John Wayne?" laughter finished the thought.

"Hello John, how are things over in merry old?" If you couldn't take a little ball busting from friends then what kind of a man were you?

"Well, to be honest we are all enthralled with the intrepid exploits of our plucky American friend. The office and all the finest pubs are a buzz, though there was not a one of us who would've thought," he guffawed twice.

"Yeah, well, you can put me in the column of those who never would've thought. And you may tell them all I did not intend to do any such thing. I was attempting a cowardly, undetected escape when the bar stool had other ideas and thew me into the midst of instant fame!" He actually laughed, not a false bravado kind of thing but an actual 'see the folly of life and your part in it' laugh. He had to admit, when he said it out loud it was even more ridiculous than when he remembered.

"That's my boy! I knew you were a true coward at heart! Though the reports we were viewing over here had me worried that you had become the Rambo of Rock and Roll. Managing artists by day and crime fighter by night! We love you just the way you are, our lovely melt." Ian had put him on speaker so Maggie could listen in and now, all three of those partaking the conversation were laughing—two in the cramped sports car one in his office in London—as if all had the same visual of Ian as Rambo, in his late fifties and not in Ramboesque physique.

Ian felt he'd had a thousand-pound weight lifted from his slender, crowded shoulders. The last thirty-six or so had him running and hiding from reality, now John Lennon—not that John Lennon, but with the name of that someone who knew when life was having a good old time with him—record producer extraordinaire had brought back the perspective. This too shall pass, if he survived the adoration of the unwashed masses.

"Why don't you hop the next trans-Atlantic and spend some time over here. I've got a lovely flat no one is currently using and you and your lovely wife would be more than welcome guests." It almost sounded like he'd just come up with the idea rather than it being the reason for the call.

"Excellent idea!" Maggie chimed in.

"Ah, there you are, my love! Shove your superhero husband in a carry on and we'll have us a weeklong bash. We can trip the light fantastic, hop from venue to pub and pub to venue hearing every artist we can find, stay up all night talking, reminiscing, lying, and then Ian can regale us with stories of saving the world one pub at a time. Though I cannot promise the kind of excitement he is used to, but still we can have a few cheeky pints, get pissed and let our boy see all the fun he is missing in life!" If they weren't warming to the idea John was on fire.

"I don't think he needs to be reminded of all the fun he has had and no longer misses in life, but I think this is a wonderful idea." She gazed at her love to gauge his interest, he seemed reticent. She got it. "How's the fame level of our intrepid hero over across the pond? We live in a world connected by internet and gossip which means nothing good every goes unpunished, or somesuch, and Ian needs to get free of the worship and back into his comfort zone, music, and someone else's quest for fame."

"Well among those of us who know and love the old man, we think it quite a bit silly but, since we love him, also a mystery. Everyone would love to hear the story from the hero's mouth, so do come. I am glancing at the schedules from Cleveland, yes? To London and there is a flight leaving out this evening. Grab the passports, a few quid and leave us laugh!" He waited for confirmation.

"I think we can make all the arrangements and getting away from here would be just what the gynecologist ordered!" Ian's mood had lifted noticeably. They hung up on the promise of a few weeks' decompression. Now, they just had to figure how to accomplish the feat without alerting the media and the mongrel hordes.

"You know Betty, who lives over on the west side? She's a makeup artist for the Playhouse, maybe she could rearrange a few features so you don't look so much like you." Maggie's face lit up with her brilliant idea.

"Excellent, and when we try to get through security and my face doesn't match any of my ID, then what," He didn't mean to say it with such a denigrating tone, but he was tired and he wanted this to work but they need a better plan.

"Sorry," she shamed him with the hurt contained in those two syllables.

"I'm sorry, I don't mean to be a dick. I've just been dealing with this crap for a few days now and I need peace." He reached across and rubbed her back while gazing apology into the eyes. Something that had worked a thousand times, but, apparently, not a thousand and one. He was going to have to really work for this forgiveness. He couldn't blame her; he'd been coarse with his words to her, he would have to find a way to forgive himself and that would lead to the path of her forgiveness.

She slipped the car into reverse and backed out of the alley before winging it around and smoothly shifting to first and as they pulled out on the main thoroughfare heading east, she ran through second, third and settled comfortably into fourth. She was heading out of town, to farm and ranch country where she could think and allow the hurt to melt from her heart.

"Does this mean I don't have to get back in the trunk," he gently prodded.

"That is yet to be seen!" But she smiled. Good, they were heading in the right direction in all aspects of life.

"We need to find a way to get back into and through the airport without anyone noticing. We can throw a hat and glasses on you, as per Clark Kent, get you some clothes that don't scream look at me, and come in under the radar." It wasn't much of a plan, yet, but she'd only started driving east a few minutes ago. This would be a project in flux while they figured out the details. Shit, if they didn't know the details no one else could get ahead of them.

K. Adrian Zonneville

Two, With a Schmeer

As the elderly couple muscled their way through the airport one had to wonder if the woman pushing the wheelchair was his wife, nurse, or warden. Or possibly all three. She had a demeanor about her that moved people to the sides. Never had to say excuse me, pardon us, please let us through, you either did or she'd run you over with the old man in the chair. No one had time to look at them except briefly before scurrying to the side. That hadn't been the plan, exactly, but she had tried to be kind and ask people to make way, which lasted all of two minutes before being ignored for the umpteenth time, and she lost her shit. Now, she was on a mission, a mission that would not be denied.

As she rolled through the TSA toward the Trusted Traveler line one of the burly agents thought, though briefly, about stopping and questioning the couple. He took one look at her and stepped back out of the way. She rolled on up to the small booth that would be their last impediment to the international gates, slapped their passports and boarding passes on the counter and waited.

The tired, bored individual looked at the couple—the war-lord driver of chair and her charge. She had the hardened look of a lifer prison guard or someone's very evil auntie and the near corpse in the chair looked to be wishing that last breath would arrive while he could still enjoy it. She wore white nurse's clogs that squeaked with each movement on the linoleum, a cardigan sweater one size too large, buttoned up to her neck, and baggie, waist-tied scrubs. He was slouched in the chair head down, oversized sunglasses that wrapped almost completely around his head, a worn and torn fisherman's bucket hat, sport jacket, t-shirt with the name of a rock band from 1963 and sweats. Oh, boy, just when you thought you'd witnessed everything God could throw at you.

He glanced at the names on the passports before looking up with interest. Before he could open his mouth, grin, and ask for an autograph or say so much as a 'gee, pleasure', he saw the look in her eyes and instantly decided he would like to see his wife one more time. He handed back the passports and boarding passes and waved them through. He was slightly taken aback when she reached over and patted his arm and mouthed 'thank you', before rolling, rolling, rolling.

"Well, that wasn't too bad," Ian grinned as she pushed him towards their gate knowing they would make the flight by the skin of their teeth. "Those people all had terror written in large letters across their foreheads, remind me I never want to see how you glared at them."

"Oh, you've seen it," she chuckled.

"Oh," he winced, "You didn't."

They were the last two loaded onto the plane, but since they were in first class it mattered not, their seats were waiting for them. Settled in and drinks ordered, vodka and tonic with a lime for her and a diet cola for him, they relaxed and prepared for the long journey across the pond. It had taken a bit of doing but she had found them a direct flight to London. No stops! So, they could lay back, sleep the sleep of the unknowns, and wake up refreshed and ready to relax with friends and fine food.

Two bored goddesses watched the ordinary play out. There would be no terror in the sky, the flight, Fate knew, would be without incident, unless...

She chanced a glance to where Fame had sat up with a disturbing expression on her perfect face and saw the ripple in the waters of life. Fate wished Fame would give her a heads up but also would not give the other goddess the satisfaction of knowing she had surprised the goddess of destiny. She'd have to hang on and ride whatever Fame had put in motion.

Somewhere mid-Atlantic Ian awoke with a start before realizing where he was and relaxed once again. Maggie was snoring softly in the window seat next to him, he loved the soft purr of her snores, it meant all was well in the world. They were at thirty-five thousand feet above the ocean and no one could touch them.

Out of the corner of his eye he noticed the Zaftig woman with the multi-hued hair and outfit across the aisle shove two olives from her drink into her mouth before releasing her seatbelt to make the trip to the rest room. She caught his eye as she bumped into him, he smiled in a gentlemanly way just before they hit an air pocket and the jet dropped precipitously allowing the copious weight of the woman to land fully in his lap as the captain righted the plane.

He tried to help her up from his seated position but she was a load and he didn't have the leverage. It was then he heard something that brought terror to his heart. She was choking. Apparently, the abrupt decent and landing in his lap had lodged the olives and she was gasping for air. Well, shit! Desperation filled him, he grabbed her by the shoulders, trying to pry her from his lap. But he didn't have the strength and she couldn't get purchase with her legs and was more concerned with the lack of air to her lungs. He did not need this woman dying at thirty-five thousand feet in his lap

He'd had enough! Losing any semblance of decorum, decency, or humanity he began to pound on the woman's back to make it known he was not happy with the situation. Maggie woke up to the sight of a well-endowed woman apparently performing oral sex on her husband at thirty-five thousand feet and was choking on him. Well, that didn't seem right! She was about to have a word or two with this hussy when Ian pounded one last time on the cheeky bitch's back and two olives came flying out of her mouth pelting Maggie in the gut. That was when the flight attendant arrived. He pulled passenger A out of passenger B's lap before passenger C could commit a crime she would regret. Passenger A was gulping in buckets of recirculated air and attempting to thank passenger B for saving her life and passenger B was attempting to explain to passenger C he had done no such thing he was trying to push her off him. But passenger C was having none of it and the rest of the crew and first class were shouting, clapping, and proclaiming him a hero.

Fuck!

Somewhere in the heavens was the sound of giggling.

That was when the phones came out. Pictures were snapped, a back was slapped over and over, kisses were awarded and a wife sat and stared at the imbecilic moron sitting next to her.

"Do you have any idea what you've done?" she hissed.

"I was trying to get that oversized behemoth off of me, that was all. There was turbulence, olives, a lap, and an attempted escape. That is what happened in Miami!" He knew his hissed explanation sounded petulant but it was all he had. His defense fell on deaf ears.

Ian didn't think a jet could become absolutely quiet with people coming out of cockpits, bathrooms, and steerage to congratulate him, ask for his autograph, and snap a selfie, but by God, it was almost monastic. He could only assume partially because he sat in the cone of stony silence emanating from the seat immediately to his left.

But it wasn't his fault! Damn it! He hadn't tried to save anybody in Miami and he certainly hadn't tried to save this woman on the plane. Karma was fucking with him and he had to discover why. He wanted his old selfish, self-absorbed, behind the scenes life back. WTAF!

They still had several hours before getting into Heathrow, maybe he could get some shuteye. And maybe he'd grow wings and fly his own way across the pond, be met by a band of fairies who would shower him with love, sexual favors and a pound of really good weed. Fuck! His brain was engaged and would not get out of first gear. What had he done in his past that Karma decided to fuck with his whole future? That was the question.

He knew ninety-nine percent of people would be so envious of the adulation being rained on him they would have sold their souls for a piece of it. Though apparently, they didn't want it enough to save people or put themselves in the line of fire; either figuratively or literally.

He just couldn't fathom 'why him'? He wasn't a bad person though not a saint. He was just Ian Patrick Sperling, friend to the gifted, manager behind the curtain, fan in the wings, and decent fella. He had lived his life by his father's brilliant admonition and advice; 'Don't fuck with the artists money! Don't handle it unless necessary and you don't take a nickel. You give it all to the artist or their business manager or whoever handles that end of the biz, but you do not handle the cash. They pay you. So, if something goes awry, you ain't in the middle.'

It hadn't always been easy. There were times, especially in the early days when his artists were just starting out, that times were lean. He could've used a couple extra bucks for food, rent, utility bills, phone, shit, a twenty to try and impress a girl enough to sleep with him. But he hadn't taken a nickel. He'd gone hungry. He'd slept in the cold and dressed in the dark. Walked to gigs and avoided the super. But he'd slept knowing he'd done what was right. Nobody cared if the manager was hungry, they cared that the band ate so they could do the shows. He drove through the night between towns so they could sleep. Well, until the time he'd almost killed them all. Asleep at the Wheel is not just the name of a band! He'd eaten an energy bar and snorted a gram to make it through the night. No wonder he'd gained so much weight once they had the financial wherewithal to eat and sleep regular. Shit, he was hungry.

Even once they got into tall cotton he'd lived by that same motto. Temptation be damned. As fame grows so does the paycheck, and a lot of the time, especially in the early decades, in cash money. It's one thing to look at a grand in an envelope and do the right thing. It is quite another set of morals for someone to hand you a briefcase with nearly a million and sit back while it was counted. That was another rule, count the cash in front of each other so there would never be any questions.

Did you ever count eight hundred thousand dollars? He asked the interviewer in his head. Well, let me tell you this, that will change your perspective on life. He'd be lying to himself, the world, and the littlest angel ever born that sat on his shoulder, if he didn't admit a bit of temptation to Steve Miller it. (Whoa, take the money...) But he never had.

He'd had visions of a quiet island somewhere down in the South Pacific, surrounded by pretty island girls and coconuts, palm trees wafting in the breeze, pot plants the size of those palms with buds the size of your head. But then reality would break in, if he ever did that the music would be gone. Not just as a manager but his gift, the one thing that set him apart from the rest of the pack, the knack most ingrained in his soul, his heart, him, would be gone. And there just wasn't enough cash on this planet to betray friends and his muse. So, it wasn't that he was pure, he was purely terrified of the consequences.

And he knew in his heart of hearts this too would pass. Yes, he'd had a couple close calls with fate, but fate and Karma would get tired of their little game and let him move on.

Fate grinned evil intent. So, he thought he could outwit or outwait her. She would prove the wrong of that. And the best part was he was blaming Karma as much as anybody else. Well, she would not disavow that belief. And she wasn't going to share that bit of information with her partner. Fame would get no credit for any of this. The plan could not be more delicious.

His thoughts had carried him the rest of the way across the Atlantic. Wheels down, he was back in his favorite city in the world. Literally, there was no other city on this planet that had claim on his heart like London and had since the late sixties!

He'd backpacked across Europe for six weeks back in sixty-eight before landing in London quite by accident. He had been hobnobbing in Gay Paree for a few weeks! But political unrest had chased all the Americans out, scattered them to the four winds, and this little hippie had landed in London. It had been a gift from the gods! He fell in love with the town before he unpacked his suitcase.

It was music centric and he knew most of the musicians. Hell, they had played his dad's rock club outside of Cleveland during his formative years. He found himself sitting in the lap of cutting-edge music, cutting-edge fashion, cutting-edge political change and cutting-edge organics and chemicals. Yeah, this was his kind of town. He partied like a rock star with the actual rock stars. He tried university but he couldn't keep his grades up. He was a young innocent boy away from the nurturing of home, friends, family, and familiar, comforting surroundings. So, he floated in and out of the music clubs, hung at Jimi Hendrix's apartment, soaked in every band, every act, every kind of pop, rock, psychedelia he could find. And now, once again, he was back!

"Are you alright?" the words quiet, full of concern and love. Her eyes searched his face, each crease, trying to see deep into his eyes, trying to discern his condition. Wow! What had...?

"Yeah, why?" He almost broke down with the love on display. When he'd dozed off, and he had to believe that he had, she was pissed, now her countenance was one of disquiet, unease. God, how he loved this woman. An entire life together and she was as brilliant, life affirming, and vibrant as the first time they'd met. She was his other half, truly, his better half, she completed him.

"You were tossing and clenching in your sleep and you were talking," but there was more he could tell.

"What did I say?" Oh, the horror of an unkind word could destroy them both.

"You were talking to Michael." And there it was. She touched his arm and he raised her hand and kissed it hard. They enveloped each other as if they could wrap themselves in a protective shell.

Michael had been best friend, closest confidant, his first act, his soul brother in every sense. And he had been gone these past ten years. It still sliced his soul into a million pieces. He had only ever loved three people that deeply. One sat next to him, one was married to their wonderful daughter-in-law and one had passed a decade before. He couldn't allow himself to think on it or he would go insane. And he shared Ian's older brother's name. How close could you be to one person?

"Sorry, I don't do it on purpose," he apologized for loving when he knew how dumb that was.

"I'm not. We should never, ever forget."

The jet pulled up to the jetway and the people all stood, as if the service was over and the football game was coming on soon. The clapping started somewhere in the economy section near the back. You could hear as each row began to take it up and then came the cheer as people got the overheads open and luggage was being pulled down. It soon became a cacophony as the passengers and crew took up a chant of his name. Oh, what the fuck.

He pulled his hat down to the point he thought he might choke himself and then thought what a lovely idea. The largish woman threw her flapping largish arms around the diminutive man and hugged him until he hoped he would pass out. Instead, Maggie dove into the pool of flesh grabbed him tight and pulled him to the surface making for the, now, open exit door. The captain and flight crew thanked him profusely as the two Americans made for a brisk escape.

They were met at the gate by a throng of humanity all waving, cheering blowing kisses and asking for autographs. Maggie assumed her Nurse Ratched attitude, put her head down like a bull and an aisle cleared. They quick walked through the massive airport to the awaiting limo John Lennon had sent. Diving into the back seat, Maggie was handed a cocktail and a hand carved wooden pipe was shoved in Ian's general direction, Maggie intercepted with an apologetic shrug before taking a deep pull and passing it to him. He grinned; she'd earned it!

The Fool For The Thrill

They had settled into their favorite hotel in the SoHo/Covent Garden district of London. It was centrally located without being actually right in the heart of the happening neighborhoods, foregoing John's flat which was on the outskirts of the great city. They were close but could escape back into sanity within moments. He lay on the bed allowing the stress of fame to dissipate from his body into the surrounding atmosphere, like heat dispersing into a cool afternoon.

"Want to go for a walk and maybe grab a sandwich?" Maggie tested the waters.

"I don't know, it's a little scary out there right now," as visions of their ordeal on and off the plane, running the gauntlet and diving into a limo like some bad action flick were still fresh in the brain pan. He shivered.

"C'mon, this isn't the airport, it is central London, nobody gives a shit about you here," she laughed as she lay down next to him and hugged any hurt out of the words.

But there was no hurt, just honesty. And she was right. This was London, his London. The town he had fallen in love with five decades ago. His second home. From the moment he'd set foot here in '68 he knew he belonged here. It was everything he'd longed for in life. This was the city of Peadar 'Pete' McCarthy, Ian's childhood rock hero, and his band the Mersea Beats, who had changed music and Ian's life forever in the early sixties. They were young, hip, played their own instruments, wrote their own songs, and were smart, clever, and irreverent. Shit! This was the birthplace of every great rock act of the early sixties. Of Victoria, Elizabeth, and Mary Queen of Scotts. Henrys and Georges coming out the ying-yang. When you walked the streets where kings, queens, and every other bloke or dame was more famous than the last one. The citizenry were kind of immune to fame, weren't they? Too much of a good thing inoculates.

"You know what, light one up, let's go out on the town."

One of the things they loved about this hotel was they could get a room five floors above the hullabaloo below. And it had a balcony. They could sit out on the veranda like normal people having a cuppa and smoke a toke or two to get ready for the evening. Relaxed, giggling and now ready for some munchies, they headed out.

As they walked out the front entrance and onto the thoroughfare they were accosted by John Lennon, not that one, the other. "I thought you two would be resting and recouping for a bit. I was popping in to see if maybe you'd like a little libation and something to nosh." His re-welcoming smile and hugs all around were the extra rejuvenation required to put a little lilt in the step.

"We did, we have, we are," quote Ian, "and we're buying. You pick the spot; we'll pay the tab!"

It was just what the doctor ordered. A quiet, though not too quiet, corner pub with both carnivorous and vegetarian seafood fare, music just loud enough to drown out the room but not each other's conversation and no one bothering them. Heaven. Wood paneling, smartass barkeep, well-worn wooden floors, and the scent of stale beer. Home.

"Things have settled down?" John smiled as the first round of snacks and drinks showed up.

"Nicely," Ian grinned back, "It is one of the most impressive attributes of this wonderful city, fame means nothing here. Hell, you almost have to be famous to walk down the street here, I think they check your IMDb and Wikipedia stats before renting you an apartment." To which they chuckled and he relaxed completely.

There is nothing more comforting than friends; old, trusted friends. People who knew you not as a star or celebrity but as a human being. People that kept you centered and grounded. When Ian considered, while sipping his warm diet cola, it was one of the most important aspects of his job as personal manager to his artists. Yes, he was a fan, he had to be a fan of the artist, their music, who they were as a person, but mostly he had to be their friend and confidant, someone they could talk to and who would be honest with them. Every artist of every caliber and level, whether local garage band fame or selling twenty million units a year, had enough folks blowing smoke up their asses. They needed someone who didn't want anything except what was best for the person. A friend. He treasured his friendships more than his access to fame. He hated fame, as it was an empty commodity, a container with a hole in the bottom that required constant filling. And he hated it much more now that it was forced on him.

John had worked with some of the best, it was his job as a producer. But he, like Ian, only took who he wanted, who he respected. When you can ride any horse in the barn why not ride the one you loved.

"How long can you stay?" John couched the question to convey a hope for a long stay.

"Shit, at this rate forever," Ian absently took Maggie's hand and held it. With the touch came all the promise of a perfect future. "To be honest, I really don't know," she tried to pull her hand away, though not too hard. "The problem is one of time. I need all this bullshit to settle down and I have no idea how long that might take. A week? Two? A year? Who knows? I am hoping some disaster happens to shift the focus of the public's miniscule attention span to death, blood, gore, and destruction instead of Sperling!" Now Maggie did pull her hand away, leaning back and glaring at him with a shocked, horrified expression.

"I'm kidding!" he half lied in defense, "We just need something to pull the public eye away from me and onto something important." He eased himself out of his chair, glass in hand, shaking it to emphasize, "I need ice! I love this town but...warm cola?"

"You have to excuse Ian," Maggie said unnecessarily, "this whole thing just has him way out of sorts. We've been together over forty years and I have never seen him where he's so lost, he has no idea where to turn or what to do."

John leaned across and hugged her. "We'll get him through this and we'll have our old irascible, whiny Ian back again."

Just then something happened in the football game on the telly and a great cheer went up in the pub. People were jumping, clapping, screaming, and banging on tables, walls, the bar top, anything that would make noise. Ian looked up just as the innkeeper attempted to put his change on the bar. Instead, he dropped several of the five-pound notes on the floor, as he wasn't paying attention to Ian but the pandemonium in his pub. As Ian bent down to pick up his change, one end of the massive sign with the establishment's name on it broke lose above his head, due to the hard banging and stomping of the packed house, swinging down catching the barkeep in the back of his head knocking him across the bar. The sign swung back as Ian stood clutching his change in his right hand and it completed the pendulum move knocking Ian ass over teacup onto the top of the unconscious publican's chest. Ian attempted the dismount but slipped in a puddle of beer, splashed during celebration, on the floor causing himself to fall over and over on top of the man's chest. Restarting the heart within, which had stopped with the blow to the head.

Ian finally found purchase and raised himself like a breeching whale off the floor to stare down in horror at the man lying beneath him. Of course, a Bobbie walked through the door to see what the commotion was about, saw the prone publican on the floor, yelled over the din asking for any medical personnel, a slightly tipsy doctor three stools down jumped from his seat, tipping the chair over in the process and made a quick examination. Pronouncing the innkeeper's need to be hauled off to the nearest medical facility as he had suffered a heart attack and would most likely be dead were it not for the ministrations of the shocked gentleman standing right there.

John and Maggie could do nothing but stare! What the fuck! They had observed the entire incident as if it happened in slow, agonizing motion. Maggie wanted to shout for Ian just to lay still but she couldn't. If she had, the man on the floor would be dead and she would have killed him. They had to get out of there before questions were ask, identities provided, and nightmares continued.

Ian threw some cash on the table before shoving his wallet where his pants pocket should be and they ran for freedom.

"You saw! You both saw it!" He tried not to scream but the thread was about to snap. This was insane and getting more so by the minute. This had to stop, he couldn't save the world even if he had any desire! Saving people was killing him.

"Is this how it always happens?" John couldn't grasp what he'd just witnessed, heroism by default. "I mean, it was like a bad movie in slow motion. I wanted to jump in, to stop what was obviously happening, but I couldn't. It was horrific, truly bizarre."

"Yes, there I am, minding my own business and the next thing you know I am raising the dead. Next thing you know I'll be running around with loaves of bread and pockets full of fishes! I need to lay down, sleep for fourteen hours and wake up from this tortured fantasy and get back to life!" Ian was openly weeping as they hailed the cab.

"At least no one will know it was you. No one got your name and no one knows you here," Maggie shook off the feeling of doom as they pulled up in front of the hotel. "You paid cash. Right?" it was the last thing he heard before nodding and sleep walking to the elevator, down the hall, opening the door, finding the bed, then nodding off to sleep.

The next realization Ian had was that he was deeply imbedded in the dream state. Which was odd because he never dreamed, certainly not to this degree. Oh, a patch of green grass here, a hobgoblin there just to assure he was paying attention but never 'dream', where you cannot tell reality from fiction, fiction from the humdrum existence of life. Or the formally humdrum existence. Now, he knew. He knew in his bones and his unconscious consciousness; he was in the dream state.

And he hadn't dreamt like this since he was a preteen. When there had still been some dispute as to who or what he would become. Right before his thirteenth birthday, maybe a week before his gift came to the fore. The timeline was fuzzy as he couldn't remember exactly when the change came. Though, he remembered that night, that dream, as if it was chiseled in his soul; and maybe it was. He was sitting around with some acquaintances; he didn't really have friends. It wasn't that he was unfriendly, he just didn't connect with other kids on more than a plutonic level. There was something that blocked the connectors with other humans. Then came the night he discovered why. In the dream they were playing some innocuous game that involved killing each other or harming small creatures as young boys are wont to do. Ian had hated these displays of manliness and machismo since the cradle but sometimes you've got to kill something weaker than you to get along. And somewhere out of a bedroom or living room window a song began to play.

There was something about the song, not the lyric or the melody but the production; something wrong. It didn't fit what the artist was trying to convey. Ian couldn't tell what or why, it just rubbed the inside of his head the wrong way. It made the point where his brain touched his skull itch. He wanted to find where the music was coming from and stop it. He followed the sound like a dog on the trail of a wounded squirrel. He could hear its cries and had one thought, to put it out of its misery.

Just as he crept up to the open window where the suffering called to him the song ended. And a high energy, fast talking, giddy idiot on the small tabletop radio said it was some new drivel from a rock idol and he wanted to know what America thought of it. Stupidly, he gave a phone number to voice your opinion.

Ian threw down his stick gun, ignored the shouting of his comrades in arms and marched home to the phone where he had a bone to pick with a crooner. The phone on the other end rang once, twice, three times, fifteen times, thirty-seven times. Ian didn't care how long he had to wait; someone would know the outrage this cacophony was creating. Christ on a premium saltine, this could easily cause riots in the streets, the break-down of society, headaches, thrombosis, anal itch, and bleeding.

At long last redemption answered with a cheery 'W-I-E-N radio, what's your request.'

"Never to hear that 'song'," and though Ian knew the voice on the other end of the line couldn't see the air quotes, he was going to give him both fingers, "again."

"What song is that, sonny?" This jock was not endearing himself to this particular listener.

"That horror you played an hour back." Which he realized was exactly how long he had stayed on the line in his dream waiting for an answer.

"You didn't like it?"

"No. Oh, the words and music are alright but the instruments are fighting each other for dominance, they grate and rub against each other like cats about to fight." Ian immediately realized he didn't have the vocabulary to describe the perturbation this diseased and dying thing had unleashed within his psyche.

"Thanks, kid, I'll let the muckity-mucks at the record company know your thoughts," he laughed as he hung up the phone.

That's where the dream within the dream ended and realization took hold. If Ian was going to expect adults in the music biz to take him seriously, he was going to have to learn the lingo. He had found his calling in life. That was the last time he dreamt of anything. From that moment on he didn't need dreams, he had purpose. He knew what needed doing and he was just the teen to do it.

Yet, here he was, for the first time in decades, up to his ears in dreamland. He'd forgotten how unpleasant that could be.

His new life came at him hard and constant. Walking down the street without a care in the world when he came across an orphanage on fire with hundreds of small children begging to be saved. He tried to ignore them but they jumped, one after another, landing softly in his arms. He would set one down just in time to catch the next. One after another like an endless stream of teeny human droplets falling from the sky. He set the last one down and ran, right into a collapsing building. Ten thousand human beings standing in line waiting for him, the savior of humanity, to come for them. There was not near enough time to save them all, yet none would be denied. Running out of the collapsing structure he saw his childhood home, safety! Except as soon as he walked through the front door his dying mother threw herself into his arms begging him to save her, his father begging him to save her, the world begging him to save his own fucking mother.

The loud banging followed immediately by violent shaking saved his frayed sanity.

"Ian! Ian!" Maggie was shaking him hard. "It's just a nightmare!" She said over and over to convince him he could come awake and it would all be gone.

John was forcefully telling someone in the outer room of their suite that Ian was not to be disturbed. Though whoever he was trying to convince of that fact didn't seem to be in the mood to be convinced.

"I must speak to Mr. Sperling in person and shall not be denied." The voice boomed.

Ian's head swam in very deep and swirling waters and he prayed they would allow it to sink to the bottom. He'd had enough and didn't care who needed, wanted, or desired to see him, he was not saving anyone else today!

The soft knock on the door derailed his thoughts. The knob turned and the door creaked slightly ajar

John stuck his head through the meager opening, "Excuse me Ian, Maggie, but there seems to be an official contingent out here that would like to have a few moments of your time. And they are quite insistent."

Ian sat up; Maggie handed him his pants. Oh well, if you had to face the headsman might as well have trousers in place. Maggie looked at him as if this would be the last time she would see him. He was off to the gallows again and this time she didn't think he could outrun the fame. It would appear it had attached itself to his fate. 'Til death do us part.

Ian came through the doorway to find several official looking gents and a lady standing impatiently in the sitting room. Two Bobbies, one politician and a woman who must be the president of the local floral club. If only they'd brought some pot.

"Mr. Sperling, I presume?" spoke the politician appearing so and so. Names would not be of great import here, just appearances. "I believe this is yours," he handed Ian his wallet. "It was found at the scene of your heroism, where you saved the life of a well-known publican, and all agreed you were the person to whom it belonged."

"Well, as it has my license, Global Entry card and photos of my wife, I guess I cannot deny the truth," his attempted levity fell as flat as his mood.

"Yes, and we would like to return it and all included with our undying thanks for your heroism and selflessness in your actions today. We would also like to present you with this certificate of our appreciation for saving the proprietor of the 'Stinking Hole' publican house's life." He handed Ian a handwritten, on parchment, beautifully framed certificate. The calligraphy magnificent, the official stamp, official, signed by the mayor, the president of town council and the aforementioned president of the floral club. Who now handed him a lovely bouquet of personally grown flowers.

Ian handed the flowers to Maggie, the certificate to John and straightened himself to deliver a very poignant soliloquy. Before the first syllable could fall from the tongue, the tallest Bobbie, the Sergeant, if Ian was any judge of officialdom, took a step towards him. Oh, Christ on cheddar.

"Mr. Sperling, once we discovered your purse, we had to go through a bit of unearthing to find you. While engaged in our search we found you seemed to practice this sort of activity quite often back in the states. Which considering the reputation of your fine country of residence, I suppose is quite necessary. We read the periodicals and know that you blokes over the pond seem to quite enjoy knocking each other about. Lots of shooting, stabbing, punching and robbing sort of thing. Well, we don't cotton to such here, we like our peace," he was ramping up to speed when he hit an Ian speedbump.

"Yes, I noticed that when last in Ireland and several of the other colonies," he had meant to think it but sometimes thoughts solidify into verbal communication.

"Be that as it may," the Sergeant cleared his throat, "we would prefer you save your holy quest of lifesaving miracles for America, not here." He stomped his foot for emphasis. "So, I present you with a Cease and Desist order against saving anymore lives while on British soil. We have enough to do without Yanks zipping over here to save lives and then wish statues erected!"

Ian stared at the man. Was he insane? He then turned to John, "Can they do that?" Before John could utter his own syllable, Ian shook his head as if dislodging something of extraordinary unpleasant taste, "Can you do that?" he almost screamed at the Bobbie. "Number one, I did not come here to save anybody but my own sanity. Numero Dos, I don't think you can stand in the way of people falling over themselves to get to death's doorstep—which, apparently, happens to be wherever I am standing and I am the doorman—waiting for me to somehow accidentally save them. I'm, I'm, I'm, shit!" He stammered and stuttered. Are these people out of their fucking minds? "I don't wish to save anybody, I never wanted to save anybody. They can all fucking die for all I care but fate or Karma or your old aunt Martha is fucking with my life and they keep throwing this shit in my fan. If you can stop it, do so. But until you can do that, please leave me alone!" He pointed to the door. He had no idea if they would follow his order but better prison than this!

Each eye stared in astonishment from one face to the next to the next to, well, you get the idea. Finally, John stepped to the fore.

"Mr. Sperling has a point. I witnessed the entire event, it was, without any doubt, a succession of accidental events of which he had no control nor want. I am not certain you can legislate or cease and desist anyone from committing an accident," John wasn't certain of the verbiage or proper use but he was attempting to sound like a solicitor, which he wasn't.

"Well, we shall endeavour to discover the truth of that," the Sergeant allowed his words to carry himself and his assistant to the door. The politician and the president of the floral club hot on their heels, miffed at the rudeness of the hero. Alas, when one considered, he was, after all, an American, well, one cannot fight one's own DNA! "Mind yourself as we will be minding you!" The words closed the door.

"I'm going back to bed!" Ian was as downcast as Maggie could ever remember. "I have loved this town for fifty years, it is my refuge, my sanctuary away from the madness and the madness has descended upon my peace! Well, I shall not be moved! This is my haven, I will not be chased by fortune, fate, Karma, or insanity from here!" He allowed the closing bedroom door to softly put him and his words to bed.

"I'm really afraid for him," Maggie chewed at her bottom lip, arms wrapped around herself as if for warmth or comfort.

"I must admit I thought you two exaggerated this affliction, but having witnessed it in action, well, I am aghast. It is like some sort of hoodoo. As if a curse has been placed on your husband by Marie Laveau herself and he is fated to return those who should be dead to the living." John sat heavily in the overstuffed chair overlooking the busy throughfare and bustling city five floors below.

They sat in silence for a half hour, neither knowing what to say. What could you say? Should they be like the Sergeant and demand he find a way to stop saving people? He couldn't do that because he wasn't actively attempting to help anyone. In fact, if push came to shove, which apparently it was going to, he was falling all over himself trying not to engage in such. It was not that Ian was a bad sort, he just preferred to remain in the background. Let the other fellow have the spotlight, the glory. Ian was quite prepared to live in the shadows of those he loved and respected. They'd earned the right. They'd practiced, plied their trade in dumpy, divey bars, hellholes, biker bars, strip clubs and starved for the right. He had only fallen into everything since the beginning.

Every few minutes their eyes would wander the silent room seeking answers to questions that couldn't be asked. Those probing orbs would meet and then slide off in opposite directions searching territory already well combed.

"He's always had a knack, hasn't he?" Maggie couldn't tell if John had found a foothold or was just tired of silence.

"Yes, it would seem he was born with this innate ability to hear the slightest grating sound in a recording. When notes didn't quite mesh, an instrument slightly out of tune, a missing piece. That something that no one else ever noticed. And he has no training, not in music, production, recording, nothing. It's like a supernatural ability to tell when something just doesn't 'fit'." She sighed. She had never understood exactly what Ian could do, but she could feel when he changed something that it was right. "He has the same ability with people; his clients."

"Really?" Now, she had John's full attention. He had never really delved into what it was that made Ian so special, he only knew that the man was.

"Yes," she nodded, "he can tell you within a moment whether he will manage someone or not. There is a, oh, what did he call it? An immediate electrical, psychological, connection, as if they had known each other for a thousand years. Did you know he told me within five minutes of meeting me he would marry me?" She nodded as she said the words remembering not a cocksure arrogant man but one who somehow knew and would make it happen.

"So, do you think it was meant to be or that he decided something and he was going to do whatever it took to make it happen?" He leaned back in his chair as if they were in a session and he found her answers quite revealing.

She considered the question for several long seconds. "No," she leaned back into a booth in a bar forty some years in the past. The music pumping in the background, a cold drink on the table, she took a sip, she could still taste the vodka tonic, as she considered the young man seated next to her, "It was almost as if he was a fortune teller gazing into my future and telling me what he saw. He wasn't challenging or daring, just stating the facts, natural as if he complimented my outfit." Her smile told John all he needed to know about these two that he'd never thought to ask. "But I met him when he already had this ability, maybe we should get in touch with his older brother, Michael, and see if he can shed some light on 'Ian; The Early Years.' See if he had this since birth or if it was an acquired mojo. "

By God, he thought, she loved him from that moment on. What must that be like? And he shivered. And what must it be like for her now? Now that his certainty, his awareness of who, what and where he was teetered on the brink of uncertainty. And how had this possibly shattered Ian's own concepts? He no longer was the master of his future or himself. The man must be terrified for the first time not to know which door to walk through. Could he do that blindly?

The soft knock on the door startled them both out of their reverie. Maggie shot a questioning glance at John who rose out of the chair. She motioned for him to stay where he was and got up to answer it. "Maybe those four forgot to actually thank Ian and have come back to apologize." She grinned.

As she opened the door, John couldn't see who stood in the hall from where he sat, he could see Maggie's reaction as the blood drained from her face and shock froze her features. He immediately got up to find out. His shock must have registered as intensely as her own. There, stood Sir Peadar 'Pete' McCarthy smiling at them both from the hallway. "May I come in?" He quipped.

John opened the door wide so the Knighted man could enter properly and stole a glance up and down the empty hallway before closing and double locking the door. Though whether to keep others out or Mr. McCarthy, in he wasn't certain.

"This is the room of Ian Sperling, is it not?" Pete asked as he twirled his baseball hat in his hands, assuring himself he had not blundered into a very wrong situation.

Maggie stared. Somewhere in the deepest recesses of her memories she could hear Ian saying something about meeting the one person whom he could never think of as a 'person person' but only as 'HIM'. Ian had met, worked with, friended, interacted with, and turned down some of the biggest names in music, but this man was his childhood, adolescent, young adult, and adult hero. He could manage to speak to the man but only by either closing his eyes or pretending to look elsewhere. And here he was, in the flesh standing in the sitting room while Ian lay in the bedroom.

"Peadar McCarthy," he held out a hand to Maggie in introduction.

"Oh, fer fucksake, I know who you are," she blurted out and then turned a bright red and covered her mouth with both hands. "I'm so sorry, that just came from somewhere, from shock, from, oh, God, I didn't mean that..." the words piddled on the floor like a bad puppy too excited.

"Maybe I should introduce," John stepped to the fore, "This is Maggie Sperling, Ian's wife."

"And mouthpiece," Pete's joyous laughter filled the room and tension dissipated like a light fog in brilliant sunshine. "and you?"

"I'm," and he stopped himself. He was known as a producer but not well-known, it was possible that Pete might even have heard of him, but to stand here, in a hotel sitting room and say his name, well, he took a deep breath, "I'm John Lennon." Silence. A silence so complete it was tied with a bow and waited patiently under the tree.

Again, Pete's laughter filled the room. If there was any band that could match what the Mersea Beats had accomplished it was his best friend, John Lennon's band, he reached over and hugged both his hosts. "This makes everything just perfect." He glanced towards the heavens and shook a finger. "Ah, you old...you know he was a dear mate of mine, don't you?" John nodded. "Well, where is the life of the party? Out saving the world one body at a time?" From another it might have seemed curt or in bad taste, but Peadar McCarthy could tell you your mum was in hospital and you would be assured. He may have been a rock idol but he never let that interfere in relationships.

"He's had a rough few weeks and more days of late. He's taking a lay down in the other room," Maggie said softly.

Pete self-shushed in apology for his loud barks of joy just as the bedroom door opened.

Ian's groggy form stood half naked as he was about to beg them for silence so he could rest. The words stuck in the back of his throat as he took in the man sitting on the upholstered chair and smiling at him.

"Ian!" chimed Pete.

"Peadar," croaked Ian.

"Ian," shot both Maggie and John miming that he might wish to robe himself in the presence of the almighty.

When Greatness Comes to Call, Pull on Your Trousers

"I'm sorry, Mr. McCarthy, Sir Peadar, uh, I have to assist..." Maggie ran out of steam and allowed herself to exit the sitting room and go help Ian dress himself.

John began to apologize and offer Sir Peadar something to drink before the Rock God reined him in.

"It's really quite alright," the Knighted man said to his former best friend's namesake. "I'm happy to have a mo to rest. Glad they found lodging on the fifth rather than fifteenth floor." He shot John a quick grin and nod.

'You walked up?" John didn't know why but the thought of this man walking up five flights of stairs, especially when the first flight was actually a flight and a half, horrified him. Shouldn't he have a cadre of eunuchs to carry him about so his feet don't touch the ground? He had penned and performed some of the greatest hits of the 1960s. He was royalty.

"Yes, we discovered back in the ancient times, pre-Captain album," their genre shattering masterpiece that established them as the preeminent rock act of the century, "that no one considered the fact we were young and could comprehend how stairs worked. So, while the mongrel hordes always waited to ambush us by the lift, we snuck up the wooden hill with no one the wiser." He barked a sharp laugh just as Ian and Maggie reemerged from the boudoir. "Really, why I'm here." He flicked a hello wave at Ian, "To help an old chum with his fame."

"Can you make it disappear?" Ian's tone was one of defeat yet joy at seeing his old friend. Though in his mind 'friend' might be stretching the definition of their relationship. Chum seemed to chafe less.

"I have been reading on your exploits and following the chase on the telly," to Ian's surprise Pete hugged him close, "Sorry you have to experience this. I know it has always been your want to remain in the shadows. More the Wizard of truth than of the fame." They both took seats across from the couch, which now was populated by Maggie and John.

"A place I hope very soon to return," Ian shook his head mournfully.

"Then you've got to stop saving people!" Sir Peadar clapped his hands as if that solved everything. "Quite a hobby you've picked up, not one most would consider."

"I had no desire to have it land in my lap. I was happy letting people die at their pleasure when and where they wished, without interference from yours truly," he shook his head violently as if he could shake this reality loose and allow the other to find its way back in. "I mean, there I am minding my own business when out of the blue someone who either has dastardly intent or is distracted sets desolation in motion and all should come to destruction. Instead, fate or destiny, pulls my sorry ass into this tragedy. Leaving me holding a big bag of 'local boy saves dolphin from drowning and worshipped as hero'. Makes one want a little payback for the intrusion." It made no sense to anybody in the room except Ian, but that was enough. "And I certainly don't wish to spend a few nights locked in the nick!" If Ian remembered right from his rowdy days in London in the 60's that was what the toughs called a jail.

"No, we wouldn't want that!" Pete mimicked seriousness while mocking.

"So, how did you handle the fame, the fans, the insanity. When we look at the old newsreels from our misspent youth it is surprising any of you survived at all!" Curiosity mixed with admiration to form the question.

"Well, mate, first off you have to remember there were four of us and the infatuation of the teenage girl can flit from shiny object to thumping bass drum. One day all the girls would be crazy over me or Jack, so, even though the reels didn't bother to chronicle it, Richie could walk down the street completely unnoticed by thousands of fans. The next week it would be Gerald's turn at anonymity. He'd sit in a park and feed pigeons while the rest of us hid in a loo or the boot of some coppers car." He shook himself out of a particular memory before continuing, "The thing to keep in mind is it is only temporary. Fads come and go, right now you are a fad, kind of a return of the Christ fad, but a fad none-the-less. Try to be less conspicuous by trying not so hard to be less conspicuous."

Ian's confused, blank expression begged more information.

"See, people can sense when you're trying not to be noticed. It's like a sixth or seventh sense, they pick up on the vibration of desperation. They can pick you out of a crowd because you are trying so hard not to be noticed. Whereas if you just live, smile, say hello, in their brain they are thinking, 'was that? No, it couldn't have been, he/she was too normal to be that hugely famous bloke. By God, he said hello to me, probably an impersonator.' " He sat back in the upholstered chair and waited for the brilliance to sink in. Apparently overestimating the thickness of the preset.

"So, you're saying if I just don't care then the public won't either?" Ian looked from Maggie to John and back again to see if they grokked any better than he.

"Get your hats and coats, all of you, and let's make a foray into the wilds of London," Sir Peadar stood putting word into action, the other three could do naught but follow the idol.

Pete wore an oversized blue overcoat, not a heavy wool one but a light cotton/nylon weave, his baseball cap, tennis shoes, Chuck Taylors. Ian slipped on a poncho against the drizzle outdoors, hood down, baseball hat, John had his usual dark blue topcoat and Maggie was stylish in blue jean slacks, light sweater, and simple rain smock. They looked nothing more than four friends out for an afternoon nosh and hot toddy on a cool afternoon.

Which is what Pete was going for. They strolled through the lobby of the hotel evoking a few curious glances, one or two slight gasps followed by the shaking of heads before the almost shocked returned to whatever they had been engaged in. Pete smirked as they fled the constrictive lobby to the freedom of a crowded London street.

Ian's furtive glance gave his trepidation away as surely as if he walked down the street naked with a large pink Flag and a neon sign proclaiming, 'Here I am! Please don't look at me'. So, of course, people did. Pete grabbed Ian by the collar and pulled him into a small milliner, the other two being dragged and towed in the wake.

"Do you see what's happening, mate?" Pete turned Ian so he could observe the crowd gathering outside the large glass window.

"Yes," was Ian's sheepish reply.

"Well, that's what we wish to avoid," his smile was so genial Ian could not help but relax. "Take a deep breath in through the nose and out through the mouth." He held Ian's shoulders steady, eye to eye, breathing with him. Well, attempting to, but Ian was still gasping and gulping large mouth's full of air and staring at the growing crowd outside the window. "Don't look at them, look at me, look at Maggie. John, Maggie, Ian now focus on me and all together now, breathe in, slowly, slowly, and out through the mouth. Relax, we're just going to get a pint, mate."

"I don't drink," eked out the hero.

"Alright a diet and a gummy. Would you like a gummy?" asked the former Mersea Beats man, fishing around in his pockets.

"I would fucking love one!" Ian stood like a man to his full height.

"Then let us pretend to do a bit of shopping and browsing," They made their way towards the back of the shoppe.

As they browsed, trading baseball caps for fedoras, fedoras for trilby's, a beret for a white straw hat which only induced a few two steps and bows to the crowd. Ian chewed half the gummy sharing the other half with the lovely Mrs. Tension eased in the little shoppe as the gummies took effect. Pete handed the man a ten-pound note for his time and the three eased back onto the lane.

It was like a magician's trick where the four of them disappeared into the crowd without anyone taking note. The impossibility of it struck Ian. Here he was, his face splattered all over the front pages of papers, on the BBC screens everywhere, walking down the street with a Rock God and no one seemed to notice. They were just four anonymous middle-aged folks walking down the boulevard seeking libations. Suddenly a Rolls Royce pulled up at the high-end jewelers across from them and the crowd once so taken with this quartet had their attention snatched towards whoever might be exiting the luxury sedan across the way. Brilliant. It turned out to be someone none of the four recognized, but apparently famous for a moment long enough, at some indistinct point of time, to drag the fame horde with them.

They found a quiet pub several blocks from the hotel and popped in to grab a bite. All this skullduggery and avoidance, combined with revelation and relief, had sharpened appetites.

"That was the most brilliant revelation of my life," Ian breathed in the fresh air of perceived freedom along with the acrid scent of stale beer, vomit, and shattered dreams.

"It was something we noticed as the fame came and flew. The more we attempted to avoid, the more they attempted to intrude. Briley's idea really," Pete tipped his glass of Best Bitter to clink with Ian's diet, Maggie's vodka tonic and John's dark Guinness. Like any good Irishman he drank only Irish in an English pub.

"Really?" Maggie was now intrigued or just stoned enough to be polite.

"Well, it's only right, as he was partially responsible for the whole mash anyway." They may not have been paying close attention before, which of course they were, how could they not? They say, even in a crowded, noisy bar you can hear the words of a Rock Legend. "Yes, he had seen how some of the lasses would respond to the band. Of course, some drinking might have played a wee part, but I digress. Briley, our manager of the time, noticed how some of the lasses would stand in front of the bandstand, not dancing and moving to the music, but weeping with love in their hearts and willing on their lips, and thought, 'maybe we can build on this'. Memories of old Frank Sinatra reels found their way into the plot and he and the record company thought, 'Why not goose the reaction with a few paid shills!' Brilliant. It got the press and radio attention that there were these four blokes creating a storm over in Liverpool and the fans just took it over." He sipped his Best Bitter.

"Wait," Ian set his diet on the table, "the whole screaming and chasing, the pulling of the hair and ripping of the cloth, that was set up?" He was incredulous through the haze of the high. He felt as though his whole world had been pulled away. This was bigger than the life-saving bullshit.

"No, no, no," Pete gestured for peace and half a mo to explain.

"They goosed it, they didn't start it, but they had no idea how it would get out of hand. The pulling of locks was quite real, I'm still scarred. We used to travel with several changes of the same clothes. Because you couldn't walk onstage with ripped shirts and jackets. It was all quite real, and, I might add, quite frightening." His shiver and deep quaff of the bitter gave truth to the memory.

"It was also Briley who noted that on certain days the fans only seemed to notice two or three of us, there was always one lucky mate who could live a normal life for a day." A wistful grin shadowed his thoughts, "though it was seldom me. Once we discovered this other bands picked up on it as well. Even your namesake," he tipped his glass in John's direction, "was able to find a few days to enjoy. I think that was why he loved New Yorkers so. They were more jaded than in other cities. Kind of a, 'you think you're famous, well, the most famous people in history have lived here. You are but a five-minute meal in a fifteen-minute restaurant.'

"New York City suited him. He could be famous and loved when he needed it and left alone to walk the streets in anonymity when the mood was on," he set his glass on the table as their order came. Two vegetarian platters and two fish and chips.

The vittles were greeted with cheers, laughter, and another round.

From the small two-top nestled in the corner of the pub where no one but those seated at it might notice, a small fortyish looking man in clean workman's uniform, newly trimmed and combed black hair, and, apparently, recently polished and shined shoes quietly made his way to the table of the celebrants.

He stopped at the head of their booth and took in each of the four closely as if inspecting for unwanted vermin. Ian tensed up slightly as he came in for a second inspection.

"Excuse me, as I don't normally complain nor comment on the revelry of others, but your boisterousness seems to be intensifying and I am attempting a quiet dinner with my girl," and at this she snuck her head around the corner so as to give proof to the aforementioned, "and we both enjoy a bit of the old cheerful gaiety ourselves, you see. But this eve was reserved for a meet of some import." And here if the man had a cap, he would've removed it so as to twirl it in hand. He leaned in so he would not have to raise his voice above a whisper.

"I am hoping to ask for the young lady's hand, as it were, and could use a softening of the tone, if you get my drift." He nervously looked over to the soon to be betrothed hoping he had not spilt the contents before the intended moment.

"Sorry, sorry, we'll keep it down until you give the high sign and then drinks shall be on us," said Pete, "That is if the news is as expected."

"Appreciated." And he was gone.

The four sat in stunned silence as Pete's theory had played out before them. This ordinary Londoner had approached a table of one hero, his bride, one an actual rock legend and a namesake of another and hadn't batted an eye lash.

Several minutes later, the man and his, one could assume, now happily betrothed, came back to the table to show off the teeniest engagement ring Maggie had ever seen, though their smiles, ear to ear, gave all the brilliance any engagement could ask. Ian ordered a bottle of their finest bubbles, another round of drinks, and the gaiety was cut loose. The two smitten and now, betrothed, never remarking on the curious company they found themselves in. Maggie did notice the youngish woman taking in Pete from the corner of her eye, whether from recognition of Mersea Beats or just of an extremely good-looking older man, she couldn’t tell.

Pete's impish smile saw he noticed Maggie taking in the interplay. He tipped his new Trilby at a natty angle which Ian thought made him look a little goofy, like when they did photo shoots with the four lads and all had to mock it up a bit. But since he had never been, was not now, nor ever would be a rock legend he kept his thoughts to himself. All was well with the world and God's children were safe in their beds.

Pete took off the trilby and tossed it on the table replacing it on his perfect head with his old baseball cap. "Shall we once again venture forth and see how the theory plays out?" He held out his arm for Maggie who eagerly took it and they strutted back into the thriving vein of London town.

As Fame smiled her appreciation of this wrinkle by Fate, she was still vexed that Ian had not fallen in love with her. All humans loved her; it was in their very being. They craved Fame, would do anything for Fame, as evidenced by the current state of affairs, where every child with a voice or the ability to type chased her with a single-minded resolve; talent be damned. What she was attempting to accomplish was to bring dignity back into her essence. It was not going well, though she would not, under any circumstance, let Fate know.

"That was lovely," she complemented Fate on the introduction of the couple. "Though shows I have my work cut out for me, doesn't it?"

K. Adrian Zonneville

All That and a Kettle of Fish

There are many people who have spent lifetimes traveling to the four corners of the earth and most of the straight lines and angles betwixt and between and all the ships at sea. There have been those who have climbed to the very top of Everest and plumed the depths of the Mariana, traversed the deepest, darkest jungles of Africa, the sands of the Sahara, the plains of the Serengeti and forests of the Amazon, the mountains of India and the neighborhood deli, who claim London is the greatest city in the world; and not all of them live within its confines. Ian was one of them.

It had everything any civilized man could desire; incredible museums, symphonies, the greatest in Rock and Roll, artists, cuisine from every nook and cranny of the world, cultures of every civilization, without the overcrowded depravity of a Mumbai or Mexico City, nor the snootiness of Rome, the attitude of New York, the spiteful maliciousness of Gay Paree, nor the kindness of Oslo. It was London. The people were polite, well-mannered, cultured, if not overly welcoming certainly decent. They had no attitude as it was assumed they were the greatest city on the planet and they had nothing to prove. They were obliging and amiable unless the footballers happened to be in the corner pub. Or to be honest, near your neighborhood or district, within several blocks of your home or screaming at any screen, but sports fans will be sports fans, most of London preferred to send the fans on the road with the teams.

So, it was with gay abandon that the foursome once again set out to prove or, heaven forbid, disprove Sir Peadar's hypothesis. The weather was London, overcast with the promise of sprinkles and showers when the sky felt the urge. The first few blocks of storefronts and knick-knack shops seemed to bear him out. The grand mass of humanity was far more intrigued by the gewgaws tempting them from every window. Ian could feel every muscle relax. Well, every single one but that tight SOB in the back of his neck that acted as if it were sensing danger ahead no matter the evidence, nor the proof of his own eyes and ears.

He stepped lightly hoping none of the others would notice. Pete, of course, slowed his pace ever so slightly to match Ian's own. "Everything copacetic, mate?" He spoke out of the corner of his mouth in a nonchalant way, never taking his eyes from their focus forward.

"Yes," said Ian matching Pete's tone, "why would you ask?"

"Just sensing a bit of tension," he chuckled, "as if you are anticipating."

"I can't just block out what my brain seems to be focusing on; possibilities," he tried to shrug it off, unsuccessfully. "My brain sees so many people, so many possibilities of someone attempting to die, and my being drawn into the melee." He barked a humorless laugh. He could feel it coming, he knew in his bones some disaster was creeping up, though none of the others noticed. His spider sense was tingling like a coke fiend just needing a bump, shit!

Ian did everything he could to shake the feeling of impending doom. It was stupid and a distraction from a lovely day. Here he was in his favorite city with his perfect wife, an old friend and fucking Pete McCarthy strolling down the main chocka-block with humanity. The sun was now attempting to force its way onto the avenue and make a grand entrance. It was time to put the past where it belonged.

What had happened was pure chance, it wasn't fate or destiny, he was not put on this earth to be a savior. Hell, he could hardly save himself. If it wasn't for Maggie, he'd probably be living in a one room walk up in the Heights surviving on opium, Jack and Tab, and a stipend from some local band trying to find a nice way to tell him it just wasn't working. He had fallen into every opportunity in his life.

Shit, why not wallow in the deep end of his depression, maybe this time he'd drown.

He had been lucky, what was wrong with that? He'd taken chances out of pure ignorance and they'd paid off. Some would call that instinct! He'd been given a gift, his feel for music and instead of cashing in just for the financial reward he had tried to do something decent with the ability. He'd made every attempt to help those on the way up. And cushion the landing later in their careers. He'd been one of the good guys, hadn't he? So, why this turn of events?

Did the muse of music think he wanted some reward other than the great one he had? Did she misinterpret some whacky thought that had passed through the pumpkin? He could not remember ever thinking he deserved or desired more than he had. He was happy. So, shove it muse, fate, or whatever god of fortune, and leave me alone.

He shook off the funk and put a little life in his step. Maggie wrapped her arm through his, soon joined on either side by John and Pete. By God, they were the new Mersea Beats!

It was a good thing that minor goddesses could no longer read human minds. There had been a time when they could. So it was, that the two goddesses plotting the journey of four seeming average individuals through the avenues of London town were completely clueless as to what their main subject was thinking. They would have become quite miffed if they could hear Mr. Sperling's ruminations. Instead, they observed what Fate had put into motion.

The crowd thickened as they made their way through the shopping district. People nodded their apology for bumping into or separating the four. That was London, polite to a fault. A protester of questionable repute marched up and down a small block claiming some imagined slight from either shopkeeper, government official or lover with a large sign detailing said slight; though to Ian the sign made absolutely no sense, more a cry for visibility to an uncaring world. People flowed around him, as if he were a large rock in a small, swollen stream, pushing some dangerously close to the line of automobiles and buses running without cease feet away.

Pete nodded for them to make a quick right to avoid the masses. The lane he'd picked was bustling but not jam packed. Here was a back lane with carriage rides, hawkers, street vendors, and beggars. It was the backside of London, the view few tourists get a glimpse of. A London of old, a London the tourists walked by without notice.

A woman with three small children, an infant held close to the breast, a toddler attached at the hand and a youngster clutching skirt, made their way towards the foursome. The unattached boy kept trying to pet the horses parked at the curb as they passed, his mother pulling him back into orbit. Ian thought she might do better to let the kid get a pet in, then he might focus more on keeping up with her rather than dragging behind.

It was then that the toddler pulled her attention to her right, the infant squirmed and the youngster cast himself free. He wandered over towards the large Percheron attached to the white carriage. Somewhere just up the lane, maybe a business or two, a woman leaned out the second story window to shake a rug, the frame gave way causing the window within to fall two stories onto the pavement, crashing with a loud bang and startling another horse, who's driver was not in attendance, and causing it to bolt free down the lane, just as the youngster walked into the middle to try and pet the draft horse of his attention.

Ian was right in front of the action, he tried to step back but a man walking a large Irish wolf hound passed behind him, the dog of enormous size knocked into the middle of Ian's back pushing Ian into the lane where he would have no choice but to save the child.

As Ian fell toward the child, the kid started, saw the strange man lurching towards him and bolted towards his mother. Ian righted himself just before the large horse trampled him. No one was hurt. John and Maggie pulled Ian back onto curb, brushing him off and inspecting for any cuts, bruises, abrasions. Satisfied they continued their stroll down the lane.

Except Pete, who stood rooted to where the action had taken place with a look of incredulity seeming to hold him fast. Ian, John, and Maggie quick stepped to collect the stunned legend and continue their progress.

"I need a pint," was all he said and they sailed towards a port of entry.

They found a booth over in the corner of a quiet small alcove well away from the front door. John took the order and headed to the empty bar.

"I mean, I saw it with my own eyes, but I still don't believe it. I watched, like it all happened in slow motion. I wanted to step in, to stop the action as it were, but I couldn't move. It was as if I were planted there to observe and couldn't interfere." He spoke as if in a dream or recounting one. He didn't look at either Ian or Maggie, rather staring off into the upper far corner where walls met ceiling and seemed so solid.

"Well, I'd only been part of two of these occurrences, now three, but that seems to be how it happens. We are bit players in this production. We have no lines, no actions, it is quite surreal," Maggie reviewed in her own mind, step by step, what had just occurred. Or almost occurred, because something had stopped the preordained conclusion of Ian saving the kid by default. But, why?

"I heard the crash," Pete was now doing his own deconstruction of the event, "I looked up. Saw the woman shriek, then relax as no one had been hurt, the horse jumped, startled, shocked not to have his owner nearby, I can only guess, and bolted. The child in the middle of the lane was a goner, for sure, but he wasn't. I hardly noticed the bloke with that huge, monster of a wolf hound, but saw the dog almost purposefully bump hard into Ian and push him into the lane. The dog pushed him into the lane!" He shook his head in amazement, " I wouldn't believe that if the real John Lennon came back from the dead to tell the tale!"

Instead, the other John Lennon showed up with four glasses, two with amber colored liquid, one with diet cola, and one with a vodka and tonic. Ian fished in his pocket for the gummy he knew had taken up residence within. He smiled in relief as his fingers closed around the little bear.

John pushed the glasses around to their proper owners with a flourish before picking up one of the beers with a great shit eating grin. "Well, everybody let's toast!!" He was overflowing with the love of life and the joy of human kindness.

"You seem in a glorious mood," said Ian as he popped the little bear into his mouth.

"We're celebrating, ol' chum, lift your glass!" He waited. Each in turn cautiously enveloped their own glass and half masted for the toast.

"Come on, ya maudlin bastards, it's over!" his face lit up like Piccadilly when Jolly Old was being celebrated.

"What's over," ventured Ian.

"The bloody curse, ya dumb yank. Dontcha see? The curse of saving people has come to an end?" He looked each in the eye before clinking glasses and taking a long draught of the drink.

"How do you figure," now it was Maggie's turn to let optimism seek the sunlight.

"Ian didn't save nobody back there. It was as ripe a situation as has ever been created but it righted itself without him. As a matter of fact, it seemed to have pushed him right out of the lifesaving business. A child! A child, he could've saved, but no, he scared the little blighter back into his momma's arms. The dogs and horse be damned, ding-dong the witch is dead! Put a fork in it. The fat lady has sung and left the building! Our hero is retired." and now the other three raised their glasses in understanding. It was over, the nightmare of decency had come to an end.

Peadar was quiet for several long seconds, his eyes and face downcast and deep in thought.

"What is it?" asked Maggie who had, of course, noticed.

"It's kind of sad, idn't it?" he sat back in the booth, legs stretched out with a wistful expression taking a stroll about his features. "I just got here. I saw something so bizarre and unreal; I still don't believe it happened. I know what I'd heard, what the witnesses said, but I hadn't actually seen it with my own eyes, and now it's done. I don't know, I almost wish..."

"Well, I don't," said Ian with much force followed by an 'Amen' from the wife.

"We would like our pitiful, sedate, anonymous lives back, thank you very much," and now Maggie took a deep gulp and then another of her drink.

"Of course, it's just..."

The two naked goddesses were startled by the very loud and abrupt, 'Ahem', and ripped their gazes from the swirling waters of life to the large, thickly bearded man standing looking over their shoulders.

"What have we here?" Asked the giant.

"Nothing just bored and watching humanity," they giggled.

"There's something about these ones," he scratched his chin. "something musical."

"You imagine something when there is nothing to be seen," chastised Fame. "If there was anything of interest you would've known the moment either of them came into the world."

"True, true," he said, still staring hard at the elderly, chunky one with the pure white hair. "Though there is something..."

"There is nothing," spoke Fate quietly, "or I would know by its path, and there is nothing but ordinary life ahead for it."

Apollo nodded reluctantly as he moved past them to listen to a symphony just taking wing somewhere near Berlin.

You Can't Always Get What You Want

The parting at the door to the pub had been heartfelt. Pete hugged all three deeply. He told Maggie to watch over Ian, whom he had come to feel very close to after this afternoon's adventures. Pete and Ian had run into each other at fundraisers and award ceremonies, had worked on a few projects, and Pete knew that Ian had worked closely with Richie, his bandmate and drummer, over the years but they had never been close. Something about the events of the day had ignited an emotional response he hadn't expected. Maybe it was Ian's response to fame. Maybe it was his remembered terror when thousands of fans would try to 'get a piece' of him, to touch him, grab a lock of hair, a swatch of fabric, he knew they only wanted to touch fame, an idol, but they encroached into personal space so treasured he had felt violated on a thousand occasions. He knew in his heart and tattered soul how Ian felt. Or did he? He and the boys had sought the fame even if they didn't really understand what that meant. They wanted to fill clubs and halls, they wanted to sell records and appear on every show on the telly. They had watched fame growing up. So, had Ian, though he had chosen another course, one where he could safely enjoy all the glory of watching those he loved and helped from the wings of anonymity. Yes, it was quite different.

When he hugged John goodbye he had to laugh and then he hugged the man tight as if taking this chance to really say goodbye to his dear friend and brother, something he had been denied so many years ago. They promised to share a pint from time to time.

Before Pete could quite tear himself away, he turned and caught at Ian's sleeve, "Hey Mate, how long are you staying in London? Or are you headed back to the states right away now that the crisis has passed?"

Ian shared a moment with Maggie who took in his meaning and shrugged as if it made her no nevermind, besides that's Sir Peadar McCarthy. "It's London, our favorite city, we have no pressing concerns, I could use a little time just touristing, no hurry, why?"

"Well, I am working on a new project and have a couple tunes that just are not coming together, I thought, maybe, if you're not in any hurry, you might take a listen." He grinned knowing Ian's reputation, therefore knowing he couldn't turn Pete down.

The five-year-old that lived in the forever land that was Ian's soul jumped up and down, screaming in excitement and joy, while Ian pretended to think about it. The slap to his shoulder from Maggie told him she had made the decision if the damn kid couldn't. "I would love to."

Pete wrote down some studio times, the address, though Ian knew exactly where the studio was, and shook Ian's hand on the deal. "I'll take you all to dinner when we're done, all three of you," he pointedly included John in the arrangement. "Maybe we can get Richie to come along."

"I'm sure he will as long as he's not paying," Ian spoke softly, though not so softly Pete didn't hear. He laughed as he walked away.

"Oh my god," Maggie grabbed her husband by the lapels and pulled him in for the long, passionate kiss, "You're working on a Mersea Beats album!"

"Well, technically it is Pete's," he chided. "John, I guess we'll be seeing more of you over the next few days. Keep your dinner schedule open for the big night."

Back at the hotel Ian threw himself on the bed.

"You're not going to sleep, are you?" Maggie sounded disappointed. She stared at his silent, prone form. "You can't! How can you possibly think about sleeping when you have been offered to work with Sir Peadar himself? A rock legend!" She didn't know what else to say. What could you say? If working with Peadar 'Pete' McCarthy didn't wake you up you were already six feet under!

"I'm exhausted. This has been a whirlwind to end all whirlwinds and it ain't over. But maybe John is right, the other thing might be. I am going to take a nap and hope when I get up the world will have righted itself, fate or fortune will leave me by the wayside and we can get back to our regularly scheduled program."

"But I thought we'd go out, have a lovely meal, catch some music, make a night of it," she tried to pull him into a sitting position. "Celebrate!"

"Maybe later, right now I am going to dream of peaceful rock shows, long hours in the studio, and listening to horrors that need correction." His snores, whether real or feigned, told her there would be no further discussion.

Ian slept for two hours before hunger and Maggie's insistence roused him from the very comfortable bed. Showered, attired in clean London wear they trundled off to Mildreds Covent Garden. They knew from experience Mildreds had vegetarian and vegan fare and was open until eleven p.m.

Bellies full, thirst sated, they walked arm in arm through the bustling streets of SoHo, up towards Leicester Square until the sound of live music drew them into a half-crowded pub down a side lane on the cusp of hipster and transitioning. The sad thing about civilized society is that when an impoverished neighborhood, one that is relatively cheap and affordable to musicians and artists, becomes known for same, then the wannabes begin to filter in so they can live with the hip. This then forces the prices of real estate towards the sky, the area becomes gentrified, and the artists, musicians, clubs, and galleries are forced out by those they brought in, removing the entire raison d'etre for anyone to be there.

This had not happened quite yet and Ian and Maggie found seats in the back of the pub near the bar where they could hear the music but not be blown away by the volume. Ian had not yet ascribed to the 'it's too loud' generation, by age maybe but not by volume. Of course, he was three quarters deaf. A life living with bands can do that to a person. But Maggie preferred to keep what hearing both of them had hence the back of the room.

The band was good but could have been much better if only they had a sound man who could hear. Christ on a woofer, Ian was near deaf and he could hear the mix was awful. Certainly, there were more musicians on that stage than a drummer and a bassist.

Maggie saw him fidgeting and knew it was only a matter of time. She considered telling him just to relax or if it bothered him that much, they could leave. And just as quickly realized that he was falling back into Ian. Tuning in a band was as much a part of him as tuning in a song in a recording studio. If it was wrong it grated on his nerves to the point he couldn't let it go.

He apologized, as he stood up from the table just as the drinks arrived. "I'll be right back," he kissed her cheek.

He didn't have to push his way through to the soundboard, there weren't that many people in the club. He tapped the 'soundman' on the shoulder and the guy brushed him off. He tapped the 'soundman' on the shoulder again and pointed to his ears, the guy brushed him off, again. Apparently, he thought Ian was some old guy complaining about the volume. Ian tapped again. Now a young, long-haired, fellow with a cute girl attached to his arm came up to Ian and seemed to be shouting in his ear. Well, of course, he was, it was the way rock people communicated. Finally, Ian pointed to the door and motioned for the young guy to step outside.

Maggie threw a ten-pound note to the innkeeper and motioned she'd be right back, maybe. As she exited the club, Ian was nose-to-nose with the guy and she heard him saying with a great deal of emphasis, "...manager of this band you should give a shit what they sound like! Give me three minutes with that board and I'll show you what they should sound like!"

Maggie recognized the tone, the attitude, and his posture, Ian was about to get thrown out of a night club, again. She had seen this before, she wished he wouldn't, but she also knew he just could not countenance bad sound, bad musicians, bad show. If you are going to be on the stage, when a hundred other bands were vying for the same, the very, very least you could do was be professional about it. Ian was daring the guy to let Ian show him some old, damn near deaf guy could do a better job than his young stud.

At long last, just before ejection, the guy motioned Ian inside. With a massive dose of attitude and want of seeing this old codger get his comeuppance, he decided, 'Let's see what the old man thinks he can do.' The manager motioned the sound guy to step back and let Ian in. Ian studied the board, the markings on the tape telling him what was plugged into where. He sat. And his hands moved as if by divine intervention. The drums settled into a nice cradle with the bass, supporting but not overpowering the keyboardist, who was very good when you could hear him. His fills tasty without taking away from the female vocalist, the rhythm guitarist, background vocals or the sweet play of the sax. It all fit together so nicely; it was like a beautifully well-crafted quilt. It was still very loud, but it was comfortable, it didn't grate on the ear. It enticed people to listen and when the song ended, they were greeted with a rousing round of applause.

Ian shook the manager's hand, and in a magnanimous gesture shook the sound guy's as well and they shared a smile. Maybe they learned something from the old guy after all. This played out as Maggie hoped; a large dose of anxiety, a moment of confrontation followed by conciliation, a heaping of learning and a desert of everyone becoming a friend of Ian's. Every interaction, or almost every interaction, with Ian ended with becoming friendly, if not friends. It was how he operated; it was in his DNA. Either that or ejection. Luckily tonight was friendship.

He came back to his diet and they listened for another half hour before making their way down the avenue. It had turned into a lovely evening of good food, decent music, and the two of them arm in arm.

Look Through Any Window

Ian's dreams were filled with broken pieces of reality and coulda beens, if onlys and what ifs. It was weird in a cerebral, scientific sort of way. A way of seeing and analyzing one's life from the comfort of an easy chair, if life could sit in an easy chair.

What he discovered was those things he considered missed opportunities were actually drive-byes that coalesced in a jigsaw puzzle life where it all fit if you could just note the pieces. He had wanted jobs at certain radio stations only to be denied or given the gig for a minute before losing it to someone not near as qualified only to fall into managing an artist he loved but thought the chance would never materialize. One door closed and closed so hard it slammed his ass into the next project.

He would lose an artist to another management company and someone he respected would recommend him to another artist he respected even more, so they could mutually respect for a couple years before separating as friends. Always as friends.

Ian had never had piles of cash, just hundreds of friends and friends of friends drawn together by mutual love and respect. People he knew he could call on in any emergency and they would be there for him. His dream a second before waking was of his idol. There was only one who Ian could never get past his adoration of and that man had come to stand by his side in his one true hour of need. Who else would understand the horror of almost instant fame than one of the Mersea Beats? And he had come, that was not a dream. And now he had to wake and meet the rock star to help this man, whom he idolized, with a recording project. It wasn't often Ian woke with a smile on his face, but this one would not be scrubbed off, not for a long time.

As he showered, brushed teeth and hair, not with the same brush, and dressed, Maggie brought him a hot cuppa and some fruit for breakfast. "How long do you think you'll be?" she asked noncommittedly. They had been married a very long time and she knew when he was involved with a project, time meant nothing. He would be done when he was done. She only wished to know if this was a movie day or a museum one. Planning her afternoon was now her top concern.

"Don't you want to come and stick an ear in?" he seemed surprised, though she very seldom wanted to spend the day in the studio. Well, unless it might be Jax or some other artist she really loved.

"I don't think Sir Peadar would appreciate having me hanging around while he's trying to work," she shrugged her almost apology.

"You might be right on alternating days or realities, but I think he wouldn't mind if you stuck your head in for a while." His confidence was disconcerting. He knew something she didn't.

"And how would the great Ear know such a thing?" she japed.

"Because of this," and he tossed her his phone.

There was the text from the great one himself asking if Maggie would be joining them at the studio. He would be honored if she would and would leave both their names at the gate. The Gate, that could only mean they were not going to the small studio Ian had told her Pete liked to use on his solo projects, but Apple. The Apple, The Gate. Shit, yes, she wanted to go!

"I guess I could come along for a while," the absolute embodiment of decorum.

"If you think you can tear yourself away from the halls of the dead," he tossed her rain jacket to her and slid his arm around her shoulders.

Normally on her best day Maggie could take a couple hours hanging around a studio while the band set up, tuned up, and ran over songs they had played a thousand times. Now hoping that playing them for the thousandth and one time they would get them perfect on this specific day. No matter how much she loved an act or their music, no matter how catchy the tune or how the lyric brought you in, by the fiftieth time you'd heard it, it lost its luster. And that was the studio. Trying time after time to get that perfect take. The one without any obvious miscues, everything tight, sounding like it was fresh out of the blocks while being the thirty-fifth time they'd run through it in the last three hours. It was mind-blowingly boring for those in the booth.

Here they walked into a studio with more history than any other in the world, you could feel the presence of those who had gone before as you entered the control room. This is the studio of Roger Daltrey, James Taylor, Badfinger, Nilsson, Tim Hardin, Let it Be, All Things Must Pass and hundreds of others. And they walked into a session in its final throes. The mixing. The repetition had been completed, the tracks were down, had been down, they just needed another ear. Ian.

The hellos were brief, beverages were offered and accepted or turned down and the tape began to roll. Apparently, Mr. McCarthy preferred tape to the more modern digital, computerized method. It's warmer, he said. Everyone settled into their designated seats and Ian, disdaining headphones, closed his eyes to listen.

This was something Maggie never tired of because she couldn't understand, just could not grok nor comprehend, how Ian did this. She didn't think he knew the how, just that he knew he could 'hear' what most others couldn't.

The first song played was beautiful. Perfect, she thought. Almost a 'Yesterday' but different. It was sweet, loving, tore at the soul in a soft, caring way. There was nothing Ian would find here. Though when she gazed at Pete, she could see his face scrunched up as if tasting something bitter. He stared at Ian who sat, eyes still closed shaking his head.

"Play it again, please," he said without opening eyes or making any outward contact with the others.

A minute or so into the second listening he held up his hand to stop the tape. "Back it up fifteen," he asked the engineer. Who, after seeking approval from the man whose session this was, did as asked.

"There," Ian whispered, "in that passage, right there, solo the strings for me." The engineer played it one more time.

"There it is. That's where it starts. Can you just give me the viola with the others softened?" Ian asked.

And sure enough, Maggie, though late to the discovery, could hear. The instrument was slightly out of tune with the other three.

"Schedule a couple hours Wednesday," Pete told the woman standing next to him, "We'll have to rerecord that bit and check the rest."

"You might as well plan on the whole tune, if he's out there, he's out all the way to the end." Ian shook his head as if to dismiss the song before heading onto the next.

This continued throughout the afternoon. Watching a master smooth out a few wrinkles to make something palatable to all ears. It was never perfect, music, like all art, should never be perfect. It was the imperfections that added to the beauty. But you didn't want it to grind on the nerves, either. Sometimes it was the discord between the same note on different instruments, some sounds just did not play well together. And other times he suggested something he heard that Pete had not; the great benefit of bringing in a set of ears and experience you trusted. He was creating magic in his own way. This was another way Ian could be involved with the creative without the fame. He was just not a famous person, it didn't fit. Though he loved being with famous folks and aiding in their endeavors, when all was said and done, he was happy to fade into the background and enjoy the obscurity.

The half dozen songs Pete wanted his help on were soon diagnosed with the day still young. "I shall send a lovely check to cover your missed day of holiday." Pete gestured to his assistant.

"No," Ian said softly, "that won't be necessary. This, this was exactly what I needed. This has healed the broken soul and salved the wound. I should pay you." He smiled at something only he could see or feel. "Thank you."

"Then dinner with you and the lovely Maggie. I have a room arranged at a fave place where we won't be bothered. See if Mr. Lennon will join us with a guest, of course. And" he grinned, "I have it on good authority that Mr. Stainesby will put aside his banging and would be delighted as well." He clapped his hands together in a gesture of joy before gazing at the two other occupants, his assistant and the very capable engineer, in the room, "Join us?" And dinner was set.

Ian and Maggie took a taxi back to the hotel. Ian loved London taxis and taxi drivers, there are none in the world to compare. His mood was as jovial as she could remember. He and Maggie cuddled together as the vehicle made its way through the busy streets of London town. Nothing could destroy this mood. And dinner with not one but two of the Mersea Beats, yes, it would be an evening to remember.

They napped, showered, smoked a bowl out on the balcony, dressed and made their way down to the concierge. Taxi called and acquired. Though Maggie had pled her case for the tube, her preferred way to travel in London. Ian wasn't quite sure where the restaurant was, though his wife assured him she was quite certain of the location and the best way to get there. She knew London as well as most of the cabbies, though she preferred the Tube. Still, since he was having such a wonderful day, she acquiesced to his wishes.

The cab ride was non-eventful and they showed up at the quiet, out of the way place early. Just as well, thought Ian, it would allow them to ease into the evening.

The Stainesby's, Richie and Barb, had also arrived early and it would appear Pete and entourage would be late. He had stayed in the studio longer than he'd planned, gone home to take a quick nap, which turned out to be less quick than planned, and was running a half hour behind. The Stainesbys and the Sperlings would keep each other company until the other Knight showed.

Richie Stainesby, the former drummer for the Mersea Beats, and Ian had known each other for several decades, as Ian had helped put together some tours and he had managed some of Richie's friends for decades in the late 80s and early 2010s. They knew each other.

"How's Joe," asked Richie jovially. It dawned on Ian that Richard always sounded jovial.

"Well, I talked to him a couple weeks ago and he sounded," Ian search for the proper term, "antsy."

"Not playing, is he?" Richie laughed. He knew Joe as well as any -body and knew if Joe wasn't playing Joe wasn't happy.

"You know him. It makes him nuts that no one loves to tour like he does. He could go in the studio but that doesn't scratch the itch. He needs live!" And they both shook their heads in agreement.

Barb and Richie sipped their juice mocktails while Ian ordered one for himself and a glass of wine for Maggie. The three had lost years, friends, and too much cash to over imbibing and each now had decades of sobriety behind them, but they did not begrudge Maggie her wine. One man's sin is another woman's pleasure. Don't judge others by your actions.

Small talk and catching up pleasantly filled time until John and his date, a robust man of approximately the same age, though smaller in stature, showed. Ian left the introductions up to John. John began by reluctantly introducing himself. Richie was slightly taken aback at the name before he, too, found great humor in it, as Pete had earlier. Richie had known and was close to the original Mr. Lennon as well. He looked to John's date and asked, "Your name doesn't happen to be George or Paul, does it?"

"No," he assured, "it's Nigel." Of course, it was and they all roared with laughter.

"Did I miss something?" asked Pete as he made his entrance.

"Nothing important," smiled his old bandmate, "just making acquaintance with the namesake."

"Ah," smiled Pete, "Angela shall be a bit tardier than I and William had to tidy up the studio before closing shoppe. Everyone have something to drink? Good. I called ahead and ordered a plethora of appetizers to nibble on while we wait." He smiled his thanks as the waitress set down his own fruit juice mocktail, tonight he was in work mode and there would be no alcohol. He enjoyed a beer or wine from time to time but not when work was involved. Finish the project, then sit back and enjoy a glass.

"So, what are you and our hero talking about?" Pete asked his former band member.

"What's this? Hero? Why I had no idea. Maggie what have you been up to because we know whatever it was it couldn't have involved our intrepid leader of the noninvolvement club," Richie laughed as he patted Ian on the shoulder.

"Actually, he is the man of the hour," Pete sipped, Ian cringed.

"What say you?" Now the drummer's interest was piqued!

"Yes, it's true. It seems when our good friend Mr. Sperling is not rescuing my pitiful recordings from banging against themselves, he also has a side career rescuing people from certain death and dismemberment," Pete tipped his glass in salute and though Ian would've loved to have told him to stop, he was an idol. "Don't you watch the BBC America?"

"Afraid I have thrown the telly out with the rest of the trash, especially when it comes to 'news' from across the way," his scowl said everything he wished not to vocalize, "nothing but gossip, political gamesmanship with that despicable man, and sports which I have no interest in whatsoever!" He leaned back in his chair and stared at Ian. "Well?"

"'s nothing," the subject under scrutiny mumbled.

"Ho-ho, I would hardly say nothing. Look, mate, it's just us here and we have little or no secrets among the chosen." If Pete was waiting for Ian to launch into a soliloquy espousing his heroics he was in for an interminable pause in the conversation.

"Right then, I'll give you a brief synopsis," Pete described the several instances he knew Ian had been involved in over the last couple weeks. Of lives saved, heroics performed, and humble pie devoured.

"Well, well, well, I would never have thought such grand exploits from someone I know hates the spotlight as much as you have proclaimed!" The percussionist clapped his hands in joy at Ian's discomfort. "And here I thought you a devout coward of the nth degree. I remember one night when Joe tried to drag you onto the stage and you ran hell bent for the locked dressing room. Why the change of heart?" Now his tone softened from one of playful mockery to concern. He could see Ian was becoming overwrought and he was a friend. Enough of the ribbing, time to dig for the why.

"I, well, you see, it all just literally fell on me, or I on it," Ian stammered.

"He didn't mean to save anybody," Maggie chimed in helpfully. "He saved people completely on accident. Really! The first time he was trying to escape what would have been a massacre and his bar stool flipped over landing him on the assailant. The second the woman literally fell into his lap and he was attempting to get her off him. And the one over here, and John will attest to this, he got clocked, went down, tried to get up, slipped several times, falling again and again on the proprietor until the man's heart started once again. No heroism for my boy, just weird, dumb luck." And she nodded once emphatically to indicate all had been settled.

When Ian heard it put so succinctly and so plebian, well, it just sounded so ignominious. It was true he had never been known for his bravery, stepping into the fray, as it were, but he'd been a good man. He had never intentionally harmed another, taken what wasn't his nor had ever forgotten a birthday, an anniversary, or to send a card when some adversity had befallen a fellow. He always sent flowers to funerals and treats to those with new canine additions to the family. No, he was not one to volunteer for the front line of active military duty but he had acquitted himself many times over the years promoting fundraisers, benefits, and contributions to musician's funds.

"Well, I don't know if I would use the word coward, exactly," he began his defense. It wasn't that he wanted glory or praise, especially from friends, but the little devil residing on the left shoulder was prodding with the pitchfork for a bit of recognition. And would that be so bad? Yes! Quoth the angel on his right as she banged his ear hard. Ian had never had to fight the battle for ego. His was as balanced as any man could ask, but now he wondered if basking in a little glory would really be all that bad.

On a mountain top thousands of miles away, a beautiful, naked goddess jumped up and down clapping her hands in joy. "I told you he would come around! I told you he would fall in love with me!"
The other perfect form reclining against the mount, frowned her acquiescence

"No, no, no, no," begged the bearded drummer, "don't denigrate the beauty of cowardice. I truly believe it is the one thing that keeps civilization from destroying itself." He took in the confused, wry glances from around the table. "Cowardice is the last defense of the sane. We promote bravery and heroics as if that is something all should strive for. Think about it. When old men decide to go to war with other old men, they pump up the nationalism, patriotism, and talk of those who went before in the defense of their country, their people, their families. Repeating stories of great bravery in the face of odds the gods would recoil from. Whether true or not. Exaggeration is the feast of the jingoist when goading others to do horrible acts they would never consider themselves.

"They play to the softly molded parts of the youthful brain, goading them, shaming them, demanding they show they are not cowards, to the point there are no places left for the cowards to hide. So, they suck it up, pretend they are brave, and take their shaking, quivering mass of human flesh to sacrifice for the better good." He took a breath.

"Wait, hold on, are you going to defend cowards as heroes?" It was John who spoke up for the first time.

"Shush," Sir Peadar giggled, "he's just getting warmed up. This is the best part of the film."

"Thank you," Richard half bowed his thanks from his chair, "and, yes, I will defend the coward. For if the coward only had an ounce of moral fortitude to steel his spine, he would refuse these entreaties for his sacrifice. He would say, 'I'm not going. I have a future here. I'm in school to discover how to help mankind, to stop this insanity, to find ways for all to live together and evolve into a better species. Go fight you're own fucking war', and he wouldn't care one whit what anyone else thought of him. And maybe others would say the same, until all the young men and women of the world stood up to say they would no longer be cannon fodder for old men's blood lust. And if everyone refused to go along with the bravery and heroics, then maybe just maybe, we would have flying cars, no babies being still born, cancer could finally be conquered. Instead, we die over some wasteland that nobody really wanted anyway all in the name of bravery and valor. We could colonize the moon, fly to distant corners of the galaxy, and live long, happy lives rather than in fear of someone trying to take from us what little we possess. Everybody would have what they needed so no one would need to take anything from anyone else," he ran out of petrol and eased back in his chair once again. Grabbing his fruit juice mocktail he raised his glass, "To the cowards, may they finally conquer human nature!"

Followed by hearty 'here, here's' all around.

Ian thought, 'in a weird way he's right, the cowards are our future.' But then again, there seemed to always be those who would wage war whether the other fellow wanted it or not. And as long as the warlord could find a few that would fight, then the others had to keep their fair share of those who would do the same. It felt overwhelming in its spiraling descent into madness. Was there nothing humans could do to change? The question of the ages, he guessed, and he wasn't near smart enough to decipher an answer. He excused himself to use the loo.

It was a beautiful old eating establishment on the north end of London. It had once been a Merchants Coffee House where the well-to-do would meet over coffee to discuss trade, prices, and all things business. Ian thought this a much better use of the property. It could use some love, he mused, as he half tripped on the worn carpeting but the smells emanating from the kitchen promised heaven.

He had been a vegetarian for too many years to count but he thanked the culinary gods that taste had caught up with the fare. Veggy dishes were now delights rather than something you did because you thought it was the right thing to do. Save the planet, indeed but could we not save the taste buds at the same moment. Yes, someone had said and they were right!

Hands washed and stomach grumbling its discontent at being ignored for far too long he exited the men's loo and made his way to the back room. Unfamiliar as he was with the layout, he got confused on the way back and barged not through the door to the private room but to the kitchen where mayhem was in midflight.

As he pushed open the door, he saw flames jumping from a pan on the oversized stove, which caught the back of the cook's apron, the flames spreading quickly to the rest of his clothing. Ian turned to make a quick exit just as a busboy came through the door pushing Ian into the wall where the knob for the fire extinguisher was mounted on same. His hand up to cushion his collision with the wall he hit the trip of the fire extinguishers mounted over the stove.

He turned and gazed in horror as the other cooks and kitchen staff noticed the man on fire and Ian's hand on the pushbutton control. Flame retardant fell from the sky extinguishing the flames on the stove and the man. A cheer that could be heard throughout the entire establishment went up.

Maggie heard the ruckus and looked for Ian, "Oh dear god, where in the hell is my husband?"

Ian staggered through the door. His clothes disheveled, his hair a mess and covered in a white powder. He slipped behind the open door. Hot on his tail was the majority of the kitchen staff, the manager of the restaurant and, one could assume, the owner.

"Where is he? Where is the man who came through the door?" asked the manager in a heavily accented middle eastern accent. Ian did his best to disappear behind the door without being squashed into the wall.

"What did he do?" Maggie's voice trembled, though in her soul she knew. She could see Ian quivering behind the open door.

"What did he do? What did he do?" the man's tone was jubilant. "Nothing of import except save the life of my sister's son, that is all. We only wish to thank him, celebrate him, let the world know what a hero looks like!"

Ian caught Maggie's eye as he silently pled with her, and any other human she could psychically connect with, to not give his position away.

"He ran through here and I think bolted towards the front lobby," she pointed emphatically in the general direction of escape.

As the hot pursuit went in another direction, Richie sat back in his chair, refusing to look at Ian's hiding space, crossed arms across his chest and demanded, "Start at the beginning and leave out no pertinent detail!"

Ian slowly made his way to the head of the table, staring longingly at Maggie's glass of wine before shaking his head and slouching down into the chair.

"I had to go to the bathroom," Ian began almost apologetically.

"And that's when the shit hit the proverbial fan," Mr. Stainesby laughed heartily at his own clever quip, though the others did not jump in the same pool.

Ian took several seconds to explain in vague detail what had happened. Maggie nodded her head knowingly. John looked quite disappointed he'd missed the show. Pete groaned dejectedly at having missed this comedy of errors as well and the Stainesby's stared in disbelief. The drummer was about to ask for a further explanation when a ruckus in the outer confines of the restaurant stopped him.

The commotion outside the door, as the kitchen staff returned, turned all heads first to the sound of their fevered entrance and then to where Ian was attempting to dive under the table. Twenty years ago he might have made it but age had slowed reflexes.

Pete watched as the small mob entered the back room excitedly pointing at Ian with intent. The intent was to deify the accidental chevalier. Pete stood slowly, pushed back his chair, and walked over to stand in front of Ian.

"Mr. Abadi, please!" He did not raise his voice but his tone was insistent. "Please, settle yourself and your people!" He waited until the din could be subdued. "I realize my friend Ian, whether by accident or heroism, saved your sister's eldest son, but his wish is not to be lifted in praise. He is a humble man, not wishing honor or adoration, it would lessen what he has done. He only wishes for you and yours to have long and happy lives. That is the only reward he would seek," he patted Ian on the shoulder who was doing his best to become invisible. "Well, that and the fine meal he came here for. Do you think, with all that has happened here tonight, you and your staff can still put together the delicious meal I promised?"

"Absolutely, Mr. Peadar! We will prepare for you and your excellent guests the finest meals you have ever tasted. We shall honor your friend with a meal he will never forget! Kings and princes will be jealous of the fare, presidents and potentates will rue the day they were not here to share in this meal, the grand and the beautiful..." the words carried him out of the room as he herded the grateful back to their stations in the kitchen to create a meal worthy of the brave man occupying the back room.

Back to the questions eager to leap from the drummer's lips. "Let me get this straight," came the inquiry, "this accident, the one from fifteen minutes ago, follows the same pattern as the supposed other lifesaving maneuvers of the past several weeks?" As a man of science and knowledge, Richard wished only the facts and data that would lead to a solution for the Ian enigma.

"Well, not exactly as each experience varies dependent upon place, situation, peripheral factors and such. One time I was in a club, once on a plane, once in a pub, the externals influence the occurrence." If Richie wanted to play learned scientist Ian would amuse him.

"So, you just fall into being a hero. It's not thought out. It's not planned. It just happens to be something you trip over. Literally. Almost as if a spell has been put on you," the percussionist was heading somewhere, though it would seem only he knew the destination.

"Yes," said Maggie and Ian together, with an accompanying nod from John, though late to the table.

"Something would appear to have happened to change your mojo, as it were. It seems simple enough we only need to reverse the mojo and you can go back to being your old uncaring self," Richie gazed around the table to take in the congratulatory nods and applause for his brilliance.

"I don't know if I would've framed it quite like that," began the subject of discussion. The angel kicked the little devil, egging Ian on, off his shoulder and kicked Ian in the ear. She had had enough of his wandering ego for one night. Fame did not fit and she knew better than anyone it would chafe until he went mad. It had to stop now.

"No, I think he might actually be on to something," cried Richard's lifelong bandmate.

Just then the side door banged open as a dozen kitchen helpers and waitstaff barged through carrying trays laden with expertly crafted vegetarian fare. Dates, vegan Shawarma, toasted nuts and vegetables in sauces that tantalized and piqued the olfactory senses, spaghetti with yogurt and garlic sauce, moussaka, hummus, and falafel, every savory spice and flavor imaginable. The room was filled with smells and noise until all trays had found a home on the table at which point silence wrapped the hungry assembled.

In between bites Ian wracked his brain to remember something or someone reversing his well-ordered mojo but found nothing. He had not been near a carnival or freak show in years.

Pete's assistant, Hilary, arrived as the food was placed on the table. She had been informed by Sir Peadar of the difficulties Ian was suffering through and had caught the gest of what had happened in the restaurant on her way through. She had some ideas to assist Ian though most of them were on the far side of conventional. As she took in the assembled, she cocked her head as if asking herself a question when she saw the Stainesbys.

She nibbled on falafel and hummus before setting all on the plate in front of her. "Excuse me, Mr. Stainesby," she ventured, "but a word if you will." He nodded. She knew that The Mersea Beats had dabbled in spirituality and some occult practices at points in their lives, maybe, "Do you still maintain any of your contacts with your friends in the paranormal?"

Richie appeared startled though whether because she knew about his dabbling or because he hadn't thought of it himself, he couldn't be certain. "Now that you mention it, I think there are still a few that would answer the call." He laughed, "Why didn't I think of that? I guess I was caught up in the actual happenstance!" Again, he chuckled before pulling out his cell phone and scrolling quickly through his contacts. "There was a woman in New Orleans, Louisiana, if memory serves, who claimed to the be the great granddaughter of Marie Laveau. The Voodoo Queen. I know it sounds far outside traditional cures, but it might be the one you need." He nodded his thanks to Hilary before turning his attention to Ian, "When do you head back to the states?"

I'm A Voodoo Child

Ian had hesitantly agreed to visit with the supposed great-granddaughter of the Voodoo Queen. He hadn't wished to argue with his friend of several decades. If there was a major difference between how Ian thought of the two Mersea Beats it was that, though he had done some work with both. He had toured with Richie and his All-Star Review and they knew each other from the road. He was more pal than legend. And though he had done some projects that included Pete, Pete would always be the idol of Ian's youth. The one who personified everything Ian thought of as a rock star and human being. He adored the man and would probably never get past his worshipping of this rock deity.

He was well aware that the drummer held some unconventional beliefs but he also knew that the man was well-read and very intelligent. Besides what other options were open? Something was awry with his nimbus, whatever the hell that was. What harm could seeking an unorthodox remedy do?

They stayed on in London for another few days to allow him to soak up the good vibes and Maggie to prepare herself for whatever might be heading their way. They took in a few current plays, saw old friends, and heard new ones. They dined with Pete and his assistant one more time at the veggie restaurant where, once again, they were treated like royalty, actually better, as the royalty was not as revered as some might have thought. There had been no further lifesaving, no run-ins with fate or destiny, but the possibility niggled at the back of his brain. So, it was a relaxed yet disquieted Ian and wife who landed at Louis Armstrong airport. They had headed directly to New Orleans rather than home so Ian could beard the lion in her den and then be on his way. He didn't want to waste any more time on this errand than necessary.

A quick stop at the hotel to drop-off bags and worries then on toward the heart of the French Quarter. This would be the natural domicile of the relative of such a famous witch. They learned from the cabbie on their way over that the Voodoo Queen was buried close to the Quarter. He assured them that the Queen's great granddaughter would have access to the power within and, this close, it would be at its apex. If you believed that sort of thing; Ian was doubtful.

They had discussed the concept on the flight over and Maggie had convinced him all options were on the table. Though she reinforced the idea that if they were to have any chance of this being effective, he had to try to believe. She knew most of what religion and the occult derived power from was belief. Ian would just have to resign himself to possibility.

The home of the scion of the Queen was on a side road a couple blocks from the famous Bourbon Street. So named, Ian believed because of the reek of alcohol emanating from the very brick and mortar of the businesses. And reek was the proper term. It was as if hundreds of years of drinking, puking, and quickies in the alleys had infused the area with a smell not even hurricanes could wash away.

The residence was tucked away behind a small courtyard replete with iron worked table and chairs, pots filled with flowers and assorted plants Ian could never have identified even with a copy of 'The American Horticultural Society Encyclopedia of Garden Plants'. They rang the bell and a disembodied voice told them to please come in through the courtyard and enter through the door in the center of the townhouse.

The interior was dark though not foreboding, with the scent of cinnamon mixed with honeysuckle, he guessed that was the huge bush next to the one step porch, as well as the reek from Bourbon Street just down the road a piece.

They settled onto the antique love seat to wait for someone to instruct them from here. The room was deathly silent, not conducive to conversation. It was an oppressive atmosphere that felt designed to instill discomfort and anxiety. To prepare the 'guest' for their encounter with the seer.

A small movement out of the corner of his eye drew Ian's attention to a seated figure in the corner of the darkened room. He hadn't noticed the other person, as he sat stock still in the near dark, as if avoiding detection. Ian knew it was ridiculous but thought, just for the moment, he could recognize the other occupant. That would be impossible as, number one, there would be no reason for this person to be here. Number two, the person in question was far too rational, too reasoned to be hanging around purveyors of voodoo. Though, to be honest, until this very moment he would put himself into that same camp.

"Jax ?" Nothing ventured.

"Shit," came the rejoinder. It would appear two campers in the forest of sensibility had slipped into the grounds of the magi!

The door to the inner rooms squeaked open and a woman, Ian thought it was a woman, poked her head out, "Mr. Brahms, Marie will be with you in just a few minutes."

"Mr. Brahms?" Queried Ian.

"They asked my name and I froze. I didn't want them to know who I was," his reply was sheepish and conciliatory.

"Oh, that should work. No one would ever recognize you behind those Foster Grants," though Ian was immediately shamed, thinking of his own impotent attempts at disguise.

"So, Mr. Brahms, what the hell are you doing here?" Ian began before Maggie squeezed his knee beckoning him to silence. He wanted to hiss, 'but his name is Grahm, did he thinks changing it to Brahms would fool anyone?' The look on her face stopped the words dead in their tracks.

"Maybe he is not here for himself but to lend aid to a friend," she smiled in the darkness to show her support of a man lending support to a person he cared enough about to support. She loved Jaxson. He was a fine, decent person. Always giving to any worthwhile cause, lending his celebrity to raise cash or awareness to save the planet, save the children, save some sanity when it came to the insidiousness of the human race. He cared. She was certain that was the reason he was here.

"Well, to be honest, I am here for me. I need to get back on the road." He sighed. Ian had known Jaxson for half a century and knew him to be a musical workaholic. He wasn't happy if he wasn't writing, recording, touring, playing, sitting at a piano or with a guitar in his hands. "I can't seem to get any kind of tour together. It's like there is some kind of curse on me. Thirteen months in the studio, all new songs, new album, new desire to get in front of people with these tunes and every time we think we have something set up, it falls apart before we can get the truck loaded. It's nuts." He was at his wit's end. There was no one in music that loved to play more than Jaxson Grahm. To keep hitting brick walls had to be the most frustrating thing he could imagine.

"I would've helped," began Ian down a different road than he had originally taken. "all you had to do was ask, as a friend." He and Jaxson had never worked officially together and they both promised to keep it that way. It kept the bad blood to nonexistence. "Maybe we both could use a tour." He said to himself, though just.

"So, that's why you're here?" tiptoed Maggie.

"When there are no rational solutions one must seek the irrational," now Jaxson had some of his fire back. He was no quitter and would not lay down without attempting every possible solution. "I have never believed in any of this stuff but when all else fails..." He shrugged. "There is no rational reason for each attempt to get back on the road to fail! It has to be some imbalance in the ether." Wit's end, next exit. "If the venues and bookers won't aid and abet, mayhap the spirits will." He turned to Ian, "You remember a crazy sound guy from the early 70s, he went by Mojo or Hoodoo back then."

Ian grinned, yeah, he remembered the guy, he'd invented some kind of really powerful acid, one of the few things Ian had steered clear of back then. Mojo was a crazy fucker but a great sound man. Genius, mixer of chemicals and sound.

"I ran into him a week or so back, he's a chemical consultant for DOW or somebody now, can you imagine? I told him what was going on and he told me about this woman," he nodded towards the closed door. "He said he'd had some kind of Karmic problem and she had jumped in and saved him. I thought he was nuts, but when sense and reason have lost out, then you go for crazy. So, here I am," he shrugged his impotence. "The question is, why are you here?"

The crack of thunder and pelting of raindrops against the windowpanes seemed to augur a coming of truth between the old friends. Ian really didn't want to explain to Jaxson all that had happened. It was funny, when he thought about his experiences over the last months, they felt more dream than reality. The occurrences out of a movie, rather than reality. They couldn't really have happened; it was just coincidence. But they had happened and he had to confide. Hadn't Jaxson just spilled his guts? Ian could do no less.

"This is all going to sound quite outlandish and reek of me being vainglorious, but it is all true," Ian began, feeling Maggie's presence encouraging him.

"I would never think of you as vainglorious," replied the songwriter, "you are now and have always been the most modest person in my sphere."

"Well, you may change your mind once you hear the tale," And with that Ian launched into the retelling of the almost massacre in the rock club, the woman on the plane, the innkeeper in London and the kitchen cook at the restaurant. He decided to omit the incident with the child and the horse as nothing had happened. Nothing he was willing to admit might have been possible.

When he concluded the telling Jaxson sat quietly considering what his lifelong friend had laid at his feet. It sounded ludicrous, just chance coincidences tied to one man. But when he stopped to consider, one-time would be coincidence, four occurrences were a pattern. A pattern that could not be denied.

"And you want to stop saving people? Have I got that right? You don't wish to save people?" To someone like the singer/songwriter saving people would be the highest calling in life. He had spent most of his career highlighting man's inhumanity to earth, to man, to all creatures great and small. Why would anyone given this power, want to rid themselves of it? But then again, this was Ian.

"Firefighters save people. Cops save people. The goddamn Coast Guard saves people. They choose that profession; they want to be heroes. It satisfies some inner need, I guess, they are trying to assuage. They are humble but they accept they could have their pictures splashed across every newspaper in the country, do interviews of how humble they are while being heralded as saviors. It comes with the turf. And the thing is people will congratulate them and then leave them alone, because they were just doing their job. No big deal, 'yeah, she saved a dozen children from the burning building, but they pay her for that. It's what she does.'

"But let some schmo fall over and accidently save someone, or a room full of someones, and they hound that person to death. 'His job wasn't saving people, his job was promoting acts and making people stars. He has been in the background his whole life now we get to stick a camera up his ass and down his throat to see what makes him tick. Privacy? If the jagoff wanted privacy he would've avoided saving people. He would've walked the other way, but he didn't so now he's ours.' I have no desire for fame, no desire to be known. That's for you guys. I am happy in my little protective bubble." Ian was running out of gas, "If I could save people and remain anonymous, I would happily jump in the life saving business, but I can't and they won't leave me alone." Jaxson could almost feel the weight of the despondency, the torment in Ian's words. Maggie clung to him, ostensibly giving him strength by her mere presence.

"That's one hell of a story and one hell of a predicament. Shit, I never thought of it that way. But you can't really let people die just so you can live your life. I mean, it just seems wrong." Jaxson tried to shake the pieces of his thoughts into some semblance of order, but they refused.

"I lived for almost six decades without saving anyone. Not one goddamn soul did I save and I was happy. No one looked at me walking down the street and said, 'There goes the hero, there goes Mr. Sperling probably on his way to save a cat or a baby or something.' No, they usually crossed the street afraid I was going to ask them for money, and it was good!" Ian had never tried to defend his life before, certainly not to someone who had known him for most of it. The sad part was, when he said it out loud it sounded so shallow, so empty, so meaningless. But there had to be a happy median. Maybe he could rescue hamsters or cats. No, he had never liked cats or vermin. Dogs! He could give money to dog rescue shelters.

"It is a conundrum. How does one live a good life without involving oneself in the rest of humanity? I don't think I could do it," the musician wasn't condemning Ian just sounding out ideas. "and I don't think you can either!" He brightened up as he thought of what Ian had accomplished without fanfare in his past.

Ian didn't like the way Jax stared at him. This was the problem with having decent friends, they expected you to be decent as well. "What?" he feared the answer.

"I think you're selling yourself short." Jaxson sat up straight in his chair so he could be eye to eye with Ian. A crack of thunder announced things were about to change. "Didn't you help Joe find sobriety? Back when he was really falling apart. And that drummer whose wife left him? You stood by his side, didn't you?" he was warming to the subject and gaining steam on the downhill run. "Actually, there have been a few people that told me they'd be dead or laying in a gutter without you. Oh my god, you have been decent all along!"

"There's no need to get nasty. I stepped in to help a few friends who needed some direction. I didn't save anybody!" He looked to Maggie for confirmation but she had a contemplative, curious expression on her face. "Now, don't you start thinking what he's thinking, because I am not a decent person!" His defense of his life was really taking a beating.

"I think Jaxson is right. You are a decent person and I never realized it. I never knew. I always believed you were who you said you were, but that wasn't you at all. You're, you're, respectable! You are a nice, honest, scrupulous person." She searched his face as if seeing him for the first time. "We have been married almost forty years and I feel like I just met you!"

"I am none of those things, you take that back. I was a drunk and drug addict; I lived the life of the rock star without actually being one. I have hung with reprobates and whores. I once almost thought about cheating on you! Ha! How do you like that!" His tone triumphant. He had proven his lack of worth.

She laughed, loud and long, until tears streamed down her face. "'Almost thought about,' you slay me. You almost thought about it," she said with more emphasis, "Shit, you couldn't even really think about it, you're too decent!" she poked him in the shoulder.

"You take that back!" He shouted at her and immediately regretted his tone of voice. "I'm sorry, I didn't mean to yell at you."

"You can't even be horrible when we're fighting!" she claimed victory.

The door to the inner chambers opened and an elderly woman stepped into the sitting room. "I was just curious if any of you still needed my assistance." The slight Cajun accent lent her words humor.

She was the epitome of a Cajun Voodoo Queen. Her head crowned by a tierra topped multi-hued wrap encased in beads and small crystals, dark purple and black Moo Moo with splashes of brilliant orange and yellow lightning, the only thing throwing off the effect were the fuzzy slippers and the oversized coffee cup. Still, you took what was offered not what you hoped for.

"I'm not sure anymore," Ian glanced from Jaxson to Maggie to the vision.

"We might be alright," Jaxson stared at the woman, he was pretty sure it was a woman, sizing him up.

"I'm not going to charge you for this, though I should. You all think you came and met by accident, don't you? Just happened to walk into old Marie's sitting room and run into each other. Maybe you all happened to come here at the exact same time so you could figure out how to help each other out. Kind of like magic, ain't it?" She took a deep draught of coffee and popped out a silver cigarette holder from somewhere in the Moo Moo. She opened it, took out a home rolled smoke and struck a match between her fingers. She was good. Taking a deep pull, she coughed once, blew out a cloud and turned to go back the way she had come.

"Wait a minute," Ian asked through the cloud of ganga smoke, "Are you telling me you knew all this and brought us here, to work out something we still haven't worked out and are not going to tell us what we are supposed to work out? And you're taking the joint with you?"

The three who had come for advice and some kind of supernatural help glanced helplessly at each other. How could this woman have known what they were here for? She must have some kind of power, some kind of mojo, some enchantment that could help if she could read their thoughts so easily. Maggie asked the question.

"I listened at the door," said the Great Granddaughter of Marie Laveau as she turned her back to them, shook her head, "sheesh, white people, so easy. But I can help." She went back into the other room and came back with a large plastic bag which she handed to Jaxson. "when you get back home, take this baggie and roll your own. Sit with some friends and discuss what you want to do. Mr. Sperling here probably would be of some use."

"What's in the bag?" Jax, not wishing to smoke anything that might be harmful to the environment or his own health.

"Don't worry, homegrown. And infused with a bit of love and generosity. It will bring together those you want to be together with. The musicians, the crew, staff, techies, you name it. It's good stuff. Now go and save the world, I need a nap." She turned towards Ian and Maggie, "And you," she said gently, "ignore the glare of the spotlight. They really don't give a shit about you, listen to Pete. He knows," she shrugged. "And you," she hugged Maggie, "try to survive living with a whack job like this. Send him out on the road when you need a break." With that she disappeared back into the dark on the other side of closing door.

Her 'assistant' met her with a large jigger of brown liquid. "I thought the get up was a bit overboard," she said as she took in the whole picture and handed her friend the glass.

"People like this want a show, not some grandmotherly sage wisdom, they want magic and dead frogs, snakes and lizards, lotta smoke and mirrors. It helps sell the product."

"I guess," replied Fame, "Many of the performers who believe in me do the same thing, it seems to work for them."

"Of course, it does," smiled Fate, "And it is working on those chuckleheads right now. They don't have to believe completely they just have to let the seed grow." She giggled. "Let's get back to Olympus. Humans make me itch."

"Well, that was interesting," Ian spoke dismissively.

"I don't think you should be so quick to pooh-pooh what she's saying. Pete did try to tell you the same thing," Maggie cautioned.

"Yeah, and then the great Ian saved another human and the crowd went crazy, again." He shook his head, "I just don't know. It's all just so insane. Here we are three supposedly intelligent, rational, clear-thinking people wrapped in a voodoo spell. Jaxson has a bag of shit, or something just like it, I have a brain filled with shit and you are married to shit." He tried, unsuccessfully to laugh.

"I don't know," Jaxson scratched his head and studied the plastic bag in his left hand, "Maybe she's got a point in there somewhere."

"You're going to smoke that shit and see if people come to you, aren't you?" Ian laughed, "Let me know when, I'm coming to help. But that had better be some good pot." The more he considered the idea the more it appealed to him. It was like a college party with live music. And what the hell if it worked then so much the better.

"Well, that, but mostly, maybe we should do a tour together." Now Jaxson's eyes became keen with concept. "You know how you put Richie's shows together?"

Ian nodded cautiously.

"Why don't we do something like that, only a bit more laid back. We'll get some friends, a back-up band, some singers, road crew, people we like, people we trust and do a tour. I hear the road; it's pleading with me to come back. C'mon Ian, when was the last time you came out on a real tour." He was pushing the case but he needed an ally. "Maggie, talk to him. We'll get a bus just for the two of you, your own private coach. See what Lee Starling is up to, Russel Crunk has been sitting on his ass for two years, time to dust him off. We need a keyboard player, a guitarist, Ian you know everybody let's go have some fun and make a few dollars while we tour our blues away!"

He could tell by the faraway look in Ian's eyes the band was coming together.

"Look I know we said we'd never officially work together, manager and act, but this is different. It'll just be two friends putting together a bunch of other friends and spending a few months on the road making music. Fun, like it used to be." Jaxson make the final pitch.

Maggie grinned a huge grin thinking of how much fun it could be to do a real tour with folks they had known for most of their lives. Yeah, this could be good.

1) Put The Band Together

2) Save The World

The lineup was coming together nicely. It would be a concert of lifelong friends. People who had toured, sat in living rooms, had relationships, made music, made love, sang, played on each other's albums for decades, and who enjoyed each other's company. Not drama queens or kings. No current addicts or alcoholics. Recovering? You betcha, they would support each other. No one who would bring bad vibes or Karma to the tour. This was to be fun, wide open, freeing and a trip of love and music. That's all. Leave your baggage at the station you can pick it up when the gig was over.

It would be some of the finest acoustic, light rock, rock, jazz influenced, writers, players, and singers. Everyone would get the spotlight and everyone would back each other up. One band for all and all for one band. It would be the musical trip of the twenty-first century. A little Woodstock, a touch of Electric Kool-Aid, a dab of 60's revival, and a massive dose of damn good music. Not an oldies show or nostalgia, but a show of hits and new material, stuff never heard and stuff heard way too often.

Maggie loved the idea because she loved the music and the artists. But mostly she loved the affect it was having on Ian. He was so involved in putting the lineup together, the routing and logistics through most of North America to start, that he had totally forgotten about all that had led up to this. He hadn't saved a life in weeks and she didn't think he would have the opportunity to, considering all he was neck deep in.

There were hotels and buses, and food for over a hundred people at every stop. Backline to have ready at each stop so they didn't have to carry dozens of amps, drums, or their own sound equipment.

Anything they could cut back on to make the travel easier, they did. Sacrifices were made, though some things musicians just could not be without. They needed a separate trailer just for guitar pedals, extra cords, and cymbals. Ian managed to put it all together. Roadies who could be counted on to do more than one job. Keep things to a minimum with professionals who could setup, do sound if needed, guitar tech and drum tech. Load in, load out, drivers who could sleep while the others worked so they could drive all night while the others slept. Ian and Maggie would share a bus with others, not get their own, it was his decision, his choice, they loved to travel with the band. They always had.

There is something about three o'clock in the morning when most of the world is asleep. You are still up, still jacked from the show the night before. The buses are rolling down the highway and it's quiet. You would think that musicians who had played for three or more hours without break would be worn out and sleeping but some of the best jams happened as the whine and slap of the bus tires provided rhythm and key.

Someone would grab an acoustic and just start picking, then another, then a few lyrics, more voices, a fiddle, a sax, someone beating on the side of a trap case. Bands traveled by private jets in the modern era but many, like this caravan, would travel like musicians. There is a camaraderie created by sharing a bus or two. It creates the team, the band, the shared discomfort. Leaning on each other, respecting each other's space. Busting balls. That might be the best part, you knew you had become brothers and sisters, family, a band, when the ball busting began. You had to love someone to truly bust chops. You can't bust balls to bust balls, it can hurt if done wrong, but if it is done with love and respect, everyone laughs, everyone slaps a back or a thigh and hugs are shared. It is good.

And it ran through Ian's veins, thicker than blood, more lifegiving. The frontmen/women to begin the tour would be Jaxson, his close friend Bonnie Welch, and James Nash, one of the greatest singer/songwriters of the past fifty years, who would help kick off the tour and try to stick around for the first week or so of dates, Graham Young thought it was a marvelous idea and would join up halfway across the country. He would sing some of the old songs he had made famous in the sixties with two close friends. Josef, formerly Steven Gatos, though busy with his own projects, thought this would be a wonderful opportunity to add his voice back in the mix; he'd meet them when he could. He had been part of the movement back fifty years ago, he could reacquaint himself with old friends and make new ones. Kenny Masara thought he could do a date or two if his health seemed to hold, as did Jesse Collins. They thought they would front load a fair number of new regional acoustic singer/songwriter types. Wouldn't it be fun to expose some barely heard of talents to new audiences, like they used to?

Yes, like they used to. And that was exactly how Ian felt about everything to do with this tour. To do one last tour like they used to. For the music. Oh, they'd all make some spending money, but not what they could if they went it alone. Whatever was left after very strict production costs would be split evenly between everyone on the tour. Frontman, side man, guitar tech, roadie, driver, everybody would be equal, even Ian who usually did all the work but was paid the least. Nope, this time he'd be paid just like a regional rock star. It was good.

Rehearsals and run-throughs completed; six weeks' work readied musicians for the road. Time to find out if there was any magic left in the tank. Everything sounds good when you're just having fun, take it to the people!

It was the first night and everyone was jacked. The performers, the road crew, the audience, the promoters, everyone. They arrived at the mid-sized venue midafternoon. A lovely old fifteen-hundred-seater out in the wilds north of San Francisco. The sound crew already had most of the borrowed P.A. in place and were running cables, the lighting crew was setting up the cans along the rigs and towers and testing placement, and spotlights were being set.

Their one semi filled with what equipment they desperately needed had pulled up behind the stage. That was one of the great improvements of today over the great yesteryear. Back in the day you had to carry three semis full of gear because you wanted to make certain you had the exact stuff the band played through. It was their sound and they wanted it to sound just right, perfect. Fifty years ago, that meant carrying your own, as you couldn't be sure that Everytown USA would have the gear you required. And you weren't going to play through Sears Silvertones and Shure columns. But today, damn near every town in the USA would have a professional sound company and decent music store they could rent from. And who wouldn't want to rent to this group? Make it as easy as you can, none of us is getting any younger, from the piano tuner to the road crew there was a sea of grey and white on top of these mountains.

Oh, they still carried some amps, a Hammond and Leslie—some keyboardists were purists and only wanted the real thing not some computer simulation. Drummers always preferred their own cymbals and pedals, Guitarist just needed their pedal boards, though those could be quite large and complex. But it was still just a small semi, forty foot.

All was moving like a well-oiled machine. Ian kissed Maggie and smiled; he was in his zone. She knew he could see her but he didn't take note of her presence. She was not upset or hurt; she had known this side of him for almost four decades. This was his joy, his bliss. He was so wrapped up in detail and dotting 'I's' that he wouldn't have seen a freight train bearing down on him; and wouldn't have cared.

He stepped out of the bus and made his way towards the small camp behind the stage. This was an area filled with RV trailers and large tents. These would act as dressing rooms and dining hall for the crew and the artists. They would work together, eat together, live together. It was life on the road, the real road, not the rock star road.

He walked through the set-up to assure himself that the dressing rooms would be adequate, they really didn't need all that much, most of the primping and preening would happen at the hotel thirty miles away. The kitchen in the food tent was coming to life with coffee pots lining a long table accompanied by several tea choices and a large plastic bowl filled with soft drinks and another filled with water bottles. He thought he remembered telling everyone they would have their own disposable drinking glasses for water. Ian hated using plastic for anything, on the road it was a necessity they tried to keep to a minimum, only reusable plastic should be brought. He'd have to look into this. Plastic!

Other than those small details—not much for a first night of a tour—everything looked good. There would be beer and wine brought out but not until the show was well under way. No drinking prior to curtain! Pot and libations would come after the show, nothing was to interfere with the show. Now to the stage area.

This was, of course the most important aspect of the pre-show inspection. Whatever went on backstage was backstage but here was the show. Here was what the folks who paid the money would see and hear. And speaking of the folks with the cash he needed to check receipts and expenses again. So much to do, so little time to do it. People always asked why he didn't have an assistant or two to help with all the details. He had tried assistants but by the time he told them what needed to be done and checked three or four times to know it had been done, he could've easily taken care of the chore himself, and not been worried it wasn't done! He didn't need extra stress, neither did the cast and crew. It would fuck up the show. He was a hands-on kind of guy, he liked knowing all had been taken care of.

The road crew was easing the Hammond B-3 onto the stage and placing it to stage left to balance the large drum set to stage right. People had no idea what it took to set a stage not just sonically but visually. If it was pleasing and balanced to the eye, it would sound better to the ear. Details, details. They would have a half dozen stage monitors though most of the front folks would have in-ear monitors. So much better and far more modifiable for each singer. Tech was a wonderful thing. When it worked. Hence the stage monitors, just in case.

He gazed over his list of do's and don'ts as he walked, not really watching where he was going, though everyone else watched him carefully. He was the man in charge. The others might be the stars but Ian decided all else so they wanted to please him. The newest kid working the stage—Ian had known the rest for a few decades each—carried a small Fender Princeton and took a circuitous route around Ian not wishing to be noticed or disturb the master. His eyes on Ian instead of watching where he was going, he was not cognizant of the end of the stage. Just as he was about to step off into open space Ian reached out without looking up and grabbed the kid's collar pulling him back off the edge. He let go, again without seeming to notice what had happened or what he had done and continued to work down his check list. It hit him like a slap across the face.

Ian turned to face the dead silence screaming at him from behind. All the roadies and techs were staring at him as if he had performed a miracle. Shit! What had just happened? He was checking the to do's, saw the kid—the kid who was in his mid-thirties and had been on the road for fifteen years—almost walk off the end of the stage. He'd called to him, no he'd blocked him from, no, he'd gotten the guy's attention by grabbing his, no, he'd pulled him back. He saved him from certain injury, it was a five-foot drop to the hard ground. But still, he'd only done what anybody would have.

"What's the matter? We got gear to set, what are you staring at?" The slowly shaking heads told him they had seen something he hadn't.

And what they'd seen was the 'kid' had actually walked off the stage and Ian had grabbed him mid-air and with what looked to be no effort at all had gently pulled him back onto the stage. Though none of them were about to say such a thing. Obviously, they were all suffering the same hallucination. No way this white haired, paunchy, late-middle-aged man had lifted a two-hundred-pound man with Princeton amp cradled in his arms and set him down on the end of the stage. They shook their heads to clear what had come from tired eyes, over-exertion, and being back on the road.

"Nothing, boss. Just tired I guess," said the road manager, a guy named Ben Friedman that Ian had known for twenty years. They had worked tours all over the world together. He knew what he had seen and knew it to be impossible. "almost ready to do sound."

"I'll alert the media," Ian joked to cut the tension, "and the band."

They would do a sound check with just the players and adjust on the fly for each performer. It was the only way when you had a half dozen acts or more on a show. The list of performers had grown to include Gillian Morse, a brilliant singer and songwriter in the Americana mode. And the one and only Cinda Wilson who wanted on because she loved Gillian and wanted to sing with her.

Ian glanced at his list for reassurance and walked toward the stairs at the back of the stage.

The more he thought about the incident the less real it felt. Like trying to remember a dream, ethereal and just out of touch of the mental fingers. He was certain he had intervened only to focus the wandering preoccupation of the roadie. Everyone let their mind wander from time to time and this time, time was on his side. He had saved nothing, prevented nothing, done nothing and the rest of the road crew mistook his intervention due to sunspots. Isn't that always what it is? Sunspots. Yes.

He spied Maggie having a beverage in the food tent and reading some book or other. The woman always seemed to be reading, he was jealous. Someday he would walk away from this life and sit on a beach and read book after book, but today was not that day.

"Comfy?" he asked as he sat with pen and paper to go over the checklist for the hundredth time. It was his main obsessive-compulsive act, the list. He had tried to leave it once, many years ago on a tour with Joe. He thought it was mentally unhealthy. He had performed these duties hundreds of times and felt he knew it by heart. Well, he had been wrong. A few very important tasks had been left by the wayside. Like Joe's guitar, which turned out to be the biggie and the one that caused the greatest consternation. From that point on the list ruled the world.

"Anytime I can steal a few minutes alone with a book makes me happy and comfortable," she smiled setting the book down pages first on the table. She knew him better than she knew her own moods, he wanted to talk but wouldn't actually engage. She had to kick-start the conversation. "How's yours going?" He should be pleased as a pig in a poke to be on the road and in charge of the barge.

"Weird." There it was. Something had interfered with the routine. One word to begin a bloodletting and she was the surgeon.

"What happened?" Best to open the wound gently, especially with the events of the past half year. She had hoped this tour would cure what ailed him, make him forget the idiosyncratic coincidences of the past. She, apparently, was wrong.

"Well, it feels more dream than reality," he began and spilled what he thought happened. Then what he believed happened and what the crew's reaction to the happening had been and what happened according to what his mind remembered happening. None of which could actually have happened.

"Shit!" She thought she had whispered the epithet though his head jerked around with the sound.

"So, you agree, you think it might be happening again. You think I, Ian Patrick Sperling, of no particular exercise program except waking each morning, could possibly have reached out these mighty arms," and here he rolled up his sleeve in case there might be doubt as to the might within, "snatched a two-hundred-pound man out of thin air and pulled him and the amplifier back onto safety. You, who have known me longer and seen me naked under the best and worst circumstances, believe in your heart of hearts, this is something I could do." Before allowing her a breath to answer, he continued.

"I am not talking about pushing a chair back and falling over on an assailant, nor beating a woman to get the fuck off me or slipping and falling onto a helpless proprietor until his heart kicks in, all quite by accident. No, I am asking if you think it even minutely possible, I could reach out and pull off the greatest demonstration of strength by a middle-aged man of the twenty-first century. Me?" He ran out of breath and dared her to contradict his perfect logic.

"No, my he-man of godlike lack of physical strength, you could not," she optically shoved love and reassurance into his brain. She hadn't married him for his physical prowess, it was his brain and his beautifully off-center sense of humor. He would never wrestle a bear to save her, but he would entertain it while she got away. "But something beyond the weirdness we have already experienced is now taking place and we need to discover if what you think might have happened actually happened." The idea struck like a bolt of lightning, well, more like an idea being thrown against the wall. "The problem is the whole crew knows I'm your wife so they won't talk to me, so, we need someone they might open up to," she began and he interrupted.

"Well, they are not going to talk to someone they also know is a good friend of mine," he was ready to pull the string and make this weave fall apart.

She knew exactly what he would do and where he would go with his rebuttal so headed him off before he could get his feet under him. "Yes, I know, everybody knows everybody so we get an everybody they know but don't know you know as well as you know him." Ian's head swam in very deep, dark waters, "Just listen," she slowed the wagon, "Jaxson can talk to Lee, isn't his bass tech someone you knew from your time with Glenn and Joe?"

"Yeah, He's bass tech, guitar master tech, and co-road manager, and I've known Dugan since high school, so?"

"So, have him bring up the subject off the cuff, while everybody is eating or setting up, tearing down, loading in, loading out, whenever. Just have him ask, like he saw some weird occurrence from a distance, like a joke. Everybody likes him, don't they?" He nodded half confidently, "see what he finds out."

It was as good a plan as anything he would ever come up with and the beauty was, while Dugan was digging, Ian could concentrate on his job. Which, he realized, he was now a half hour behind in getting done. He kissed his brilliant wife, left the whole mess in her lap, and strolled off to play concertmaster.

...And The Band Played On

If there was one thing Ian was top of his class at accomplishing it was, with the exception of being broadsided by the lifesaving thing, pushing all concerns to the back of his conscious brain while he worked. The outlandishness of stepping into the middle of the death throes of another human being to stay the inevitable had thrown him for a loop. He was in the fantasy business. This was NOT his fantasy!

He promoted and managed people's fantasies, both the artists and the fans. That was the joy of the job. No one seemed to realize his main job was allowing artists to live out their fantasies, that was it. Find someone with talent, great talent when possible, and let them play rock star. It was fun. The balancing act was to allow them to believe it only so far, then you had to rein them back in. If you allowed your artist to believe their own press, the lies made up by the promotion machine, the fantasy created to sell them to the gullible, then you were in trouble. He shook his head, not the gullible, the public. People wanted to believe the illusion. They wanted to believe their rock gods lived in mansions, ate nothing but steak, lobster and weaker acts. Wanted to believe they drank champaign from golden goblets and had sex morning, noon, and night. It was the supposed dream. The reality was quite different.

Bands toured, and they toured hard. Twenty-eight shows in thirty days. Each stop a day away from the last. Sleeping sitting up and bouncing down the road. Yes, some traveled in style, but they were few and far between. Eagles, U2, Elton John on his many farewell tours, but most traveled by bus and truck. They lived for a few hours in a hotel to shower, shave, iron, grab a few winks in a bed that wasn't moving. They ate at the venue before the show, played their hearts out, then loaded on the bus for another overnighter. His job was to make them believe it was all worthwhile.

And the main way of accomplishing that was to make sure that everything was perfect when they walked on stage. To guarantee they would have no problems during the show, he hated problems during the show. They should stand out there in the spotlight, shining like wizards of old, performing magic with a guitar, a mic stand, an attitude, so the people who shelled out their hard-earned pesos would want to be just like them.

And when the applause, the screams of joy, the sound, the roar washed over that stage, he felt good. He had done his job. He could stand against the wall in the wings and let them bathe in it. He had no need for the fame, for the glory, he had this.

Ian and Maggie sat down for their lunch break before the final sound checks, the final stage checks, guitar tunings and preparation to wait for the long show to begin. The crowd had trickled in at first, but now was a teeming mass of humanity fifteen hundred strong and growing in anticipation as the day moved toward evening.

In the distance he could hear the opening strains of *'Life on The Road'*, a perfect song for a soundcheck; actually, a perfect song of love, friendship, longing, and home. Jaxson was going to give the early birds a little treat, probably play for a half hour. He must be getting antsy and fidgety waiting for the show his-own-self. Ian didn't think he knew of any other entertainer that loved to play more than Jax. He had been known to do sound checks that lasted a couple hours. He hated waiting for the show to begin.

Eyes closed, Ian let the song take him down a very familiar path. They had both traveled the musical road for half a century. They both knew the ups and downs, the joys, the sorrows of death or careers destroyed by avarice, over-indulgence, and neglect. They also had both survived and, most importantly, remained friends through it all. He took a few minutes to revel in the love, the memories, the late-night phone calls, and the time they both decided it would be best for both of them never to work together. And here they were. But this wasn't really work. This was friends on a journey together to share some songs and time.

When Ian opened his eyes, he was staring at a large Asian man sitting across the table from Maggie and himself. No, not Asian, more indigenous. But not Native American, more Mexican or South American or what? He couldn't decide.

"Mayan," said the large specimen of human around a bite of roadie chow.

"Pardon?" Ian was caught off guard.

"You were wondering what my heritage might be. I get that a lot. People are always guessing what my culture might be." He took another bite and chewed while considering Ian as much as Ian was considering him. "We are some of the last Mayans on the planet and if the leaders of Guatemala have their way, we will be the last."

Why did this large man look so familiar? Ian thought he knew every member of the crew by name and position but this guy was a puzzle. He tried to place him but only came up with roadie. The backbone of the rock industry. The unsung heroes who hauled the music, set it up, tore it down and moved it to the next town. The real road. The fella threw back a long, black lock of hair that had wandered around his shoulder and found its way into his meal.

"I thought about waiting or not saying anything but my mother says it's bad luck not to acknowledge your gift," He set his fork down and looked hard into Ian's eyes.

Ian was never a man to back down from anyone, though the thought popped up for a moment. "What gift did I bestow?" Ian had a very good memory and this was driving him to distraction. He hated games.

"My health," he grinned and a peace filled his face. "You pulled me back from what would have been a very painful injury. My mother thinks you might be a minor deity or shaman or something. I told her you were just the boss, but a good one. She sends her thanks as well." Again, that grin or smirk or childish coy smile.

It was the second time he had mentioned his mother, and though Ian was pretty sure even mountains had to come from somewhere, he pitied the woman who'd had to bear this load. It was funny, Ian thought, that guys like this always had a close tie to their mothers. Mama's boys, big enough to watch over her but never give her any backtalk. And then it finally hit.

"You're the guy from earlier, almost walked off the stage. Gotta be careful out there," and now it was Ian's turn to smile. He liked this man. He wasn't here to gush, just a quiet thank you, no more. He knew Ian had done no more than redirect his attention, though that redirection had saved him some time in the hospital.

"From what the others say I did walk off the stage. They say you lifted me back onto the stage. It was a fete they would not have believed had they not seen it," again those dancing eyes took in all of Ian as if trying to envision this past middle-aged man lifting him. He couldn't. No matter what the other roadies thought they saw. But he liked the image, the video it placed in his head.

"Well, they had to have seen something in the sun glare or imagined it. Especially now I get a good look at you. Shit, ask my wife, I can hardly lift my own ass off the couch most days," they all three laughed. Ian thought the other two laughed a bit too hard, but he let it go.

"Gabby," the large man held out his hand for Ian to shake.

"Ian," said Ian needlessly. Everyone knew who he was. "Gabby? Like in Hayes?" It was the only one Ian could think of.

"Gabby, like in Gabor. It's a Mayan name, It means God's bravest man. Guess my ma knew I was going to be big," now he laughed hard, an uninhibited, joyful sound that filled the backstage.

"How come I haven't noticed you until today? I mean you have got to have been working the last few weeks helping us get ready. And not to toot my own horn, but I pride myself on knowing everybody on the crew," this bothered Ian. How could he have missed someone so big, so extraordinary. His size and looks should have made him stick out like an orange in a plum patch, whatever that meant.

"It is the way of my people. The less we are noticed, the less those who would exterminate us are tempted to do so. We are of the lowest caste in Guatemala. Workers. Strong backs, weak minds, and they say our genetics make us lesser than others. We stay to the forests; we try not to bother anyone." Now the sad, the grief carved his features.

"Caste?" Ian didn't understand.

"Yes, like in India, where we in the Americas got our name. They have a caste system. You are born into your caste, you live in that caste, and it is almost impossible to break out of your caste. Though the upper castes would have no want to, just those of us in the lower castes," he tried to explain without accusation or hurting the feelings of the man who had saved him.

"That's disgusting! How can anyone get away with a system like that?" Ian was aghast and he could feel Maggie's temper rising as well.

"Maybe you should ask those in your own country. You have the same," he finished the last bite of casserole on his plate just as the road manager signaled that he was needed. "Sorry, got work to do. I really just wanted to thank you and let you know if you ever need anything, I'm your guy."

"Well, more conversation and a little mescaline," said Ian half joking.

"Interesting fellow," mused Maggie.

"One would think he is more than he first appears to be. I wonder why he hasn't moved up the roadie ladder in fifteen years. He seems smart, dedicated, strong as an ox on steroids, I don't get it," Ian gazed at where the large Mayan had sat talking to them. "I'm going to talk to Ben and see what he knows."

"Well, watch yourself, he already seems quite taken with you. And I really would like to hear what the others are saying. I love you, don't get me wrong, but I just can't get my head around the concept of you lifting that package into thin air and floating him to safety. You have trouble starting the mower," she chuckled and punched his arm, inducing a proper wince from the man of steel.

"Maybe it's one of those things you read about, like a mother lifting a car off her baby, kind of thing," he grinned.

"Maybe, but that is one big baby and you ain't his mother," She shook her head, "I'm going to find a quiet spot to read, let me know what you discover and try not to save anyone else."

As Ian wandered about the encampment doing a last-minute check, he heard Jaxson finish his last tune and thank the assembled for their kindness, explaining that the show would start on time and soon.

He only wished to be assured the keys were in tune, the sound was perfect so that they, the paying public, would get the best show possible. Details.

Ian caught the famed Dugan grabbing waters to put about the stage. It was going to be hot under the lights and he wanted water close to everyone on that stage. This was why he was considered one of the best road men in the business. He would also be working as guitar tech for Yogi Mahesh, known as one of the more tasteful and versatile guitar guys around, and bass tech for Lee Starling. Dugan had worked for some of the best guitarists in the world, they were lucky to get him for this run. Sometimes the stars align, the tour he was supposed to be on came down with a broken arm, well, one of the key components did, skiing accident, and so it freed him up to join Mr. Friedman and crew. As much as the musicians made the music, the roadies made it possible. Take the stress out of a musician's day and they would reward with beauty at night.

As Dugan stood, he saw Ian making his way to where he stood. "How long we known each other," he said by way of greeting, "Twenty years? More?"

Ian thought as he walked, "More, I would think. Shit, we go back to high school."

"Yeah, that's what I was thinking. Worked a couple tours, some of the Rock and Roll Hall tours, events when you were up bothering the folks in Cleveland, run ins at celebrity functions. I've seen you put together tours, a TV show for MTV when the M meant music, charity concerts," he stopped mid-thought a curious expression roaming his features. Something Ian, apparently, was going to have to get used to.

"And your point," Ian kick started Dugan's thoughts in hopes they would find the trail they'd been on.

"I've seen you lift an audience with music, lift the heart of many with charity, I ain't never seen you lift a two-hundred-pound man with amp in the air," he laughed and waved a hand full of bottle waters, "but these fellas swear by all that is holy that's exactly what you did."

"They were seeing things in the sun or the heat got to them. Everybody around here has lost their minds. Next thing you know they'll all have little altars with my picture hanging in road cases. I'll be the patron saint of roadies," Ian forced a laugh. He had to nip this in the bud, stop this rumor before it really got legs and some journalist decided there was a story. The last thing he needed right now was the distraction of fame or a reasonable facsimile. Or worse, somebody digging up stories from the recent past that had finally found their way to the public interest graveyard.

'Oh, don't worry, they are all pretty convinced they are suffering a group hallucination. Herbie, he's the drum guru, has started a conspiracy theory that one of the other guys put some mescaline in everybody's water." He shrugged his hands full of bottles, "it wasn't me." He turned to walk away, "I gotta get everything set on the stage, you need anything from me?"

"Nope, just doing my own last-minutes," he waved the road master on his way. Funny, he thought, that was the second time someone had mentioned mescaline and the first had been him! Time to focus on the show and check to be sure all the acts were close by and ready to take the stage. It was the one part of the job he least liked, herding musical cats. The lineups were posted every three feet, you should know when you were up. Sheesh.

The artists quit hiding once the first act, a North Cali artist that Jaxson had heard some of, Joan Newsom, took the stage. There was something about hearing someone for the first time that no act, be they local or superstar, could ignore. Especially when there was enough buzz. It was not even the competitive side, though that does play a role, but it was being turned onto to something new, something exciting and someone you might want to record or write with. Ms. Newsom lived up to all expectations and, since this first concert was just north of San Francisco, she was a known commodity and they loved her.

There would be a short changeover, one of the best parts of using one back-up band to handle every act, especially when it was a back-up of some of the best musicians in the world. Once Joan finished her set, Dugan and crew made quick work of fine tuning the set up. Ian stood to the side of the stage so he could see everything that was taking place. It was his perch, leaning against a trap case, arms crossed, watching every move of every person on or near the stage. Details. He could also keep an eye on the audience. Yes, this was a pretty laid-back, older audience for a laid-back kind of show but you never knew when someone would drink one too many or the gummy would kick in harder than they thought and mayhem would ensue. You could never be too careful. He loved watching the shows from the wings. The sound was awful, balanced for whoever stood closest to him but he didn't care, he wasn't here for the entertainment; he was here for the family.

James Nash's schedule had changed and he had to catch an early flight, to do a benefit in New Mexico then he'd catch back up with them further down the road. So, he was next on the stage tonight. The lineups and times would change as the tour rode across the country. That was one of the fun parts of this kind of caravan. Nobody could get too comfortable, the lineups changed, the set-up changed, the sound changed, and they had to be ready for whatever happened. He thought the road crew loved it as well because they never could get bored.

Everything was smooth and then the night got so much better as Maggie joined him with a kiss on the cheek. Yes, this was going to be a great tour. Ben came over to ask a few questions about the next act. That was why Ian thought him the best, even though he knew who was on and what they needed, he still liked to check the details.

Ben was like that; it was the main reason Ian had wanted him so badly for this tour. Most of the venues would morph into mid-level outdoor spots as the weather continued to improve. It was late spring heading into summer! So, they would both be keeping a watch on the weather prior to and close in to show day. If they needed, Ben would have options other than postponing or cancelling. Both of them hated cancelling a show, nights off on the road made people bored and cranky, and bored, cranky people got into trouble. Both road crew and artists. Oh, one night here and there didn't make no nevermind, it refreshed tired people, but too many and the stupid came out.

They had both seen tours fall apart when too many nights got pushed back because of weather, and it was late spring, weather would soon or late come into bearing. They had tried to avoid the middle of the country as much as possible, well, the southern half, Tornado Alley, at least until mid-June. They'd routed from here up through Oregon and Washington, skip across Idaho and then across Montana. Though there was still a chance they could pull off something on an off day in Coeur d'Alene, but the promoter was a bit shifty. From there, they'd work the northern tier of the Midwest, Minnesota, Iowa, though those states could be dicey as well, down through Illinois, Indiana, Ohio and onto the East Coast. It would be a little brutal but most of these folks had been sitting through the harsh fall and winter.

Concert seasons, like all seasons, come and go and winter was not the best time to be out wandering around the country. If Tornadoes could put a damper on the spring, snow, blizzards, and pileups could put an end to a tour. A tornado in Oklahoma can be avoided, a blizzard tying up the entire midsection of the country could not. Autumn had begun harsh and turned ugly. Nobody had been touring in quite some time. These were happy gypsies to be back on the blacktop, wheels turning regularly.

Ian should concentrate on the music, the show, but he had a million things running through his head. Someone has to be in charge. Someone has to worry. And it wasn't going to be the artists. And the roadies expected him to be ahead of anything they might have to deal with. Yup, he liked having Ben at his side.

James was saying Goodnight to the Pretty Ladies, an old tune he loved to close with, when Ian roused himself from his concerns. Bonnie walked out on stage to give him a kiss and tell him she'd see him in a couple, wish him safe travels and one last hug as the band eased into nice groove. Smooth as a baby's cheek, thought Ian. He grabbed Maggie to do a little dance, two, three bars' tops, but he felt good. For two people who loved music they were not much for dancing or, one should say, Ian was not much for the dance floor. He was much more at home in the wings.

The crowd that had been singing along just moments before now held each other and danced in the restricted space front of the stage and aisles provide. People were laughing, hugging, remembering. That was the beauty of this music, thought Ian, not what it had meant when it came out and people fell in love with it, but what it evoked decades after. People had spent centuries seeking the fountain of youth and it was here all along. Music. Music hath charms to soothe the savage beast, but it also had charms to make the old feel young. He had seen it a thousand times, he would see it on this tour. Musicians in their seventh and eighth decades would become kids again. Rockin' and rollin', gyrating on the stage, and high fiving the crowd. Yeah, this is exactly what he needed, and some time with that Mayan guy, Gabby. There were many questions running through his head and he thought that guy might have some answers.

The show continued with Jesse Collins, as a special guest appearance, and a closing set by Jaxson, all in all a very successful first night. There had been minor glitches with sound and lights but nothing extreme and all could be worked out before the next night in Eugene. Now was time for tear down, load up and the drive. There was one bus for the sound and lighting crew, one bus for the road crew, with very comfortable beds so they could rest, one bus for the female singers and artists, one for the band, and one for the assembled frontline artists and Ian and Maggie. Quarters would be tight but comfy and everyone could jump from bus to bus as they got accustomed to each other. Many of the artists knew each other and the members of the band, who had played with the best of the best since 1967, so Ian knew within a few days everyone would be jumping from bus to bus on a regular basis.

Musicians liked to travel with musicians no matter their spot on a show. They would swap stories, jam, try out new songs, laugh a lot, and share the road. Roadies liked to travel with roadies so they could go over the show, iron out any wrinkles, and trade stories of the best and worst to work for. They didn't need musicians listening in while they critiqued either them or their compatriots. Nobody wanted to know the road crew thought you were a demanding, entitled little priss. Of course, the way to avoid that was to not be a demanding, entitled, little priss, but what did Ian know. And the sound and light guys had their own schedule and didn't need anyone fucking it up. They wanted everything in place before the band's equipment was unloaded and scattered about the stage. So, the conclaves were set in place and the buses could get rolling.

Ian had asked if Kevin could join him. The roadie he asked just stared at him. "Kevin," Ian said again, "your boss." To clarify. The guy still stared as if he couldn't understand what Ian was saying. Then the light began to glow as understanding came to him.

"Dugan?" came the hesitant query.

"Yes, he has an actual name just like a real boy," Ian's vexation was showing.

"Guess I didn't know that. Shit known the guy for thirteen years didn't know he had a real name, always thought it was just Dugan." He shrugged and went off in search of this Kevin.

"You want me, boss?" Kevin stuck his head in the bus.

""Yeah, I always think it best to go through the proper channels. So, would you ask Gabby to ride the first leg with me? He hasn't done anything bad, I mean, he isn't in any trouble, I just want to talk to him while we have time," Ian didn't want Dugan to think Gabby had done anything so he wouldn't transmit that vibe to the asked for. He also wasn't sure he wanted anyone else to know the why.

"You want I should stick around with you guys?" Dugan asked as he turned to leave the bus, "You know these fellas aren't used to the bigwigs asking for them, let alone asking them to ride on their bus. It might make him more comfortable if I'm here. I mean I'm not real close to him, we worked together a few times. And I knew he was a hard worker and strong as an ox, but I think Ben was the one who recommended him for this tour. You told both of us you wanted people who were the best, would provide no drama, no real bad habits, I mean everybody smokes a little pot at the end of the day, has a beer or two, but no problems. This guy is the epitome of that. I'd hate to lose him," he glanced over his shoulder to see what Ian's reaction would be.

Ian loved that this man so cared for his guys he would put himself on the line if he had to, maybe he should let Dugan stay. He might have some ideas of his own in the direction Ian was heading. Though to be honest with himself, he wasn't sure what direction he was heading. "Sure, you stick around, we'll be stopping to replenish the veggie fuel in a few hours. We can share some time."

Dugan was a big man but Gabby made him look almost like a child. He was tall, broad shouldered with not an ounce of fat on him. Ah, youth, thought Ian when he glanced at his own little pudge around the middle. No matter how hard someone tried, age would have its way. Muscles sagged, that tire formed around the middle, sometimes a spare, sometimes a double truck tire. Luckily, his was still kind of a bicycle.

"You wanted to see me, boss?" Dugan might have tried to reassure the man but there would always be this separation between the boss and the worker. Maybe that was what Gabby had been trying to explain.

"Yes. If you don't mind riding with us," and here he nodded to both Maggie and Dugan, "for a little while. As long as I'm not taking you away from a card game or a round of guessing who will be the biggest nightmare on the tour?" He smiled. The crew might've guessed that the higher ups knew what they did in their spare time but Ian was confirming it.

"Nah, I don't really take part, spend most of my time reading and sleeping." He gave Ian a sheepish grin.

"You don't hang out with the rest of the gang?" Ian was slightly taken aback. He'd always thought all these guys would hang together, and they usually did. This Gabby was an odd one, indeed.

"Nah, I guess I just move from crew to crew, never really get to know the other guys. They always seem to be in the same clique, and I'm not much of a joiner. Guess it comes from my roots. We keep pretty much to ourselves out of self-preservation." He shrugged as if none of it meant anything.

"Well, your roots are what I wanted to pry out of you. I wanted you to expand on the whole caste thing and how it affects you, us, the world. You seemed to have a pretty good handle on the subject and I'm completely ignorant." Ian sat back as an invitation for Gabby to speak when he felt confident doing so. "So, if you wouldn't mind, do me some learnin'."

"Well, Boss," he began and Ian stopped him right there.

"OK, let's get one thing straight, my name is not boss, it is Ian. I may run this circus but I am not 'Boss'. I don't own nor run a plantation; I don't own anybody's ass nor do I want to. I expect to be treated just like everybody else. We all have a job to do and if we do it well, then this tour will succeed." His ire spent he sat back once again and glared at Dugan, "And that goes for you and everybody else as well. Ian! Say it with me, not boss, not Mr. Sperling, Ian." They didn't say it, but he thought they got the gist of the pissy rant.

"Sorry, Bo...Ian," stumbled Gabby. "See, with my people it is best not to draw attention to yourself or you just might wind up in prison or dead. There aren't a lot of options for those of the forgotten. That's what we are. I told you, we are workers, disposable workers. They recruit us with promises to take care of our families then march us into the deep forests to tear the heart out of the Mother and rape our sisters while we are away. We are not considered human. We are the low end of the caste in Guatemala. In India we'd be the untouchables, the shit pickers, people so dirty no one would come close. Hell, if their shadow falls on you, you had to strip down and wash the impurity off. That's some shit there.

"We are expected to get out of the way of the upper castes, all of them," he emphasized. "Just like black folks in this country have been for hundreds of years. It sticks to you like a stink. It's the shape of your eyes, the color of your skin, your name, what your father did for a living, what your mother sells herself for. We are not human so you can do anything you want to us. Black folk know what I'm talking about. It's in their DNA. Bred into them over the centuries through a dozen or fifteen generations. The upper caste, the dominant caste could kill, torture, buy and sell families, children, wives and husbands, and if anybody had anything to say about it, they got whipped and beaten, some to death. And nobody did a fucking thing about it." His voice was a whisper of hopelessness, sorrow, desperation. "That's why you see most black folk don't mix with the white. They're always weary that those times can come back. Folks you thought was friends turn on you when the majority tells them to. Protect yourself, fuck the other guy, he ain't like you." A tear escaped its prison and ran for freedom. "Sorry, you asked. That's the caste system. No upward mobility, no escape except death. No love, no loyalty, no friends. So, we keep to ourselves. We try to find others like us, but we know, for a bone they would turn you round."

Ian was shocked beyond words. What could he say? He wasn't a historian. Hell, he never graduated from high school because to him it was HIGH school. His well-guarded liberalism was punching him about the face and midriff. "God, I'm sorry. So, what can we do to stop this insanity?" He had no idea but he knew it wasn't up to him to think of a solution it was up to him to listen and help if he could.

"Not sure I know. Education, training to get out of the poverty. Hope, the children need hope. Regular meals, a vision of a future where they aren't garbage. To be lifted up with a decent job, a future, to have worth, meaning. Mixing in with the upper castes so they can see we're all the same and those of us down here just want a chance. Shit, there's so many ways to begin and none of them guaranteed to do a damn thing. Maybe you are beginning to dig why you pulling me back from the edge, whether you lifted me or pushed me or yelled, you pulled me back, is such a massive thing in my head. Why my mother thinks you're something special." He grinned.

"Well, I'm not!" insisted Ian.

"You sure ain't a godling or spirit thing sent to help humanity," laughed Maggie, joined much too quickly by Dugan.

"Oh, you're a good boss and all, don't get me wrong, but ain't nobody worshipping you, at least not yet." Gabby glanced at Dugan to reinforce the statement. "Look we respect you. Not because of what you did but because of what you do. Talking to us about shit like this, you care about the crew. We dig that. But you ain't going to change the world by yourself."

"But what if something good could be done?" Ian had grasped the last straw of a wild idea.

"Like what?" Maggie had seen this look before. Mickey Rooney just met Judy Garland and it always cost them financially.

"Well, everybody joined this tour to have fun, make music, party a little. We've been cooped up so long between weather, ugly weather, promises of better weather and whether the weather could be out weathered. We all just wanted to get out of the house and do what we do." Ian had the tail of a wild hair and wasn't going to let it go.

"So, what is your grand idea, great and noble OZ?" Maggie wanted facts, figures and to know if they were going to be eating PB and J with Campbell's soup for the next six months. Before you drag me into this, she seemed to be saying I want to know all about this briar patch.

"Well, everybody needs to pay their bills, send some cash home, eat regular and have a drink, so we set up a minimum and then jump it up a bit. Most of the artists are pretty well off, but they need something as well. We got receipts, merch, a percentage of booze at some of these places, let's work it out. We always make a profit, usually a healthy profit, why not use it to, I don't know, build schools, hire teachers, provide some food for the kids. I know we can't fix the world so let's find some places we can help." Ian's mind was turning at warp speed now. He didn't know how to help, just that he had to help.

Oh, shit, he's got that Mickey Rooney gleam in his eyes, thought Maggie. Looks like we're going to put on a show to save the town.

The Wind Changes Directions, Can The Tune?

As the bus rolled north, they discussed many details and how to bring about the change they all sought. Gabby told them they should begin with the Native Nations in the US rather than try things in Guatemala. If they tried to send cash or supplies to help his people it would be intercepted by the junta and would be wasted.

Ian agreed stating, "I have some connections to First Nation folks back east and some out west but Jaxson has much closer ties. We'll have to get him involved as soon as we stop. Shit, we will need to get everyone on board if we have any hope of this going anywhere."

"Yes, and you do need everyone on board. You don't know the financial situation of every roadie, sound and light person on this crew. Or of the band members. You need to ask them what they need, if one says no, then you have to say no to the idea. You can't single out one person who might need cash a bit more than the others." As usual Maggie was the voice of reason and intelligence. She had touched on extremely pertinent and sensitive points. Either all were in or it wouldn't happen.

"Maybe we should present the idea, the concept to everyone then have a silent, write-in kind of vote. That would also take away some of the pressure if one of the crew has a problem, they wouldn't have to air it publicly. We don't want to embarrass." Dugan always watched out for his guys.

He had to laugh in his head every time he thought of himself as Kevin or Dugan, it was like he was two different people. He grew up Kevin but guys have to give each other nicknames. The beginning of the bro culture had given him the Dugmeister, Dugerama, and the one he hated most, Dugzilla. But thankfully, he grew out of the bro period, or moved away from the bros back home. He was definitely not the bro type. He thought just Dugan as opposed to Mr. Dugan, was by far more friendly and inclusive. Besides, Eddie Van liked it and that was good enough for anybody!

They would need to fuel up once they got to Oregon a few more hours away. They could hold their meeting while the buses filled up with French fry grease and pig fat and they went into the truck stop to fill up on band chow. They could get Biodiesel in Cally but at a premium. Now, especially with the new plan, they would want to count their nickels and dimes.

Ian would run the idea by Jaxson first, as this really was his tour, but he thought he could answer any of Jaxson's questions and iron out any wrinkles before they met with the band and crew full on. Gabby and Dugan would meet with Ben and fill him in on the meet in Ian's bus and get his thoughts as well. All of the plotters would be on pins and needles until they held their prospective conferences.

The TA truck plaza near Climax, Oregon looked as though it had been invaded by a very tired hippie army. Long haired, long-bearded men, women in shorts, t-shirts, no bras, sun dresses, no bras, sandals and boots, no bras, the truckers couldn't help but notice. It was a trip back fifty years to when most of these truckers, waitresses, and cooks hadn't been born. And neither had many of the hippies, or they were just babies. It was just before the morning rush so, though the truck stop folks were happy to have the business, they also hoped they wouldn't stay past the normal influx of regulars.

After orders had been taken, coffee and tea served, and luckily for all involved no questions about organics or vegetarian fare—though a few orders for meatless breakfast sandwiches were taken and two salads—the contingent settled in.

Ian, Dugan, Ben—who had joined the cadre of converted after concerns of paying off his recent home renovation had been allayed after a conversation with his more than understanding wife. A better woman God had never put on the planet—had joined forces with the originators. They joined Maggie, and Jaxson, who had jumped on board far more enthusiastically than even Ian thought possible, sitting at a long table while Gabby sat nearby at a table by himself. Ian brought the group to attention by asking for silence. He had gained some extra respect with the story of saving Gabby though many still credited drugs. It was still a good story.

"We," and here he included all sitting next to him, "had a bit of an epiphany on the ride up thanks to an education from Gabby here. We learned some things that were hard for us to face, but necessary, about the condition of many of the people of the world. Many who are stuck or forced into hardship not because of something they or their people or, their, their ancestors might have done but because of many of ours. They are caught up in a Caste, c-a-s-t-e," he spelled it out to avoid confusion, "not of their making. And we'd" again he included all those by him and the one sitting who appeared very uncomfortable with the attention, "like to do something about it. It will require a bit of sacrifice by many, if not all, of us."

He waited for the unhappy murmuring to settle down. If you are asking a favor you have to let the asked be heard, if only to let you know you had work to do. "Understand we will not ask of you anything we are not willing to take on ourselves. As well, we will not ask anyone to bring great hardship on themselves. Also understand that if even one of you cannot or will not go along with this plan then that will be the end of it. We will try to explain as well as we can before the food gets here just what we plan and then we will have a secret, write in vote so no one has to expose anything they are uncomfortable telling the rest of us. Sound fair enough?" He waited.

"So far," came a voice from the back he recognized but let it drop. The rest had chuckled and smiled, that was good sign.

He had Gabby stand and give a brief synopsis of the caste system and what it meant to his people, the Native American people, African American people, Indian people, and the brown people now pouring across the southern borders. He didn't expound or lecture, just the facts, and only the facts of the effect this system had on people all over the world and what they hoped they could do through education, job training, and awareness. Then he sat.

Now came the hard part. Jaxson, as he was the best known among the band, the road crew, and loved by all (or enough they hoped he could carry the day) explained how they wanted to structure the finances for all. They were all supposed to get a healthy bonus at the end of the tour, they would get a quarter. Murmur, murmur. But their regular pay would stay the same. All except the front line 'stars', who would have their pay cut by a third. If they could cut other expenses, count nickels, dimes and quarters, and figuring in how well the door had done their first night, they figured they could probably reap a financial profit at the end of the three months in the neighborhood of between five to seven and a half million. That should be enough to begin a few long-term projects of building schools—trade and educational—and introducing programs to make people aware of how this system hurts not just those at the bottom of the ladder but all the way up.

Silence filled the restaurant. Even the employees had stopped to listen. One, a line-cook, came out from the back, his long black hair tied into a ponytail, jeans, white T, and moccasins with non-skid souls who took in the assembled. "I know I ain't a part of this and I should keep my words in my mouth, but, damn, that would be one fine thing on the res where I lived. We just need hope, the kids need hope and to know they ain't garbage, and where I come from those are commodities that lie far down the road from most. People on my rez are dying from a poverty of hope and opportunity. Do what you like but, damn." He seemed to wipe a little grease from the corner of his eye before returning to the kitchen to finish cooking their breakfasts.

"Well," said Maggie wiping a little grease from her own.

Thought and consideration lay like a down comforter on the entire group, You could almost feel each considering their own circumstances, adding and subtracting, considering how this phone call was going to be greeted by significant others. Car payments, rent and mortgages, schools, gas and electric and possibility. Helping their fellow man. It was a large group of hippies with full hippie hearts.

The silence was shattered by the quiet, strong voice of Lee Starling, bass player on ten thousand records, literally. Long, flowing hair, full beard and mustaches that hung past his chin, he looked over towards his long-time friend and rhythm section brother, Russel Crunk, who had damn near as many credits and time in as Lee. "I guess I speak for at least most here when I say we, as musicians, sound, lights, road, everyone here has always given back to our fellow man. It is expected and an honor. We do a certain number of benefits, fundraisers, freebies to feed and clothe the poor every year. No one can say we do this just for ourselves, we are proud and happy to help."

He took a breath to take in the nods of agreement and smiles of remembered shows. There was always a feeling, a vibe that filled every heart and soul when you gave of yourself to help others. The shows were brilliant. The artists, crews, stepped up their game, it was love personified.

"Now you are asking us to give up what was promised and expected for three months," He looked directly at Ian as he knew he was the ringleader.

"Yes, that is exactly what I ask," responsibility accepted, "but only with the permission of all."

Lee kept his stare on Ian for a few more breaths before returning to Russ for support. "That's a lot, more than anybody ever asked before." He took a deep breath and all joined in to see where he was headed. He took another long, deep breath and you could count the heartbeats before, "It would be epic, wouldn't it?" he saw Russ begin to smile. "Man, they'd talk about that long after we're stardust and floating in a psychedelic miasma." He grinned and shook his head as if amazed he was coming to this conclusion, "Goddamn, that would be something. If we could keep this group together for the whole thing, we would have accomplished something no would ever believe possible. Then let's hear them sonsabitches talk about worthless hippie musicians and friends." Here he laughed, he couldn't help it. "And if anybody needs extra to make bills or anything, I'm guessing some of us that's done well could help without nobody the wiser."

That's when the cheer went up. There was no need for a vote. Hell, even the truckers joined in and took up a collection to prime the pump. Though Ben heard one of them saying something about 'dirty hippie, commie, pinkos,' but the guy threw in a fiver for luck. The mood changed, the tired gone. They'd still make book on all their needs and there'd still be a bonus, but the real bonus was what this tour now meant.

Ian glanced over to the huge smile on Jaxson's face, man, this was right up his alley. Maggie was grinning ear to ear, Ben looked about to bust wide open. Gabby sat with a look of wonder like a glow beaming across his face and just shaking his head. What had he done? His mother would be proud.

"Breakfast is on me!" shouted Ian.

"It always is," shouted back the familiar voice, and all laughed a joyous sound.

Jaxson, Ian, Maggie, Dugan and Ben made their way back to their bus where they collapsed on the couches just inside the door. "Well, I know I hoped everyone would consider but that was just overwhelming," Jaxson sighed relief. "Lee couldn't have put it any better. This will be epic!"

"They are the best and you guys picked one helluva crew," Ian got up and shook both the road manager's hands and hugged each one. "I thought for sure there'd be at least one who would hesitate if not revolt, but Lee was just stunning. We owe him big time." Ian breathed his own sigh of relief.

"You guys should do something special for him, to thank him. I don't know what, but I'm sure you'll come up with some grand plan. You always seem to," Maggie chuckled a nervous laugh. She feared what these two idealists would pull out of their hearts, but then, she really didn't care. Lee was right, this was epic, no one had ever done an entire tour for a cause.

"He likes ice cream," said Ben thoughtfully. The others just stared.

"OK, Ice cream by the bucket if that's what it takes. Right now, if we're going to get serious about this, we have to talk to a few attorneys about setting up a charity so we're covered legally and can show we're on the up and up. Any ideas?" his eyes wandered from face to face.

"I might have a guy in L.A.," began Jaxson, " a guy I knew from the record company. He's on his own now, but it might be nice to feed him this. Pretty decent fella, for a lawyer." He grinned.

"Sounds like the perfect person to go with, if you feel confident," Ian said and the others nodded.

"So, what do you think you accomplished?" Lee had pulled Gabby off to the side. He'd put himself on the line for this, now he wanted an accounting.

"I don't know, exactly. Maybe to give some kids something I never had." He shrugged.

"And what is that, exactly," Lee emphasized the word.

"A feeling of worth, that they have some value in this world. That they are worth investing in. That maybe someone sees them as more than garbage to be avoided on the street. That they don't have to spend their lives trying to be hotshots or gansta to prove their worth. They can be trained to be productive and feel pride in what they do and who they are. I don't know, really, maybe just to let them know they are human and they count." He tried his best to find the words but he really wasn't an educated, literate man, just a worker. "That they have worth."

Lee shook his hand, "Just wanted to be sure. I'm proud to be counted in."

"It looks like you might get more than you bargained for," Fate dipped her finger in the pool of life.

"Whatever could you possibly mean?" Fame was the epitome of virtuous innocence.

"You know what I'm talking about," Fate sat up and glared truth into the other goddess's eyes. "Now they all want a taste of you."

"Just hedging my bets. Besides isn't it better to have people worship me for purely altruistic reasons rather than superfluous?" She had picked a rose from a bush that should not have grown this high on the mountain and sniffed.

When The Road Calls, Wheels Turn

Eugene, Oregon is a pleasant community of artists, musicians, hippies and those who keep the buses running on time. You cannot have hippies and musicians run towns, they just don't have the aptitude, you need the straights to collect the taxes, fix what needs fixing, take care of garbage, electric, all the necessities so the hippies can be hippies and the musicians have some place to play. And if done right it runs like a well hash-oiled machine. Eugene, Oregon is as close to such a place as you will find. And it is wrapped in the beauty of the Willamette Valley. Arts, education, pot, and friendly folks, it reeks of laidback 60s vibe.

The Cuthbert Amphitheater is a lovely intimate five thousand capacity outdoor venue. Seats if you want 'em, grass if you don't. It was a perfect spot for this caravan of goodwill. Every single participant of the rolling, 'save the world', tour was walking three feet off the ground with their decision. They would do good for others and what better place to begin raising financial resources for the crusade than this spot.

The backstage buzz was palatable. Everyone intent on making this kickoff one of passion, though nothing had been formally announced as they had barely decided this morning over a very early breakfast. They still wanted this first night of the reconstituted tour to be the best concert ever.

The crew smiled at the musicians, the musicians were happy with the sound, even the lighting guys seemed pleased with their work. Though the one glitch was with some electrical shorts after a night of heavy rain. But Jakob, one of the road crew's elder statesman swore he had met the problem before and he would meet it head on now. Just a few splices, some electrical tape, flip a switch and they could do soundcheck.

Ian was strolling along humming to himself, going over last-minute checks and hoping Jakob wasn't screwing things up worse than they already were. Jake was a good man, he meant well, but had that air of one too many tokes and three too many hits of something powerful about him. He might have quit the doing a long time ago, but it was still doing to him.

He stood in a small puddle of water unnoticed by any and all who happened to pass including Ian who was intent on his list and check marks. Just as Jakob reached down to make a splice, Ian's foot made touchdown in the small pool of water shared by Jacob's right foot. Jake touched the wrong wire to the wrong metal tool and lit up like a forty-foot Christmas tree. The shock of electrical current coursed through the small puddle and into Ian's body, causing Ian to fly to his right. He attempted to find balance when a second shock of current caused him to flop like a fish being electrocuted out of the water, he crashed like a bull into Jakob. Jacob flew four feet one way, Ian three the other and he crashed into a stone wall finally pulling the plug on all the excitement. A puff of smoke hung above his head. Ian was unconscious.

That was how they were found several seconds later by a very confused Ben Friedman. Who immediately called 911.

When Ian awoke his first thought was, 'Oh, fuck, not again,' his second was 'am I dead or alive?' Probably reverse order of what they should have been. He heard Jax strumming and singing softly somewhere in the distance which did not sooth the savage emotion. Reasoning if he was dead, he would probably still hear Jaxson, ah well. He opened his eyes to the vision of Maggie hanging over him hoping for him to breathe. Again, not consoling as he would hope his first glimpse of the afterlife would still include the love of his former.

A constant beeping, the pressure on his upper arm, the quiet but confident tone of an obvious medical person speaking to someone on a phone did, however, comfort. He was alive, they were just making certain.

"How's Jakob?" was whispered and Maggie took a deep, shuddering, emotional intake of breath.

"He'll live, thanks to you," he thought the words sounded troubled, as if she almost wished he hadn't. But he quickly realized that was not the case, she was concerned as to how this would affect him.

"He wants to come to thank you, for saving his life, I think," Ben posed the statement as if a question. There was a weird vibe surrounding the request.

"Just give me a few minutes to return all the way to the living." Ian begged.

"You know he just doesn't like being thanked for things, especially things he can't seem to stop doing." Maggie explained for her husband.

"I'm beginning to see you guys weren't kidding back in New Orleans. This is really a weird quirk he has acquired." Jaxson shook his head in amazement and realization. "Though if you have to have a weirdness about you, this one is pretty good." He laughed.

"Not for Ian," Maggie replied, "It's not that he minds saving people, he hates the notoriety that comes with it. As he has said over and over, he is not famous, he doesn't want to be famous, he gets all he needs from being with you all. Your fame is enough for him. It chafes and it would be best if everyone just accepted he has this strange talent and not get all worshippy!" Her concern could be felt by all standing around. Which included most of the crew, the band and everyone else.

"Oh, we won't," said the sage Mr. Starling, "I think everybody now believes we have the best good luck charm on the planet, maybe in the cosmos. And we ain't going to do nothing that might jinx it." Nods followed the words.

"That would be best," Maggie approved, "and he needs some rest."

"I can do all his finals," Ben stepped up, "he was pretty close to checking off the last few things anyway."

"I'll help, too," chipped in Dugan. "This one's for the untouchables and Ian!" they had unofficially adopted, 'The Untouchables Tour' while Ian was out, until someone came up with a better title.

Ian closed his eyes, laid his head back in the damp earth, and pretended none of this was happening.

Unbeknownst to Ian—though he would not have been disapproving—the company had held a meeting while he lay unconscious on the ground, head in a puddle of muddied water, and body jerking from time to time with the indelible physical memory of a massive wave of electricity shooting through his body. They had decided no one outside the current members should become aware of what had happened over the last couple days. Not friends, family, husbands, wives, lovers, children, friends of friends, second cousins or drinking buddies.

They knew of Ian's skittishness towards fame. Not others, they had earned it through hard work, dedication, and talent, but as a personal affliction. He had no need or want of the infection, quite happy to lean against a trap case off the side of the stage in anonymity and listen to the friends he had helped to achieve their dream.

He loved to walk through the crowds to check levels and reactions of the fans without being bothered by same. It was part of the gig, and he wanted to be left alone. Some had heard rumor of his run-in with fame after stopping a mass murder down in Florida, and his reaction to it. They reported that he had fled the country to flee the fame that was chasing him, only to have it land right in his lap in the middle of London. They did not want to lose their talisman.

Everyone working this tour had worked more than their share previously and they knew intimately how tours could go. They could be the most amazing trip through country and music with all becoming family and remaining so for years. Shared memories, shared stories, shared pain and suffering which only brought folks closer together. On the other hand, they could become nightmares of people trying to sabotage others so the famous would consider the other incompetent and never use the competition again. Jealousy, desire, and covetousness were not the sole property of the Illustrious and notorious.

This was a tour with a divine purpose. It was so much more than music and vibe; it was for the world. And it wouldn't be possible if everyone wasn't on board. Therefore, every person involved had to be aware of any and all disruptions to the force. Not to punish or cut them out, but to heal. This was a tour where music, song, the talent of the performers would be augmented by the talent of the crew. They were one. If they overheard someone was having financial problems they would help. If they overheard someone was having relationship issues they would listen and provide support. Maybe a few days at home would help or bring the aggrieved out on the road for a week or two, let them bathe in the light of the Untouchables.

They had all agreed to the title. It was a term used for the lowest of the lowest caste in India. And they all knew. Each had experienced the criticism and censure of society. Maybe not because of birth, color, sexual orientation—every crew had its share of lesbians, gays, people you could never tell what and with whom, but then no one cared, to each their own—drug busts, addictions of every kind, down and out and back up again. And they knew the look in the eye of normal people who would never understand where it all came from. Now they had a name, a proud name!

So, Ian was their charm. And by virtue of marriage so was Maggie and anyone associated with them. The crew would watch over them and care for them, as if they were favored pets. Oh, they would try not to be obvious, but they would be there. This part of the plan Ian would not have approved but he had no inkling and never would. He had saved two of their number.

So, he was none the wiser when they would bring him his diet cola and a bite over to the side of the stage. He thought they were just being considerate to his weakened condition and they would cease in a few days. He knew crews, they would get tired of his wants and needs very quickly.

The papers came from the lawyer in L.A. while they set up near the tri-cities in western Washington. The sun blazed from a cloudless perfect, blue, sky. It was warm without being overly hot and everyone was in their, now, typical good mood. A fund had been set up at one of the large banks in downtown L.A. so all would know it was on the up and up, nothing hidden. They could have all profits deposited, once expenses had been deducted, and allowed to grow at the going rate. Maybe they could set up investments so it would grow a little faster, if they could find a financial advisor they could trust. All had been burnt at one time or another, or knew others who had, so they would be very careful with the largess.

Word began to spread. No one knew how or from what source, but word of what the tour had become about, was the talk of the internet chatrooms, Instagram, and every other conceivable platform. Fans might not have understood what the caste concept was or why it mattered but they knew, on a visceral level, that it did. And the fans wanted in. Notice escaped the crew of the Untouchables; they were too wrapped up in their daily concerns to be wrapped in social media.

Fans collected at the gate, they passed empty coffee cans up and down for others to throw in a few bucks, change, a joint or two, whatever they thought would help the cause. Whatever the cause might be. Confusion can be a great motivator. 'What is this for?' Helping people. 'What people?' People who have nothing. 'Why do they have nothing?' I don't know, just throw in a few pesos so I can listen to the band.

It was time to do some 'splainin'. The question was, who would the 'splainer be?

When We Come Together As People, We Can Move Mountains

"There's a little brown guy out here lookin' to talk to you, boss," Regis stuck his head in the door of the temporary office of 'The Untouchables.com'.

Ian glared at the empty spot before saying, almost but not quite, under his breath, "I hate when they call me that. It just reeks of plantation, especially when a large black man calls me that. And double especially when it is obvious that man is my superior in size, strength and, apparently, sense of humor."

"They do it because they know it drives you crazy," Jax laughed, "and they do it out of love and respect, believe it or not."

"You know," Ian deflected, "coming from someone else his statement would be considered racist. Or, at the very least, offensive."

"What? About a little brown guy wanting to talk to us?" Jaxson was only half paying attention to Ian's diatribe.

"Certainly, the little brown guy part. Though when a large black man, black as a jungle night, one might add, says it, it loses some of the offensive."

After the incident in Eugene, all had become protective of each other. Accidents on tour were a common occurrence and Jakob not taking all precautions was outside the pale. He was their top electrician and for him to be so careless just threw a pall on the mood of the entourage. Ian might have pulled the plug and saved his life, but it should not have been necessary. Standing in water while working on electrical wiring, not the brightest idea. Confidence was one thing, over confidence another. The tri-cities shows had instilled a level of good humor and bonhomie, but there was still a hint of unease as they played the show in Coeur d'Alene, though Ian had stood over the promoter while he counted the money and then counted it again himself. This was no longer just money but hope and promise. No chances of any kind would be taken. They even slowed down their pace to Montana to avoid the possibility of accidents.

Ian found the 'little brown guy' easily as he stood out like an L.A. lawyer in the middle of wide-open Montana range where they stood. They were supposed to perform at a venue in Billings but a large storm had blown through with high winds and, luckily, very little rain, but had knocked the roof off the venue. They were about to cancel the show when a couple of the local singer/songwriter women showed up with an idea.

A friend had ten acres just outside of town, they could put up a decent stage, run electrical from the road to the stage, and still put on the show. It would be early evening before they could start and the show might be abbreviated, of course, there'd be no sound check. It would not be close to ideal but it would work and all would be satisfied, they hoped. The show would go on, the cash would be raised, the good deed would continue to grow. Miracles. And the two women would open the show. Luckily, they were a known commodity to the greater Billings area. Good vibes filled the Montana territory.

The L.A. lawyer, Ian would do everything in his mental arsenal to banish the little brown guy description from his brain, was wandering about the finishing touches of preparation, lightly dancing around some puddles of mud so as not to ruin his very expensive shoes. He looked L.A., felt L.A., in his clothes, his expression, his want to be anywhere else, especially if it had a lot of concrete underfoot instead of what he could only assume to be cow shit.

"Can I help you?" Ian hid his grin.

"Mr. Sperling, I presume?" asked the man with a slight, though noticeable, accent. Indian, from India, if Ian was not mistaken.

"Yes."

"I am Mr. Raj Bharadwaj, your attorney in the matter of the 'Un-touchable' account," his tone changed, sounding as though he sucked on something distasteful when he said the word.

"You are a friend of Jaxson's?" Ian was slightly taken aback that Jaxson would have anything to do with someone who seemed so offended by those he considered lower than himself.

"We have not officially met but a friend of a friend, of a friend, kind of thing, yes. Anyway, we need to talk about the account, what the plan is. Or if you have a plan. It is beginning to mount up to a relatively tidy sum." There was something about the way he said the last couple words that rubbed Ian the wrong way.

"Hey, what's going on?" Jaxson had come up quietly behind the two.

"It would seem our largess is growing and Mr., uh," Ian danced around the pronunciation.

"Bharadwaj," helped the lawyer.

"Yes, seems to think we should start doing something with the money," he supposed.

"Well, you should begin to start thinking about beginning to put together some sort of strategy of where to begin investing in the concept," the lawyer stepped cautiously around another cow patty.

"Such as?" Ian pushed.

"Well, a school here, a vocational program there, so the buying public can get a visualization of your plans for the money they are shoveling over," now he grinned and it was far more genuine and joyful. "I am curious how you came up with the concept in the first place. Not many in this world are knowledgeable about the caste system, let alone have tied it to so many other cultures as you two seem to have done. It is not an easy concept to accept or understand. We are attempting to change in my own culture, though fighting thousands of years of indoctrination. It is a concept that has existed as an integral part of our culture and has proven to be quite difficult to change. To move the humanity needle deeper into any culture is a battle. Though, now, thanks to you and your tour, many more people know." Ian and Jaxson shared a worried frown.

"I'm afraid we," and here Jaxson pointed to himself and Ian, "didn't come up with the connections one of our road crew did."

The lawyer, ignoring Jaxson's correction, took a deep steadying breath that brought out the worry in Ian's managerial heart. "It is the reason I am here. People have heard of your mission." Ian and Jaxson's expression told him he required a bit more explanation. "About your tour to attempt to change a few corners of the world or, at least, some of the thinking and castes that are ingrained there. I don't know how," he said before either could ask the question, "an overheard comment from one of your roadies, a band member on a cell phone calming the nerves of his or her spouse. I don't know but it has. Instagram, Facebook, Tick Tock, everything, wildfire! People know you and your crew are working for minimum wage and they wanted to connect. There is some talk that there is a certain magic at play here, though no one knows what form it takes, why, or through whom, but they believe. It is what I would guess hippies in the sixties felt and believed. They think they can change the world and you are the focal point."

"Shit," whispered Ian as he realized where this was headed. He wanted off this bus, not to ride it to the end.

"They tried to contact your fan clubs but all enquirers were told they knew nothing. So, people found the bookers at the venues and followed the leads to the producers then to us. And then, they shared. We didn't know what you wanted to do," and here again he took a very deep breath before the beans spilled all over the ground, "we set up a fund. A separate fund from the one this tour is amassing," he immediately added, "to keep all monies distinct. But people want to help and help they have with donations. It continues to build. They call it the tour to save the world. I believe you should keep the Untouchables, as I believe it denotes what it is you are accomplishing."

"How much money have people donated?" Get the facts before making decisions, Ian's rule.

"So, far?" He pulled out his cell phone and punched in information, "A little over a million and a half and growing."

Both Jaxson and Ian whistled. How cliché, thought the songwriter.

"Well, I guess we need a meeting and some discussion." Jaxson said to the nodding heads.

"And a more firm plan on what we want to do and where we are going," concluded Ian.

The lawyer glanced from man to man, "Who is the man who began this venture, who informed you of the castes, the untouchables, the connection between them and your society?" Curiosity is a strange thing and makes odd roommates.

"Gabby. The great big guy over there wrestling the bass bin into place," Ian said to the man's blank expression. "The rather large fellow over there with the big, black looking thing twice his size he is attempting to set in place next to the drum set. You know what a drum set is, I assume?" Always the smartass and always ready. The lawyer nodded and walked in the direction of the stage and Gabby.

"Cute," said Fame.

"What?" enquired Fate.

"You're going to tell me you had no hand in spreading the news of what this human endeavor is about?" She stood, tapping her toe on a rather large boulder before kicking it down the mountain.

"Well, sometimes destiny needs a hand. And I am that hand, it is my job, you know," she grinned, daring Fame to say anything.

"So, now they believe in destiny? And they move away from me?" Fame was not in the mood to play.

"No! It accomplishes what we both desire. It moves the needle in your direction by allowing their fans to think even more highly of them. Their fame grows and so do you," she explained the whole concept and Fame glowed as she began to understand.

The 'little brown guy' carefully made his way to the stairs at the back of the stage, wiped his shoes and tip-toed up to where Gabby had settled the large bass bin. Fastidious. That was the word that came to Ian's mind, yeah.

Mr. Bharadwaj stood taking in all that was Gabby. The large Mayan took extraordinary care in his work and the small Indian man seemed to take pleasure in watching a job well-done.

"May I have a word?" asked the lawyer.

"Well, you can while I work or you can around two a.m. while we're driving but I'm afraid I can't just stop what I'm doing to chat," the grin that filled Gabby's eyes and ran across his lips took any bite out of the words. He was busy but he would talk while he did his job. Lawyers love guys who know when the bosses are watching.

"As long as I'm not in the way," said the legal man as he took a half step back.

"Not mine but remember I'm only one of a crew. Maybe go cop a squat on that trap case over there.

The fella from L.A. took a glance where Gabby indicated a black squat box nearby and made the proper assumption. Almost intelligent for a lawyer.

"They tell me you are Mayan. I am Indian, from India," he always found it necessary in this country to expand on that tidbit of information.

"Yup," Gabby was a man of few words.

"My understanding is your culture also has somewhat of a caste system, it that correct?" Gabby turned from where he was running a cable to be certain he heard the man right.

"I think, if you take the time to study any culture in which one society runs roughshod over another and remains as their masters for any length of time, there is a caste system. Some are just more caste, older, and set in harder stone," he nodded to indicate he knew what Indian culture had devolved into over the centuries.

"Yes, well, be that as it may, I wanted to hear from you of your own. By the way, Raj, is my name, it was rude of me not to introduce myself," he held out his hand and Gabby's encased it. The strength evident almost pulling the lawyer off his case. "You are Gabby, yes?"

"Gabor," he lessened the pressure.

"Can you tell me what you hope to accomplish with this tour?"

"Shine a little light," and his smile did just that.

"On?" he should've been a dentist.

"On the fact that every culture does this, relegate certain people to the bottom. They beat them down, refuse to accept they might be human, they might have intelligence, worth, a soul. Look Mister, I don't know you from night and day but I can tell in five minutes you are one of them. The better ones, the highest caste in your society. Why you want to come here and bust my balls, I don't know. All I do know is these people here, no matter where they started, they have accomplished a lot and they care about me, at least as a human being. And they've offered to do something no one ever has in the history of this world. To completely give of themselves for another on a grand scale." Gabby took a handkerchief out of his back pocket and wiped his brow. He hadn't been aware he was sweating, either from exertion or this guy pissing him off.

"I promise I am not here to anger; I am here to learn. It is the only way we can change what is into what should be. I am of a new generation in my country that wishes to abolish exactly what you are trying to abolish, but I need to know." Silence filled the stage, "I seek guidance, a teacher. I am asking for you to help me so we can help each other."

The two stood motionless in the midst of all the activity taking place around them. It was as if they existed on a different plane and the rest of the crew, the band members, none of them took note of the two men.

"Hand me that mic cable," it was so offhand it took the little lawyer by complete surprise.

Raj gazed at the coiled black cable as if it were a snake that had snuck up from behind him.

"It won't bite you," reassured Gabby, "If you want me to teach you about my life, you have to live a bit of it. Even if the hardest part is behind me, you can see what we at this end of the ladder do to keep the machine running.

"The first thing you have to realize is we are all the same under the pretensions," began the large man to the small by size though not societal stature. "You might have money, servants, big houses and cars, no worries, but strip away the accoutrements and we all bleed, we all need, fail and succeed. And unless you do it on your own, it means nothing. Gifts of a perfect life teach you nothing. Struggle teaches you worth. Alright, now bring that mic stand over here," one step at a time he thought while the lawyer, Raj, gingerly picked up the stand Gabby had pointed to and struggled to bring it over.

"What the hell is Gabby doing to my lawyer?" asked Jaxson to no one in particular.

"Looks like he's got him a gopher," laughed Ben. "Wow, a lawyer actually working. It is a changing world."

Later in the evening as they sat around for the meet after the show, going over what was missed, what wasn't, what was perfect, and how far they had to go for the next show, Jaxson pulled Mr. Bharadwaj aside. "What was that all about today?"

"Trust," the lawyer shrugged, " I have to earn his trust so he will do something that will help all of you."

"What do you have in mind?" Jaxson pried.

"Well, if it is all the same, I would like to travel with you for a while on this tour. I have some ideas that I need to iron out and this looks to be the perfect place to iron them." He had some plan but wanted to keep it to himself until he was assured it had a chance to succeed.

"OK, first the lawyer is hanging with, and working for, Gabby, now him and Jaxson are thick as thieves, what gives?" Dugan hated secrets, especially on the road. They tended to instill mistrust and rumors. And if there was one thing that could kill a tour it was rumors.

You don't cheat on your wife or husband. You send money home for the family. You take care of business and each other. A road crew worked together for the benefit of the show. It was always about the show, when you forgot that, all else would fall apart.

"I don't know," Ben said around a mouthful of Purina roadie chow, but I have known Ian for two decades and Jaxson almost as long, I would trust both of them with my life, my kids, my wife. I think they're up to something but with this group it's usually something fine," he patted Dugan on the shoulder for reassurance. "Time for the road."

Wheels Roll, Life Moves Forward

As they came around the bend on Interstate 90 by Buffalo Wyoming into the sunrise over the wide-open plains, and began heading east towards Rapid City, their next tour stop, Ian's phone blew up. Calls in the middle of the night or very early in the morning are never a good thing on any tour. This did not bode well for the Untouchables.

It was the promoter in Rapid, things had gone insane. Fans were crowding in from Nebraska, Wyoming, North Dakota—a couple hundred miles north—and from the east. The Rolling Save The World Tour aka The Untouchables Tour, had, as Raj told them, caught fire.

The Monument could hold ten thousand, which in a state of just over six hundred thousand should have had breathing room for all. But they hadn't counted on all coming. They might need to change the venue. But to where? This was the largest venue anywhere near the city with the next closest almost four hundred miles away. Shit!

Well, if he was up then soon so would Ben and Dugan be as well. The buses pulled over in Gillette so the crews could stretch their legs, pee, and fuel up on hot, fresh coffee and a completely unhealthy truck stop breakfast. It was time for a powwow of the leaders, and Raj had texted he wanted a word as well. Might as well kill one good morning with all bad news.

Bleary eyed, though more alert than Ian would have thought, Ben sat at their table with a map, an atlas, his phone, and computer. The man was ready to go to work. Well, as soon as the coffee was poured, drank, and then refilled once.

"I know we have absolutely no desire to try this again, but there is a guy outside Rapid, on route 44, that has a huge ranch. He has power and thinks with some Jerry-rigging we could put up a pretty good staging area. Once again, we could put off the show for a day, we have a day off anyway, while we work out security, tickets, port-o-potties, whatever. It would be even more haphazard than Billings but it would work. Or we could just go with the ten-thousand-seater and save ourselves one whole day of shit trying to half-ass this." Everyone knew where Ben's vote would fall.

"I'm with Ben," said Dugan, "I know we're trying to save the world and would like to make everyone happy but we can't keep slapping together shows and venues. Maybe if we had more than one day's notice of this shit we could work out something, but this shit is getting old extremely quickly. It was fun one time, but not every fucking day," Kevin had returned and reinhabited Dugan, and Kevin was tired.

"How many people are we talking here?" Raj jumped in, "I mean are there fifty thousand? A hundred thousand? Or is it just a few thousand overflow?"

"I don't know," said Ian picking up his phone, "Let's find out." After a few questions, 'uh-huhs, Oks, that makes more sense and an I'll call you back'. He hung up. "Maybe fifteen thousand tops. I guess they're not used to these kinds of numbers this time of year and they were flipping out a little. It ain't Sturgis!"

"What do you have in mind, our one-day lawyer/roadie?" Ian asked Raj, the need to jab overwhelming, if only a little. Maggie gave him a bleary-eyed glare and he responded with a bleary eyed silent, 'What?'. Head shake.

"Could we set up an auxiliary stage out in the parking lot? Off to a side of the side, kind of thing? Everything is already there, in the building, the temporary stages, sound, all, and you could just have the people outside pass the hat, as it were." Raj shrugged assuming they would think it stupid, coming from someone who had only showed up the day before.

"It might work. It wouldn't be the whole show, but enough of it that people would be happy. They'd get to see and hear a good portion of the show, contribute and feel as though they were part of what we're doing. Plus, it would buy us some time to see if this is happening on the rest of the stops." Jaxson really hated canceling shows, he loved to play.

Everyone turned their attention to Ben, Dugan, and the road crew. This would have to be their decision, they would carry the burden, and a burden it would be. All took in each other's measure before dropping heads in resignation, "It's possible." Was all any of them would concede.

"Come on, guys, it's better than setting up in the middle of a four-hundred-acre cow pasture, isn't it? Here, you only have to carry stage sections a hundred yards not thirty miles!" Jaxson thought he could lighten the mood with a bit of levity. Jaxson Grahm is a brilliant singer and musician; he is not a comedian. His comic attempt was greeted by stares and shaking heads.

Raj broke the tension, "Mr. Grahm, Mr. Sperling, if I may have a word," Mr. Bharadwaj was anxious.

"It will have to be on the bus. We need to get rolling if we have any chance of pulling this off," Ian tried to shush all parties towards the door while handing over his credit card to the nice waitress.

Once on the bus and tires rolling in the right direction Raj cornered the two heads of the Untouchable state. "I know what he is going to say," he said conspiratorially not mentioning names, "but I think this is important. There is still a lot of confusion as to what this tour is all about. People know you're doing something no one has ever done. And they know you are doing it for the good. They just can't wrap their heads around what it is. Maybe someone could kind of explain it, from the heart, from experience, from their mother's heart and her people." The who was coming into focus and both Ian and Jaxson shook their heads knowing what the answer would be.

"Gabby." Raj almost whispered it as if an invocation.

"Gabby?" asked Maggie.

"Gabby?" Jaxson glanced at Ian.

"Gabby?" Ian threw it back in Raj's face.

And the three-time incantation fulfilled the magic as Gabby stuck his head out from where he had been resting in the back of the bus.

Well, it might have brought Gabby but it did not bring hope. They knew, instantly, there was no way he was going to walk on a stage, in front of ten thousand people, and talk. Move an amp, adjust a monitor, replace a guitar, you betcha! But talk? He would sooner die, and mentioned same, as they attempted to explain to him what Raj had in mind.

They cajoled. He dug in his heels. They begged, he remained silent. They tried to tell him it was nothing, like talking to his family. Yeah, ten thousand of them all at once. They thought they could convince him.

Were these people insane? Gabby almost said out loud, he had trouble conversing with people he didn't know. Job interviews were a nightmare. He was a single man for a reason, he couldn't just talk to a girl, a girl he didn't know, a girl in a bar or a concert. Are you absolutely shitting me?

They reasoned and sweet-talked to their hearts content; this mountain could not be moved.

"It's not a big deal," egged Jaxson, who had walked on thousands of stages in his life which was why he could not conceive why someone wouldn't want to. "Just pretend you're talking to your mom or your best friend, one of the guys from the crew!" He pushed.

"No!"

Jaxson went against type and decided to play the macho card, "I'm a wee bit surprised that a big guy like you would be so intimidated by such a small thing as talking on a stage. I mean, don't you realize you would tower over the people there? And if you look at them as a singular entity rather than a mass of humanity it becomes even easier."

Gabby would have none of it, "You have no idea how small you look on stage do you? You see yourself from inside your head looking out at the audience. But from their perspective, especially those way out in the middle to back you're about an inch tall. That's why we have all these huge screens so they can see you and that's how you see yourself, like the guy on the screen. I see myself as an inch tall, miniscule, almost non-existent. I see myself as the guy way up in the last row of the balcony sees me. I'm not doing it, find yourself another dancer."

The evidence was becoming quite evident, they could blast, jackhammer, take hammer and chisel, this was one piece of granite that would not be carved. Their time would be better spent down the road banging away at Crazy Horse. As the jury returned with their verdict it became aware to all, but especially to Gabby, he was no longer needed here. They pulled into the parking lot of the Monument Hall and he excused himself to go get his work done.

As he got off the bus and headed toward the venue he passed a contingent of Native folks making their way toward the small, dejected, group exiting the same bus. Work needed doing but curiosity overrules all, he had to see what this was all about.

The group of half dozen indigenous people waited patiently for Ian, Jaxson, Maggie, Ben, and Dugan to come to them. They did not wish to appear threatening or that they had an ax to grind; just a few knives.

"Can we help you?" Ian, as manager, took the lead.

'We have come to ask your intentions," said the eldest.

"Well, I guess since I have no other choice, I'll marry her," some things should be kept in the head, Ian realized as he took in their blank expressions. "Intentions as to what?" He straightened his ass up.

"Word has reached us that you are raising funds in the name of the forgotten," this man was not here for jokes and a show.

"I'll handle this," said the songwriter, stepping in front of the mismanager. "We are dedicating this tour to the unseen, the forgotten, as you call them, the Untouchables. Those who have fallen between the cracks or have purposefully been pushed aside." He was on a roll now, "We know too many of our brethren have been kept in poverty, poverty of soul, finances, hope for far too long. We hope to take the money raised and use that to lift them, to help them, to encourage them. To make life better for them." He glanced over where Raj had a look on his face of 'this is what I was talking about'.

"How?"

The fact that a Native American said that one word to him threw Jaxson completely off his tirade. "What?"

"No, how? How are going to accomplish all these lofty," and here you could almost hear him say, 'white man', though he didn't, "goals?" This man had dealt with white guilt and liberals full of lofty concepts too many times before, none had come to fruition just a lot of wasted time, money, and effort. He was tired and old and wanted to accomplish something before he wandered into the afterlife, not be the center of more bullshit. The road to hell had been paved, resurfaced, paved again, patched, and closed. Good intentions and a fiver could get you a shot and beer; he wasn't thirsty.

"What do you need? What is it that would make life better for you and yours?" No one was more shocked at the words than the speaker. Gabby hadn't noticed himself stop, turn around listen, and ask. But he knew the words, he knew the truth.

"Ah, the Mayan, I presume," the old man's smile told Gabby everything he needed to know. A kindred spirit. "Joseph Standing Bear," he held out a hand in introduction and welcome. "What is it you are asking?"

"Something no one ever seems to ask our people, 'what do we need?'. These are good men," he said indicating the crew forming around the conversation, "I know they all mean well, and we've talked, but no one ever asks us, our people. They tell us they are going to build schools to teach us what they think we should know. They tell us they will give us food but not make it possible to feed ourselves. They treat us like children, like invisible forgotten, we should be grateful they have come to give us all they think we might need. But they never ask."

"Now wait a minute..." began Ian.

"Let him speak," quietly but with much steel rumbled the voice of the ancient one. "You wish to use us to raise money and make yourselves feel better about who you are and what your ancestors might or might not have done, fine. We want to hear what our brother from a far southern mother has to say." No more words would be heard by anyone except words of the Mayan.

"I know you probably would have gotten around to it," he calmed Ian's ire, "but we the people, the left behind, the Untouchables, have minds of our own. We know our individual needs. Each tribe, each caste, each of us know what might help. Yes, schools, and shoes, clothes, food so the children don't go to school too hungry to learn. A hungry mind can only absorb so much when a hungry stomach calls. But instead of telling us what you are going to do with your largess, it would be nice if someone asked."

The crowd had grown with native children, indigenous families, wanting to hear what these elders discussed. They spilled out from the parked buses and onto the parking lot/concert side staging area. And even though they would've loved to hear what was being said, many of the road crew were attempting to assemble a decent stage where these folks now stood. Tow motors moved heavy pieces of staging and lighting around curious bystanders.

"You cannot teach us pride, pride in our people, our heritage. You cannot give us worth, but you could cease taking it away, either by force or by kindness. Let us live. Jobs, decent, good-paying jobs, allow us to fix our homes without your permission. Quit appropriating our land, our traditions. We are not a curiosity for you to come out here and take pictures of. 'See the colorful Natives dancing'," and here he shot a quick glance to Jaxson, "for your entertainment, we are a people. Let us be. And we will thank you." Gabby had said more in the last five minutes than he thought he had ever said in his life. "And let us live, without asking your permission."

Silence filled the gap.

A little boy who had been trying to get around his mother's legs so he could see and hear—his own curiosity could not be contained any more than the others—slipped between legs and made an end around toward the action. One of the tow motor drivers hauling a pallet of stage sections didn't see him, due to the boy's size and proximity, and drove straight for him. Just before the collision Ian, without assistance of accident or slippage, stumbling, misstep, or stagger, or, come to think of it, thinking, reached out and snagged the kid without ever taking his eyes off the Mayan and Standing Bear.

The befuddled scrum of people stood back in awe. Before anyone could utter a syllable and before the 'Oh, shit' could kiss Ian's lips, Joseph Standing Bear hugged him in gratitude. No words were exchanged. No platitudes, no cheers, ovations, or bravos, just a thanks for doing what was expected. Oh, the story would be told but only as a teachable tale of what a human being is supposed to do. Kindness to another, and in this case, to a family who would've lost a small child. Not one of the assembled seem to think more of it.

"You have our blessing," said the old Native, "You are a good man, he is a good man, I have to assume you are all good people. We accept what you do. What do you need from us?"

"Tell us what you need," replied Jax sheepishly. "I think we have some cash to divest." He nodded to the well-pleased Mr. Bharadwaj. They would have their first project.

"That was good what you did there." Maggie had sidled up next to Gabby as he melted into the background while others took over the conversation.

"I never said so much in my life, I should've stayed out of it." Gabby turned to go back to work.

"No!" She declared, the word firm, unyielding. "You saved what might have fallen apart. And you did it with your heart. That is what is important here." She took a long, slow intake of air, in for penny, "They listened because they respect you. Because you spoke truth to all, because you know the pain, the indignity, the awfulness of what they have survived unlike any of us can know. You know it in your soul, and more importantly, you know it in your people's souls, your mother's.

"You spoke for them because that was most important to you, not your insecurities, not your feeling of worthlessness, not your damned shit self-image, YOUR PEOPLE!" Heads turned their way and she silently apologized as she led him away from the crowd. She had a point to make and she was going to have her say. "You have an opportunity to do a great good here. You, Gabor of the Mayan people, God's Bravest Man, can move the mountain, if even just a fraction of an inch, with your words. I know about being terrified on stage. Those two idiots," and she pointed at Ian and Jaxson now intently discussing whatever they discussed, asking and involving the indigenous folks as well, "have dragged me on that damn stage more times than you can imagine. I swear they do it just to keep me humble. Well, it works but I'll tell you this, when you walk out there in the middle of those lights and look over the crowd you can't see but a tiny percentage of them. You see their faces, their joy. They will smile at you and you will feel their love. And you will accomplish what none of these fools can hope to." Her grin was what sold the thought. He grudgingly agreed. No one argued with Maggie; not and won.

They told the 'boys' the change of heart by the big man, he would explain at some point during the show.

"How about during *'The Cannons of Peace*," suggested Dugan.

"Damn good suggestion," smiled Ben and Jaxson, the deal was settled. Time to get this show up and running.

Both stages were set as darkness and the sunset and dark closed in. Restlessness settled, anticipation filled the auditorium and the outside stage area. The show was about to begin. And what a beginning it would be. During the interim of meeting the First Nation contingent and the show, decisions had been made concerning the opening. The show would honor those they sought to aid.

At the speed of darkness, the drumbeats began, slow, steady, like a heart, simultaneously inside and out. Sparkles of light reflected off silver and turquoise jewelry and drums sticks, gemstones and beads glistened as lights flickered, illuminating the stages. Chanting could be heard as it snaked its way out from backstage accompanied by leather soles on wood. As the chanting grew in volume the beat of the drum intensified. The audience silent. They could feel the ancestors gather around them, outside they could feel them in the air, and their giddy smiles illuminated the stage like a sky filled with stars. Dancers then filled the stage, singing story and respect to those who came before and those who would come next. Joy, hope, rejuvenation, life. The crowd might not know the lyrics but they knew the sounds. Tears filled eyes; they joined the dance. The dance of humanity. The dance of change. And just as abruptly it ceased.

Through the silence came a tall, elderly First Nation man, resplendent in Native traditional dress, Buckskin shirt and breeches with a hundred thousand beads of every color under the rainbow, Buckskin boots and three eagle feathers protruding from the crown of his head.

He stepped up to the microphone, "Welcome! Welcome to Paha Sapa. The ancestors of our people welcome these artists and appreciate what they hope to accomplish with their music and love. Know they mean what they say, their words are true. We can and will be healed by the actions of others but mostly we need to be healed by our own. Mitakuye Oyasin! We are all related!

"Let's dance!" And the drummers picked up loudly where they had left off, the dancers danced, the dreamers dreamed.

That was what Gillian Morse, Cinda Wilson, and Michelle Ranch, who was out visiting family in Wyoming, walked out to, to kick off the rest of the show. Each act melded into the next. Tonight, there would be no MC, no interruption of music, just smooth transitions with one artist introducing their friends. All proceeds from this evening, those from the gate, those collected in coffee cans and bags would be donated to the Pine Ridge Committee to use as they saw fit. With slight oversight from the legal team, of course.

Jaxson came out and played five songs before launching into *'The Cannons of Peace'*. A large, very frightened, man paced back and forth in the wings in front of where Ian stood. Ian wanted to say something to calm Gabby, but he had no words. He hoped Jaxson would get to the intro before Gabby wore a hole in the floor.

Movement caught his eye as Maggie walked to the big man and took his arm. She looked up into his face, though she had to stand on her tippy toes to do it, smiled and said something to him. He grinned back and seemed to relax, ever so slightly.

Pianissimo, Jaxson brought the band down behind. He said he had a special guest who would like to say something but was unused to speaking in front of people, so he asked the audience to be kind. It was time. Gabby walked out to the appointed mic and looked out over the sea of people.

He froze. All his words dried up like a spit of water on very hot sand. What the fuck was he doing? Terror filled his body; he couldn't even run; he was frozen in place. He was going to die of a heart attack in front of ten thousand people. Fuck! Silence.

His fervent glances sought some escape, but there was none. He saw the band staring at him, Jaxson staring at him, Ian. Maggie smiled and walked through her own terror of the stage to stand next to him. She took his arm, as if they walked down a park lane in the blossom of spring. For some reason Gabby's eye caught Lee, as it frantically searched for an avenue of escape. The ancient bass player was standing calmly gazing at Gabby with a huge grin on his face. 'What's so fucking funny?' Gabby wanted to shout, but he had no voice.

And that was when Lee started to beat on his chest with one fist while plucking a solid beat with the other on his bass. Next Jaxson took up the beat right above his own heart while Crunk took up the beat on the bass drum. Soon the entire congregation was pounding their chests in rhythm to their hearts, their love. They were telling him they had him in their hearts, they were there for him. Gabby stepped up to the mic.

He spoke from his heart, from his mother's heart and from his people's hearts. He spoke for the forgotten, the ones who had slipped through the cracks either by plan or by life. He spoke of true equality, of not separating by where in a country you were born, or the hues of the spectrum. That we could not accomplish what we hoped without the help of all. Without reaching down to lift up. Not just mouthing words and platitudes but with actions and ridding ourselves of indoctrination of concepts like Untouchables. Because when it came right down to it weren't we all, in some way, untouchables. Wasn't it time to touch, feel and have empathy for those who suffer? Yeah, stupid hippie ideals. Stupid teachings of the ones we supposedly worship. Stupid, but sometimes stupid is necessary. To believe in fairies and nymphs and the spirits of the world. A little night magic. He said many things he would never remember and each night he would adjust as the words came.

Yeah, it was going to be a good tour. Ian smiled; nothing could fuck this up!

A Perfect Day in an Imperfect World

Ian and Maggie had decided on a side trip to Chicago coming out of the shows in Sioux Falls, St. Cloud, down to Des Moines and into the Quad-cities before heading toward Champaign where James Nash was finally going to catch up to them. He had been inundated with guest spots on late night tv and filling in dates on the road. He had been missed.

As the weather improved in forecast and actual fact, they were able to produce more outdoor shows, allowing for more fans, longer shows, more acts and more headaches. Ian needed a mental health day! They shopped a bit, had a fabulous Italian meal at Topo Gigio's in Old Towne, visited some old haunts from their past; and Ian saved a guy who almost walked into an oncoming bus—he had now come to accept his saving people as an affliction like a stutter or Tourette's, people would just have to be patient until it cured itself—and bought some Garrett popcorn. They rode their joy to Champaign and their hotel.

All had a night off, which after the past few weeks was a much-needed respite, and all were in a relaxed, numbed state of mind as Ian and Maggie settled into their comfy, if not exorbitant, digs. Jaxson came down to report that Kenny Loggins had called and wanted to know if he could come down to do a few numbers on the show. He was passing through regionally on his own short tour, loved what they were doing. And of course, just wanted the hang with friends.

Ian smiled, this just got better every stop. They were on the road with a great crew, fantastic low stress artists, the numbers were exploding—they might not save the world but they could send a good dollop of hope—and Maggie was by his side. Perfection!

All were in a great mood the next morning as they headed to the stadium where the concert would take place. The stage crew was putting final touches on equipment, amps, lines, mics, trusses for the lights, and stacks for the fronts. The sky was perfectly clear, no rain in sight for five hundred miles, according to radar. People had begun gathering a day ahead of showtime and there were a hefty number camped out.

The guy's clothes caught his eye through all the buzz of activity. Ian didn't recognize him, but there was just something. He had the look of a NY Goombah right off the street, like he had been bred between a L.A. coke dealer from the eighties—shit, was that a coke spoon dangling from his one gold chain? — and New Jersey numbers runner. He was glad handing everybody he saw, laughing too loud, pants and shirt way too tight to be looking for work and shoes that would be ruined by three p.m. Even Raj had stopped to buy a pair of work boots back in St. Cloud. He could only be a record company rep. But whose?

They had more than a half dozen regular acts and others popping in and out each stop. Who would send this slimy creature into their pond? Well, Ian was about to find out. Success was drawing a degenerate element and Ian wasn't going to do that again.

This tour had nothing to do with records or companies, this was their own thing, their own windmill and nobody else was going to tilt at it for some sleazy profit motive.

"Can I help you?" Ian put on the polite, though it was not his first impulse.

"Hey, Vilhelm Wilhelm," he stuck his hand out at an awkward angle to give some kind of hipster hand contact thing. "A and R."

Yeah, there was nothing about this guy that fit with anything else about this guy. Vilhelm Wilhelm? Maybe Meato Guido, but, shit, such a nice day, too.

"Ian Sperling, I run this circus. How can I help you...William?" Ian felt like hopping back into the shower. What was it with the industry that they always found guys like this to fuck with artists, writers, and musicians?

"Vilhelm. Just checking in to make sure everybody has what they need. You know to make sure the artists are being cared for, if you know what I mean," and here Ian felt the bile rise as the wink and nod, buddy-buddy whatever, seem to indicate something of an extremely lewd concept.

"Oh, from the A.S.P.C.A?"

"I'm sorry, the what?"

"The Anachronistic Society for the Prevention of Cruelty to Artists." Ian smiled quite proud he had come up with something so stupid so quickly.

"No, not really," the man appeared confused, "I am an A and R guy." He clung to his life raft for all he was worth.

Ian nodded, "All of our 'friends'," and here Ian emphasized the word so V.W. would get his drift, "are well taken care of. All wants and needs. So, scoot along back to L.A. or whatever cesspool sent you, we're doing just fine, Wilhelm." Patience does not come in an unlimited size and Ian was squeezing the bottom of the tube.

Apparently, this guy had skipped 'Hints 101' in slimeball school because he showed no sign of grokking Ian's palpable tone. "Vilhelm. Well, I'm just going to hang around a bit to make sure everybody is happy. It's ma job, ya know." Another wink, some kind of clicking sound from his mouth and he was off.

Ian was not happy. Who had given this floating turd a lanyard with an All-Access? Somebody was going to get an ass chewing. And whose goddamn rep is he? Time for some investigative skills to kick in. Come on brain do your magic! But there was no one on the tour he could possibly imagine who would have some low-life, oily, wannabe snake like this repping them. Something smelled like shit in Champaign.

He had seen Jaxson making his way over to talk to him before he spied the slime, smiled, and did a one-eighty. Mr. Grahm would be first on the interrogation list.

He claimed innocence, ignorance, and amusement. Mr. Grahm has a strange sense of humor, funny as shit, when it's happening to someone else, though if it had been him, he'd be hopping pissed on a hot rock.

Time to check in with Dugan and Ben, they'd know something if anyone did. Show time pushing at his back he decided to wait until the end of the show or the ride. Whenever he remembered. But right now, Kenny had shown up backstage and Maggie was hogging him. Ian needed a little Kenny love as well.

Over the next few days and shows in Indianapolis, Dayton, north through Detroit and back down to Cleveland, Ian saw more and more of Mr. Wilhelm, though every time he tried to corner the guy he seemed to disappear into thin air. He was always cajoling with the road crew, the lighting folks, especially the pretty red head who ran spot, and some of the band members. Nothing outwardly suspicious, just odd.

They had another night off coming into Buffalo and thought a trip to the Canadian side of the falls would relieve some of the stress causing Ian to miss much sleep with a headache, shoulder pain, and a slight case of vertigo. Jaxson, Maggie, Ben, and Ian headed out across Grand Island and down to the Falls. None of them could ever remember stopping at this magnificent natural creation in all their cumulative years on the road. It was well worth the trip, they even decided to get soaked on the Maid of the Mist. So, with light hearts, and relaxed neck muscles they made their way to the border crossing to get back to America.

The dog sniffed Ian, stepped back, sniffed his right pocket again, stepped back and barked. Ian wasn't sure what that meant, but he was pretty sure it wasn't a happy bark. Did he have some shake left in his pocket? No, he wouldn't be that careless. There was always a certain amount of pot in any roving band of artists and crew, shit it was legal most everywhere, but still, what were the laws in NY and Canada?

"Would you mind emptying your pockets on the table, sir?" the guard wasn't exactly accusing but he wasn't requesting, either.

"Nope, whatever you need," Ian had a show to put on tomorrow and spending some time in either a Canadian or US lockup was not on the agenda.

Some change, a couple hundred in cash, mints, keys, and a roach. What the fuck? A roach? It wasn't his he could tell by the sloppy way it had been twisted. Every pot smoker knows exactly how they tie off a joint and this was not his handywork. Someone had set the man up.

"If you wouldn't mind," said the now alert border guard, pointing at a spot he expected Ian to hop to.

"I can explain," began the flustered manager before being shushed by both friend and foe alike.

As the guard continued his own search of Ian's personage Maggie dug through her small but seemingly bottomless purse. By the time he had the cuffs on Ian's wrists she had piece of paper in her hand.

"Excuse me, officer, I'm not sure if this is pertinent, but I have his medical marijuana card and doctor's orders right here," she presented the paperwork.

"Ah, geez," the guy seemed so disappointed Ian thought. But, shit, it was a roach not a pound!

As in any decent story, the heroine saved the day.

Ian knew, he had no proof, per se, but he knew in his heart and head, he knew. Maybe it was the oily tip on the roach, maybe it was the way the guy had disappeared every time Ian went looking for him, but he knew. This slimeball was trouble with a capital T. He had somehow slipped the roach into Ian's pocket, maybe with a folded bill, maybe because Ian wasn't the most observant person in the world, but he was going to get rid of the nuisance. This was his circus and he hadn't hired another clown.

When they got back to the hotel there was no sign of the 'record rep' and no one had seen him all day. Maybe Vilhelm Wilhelm had split the scene and Ian could just relax. Ian felt like the fisherman who could never get past the one that got away. He wanted to throw the guy off the circus train himself. He would have to settle for the fact the slimeball was gone. But then he discovered the woman journalist poking around and his hopes plummeted.

Now, don't get Ian wrong, he had nothing against the press, they served a purpose, especially in the music business, but this tour had been humming along nicely and without a lot of press. He wanted it to remain low key, especially with his affliction. He remembered the floodlight glaring attention that his quirk had caused and the complete takeover of his life. The last thing in the world he needed now was to have a journalist witness one of his accidental moments of restoration and wake up the publicity and stardom machine. He liked that everyone surrounding him now just accepted his little quirk.

She was a pretty woman, not TV reporter pretty but journalist pretty. She had an intelligence about her eyes and a smirk that revealed a wicked sense of humor behind the serious expression. She was all business right now and Ian wasn't. He wanted a pound of flesh and the meat locker was empty.

"Can I help you?" he was tiring of the question.

"I am Jeanette Serling, with the Times," all business.

"I am Ian Sperling, Ms. Serling and haven't been with the times since 1970," he smiled innocence. Her blank expression was all the reward he required. No, take that back, her dawning awareness of what had just taken place was the cherry.

"Well, be that as it may, we have heard of your tour in New York," she said the name of the city as if it were magical or should be to him, "So, here I am to find out about the great tour to save the world."

"Ms. Serling, New York? People in the great city are noticing our little tour? Are you ok being this far from the mothership? Do you need a latte or lox and bagels? Cheesecake? It must be disconcerting to be this far out in the hinterlands," Ian was in no mood to play, which was when he usually played the hardest.

"I'll survive, Mr. Sperling," the hackles rose and fell, the claws became nails and the temperature dropped. All business. "I really would like to know more about the tour. The reason. How it came to have such a grand purpose, all of it."

"Of course, Ms. Serling, if you can walk, talk, record, take notes, whatever all at once I would be happy to entertain any questions you might have." Mr. Conviviality.

"Tell me, Mr. Sperling, how long has this tour actually been running?" Ian was overjoyed to see this early thirtyish woman take out an official press notebook with pen in hand. OK, he would have to reassess.

"Well, Ms. Serling, we rehearsed and tried different pieces of the puzzle for six weeks. We wanted the right acts, the right temperament, the right road crew and staff. If you're going to do a palooza for three months everything has to be right. Scheduling, not just on stage, but time on and off the tour. Plugging new acts here, regional acts there. Catch someone on their own tour for a few nights, each artist only does a half hour or so, so it's not real taxing. You have to know people's pasts and who's been with who and who shouldn't be with who again. It's a labor of love, lust, and shouldn't be's." He continued walking toward the backstage area, "We need to get you an All Access if you're going to be hanging around here for any length of time, Ms. Serling." His way of determining how long he would have to live with the press.

"A few days should do it, Mr. Sperling," she smiled sweetly, too sweetly he thought. "Why 'The Untouchables'."

"To be honest, Ms. Serling, I could explain that but I would fuck it up, I want to get the group together when they're not running around with their hair on fire trying to get this show together. Maybe on the bus ride back toward Pittsburgh tonight. If you'll excuse me," he said remembering a previously unknown appointment.

"Mr. Sperling, do you mind?" she asked waving the pen in a circular motion indicating the whole of the backstage.

"No, Ms. Serling, have at 'em, Dugan here will get you your laminate." And he was off to parts unknown still with an eye out for a certain slimy record rep looking bastard.

"Mr. Sperling," she asked to his receding back, "how long?"

"Until I tire of it, Ms. Serling, until I tire of it," she couldn't see his smile but she could feel it.

Jeanette Serling was a good reporter and not just about music or culture, she had a nose and it was twitching. Not hard, she didn't have an overwhelming urge to scratch but something was out of order here. Everyone seemed on the same page. The mood of all involved almost euphoric, as if on a mission from god. But which god and what mission.

Oh, she knew about the concept of raising those from the depths of depravity, poverty, soul crushing generations of ancestors held under the suffocating power of those just above them, but there had to be more. Like, why? No one had cared about the condition of indigenous peoples, slaves, untouchables, black and brown people, for hundreds, if not thousands, of years. They were the conquered, grist for the mill. That any had survived this long was a testament to pigheadedness, no more. But wasn't that the same with women? The thought rambled through her head.

Hadn't they been ignored, used, raped, pushed down, down, down throughout history only to rise at long last to take their place just below white men? Wasn't progress slow, incremental, but progress? Ah, who the fuck knew. What she did know was that there was some stink in the ointment here or the beginning of rot. She could feel it, just below the surface of all the good, hippie, sixties, 'we're in this together for the love of mankind' bullshit. And she wanted to find that rot and expose it.

It was the way some of the crew were distracted in deep conversations with dissatisfied expressions on their faces. A dissatisfaction that seemed to have nothing to do with how things were setting up or how the show might go but with something deeper. A storm was a brewing and Ms. Serling wasn't going nowhere until she witnessed the destruction. She was a journalist.

"Really? You brought in a journalist?"

"Look you want them to worship you, you need press," There was a wicked glimmer in Fate's eyes. They had been playing with Mr. Sperling like a cat with catnip for a few months now. It was beginning to lose some of the luster. She wanted some kind of action and who better than the press?

"I suppose," said Fame thoughtfully, "Are you going to spill the beans on his history?" That should gin up the celebrity machine.

"Not yet. I see something in the future where she will add more flavor to the stew. Her destiny is now tied to theirs. It's just something I like to do. It's like juggling, the more balls you have the more interesting it becomes. Let's see where it all goes from here." It would not have surprised Fame to see Fate rubbing her hands together.

And The Sauce Begins to Thicken

The show in Buffalo had been one for the books. Ann Di Francesco popped in to sing a couple of her tunes and join in as a background vocalist with Gillian, Lucinda, Bonnie, Michelle, and Jesse Collins, it was as heavenly a choir as Ian could remember and as righteous a night as any in music. All shows were being moved to outdoor venues, baseball parks and football stadiums. The beauty of America is that cities might not have cultural centers and opera houses, theaters, and concert halls but every single one had some kind of sports facility that held large sums of humanity, perfect for concerts. Well, except for the sound, but that was up to the crew to fix, wasn't it? Gabby had even settled in a little more as speaker for the Untouchables.

Jeanette had been allowed to join the inner circle on their bus, Ian's decision, though no one could cypher why. Ian had his reasons, though mostly he hoped if she got what she wanted she'd go away. So, it was Ian, Jaxson, now Gillian and Jesse, circles change, Ben, Dugan, Gabby, and Regis, who wanted to really understand on a visceral level what all this caste stuff was all about. And to figure out where he fit into the scheme of things here. Before the doors whooshed closed Raj slipped his slight frame onto the steps and the arm of a couch. Maggie had chosen to ride with the girls in the band and some of the musicians who wanted to keep jamming on the ride.

Jeanette listened intently as Gabby explained what his mother had told him of their ancestry, of the conquerors from Spain, of their subjugation and millennial long fight for survival while first the Spaniards and then the Mexicans and finally the Junta in Guatemala, attempted to work, torture, rape, them into extinction. Raj shared his own stories from India though from another perspective. He was from far up the ladder from where Gabby stood but they stood in solidarity. Something she found refreshing.

Though she still could not understand the concept of it being impossible to rise even slightly above the station you were born into. Here she was a young black, professional woman who had come from parents that had risen from the poverty of their parents to middle class. If they could, why couldn't anyone, anywhere?

"You are representative of all they fought for, all they suffered for. The generations that lived under the chain and lash to continue the blood so you could be born into a better time. A better time that took a long time to arrive and not for all. Look around you, girl," and had this not been said by the massive Regis more words would have been exchanged, "How many don't get the opportunity you did. How many either got tore down by the system or each other? For centuries. Centuries! Our people were less than cattle, less than nothing. Could be killed without thought or retribution, for looking the wrong way or saying the wrong word. People still live that way and there are those who would drag us back to the 'good ol days' in a heartbeat. That's what this is about. That is what this tour is about, to open eyes, minds, not blame, not guilt, just shine the light." Regis had found what he had come for and he was filled with the right of it.

"You want to fill your paper with some words, you tell folks to look around, to see the condition of their brothers and sisters of all colors and persuasions, to see their condition, to lift them up. To lessen one is to lessen all. We doing it with music and love, yeah, it's stupid, should be doing it with baseball bats and guns, but these people, these musicians, they ain't above us, they don't look down on us, we all the same to all these people. That's why we are doing this. And why, even though I hear some bitching lately, most all still in full boat." He was spent. Regis was a big man, mostly a joyful, hard laughing, drinking and toking man, but like Gabby not much of a talker. He'd used up about a half year in the last ten minutes.

"So, you are going to take the money earned," she began.

"Minus expenses," Ian reinforced, "people have to be paid, fed, send money home, hotels, gas, emergencies, expenses. No one is working for free. All are paid the same."

"All?"

In unison, Jaxson, Ian, Gillian, Jesse, Ben, and Dugan, "All."

"Impressive." She nodded. "All the proceeds," she corrected herself, "go to?"

"Building, investing," now it was time for Raj to show his stuff. "We are investing in communities, schools, community buildings, approaching industries which would benefit those communities to build campuses to provide jobs, good jobs, clothing and feeding the children. Whatever the people, the recipients tell us they need. We do not dictate, we listen."

"So, mostly brick and mortar kind of stuff?" Jeanette was warming to these hippies.

"Not all," smiled Raj looking to Jaxson to see if he still had the reins, the nod told him, "We are also investing in programs to lift the souls, and maybe that is the wrong word, as we are certainly not a religious affiliation of any sort, but the hearts and minds of the children. To show them their culture, their worth in the world, the beauty of their people. But not just the people in the villages and communities. We wish to expose those who are not aware of what has been done to these others and continues. To show the world the value of all people, of their cultures, what they have contributed to humanity for thousands of years. We wish to begin advertising campaigns, programs at schools and universities to teach respect for the unknowns, the forgotten, the..."

"Untouchables," she finished.

"You'll see as we travel along. You're welcome to stay with us as long as you wish," Jaxson smiled in invitation. Ian twitched with fear of her witnessing something he hoped she wouldn't. "We can talk more as the circus continues, right now the rocking of the road is calling me to my bunk," and with that he shuffled his tired ass to the back of the bus.

Murmur's continued as questions were quietly asked and answered as best as could be before Ian perked up. "Regis, we need to talk privately, and soon."

"Oh shit, yes boss," Ian refused to rise to the bait.

As much as Ian loved to travel by bus, the hang, the camaraderie, the jam sessions, the bullshit sessions that lasted all night, there really was no privacy. No place he could secrete away with Regis to question the big man. The thing was, he really wanted to ask him about what he'd said about bitching. He'd heard nothing himself and neither Ben nor Dugan had mentioned any dissatisfaction among the crew, so who was complaining? And what were they complaining about? He knew one thing and that was if there was murmuring of mutiny among the crew, he wanted it nipped before they were left stranded somewhere without crew, equipment, or song. And he certainly didn't want to discuss any tear in the fabric with that woman from the Times sitting right there!

It was then the change of mind took hold. Ian decided there were enough secrets and this would not be one of them. Honesty was called for and if they wanted the Times or anybody else to trust them then they had to be honest among themselves.

"You said something interesting a moment ago and I'd like to delve a little deeper into the subject," Ian tip-toed but attempted to put on his big boy pants. "You mentioned some folks are bitching about something, what might that something be?"

"Well, I shouldn't have said anything. It's really nothing to be concerned with, boss," he grinned.

"And you can stop that shit right now as well," Ian would not be distracted. He wanted to know what was happening with his crew.

"Alright, Ian, some of the guys have been hearing about how people are sending in a lot of donations for this thing and they're wondering why they can't get full pay and bonuses like they were originally promised now," Regis spoke as if a gun was at his head and the words poured out.

"And where did they get this information?" It wasn't really private or a secret but it wasn't exactly public knowledge either. He glanced at Raj, he had all the info, didn't he?

"Not me!" Raj did not wait for the question.

"I'll be honest, I'm not sure. Though maybe some reporter said something in the press, God knows they can see folks collecting at the shows and it ain't no secret some are contributing to online shit. GoFundme and Donorbox, Indiegogo, they're all over the fucking internet. I didn't say nothing, you can be sure of that." Regis, for whatever reason in his former life, felt the need to defend himself though he had done nothing.

"He's right," jumped in Gillian, "I funded my last recoding with Indiegogo. Fans love it, they get to feel like they are a part of the process."

"Alright, alright, settle down, I'm not accusing you fer Christ's sake. It just bothers me that the crew is saying anything. I thought we were all supposed to be in this together. Looks like a meet is in order. Regis, thank you. I will not forget you stepping up. You might have saved the tour," he actually stood up so he could hug the big lug and let him know all was well between them.

What the hell had gotten into the crew? He would find out on the morrow before setup.

Routing and availability had made the Pittsburgh stop necessary. Once things began to move outdoors, they had to work around sports and event schedules to get the venues they needed. So, a quick five-hour overnighter to Pittsburgh and PNC park. Ian couldn't, if he was honest with himself, tell if it was availability or his penchant for the game of baseball but he preferred baseball parks to football stadiums. There was more history, more intimacy, more peace in a park than a stadium.

He'd planned on having a meeting with everyone, and he did mean everyone, right after breakfast but it soon became clear that would not happen. One of the equipment trucks had an axle overheat and broke down just north of the city. The people who were supposed to be at the park to set up the stage early were very late. Though by the time the troop arrived they at least had the stage in place and the local sound company had loaded in. They were scurrying to get caught up to schedule.

The talk would have to wait, plus showers were poking their ugly head across the radar screen. Not what Ian needed today. And for some reason, which no one could fathom, Jaxson was not happy, though Ian thought it was probably because he had done so many shows in a row and the road was wearing on his old body. He could use a night off or two. They needed somebody to step up and fill in who could satisfy the throng.

His phone rang. Josef had just landed at Kennedy and wanted to know if he caught a flight to Pittsburgh whether there was a guitar he could use for a couple songs. They'd cut Jaxson back to three tunes tonight and let the man rest. Magic.

As much as Ian wanted to iron out whatever was bugging the crew, the show always had to come first. Somehow the phone call from Josef was discovered and leaked, or the rumor thereof, which took off on radio and tv at the speed of sound and light, and the crowd of twenty some thousand had now swelled to almost double that. Ian might not like rumors but they certainly helped ticket sales.

Josef, formerly Steven gatos, had not performed on a live stage for a long, long time due to ignorance, misrepresentation of things he never said and religious bigotry, so this, if true, was a huge deal. Extra security had to be found, more ticket personnel, food, drink, merch brought in. It is not a simple thing to add thousands to a concert. Plus, with the breakdown, the hustle to get equipment from said broke down truck to stage to ready, well, that was why he had wanted, and gotten, the best of the best for the road crew. They were ready.

Jaxson seemed slightly more relaxed and at ease knowing some of the weight had been lifted from his very capable shoulders, but even the strongest can tire. The rest of the cast and crew were excited and abuzz with the new addition to the show. They didn't care if he did one song or twenty, most of them had never had the chance to see, hear, Steven Gatos live. This would be beyond epic. Josef joining James and

Jaxson for a triple headliner kind of night. Not to take away from the rest of the cast but these guys had weight.

Yeah, this was definitely the tour of tours, Ian thought, and this little wrinkle in the fabric might just have helped iron out some of the crazy but it was still there, festering in the minds of the crew. He still wanted to nip it quickly.

Though the skies threatened throughout the afternoon, glimpses of sunshine provided hope all would go off without a hitch. Some sprinkles just before they opened the gates dampened spirits for about fifteen minutes before the gods smiled and the clouds broke. It would be a great afternoon and evening.

Ian begged the local constabulary for an escort to get Josef from the airport to the Park and after much negotiation and promises they conceded. Josef was on his way. Ian didn't know who was more excited, him or the crew. He had known Steven since the very early seventies, they hung, Ian loved his music, they both loved opium, it was a friendship made in music. Ian played him on the radio, the record company loved and appreciated him for it, they got to hang.

They had remained close until Steven dropped out of sight in the late seventies after finding what he had sought all his life. Peace, love, family, life. Then they reconnected at the turn of the millennium and had remained working together and friends for two decades. But opportunities to actually share the same space did not come often enough. Ian was going to try and convince Josef to hang and play at least until they got to NY.

They'd be there in a week and half and then set up residence at the Beacon for a week, a much-needed rest stop. Yes, they would be doing shows every night with a rotating cast of artists but they would sleep in real beds that weren't moving, bouncing, and jouncing all over America's much in need of repair highways and byways. They could eat regular and healthy, not that most of the crew wouldn't miss truck stop chow, but it would be good mentally and physically for all involved.

There were already rumors of who would be stopping by the Beacon for guest sets and it was wild. Even Ian, who had been in this business since he was knee high to Keith Richards, was surprised at the names being thrown about. Rumors sell tickets. If half of them showed up, shit, if a quarter of them showed up, it would light this thing like a rocket for the rest of the country. This was the tour of tours and the one to be on. He hoped the grumblers in the peanut gallery would remember that.

Maggie found Ian off the right side of the stage as he intensely watched the final setup and the multitudes entering. "Jeanette wants to know if she can share your space, to see what it is you do. I told her I would intercede on her behalf."

"Ah, the manager's wife now picking up her own clients!" he mocked before hugging the woman he loved. "What happens if..." He left the question hanging.

What this close-knit community had come to accept as his oddity he knew would only take one incident to blow up all over again. He'd fought the ego and draw to the limelight once before, and thanks to the strength and wisdom of this very woman, standing looking at him with love and sympathy in her eyes, he had found his own strength. He didn't know if he could again.

"Then we'll deal with that. But I think she really is caught up in this and seems a good egg." She shrugged.

He loved and trusted this woman more than any other person on the planet. "I'm here."

Maggie went to bring Jeanette to 'the spot', Ian's spot.

"What is it you are looking for, Mr. Sperling?" She remembered his little game as she asked, watching him watching everything happening in and around the stage and throughout the infield and park.

"I guess anything that could possibly go wrong, Ms. Serling. Any detail that I, or God forbid, either Ben or Dugan or one of the crew might have missed. To make certain all the security is in place, to watch the crowd to see if any up front are inebriated already or if, if, if. A thousand possibilities." He gestured to the mass of humanity.

"And if something should arise, Mr. Sperling?" she raised her right eyebrow in question looking at the tired, past middle-aged man standing before her.

"Then I want to get in front of it immediately, Ms. Serling. Or I should say, I want them," and he pointed to the smiling, large men in front of the stage, "I want them to get in front of it." He smirked. "I also want to see how the crowd reacts to the way we have the show set up. Too much of this act, not enough of that, too many folky, singer-songwriter types without enough rock and roll. It's a long show, I don't want people getting bored. Bored people are trouble on several levels, and trouble is what we avoid." His eyes never stopped moving, taking in every little thing he could.

Jeanette was impressed by his complete commitment. They had been on this particular road for a month and he still watched each piece of the puzzle. He had to be as tired or more so than anyone here but he would not leave to others what he thought he had to do.

"Come, Ms. Serling, let's wade into the sea before the waves begin to crash," he held out his arm for her to take before they moved down the stairs to backstage and from there out front. "Let's see what things look like and sound like in the cheap seats." He moved her against the current of humanity away from the outfield and towards the actual seats of the ballpark. Bill Deasy, someone Ian knew from the eighties, had put together a trio to open the concert. This would provide Ian with the opportunity to listen, check lighting from far afield, and gage qualities it seemed only he could discern.

They made their way up into the upper decks where a small quantity of humanity had taken up residence. A large percent of people wanted to be right in front of the stage, heads stuck deep in bass bins and losing hearing by the song. But many liked to be up here in the stratosphere of the venue where the security would leave them to smoke a few bowls, take up as much room as they needed, watch the big screens, and enjoy the vibe.

As they climbed into the second deck, she noticed some of the early arrivals were beginning to sway to the music coming from the P.A. before any band could take the stage. They seemed pretty high from what she remembered back in the old neighborhood in Philly. To each their own. One stoner, accompanied by a couple young, well for this crowd, ladies, early forties she guessed, was weaving his way up the steep stairs with a tray of beers and some nachos. Ian and she were cutting across the aisle of seats several rows below to get by them. Ten feet separated the two groups when the stoner missed a step and was about to fall backward down the steep incline.

Later she would be quite certain that what she saw could not have happened. As they walked—Ian with his head turned away from the group in front, talking to her—she was certain the stoner was about to fall to his death down the concrete stairs right in front of her. The stoner teetered on the missed step, fell backward but before he could actually fall Ian's arm snaked out, wrapped him around the collar and pulled him back to safety. Ian never turned around and seemed to not have noticed himself save the man's life. Imagination, what a wild thing, for certainly she had not just witnessed what she thought.

Ian continued on the line he was walking, as if nothing had happened, though the expression on the faces of the women behind the stoned man told her she might not have such a vivid imagination after all. They found seats so Ian could sit for a few moments and listen to the recorded music from on high. Satisfied with what he heard they got up and moved to the interior of the ballpark.

Once back inside the bowels of the great structure Jeanette could convince herself that what she thought she saw was actually an illusion, a trick of the light, between the western sun's sharp rays and the passing dark clouds, shadows, and mind games. There was no way this slight, aging man could've pulled that man from tumbling down the concrete stairs. They both would've gone down. She was tired, that's all. She wasn't used to traveling like this and hadn't slept well on the bus.

Steadied and reassured she followed Ian through the throng of fans heading their way out into the, now, live music. Bill Deasy was playing and the melody pulled the people to listen in the open air. There were still folks lined up to get sandwiches and drinks, good vibes filled the air.

The crackle of electricity caught her attention. Ian was telling her about food and drink sales and how he wanted to check the merchandise tables to see if people were buying and then they'd get back on the field. When a soft pop and fizzle drew her attention to where a young hot dog vender set his box on an exposed cable. Apparently, the box blocked his view of the shorting cable. As he set the metal box on the electric cable a current of electricity shot through him. Before she could scream or shout or call attention to anyone who could help, Ian, who had not been paying any attention at all to the situation tripped over the cable, unplugging it from the wall and severing the connection.

The kid sat on the hard concrete, breathing hard but ostensibly physically fine. As he regained his equilibrium he grabbed the box, slung the strap over his shoulder and marched on. She stood stock still staring at Ian as if he had just performed a miracle that no one took note of. This was impossible. The man had accidentally saved a life and no one but she noticed. Not Ian, not even the kid he'd saved, both continued through life as if nothing had taken place. Ian continued walking and talking about t-shirts and koozies.

She shook her head and scrambled to catch up. She needed to lay down and close her eyes. It was impossible, or at the very least improbable, that this man had in a matter of moments saved two lives and no one cared, as if it were a given. Something that happened every day.

She checked her head for fever. Nope. She focused her eyes on people and inanimate objects near and far to test her eyes. Nothing wrong there. Maybe she should call her shrink and see what she had to say about these hallucinations. God, she couldn't be having another breakdown, could she?

All things passed Ian's inspection and they were back on the field. The three women, Michelle, Gillian, and Ann, were singing angelic harmonies, weaving in and out of each other's voices, taking the assembled mass of humanity down an old country road to a time of sitting on the porch and sharing an afternoon. These were old songs from Appalachia which some in the crowd knew and added their own voices. Traditional songs were meant for just such an occasion.

Ian listened with a fine-tuned and practiced ear, not to the music, he told her or the song but to the sound. He would move from spot to spot throughout the ballpark listening in each to assure himself of the quality of sound. He wanted it crisp and at a volume that was loud yet pleasing to the ear. She was duly impressed, again, by his attention to detail.

It was then she noted the speakers placed around the infield. She had attended concerts and knew from experience they usually had all the speakers up front, on or around the stage, but here they had placed mid-sized speakers throughout the park.

She caught Ian's attention and brought it around to these. "Why, Mr. Sperling?" she asked pointing at the mounted speakers.

"It gives a better quality of sound, Ms. Serling. One of the guys decided he wanted to try this out tonight. So, rather than push the fronts to the edge of distortion we can run at a more comfortable level and still reach the whole audience." He grinned at the result.

"Aren't you afraid...?" she began.

"What, that they will get stolen or fall or something, Ms. Serling?" he finished. She nodded. "Nope, they're up there pretty solid and we have enough security no one will fuck with them."

Her eyes followed his finger up the seemingly fragile stand to the three-foot square black boxes and wasn't positive she agreed. Then, as if to prove her point, the speaker perched there vibrated with a heavy bass line from the band and trembling its way to where it teetered on the edge of the small platform. Right above a family of three sitting having lunch while listening to the music, unaware that they were about to be crushed.

Ian seemed to notice the family at the same moment, though Jeanette was quite certain he hadn't noticed the speaker. Casually, as if in slow motion, he walked toward the small child with a t-shirt he'd picked up at the merch table. The kid saw the shirt and bolted toward Ian. The parents jumped up, too late to grab the urchin, and had to bolt after him. The speaker landed with a thud where they had been sitting.

Ian gasped, a look of horror stretched across his face, as he took in the family holding their child, the speaker and the look on Jeanette's face. "Oh, fuck." Was all he had.

Ian took a long, slow deep breath while he composed his features. When he felt confident, he affected a look of surprise, not quite shock. He didn't want to overplay his hand. "Wow, that was a close one, wasn't it? Weird how that speaker fell like that. The guys promised they would secure them so that couldn't happen. Guess I have some questions to ask," he gestured they should head back toward the backstage area.

"I believe we all have some questions, Mr. Sperling," though she would have to sort out some facts from suppositions. What had she actually seen and what had she only thought she'd seen? There was definitely something weird going on here, of that she couldn't argue with the man.

"Ian," he gave her a conspiratorial cockeyed grin.

"Ahem," she made her way backstage.

As soon as Ian got backstage and divested himself from Jeanette, he made a beeline for Maggie. She was his only hope. In a few short and breathless sentences, he told her what had happened and Jeanette's reaction.

"Did anything else happen while you two were walking around?" If she had been any other woman and this was any other circumstance, he would know she was asking if he put the moves on the younger woman. But he was almost sixty, Jeanette was in her early thirties, and he loved his wife. He knew she was asking if he had done anything else to save or help other people. Damn, he was so wrapped up in showing the woman around and explaining how things work on a show like this, so wrapped in his own thoughts and his love of the job, he really didn't know. He couldn't remember.

"I don't think so, but I can't be sure. And the way she looked at me, like she'd seen an apparition or witnessed a miracle. Shit, I don't know, but she seems to have taken to you since she arrived. You need to find out and stop her from printing any kind of hero crap. God, I don't think I, or this tour, could survive another bout of hero worship." He paced while he talked. She kissed the top of his bowed head and took the mission.

Maggie found Jeanette sitting in a folding chair just off the back of the stage, eyes closed, listening to the beauty of Jesse Collins. The man had a voice and guitar style that can only bring smiles.

"Interesting afternoon with Ian?" she posited.

Jeanette did not open her eyes but nodded her head. Silence.

Maggie grabbed another of the chairs and sat across from Jeanette to wait.

Clouds skidded across the darkening sky. Jesse completed his set as Cinda came on, soon to be joined by David Grisman. If you had to pass some time, there was no better way.

"I know you'll think I'm imagining things or losing my New York mind but I could swear that man," and she indicated with a nod to where she thought Ian was probably standing, "saved the lives of three people today, and not one other person noticed." Her face screwed up in total disbelief as she opened her eyes and gazed directly into Maggie's eyes. "And the thing was, each time it was quite by accident. I'm not even certain he knew he was doing it. Shit, I'm not sure of anything I saw today except the family and the speaker." Her eyes pleaded with Maggie for explanation or, at the very least, confirmation. She needed to know she wasn't losing her damn mind.

"Yeah, he told me," there it was. Four words to save the sanity of the nice journalist. "It's really not a secret, I guess, but we'd hoped it would all go away." And so, the history had to be told. Honesty is its own reward, secrets only nurture suspicion. The story of the rock club, which Jeanette immediately called up on her phone so could read the account herself. Muttering 'oh shits' and 'what the?' to herself.

"Let me get this straight, you are telling me your husband saves lives by accident? It's not a conscious decision? More like an involuntary muscle convulsion?" Jeanette was doing everything she could to wrap her head around what Maggie was saying.

"We think of it more like a lazy eye or a third nipple. Something that, once you get used to it, you don't really notice anymore. Others do, but we don't so much. It can take on quite interesting characteristics," and she told the tale of Ian lifting Gabby and setting him back on the stage.

"Get the fuck out of here!" Jeanette gasped. That was one visual she didn't think she could ever set in stone.

"See, the thing is, we really would rather not stir any of this up again. It almost drove him out of the business before. He has no desire for the notoriety or acclaim. He does that for others, it does not fit him. He is NOT a famous person, he likes his spot in the wings listening, loving his artists, proud of what they accomplish. Watching them bask in the adoration of people who truly love, respect, and need, I guess, the music that his friends produce." She knew she shouldn't ask but that was why she had come, "We are kind of hoping that, as a friend of what this tour is about, and someone I think, I hope, I have made a connection with, you'll kind of forget this aspect, this quirk of my husband. I know I don't have the right; you can tell me to shut up any time now," Maggie shrugged her impotence.

"It's really not part of the story, though I think it should be. And I don't want to jinx anything here, so ok. But I just cannot believe this hasn't spread like wildfire and every single person here isn't talking about it. How have you kept it quiet?" Jeanette would have some answers for her silence.

"They all feel that Ian is like a good luck charm, a talisman for the tour, if anyone said anything they are afraid it would all come to an end, and they are having too much fun to let that happen. Musicians, roadies, crew, they are of a different cloth, a different world, different superstitions, magic, and pixies and wood nymphs, and belief in the melody. You don't fuck with the melody."

"Artists. Yeah, I guess I get that. I got friends," and she allowed the thought to ride.

Ian's grin was a permanent fixture on the side of the stage. He loved listening to the music, the harmonies, the glory that was the joy his friends created. The sound was unbalanced, vocals too hot here, bass too hot there but that was stage sound, not the fronts. He could tell by watching the euphoric expressions on the faces of humanity that the fans were getting their money's worth. They had discussed raising the ticket prices as the tour had grown in stature and more artists were asking about coming to play but had decided against such brazen unrestrained capitalism. That was not what this tour would be about.

Yes, they wanted to raise money for the Untouchable cause, to build schools, community centers, feed and clothe people, give hope but folks all over the country were contributing in their own way and that was how it should be. Organic, of the people, by the people, for the invisible. He still had trouble comprehending how many people were left out of so many societies, including his own.

Progress had been made, hadn't it? We had moved on from slavery, hadn't we? Yeah, he admitted to Jim Crow, redlining, separate but equal. Lies, all lies. They couldn't change the world but maybe they could change some minds. Some would never believe. They bought into the great American myth that it was up to the individual to make it and if they didn't it was their fault. Of course, when a society stands against the individual, improbable is the kindest way to think of the possibility of success. It happens but it was the exception not the rule.

These were the thoughts that ran through his brain as he watched the crowd ignite. The rumors were true. Jaxson was introducing a man whom none of the assembled, or certainly very few, had ever seen or heard live. Whatever they might've paid for a ticket, now, was the greatest bargain in the history of music. Josef, aka Steven Gatos, humbly walked to the center microphone. He gazed over the assembled thousands, smiled, turned his head to announce a key, the band nodded, they knew his music, some had played with him fifty years ago, and launched into his very first megahit. The crowd went crazy.

And the memories came back thick as molasses. Their first meeting, hearing of Steven's illness, his time off writing four of the most brilliant albums of all time within a year. The journey of the songwriter, his absence from music for two decades and his subsequent return. The ignorance and hate of people, the threats, and then, this. Ian hadn't realized the tears until they fell from his cheek. If there is a heaven, he stood in the center of it.

And then his eye caught a flash of color, a bobbing head, the gold chains. That sleazeball, where did that sonofabitch come from and where did he go? Ian ran to the backstage area where he could radio security to find that guy. "Just look for a gold chain, you can't miss it, it's got coke spoon hanging from it."

He didn't expect security to shut down the concert, just keep an eye out for the slimy bastard. He should be easy to spot with a hundred eyes keen on spotting him. Yes, there were thirty thousand people, but they were old hippies from the sixties now in their seventies and eighties reliving a time when they were in their twenties and dressed like it. Tie dyed over paunch, jeans that fit a decade or so back, breasts a little too low for that top, long unkempt hair, except those who'd bought into the American dream. Though they were inconspicuous in their conformity. The object of his attention looked like a bad extra from a horrible eighties' movie involving a huge pile of white powder, large breasted women in postage stamp bikinis, driving very fast cars and shooting each other while smirking for the cameras and each other. Right off the central casting lot for low budget films. He should stick out like an oil slick on a ducks back. And Ian wanted him washed from here.

But no reports came in. How could that be? There was no way he could've fled the ballpark without one security person noticing. But there it was, like Houdini he had escaped. This was very odd and Ian didn't care for oddities at a show. No drama, no surprises, no slimy personages skulking around. He was certain the rep had slipped the roach, just big enough to be found, but not big enough to draw Ian's attention, into Ian's pocket. The question remained, why? What did he hope to accomplish? Even if the border guys had busted him, Ian would've been back on the free side of living within a day. It was an annoyance, nothing more. Just being an asshole to be an asshole? Ian hated puzzles and this was a big one.

'Train of Freedom', this would be the final encore. Everyone that wasn't on the stage previously was now filing on to add their voices to this choir. Each fan took up the lyric and sang from their hearts, each singer, each band member filled with the joy of remembering and the vibe of tonight. Yeah, flush that turd and sing from the soul. Ian grinned ear to ear, Maggie joined him at the side of the stage and they held hands like teenagers, laughing and hugging. It was good.

When they had decided to put this tour together Ian and Jaxson decided they would prefer to stay in second tier cities not the major metropolitan areas. More laid back, relaxed, smaller, easier to control and less drama. Pittsburgh was a city of medium size but over average population and was at the edge of where they wanted to be. They wanted a fun tour, not a major one. Though the best laid plans and such, as the tour grew so had the need for larger venues. Neither man liked it, but they were on a mission and the mission would not be denied.

Their next stop was to be Trenton, New Jersey at the ballpark of the Trenton Thunder, capacity six-thousand four hundred seats and maybe another eight to ten thousand scattered around the field. Normally a wonderful number, but ticket sales had reflected rumors and they needed to make some decisions. The closest larger venues were in Philadelphia and none were available for the dates they needed. Renovations and ballgames took them out of contention. Ian would have to meet with Dugan and Ben as they drove east. The last thing they wanted to do was surrender to unrestrained capitalism, they would not whore this tour. But first, he had to meet with the crew and get whatever was bugging them settled.

They would have a meeting once load out was completed. He knew everybody just wanted to get on the road and rest but this was more important.

Cards On The Table

Meeting behind the stage area where the trucks and buses were parked, the crew gathered around, leaning against the buses, the trucks, each other. Sitting wherever there was a flat enough surface or on guitar cases or the earth. They were a tired group. They wearily watched as Ian took center concrete.

"I know you'd all rather be riding right now. You're tired, worn out, shit I'm tired and worn out, but something has surfaced that I think we need to address. Apparently, there is some dissension in the ranks and some grumbling about, well, I'm not sure what, but would love to find out." He assiduously avoided eye contact with Ben, Dugan, Gabby and, especially, Regis. He wanted no one to know where the info came from. There would be no blame, only discussion. "If there is something I need to know please tell me. Is it the schedule? Do you need more time off? I know we've been busting ass but that's a tour. If someone needs a day or two or three, let me know. We'll do what we can. You know New York is coming up and we'll be there a week, maybe we can rotate some schedules." He tried to read faces for some reaction but nothing.

"Are you getting pressure from home about bills? Being gone? Do you need some extra cash for stuff out here? What?" he knew he was half pleading but he needed to know.

Silence. Furtive glances told him they wanted to say something but they were waiting for someone to bust the dam and no one wanted to handle the sledgehammer.

"See, it's like this," said one of the lighting techs, it's always the lighting techs, "We've been hearing about people setting up GoFundme pages and other stuff like that. Also, that people have been donating like crazy to our own 501c3 to the tune of millions, if not tens of millions." He glanced around him for solidarity. Nods encouraged him to continue. "we're just wondering with all that cash coming in why we can't go back to the original deal, bonuses, pay, better digs, you know, like we agreed to when you asked us to join."

Now all eyes were on Ian. He mentally kicked himself in the ass for being so stupid as to not anticipate this. He should have seen this coming from a month away, but he hadn't. Now he had to save this tour.

"Because it's ours." He said simply. "Because we all decided to take this on. I'm happy people are getting on board, setting up their own fundraisers, contributing to ours, but they were not part of the agreement we all voted on. We decided to do something no one had ever done. To dedicate ourselves to a greater good, a cause bigger than the tour, bigger than ourselves. To do for folks who had been shit on for generations. To let them know, they might have been forgotten for centuries but they were not forgotten now. That you cared enough to put yourselves on the line for them and give up some of what we had for them. Because we cared. Because helping them was more important than enriching ourselves.

"Look, I know it's been a strain, we all feel it, but if you need some help let me know. Shit, if I have to, I'll give you money out of my own pocket," he couldn't be absolutely certain, but he was pretty sure that the muffled groan he heard came suspiciously from the direction where Maggie sat, but he meant it. This tour had come to mean the culmination of what the music was supposed to be about and he wasn't going to lose it. "How do you think the fans would feel if they found out we set our wants above the needs of those we said we would serve. That everybody was getting paid full boat, bonuses, staying in better hotels, comfy, not having to sacrifice at all. With all our righteous indignation, our railing against the inhumanity of it all while we drink champagne and eat steak. I'm not saying you guys aren't worth it, you're the best damn crew, band, people I've ever shared the road with in over fifty years of this. But we can't have it both ways," he glanced over to where Jeanette was taking all this in and taking notes. Ah well, honesty, openness, truth, they would be their stock in trade or they'd have nothing.

"Here's the deal, if anyone wants off the Untouchables Train, you are free to go. I would ask that you stick with us until NY, but if you don't feel like this is for you anymore, I'll pay you off in full. No hard feelings, no recriminations, just best wishes for a great life and, honestly, a thank you for all you have done. But the tour will continue, if I have to roadie, run sound and lights myself. I've done them all and I might not be the best, but I can still carry an amp." He saw each of the road crew peek over at Gabby and remember. This was greeted with chuckles and a few catcalls of wanting to see him wrestle the bass bins, but it was done with their usual good humor. The vibe was coming back. The tension was clearing. "If you want, just let me know your decisions once we get close to the city. I'd appreciate it. But right now, I have another meeting while we drive about the logistics for the next week. I think we have some cyphering to do. And I'm already worn out, beat up, and old. If you'll excuse me, let's get wheels up and rolling, the road is calling."

In any other conveyance it should have taken only six or so hours but when you have a caravan of four buses and now, two semis, yes, they'd had to add more equipment as the tour had grown, it adds to the time required to go from A to Z.

Ian, Ben, Dugan, Maggie, and Jaxson had the lead bus and the most to do. They had five days and three shows before they would arrive in NYC. It wasn't the time or the shows, but the number of people who wanted to crowd into the limited venues they had reserved. There really was not much they could do. They had what they had and that was all they had.

The most pressing concern was tonight. Trenton had been chosen because it was a minor league stadium, the Thunder were on the road, it was a beautiful spot, set next to a lovely river and was close to Allentown and the outskirts of Philly. Too close, it now turned out. The tickets had been gobbled up by those caught up in the music and the mission of the Untouchables. They hadn't counted on that. This was supposed to be a relaxed, fun tour with friends and family. It had turned into a three-ring circus that had annexed and built extensions all around. It had morphed into the octopus of touring companies.

They needed more room but there was no more room at the inn. "Maybe we could get them to add another date. The baseball team is still on the road for another two days," suggested Dugan.

"The guy told me when we booked, they needed two days to prepare for the team's return. They'd never go for adding something on to the tail," Ian shook his head. "we'll just have to swallow the pill. We got what we got."

The meeting unsatisfactorily concluded about three in the morning. If Ian thought he was tired when they left, he had no idea how tired he would be when the phone rang at five-thirty in the a.m. 'Who the fuck?' was all he got out before answering. Nobody calls at five-thirty in the a.m. if it ain't an emergency.

"Is this Ian Sperling," asked the gruff, obviously, just waking voice on the other end.

"Yes," he sighed into the cell.

"George White," now why did that name sound familiar, "I'm the president of the Trenton Thunder Ballpark." Ask and ye shall...

"Yes sir, how can I help you?" Now Ian was awake.

"We have a minor problem. It would seem your little show has created quite a stir and now we have far too many people and far too few tickets available." He sounded apologetic, that might be good.

"What can I do? We've become the hip thing for the moment." He tried to keep it light.

"We've been banging around ideas all night and the only thing we can come up with is, if you guys can maybe stick around town for a second show tomorrow night as well," Talk about ask and ye shall...Ian sat up in his bunk, banged his head on the upper, before stuttering out he thought they could work something out. Sometimes the gods of the music biz just decide it was your turn to get a little candy, so enjoy it, because they could just as quickly decide you'd had enough.

Breakfast was very early, again, that morning. The hotel, obviously, had not been prepared to be invaded at the break of dawn, or close enough to it, so Ian had found a place they could squeeze into to feed the hungry, sleep addled masses. All were elated at the addition as 1) it would pad the pay envelope just a tad, and 2) they could sleep in the same beds for another night.

Life on the road can be exhausting with the constant movement, the different bed every night, the shows, too many back-to-back nights, setting up, tearing down. But nights off cost money and trouble could ensue with tired crews, a few dollars in the pocket, and an open bar. Still, this was the best of both worlds with an extra night of work in the same locale. It would help refresh the crew before the quick push into New York.

The crew was in lighter spirits as they checked into their rooms. The hotel staff was beaming and efficient as they filled their rooms. It was a good morning, indeed. They also knew that after resting up here for two days they were heading towards the ocean. There is something about the sound of waves and the movement of water that soothes the human soul. Yeah, Ian was tired but the mood lifted his energy as he set about getting life in order before heading to the ballpark.

When the tour took on new meaning and the fans embraced it whole heartedly, they knew they had to up their game some, but he still didn't want to lose the feel. They had discussed where to move concerts, when possible. What kind of surroundings, what they wanted to do to keep that vibe. Ian had posited the concept of ballparks. He loved the game, the waste of a day in the sunshine while a baseball game lazily went on. Talking baseball with whomever was by him—all baseball fans will talk baseball with anyone at a ballpark or bar—while munching on nachos and drinking a diet. It was the best way to spend a spring or summer afternoon. He thought it would lend to the original concept of the tour. He had been right.

As he rode down to the venue with Dugan, Ben, Gabby, and a few others—Jaxson decided resting was the better part of valor for him. Ian really hadn't taken note of how exhausted his main act was, he needed to keep an eye on the man—his thoughts settled on the night before and the meeting. He wondered if he had overplayed his hand with the crew. He had given them options. Obviously, no one had come up to him since, he hadn't expected anyone would jump right away, but he wanted peace. He would rely on Dugan, Ben, and others to report back. Though if he was honest with himself, he knew the crew would keep their decisions close to the vest as they knew that this group would report back to Ian. Which is exactly what he wanted! Openness, honesty, if there is a problem get it out in the open.

And why had they all-of-a-sudden decided this? Or so it seemed. They had known for a month that people were contributing to their cause in several ways. They had agreed it was a good thing because it meant that not just the crew was invested in this tilting at windmills, but the fans had gathered their horses as well. Maybe, just maybe, with all these people working, trying, adding their weight they could topple one or two of these giants. So, why the slight mutiny?

It didn't make any sense as it ran faster and faster around Ian's tired mind. Put it on hold, he kept telling himself, all things will be revealed in time. Until then, they had a show to put on.

He was happy to see the stage in place as they came through the tunnel and out to the field. A group of business casual gentlemen and one woman were clustered in front of the stage and looked up as the rag-tag group came onto the field. This must be the brain trust of the Trenton Thunder, thought the boss of the hippie army.

"Mr. Sperling," the leader came up and shook Ian's hand, "George White, president of the Trenton Thunder Ballpark." His smile was genuine, his handshake firm, but there was something. Oh yeah, businessman, there were dollar signs behind the smile. Oh well, can't blame a man for making a living.

"Nice to meet you. And nice ballpark," Ian said taking in the beauty of the minor league park sitting on the river.

"Fan?"

"Love the game," and his smile gave truth to the statement.

Now the grin on the president's face was one of pride and his own love of the game. "Me too, since I was a kid, though never good enough to play very far up the ladder. This was as close as I could get," he beamed at his 'home'.

Ian liked this guy. How could you not like a guy who loved his job this much? Especially a baseball job!

"Sold out? Eh," ventured the rocker.

"Shit, we could've sold this thing out four times over, I appreciate you guys sticking around for another show tomorrow, that really helped placate the masses. Though not everyone is happy," he shrugged.

"When is everyone happy? Let's make sure the electricians and roadies are going to be happy." Ian pulled out his list, his contract, his rider, he was now at work.

Ben and Dugan checked out the stage, the backstage, the 'dressing rooms', i.e. RVs, access for the trucks, the ramps, the crew. The cool thing to them about working these venues was the lack of attitude. These places knew they were minor league and the fact some rock and rollers thought this would be a great place to set up a concert thrilled them. They weren't put out like a major city facility would be, they would bend over backwards to make certain everything was just the way the crew wanted it, and they'd throw in a nice lunch.

Yeah, a nice lunch. Ben thought about that gig in—where was it?—Nebraska, he thought, some little dot on the map and they had to put on this show. It was a country band of regional fame—what the hell was their name? He couldn't remember—the town was so excited these guys were coming to play their fairgrounds that the ladies of the town had put together a homemade lunch and dinner for the entire band and crew. Worked all day to cook for these road weary guys. Best meal ever in thirty years of music. He smiled. Yeah, we like small towns.

The trucks showed up around ten, the roadies at ten-thirty with the lighting guys right on their tails. The trucks were unloaded, the sound set up, the stage set up, the lighting set up and lunch was brought out by the caterers. The show would be on time, gates at three-thirty.

Ian couldn't get rid of the itch at the back of his head. Everything was too good, running too smoothly, something was going to blow up and it wasn't going to blow up at a convenient moment. Someone was about to shit in his pudding and he hated the anticipation.

Ian's paucity of prescience proceeded his gloom, in other words, he was wrong. The show found new heights to climb and climb it did. It was as if each performer found new energy, new joy in old songs and stories. They fed off the excitement, the celebration of giving of the fans. People came not just for the music, the show, but for the hope, the promise that this tour brought.

Many came to learn. They had no idea that so many humans were treated as nonentities in this world. Hell, many had no idea of the conditions in their own country. Of the abject poverty; of the reservations. How could people be hungry, starving in the land of plenty? How could we allow human beings to live in hopelessness, devoid of a future, abandoned and forgotten in the 'richest country in the world'?

So, they brought their optimism, their empathy to the show. They filled the small ballpark with cautious enthusiasm. Many of them had lived through the sixties and thought they could, or did, change the world only to have it change them or their friends. This might be the do over.

The best part of the tour for Ian, and Jaxson, was the number of Gen Z's or millennials, or alphas or whatever they decided to call the younger generation. At the dawn of the tour most of the crowd had been what you would expect, folks in their sixties, seventies and wheelchairs though as word spread of the purpose the ages had begun to drop. The 'kids' were digging the mellow, as they used to say, and the depth of the songs. And they had the vitality to drive the show and those around them.

Here were twenty somethings dancing with seventy somethings who encouraged the eighty somethings to do something. They shared picnic baskets, bottles, and pipes. Old folks boogied while trying to get gummies out of partials and bridges. And, of course there had to be those who showed too much of what life had done to their bodies with pride and defiance. All any of the performers could do was laugh and encourage. It was the free for all of free for all's.

Gabby blushed when the granny flashed him but Maggie thought it also helped him relax a dab during his 'speech'. He would never be comfortable in front of people, especially that many people, but he was trying. The word had spread of the beating heart so every time he took the stage every person present took to pounding their chest to let him know they had his heart in their hands. He was safe. It was an amazing thing. Tomorrow would be a wonder.

Ian's prescience decided to kick in on overdrive.

He didn't sleep well, which usually happened when he was exhausted. Dreams came, nightmares followed, he woke up covered in a sheen of sweat, remorse, though over what he had no idea as the night's exertions had fled, and he was more drained than when he had laid down. The dark circles under Maggie's eyes attested to his thrashing in the night. This was not how he wanted to start the day. Nor was the drizzle he saw out the window.

What the? The weather people on every local had promised warm and sunny, perfect. Not hot, not muggy, NOT drizzly; warm and sunny. He wanted someone's head on a platter. The knocking on the door beat in rhythm to the headache forming in his left temple. Shit!

"Boss, we got a problem," said Ben as Ian opened the door. Couldn't he wait one second until the door was fully open?

"What?" the exasperation in his voice made Ben wince but he was not one to hold back facts, and there were some nasty facts.

"Somebody fucked with the sound," the nutshell.

"What?" not Ian's finest linguistic hour.

"Some wires cut, some missing, a few speakers busted and cabinets tossed into what is now mud," Ben was as pissed as Ian was becoming.

"Where was security?" they had several trustworthy guys keeping an eye on things overnight, why hadn't they stopped this vandalism.

"Apparently, they were drawn off by some disturbance outside the gate," Ben winced as he knew what was coming.

"What the fuck were they doing outside the gate?" the fact that his voice remained calm, almost devoid of any emotion was worse than if he had screamed. "The city takes care of what happens outside the gate, not our guys." Right before the words declaring their termination, he stopped. Something was definitely wrong with this scenario and he wanted answers more than heads.

The rain fell harder with Ian's darkening mood. If it didn't stop soon, and he meant very soon, the infield would be a mud pit. They might have to cancel the show. He hated refunds.

"Let's get down there. Give me five to change and grab some hot tea." He closed the door softly rather than slam it like he wanted to. Control.

The rain had stopped by the time they pulled up behind the ballpark, count your blessings, he counseled himself. As they came through the back gate he saw the four security guys, heads down, waiting for the ax to fall. They knew they'd fucked up and they knew they'd be done.

"Anybody want to take the lead on explaining exactly what happened here?" Ian did his best not to sound livid. Partial success is still success.

Andrew, he was pretty sure that was Andrew though he looked worse for the fuck up and loss of sleep, stepped forward. Ah, a man to take responsibility, already he rose in Ian's opinion. "Well," he sighed and then stood up straight to face the hangman, "you know we got a bunch of folks camping outside the gates, right?" Ian nodded. "Well, about three in the morning we heard this screaming and shouting. We had to investigate, as it sounded like someone was being beaten or killed or who knew what. We get out there and there is this scrum going on. Wasn't really a fight more like people just fucking with each other. We kept an eye on it for a few but didn't leave the park, honest." He looked to see if Ian believed. Satisfied, he continued, "It looked stupid enough we called in to the local cops and went back to our job. And this is what we found. Couldn't have been gone more than ten minutes, fifteen outside, and someone did this."

Ian could see some of the bass bins laying facedown on the wet ground, speaker wires had been cut, and someone had taken a large screwdriver to some of the other fronts. It was a mess but at least the stage equipment seemed to have been left alone.

"Make a list of what is damaged, what is broke, what needs replaced before the show, then find it. If you have to run into Philly or fly to Mozambique, I don't care but get this shit up and running before the gates open." He shook his head, who would do this? And why?

Andrew hesitated for a breath before realizing he still had a job and if he wanted to keep it, he had best get moving.

As Ian took in the damage, he realized it was not designed to ruin the show but to be a pain in the ass. Someone wanted him or those in charge to know they were out here and willing to fuck with him for the sake of fucking with him, and no other reason; it was personal. Kind of like the roach in his pocket. Hmmm.

Obviously his first thought was of Vilhelm Wilhelm the slimy record rep. But, again, why? What would he gain by screwing around with the show? If he was repping one of the acts, wouldn't he want the show to be a huge success? None of this made any sense. This was a minor disruption, though a disruption none the less.

Then again, it could just be vandals in a small town who couldn't get tickets and decided they wanted to screw up everybody else's day. Karma would get them in the end. And maybe Karma was biting Ian's ass right now. They'd had a really good run considering the pressure of the schedule. Twenty-four shows in twenty-eight days on the road with only a few small breakdowns, that was a damn good run, especially considering all the readjustments, added nights, tired crew. It could be as simple as shit happens on the road and you deal with it.

Ben called over to the hotel to get some of the crew over here to begin cleaning up the mess and seeing if they could save anything. This would be an expense they'd have to eat. Ian didn't think the president of this collegiate minor league outfit would foot the bill. He didn't hit Ian as the head of an organization flush with cash. He'd let Ben and Dugan deal with the damage. He wanted the lighting guys to come check their shit before they went shopping as well.

Now to check the condition of the infield. If it was soupy or sloppy, they might have to restrict where folks could set up their lawn chairs and blankets. He didn't want to screw up the field for the returning ball club or word would spread and the other parks along the routing might get cold feet.

Surprisingly for a small market minor league park this joint had excellent drainage, not usually the case. Someone cared about the game in this town. That was one big monkey off his back. Now to get back to the hotel, make some calls to shore up the rest of the week and confirm all reservations for NYC. He would assume, and he knew what that meant, that since no one had approached him about leaving everyone was still on board.

He'd gotten a deal a few blocks from the Beacon which he found a wee bit annoying considering the Beacon had their own hotel right there, though price was price and they had to save a few bucks where they could. The Lucerne offered them two floors for the best price and they were close.

His phone buzzed as he worked details and arrival times, he didn't want to hit the city anywhere near rush hour. Even though they'd be heading in while the rest of the world was heading out it was still a massive headache. Shit who was he kidding? New York city was a nightmare twenty-four hours a day. It's the price you pay for success.

The number on the phone was restricted, could be a bullshit spam call or could be someone important, roll the dice. He answered.

"Ian Sperling."

"Hello, mate," came the familiar voice on the other end. It was the only voice in his fifty years in the business that still gave him chills. Ah boyhood idol worship cannot be destroyed.

"Hey, Pete," did his voice tremble. Come on, he had spent time with this man in London only a little while ago. Suck it up, Sperling, the guy likes you. He goes out of his way to try and make you feel like you're just like him. Yeah, if you were a megastar; and the best megastar in history at that.

"I have some business in New York next week and I see your little caravan is winding its way through the big city. Would you like a few guests to show up? Would that help the cause?" Pete's grin could be felt through the phone thirty-five hundred miles away. He thought this would be a fun idea and that meant he wanted in. If Ian had learned nothing else about Sir Peadar, it was that he loved to have fun especially when it came to music.

"Are you shitting me?" he might have phrased that better had his brain not froze at that particular moment.

The laugh on the other end of the line told Ian all he needed to know but Pete added, "See you next week."

OK, the day was improving with each passing minute but he was still pissed about the P. A. and wanted a few ounces of flesh. And to know what happened to Herr Wilhelm. He didn't like that sleaze wandering around unescorted.

Now, to be perfectly honest Pete hadn't said he wanted to be a guest performer, just a guest. In any case having Sir Peadar in the room was enough to cause a huge stir of publicity and buzz. The man could stop traffic just by walking by. The thing was, Ian told himself, he really didn't want this to get bigger than it already had become. They were being forced into either larger venues or more shows as it was, did he really want to turn this into a massive, superstar, studded, mini-Woodstock everywhere they went?

Time would tell, but he wouldn't. This would be his secret. If others were keeping things close to their chests, he would keep this close to his. The tightrope would be whether he told Maggie. He had no secrets from his wife, he never had, not even minor ones. Oh, a surprise birthday party or when he'd bought her a horse without her knowledge. But she knew the horse and it was for sale and he was flush at the time. That had been a long time ago. She still had the horse though he was far from flush these days.

His mood lightened with Pete's laugh, it lightened a bit more when Dugan explained they always had plenty of patch cords, spare speaker wire, and connectors. You had to when you were on the road. Shit broke without vandals, setting up and tearing down every night is hard on equipment. They had spare amps, speakers, cabinets, everything they would need to repair and keep traveling. Gypsies' plan for failure so failure doesn't stop the circus.

If You Want The Best Hire The Best

The reason you find the best crew you can find for a tour like this was this show and this crew. No one would ever have known of the destruction that morning. Sound, lights, perfect. The performances would be stunning. The mood of the entire cast and crew was ebullient. Everyone knew they were headed for a residency at the storied confines of the Beacon for a week but first they were to head up the coast. There would be water, lots of water, an ocean. Maybe not as big as the one they left more than a month ago, still, it would do.

There is something about the sound of waves, the constant perfect rhythm that touches the human soul. From the waves we came to them we return. One of the road crew had somehow snuck his surfboard in the equipment truck. Yeah, waves. If Ian hadn't been in such a good mood, he would have read him the riot act. Pete was going to be in NY!

And then it hit him. If the word got out—when the word got out, he corrected himself—that McCarthy was at the show and probably would be each night, people would lose their minds. For an eighty-year-old guy, a former member of Mersea Beats was still a former member of Mersea Beats to millions, they would want to come if just for a sighting. Tickets would be at a huge premium. The scalpers would be out full force; Ian hated scalpers, they were the bane of the industry and had been since the dawn of time. He wished he could come up with a plan to deny them screwing the fans, though no one in the history of entertainment had ever devised such. But he might have an idea and he needed to call the Beacon anyway, to tell them they'd probably need the next week as well. He hoped they would agree.

He needed to talk to Jaxson to get his thoughts. Shit, he might have to spill the Mersea Beats beans to him and that meant he would definitely have to tell Maggie. The last thing he needed on this tour was a pissed off wife or even a dissatisfied one. Ah, well.

He found Jaxson still in bed. That was highly unusual. Not that he was an early bird catches the bus kind of guy but noon o'clock was still a bit on the late side. They really didn't need to do another sound check; they'd played the night before. Even so, Jaxson was a guy who loved to play. Even if no sound check was needed, he would want to go up and play for an hour or so.

Ian knocked, knocked again, waited, then knocked harder until the voice said, "hang on."

Jaxson looked disheveled, tired, he had dark pools under his eyes, as if they harbored deep forest ponds that held unfathomable terrors. The tour was wearing on him. It was wearing on everybody, but they'd stayed in one spot for two whole days, he should've caught up on rest.

"You OK?" Jaxson wasn't a client of Ian's, they were friends, had been for a half century. This little romp around the country was supposed to be a relaxing thing, not the Bataan Death March. Ian hated to cancel shows but sometimes the better part of not killing your friends was to take a night off.

"Yeah, just got this head/sinus thing that hit me like a sledgehammer when I got back here. I'm coughing, my lungs are wheezing, my sinuses won't stop draining and I think I might have died around five this morning." He coughed a laugh.

"I'm calling someone, there has to be a doctor near that works in the twenty-first century," He had his phone in his hand punching in the number for George White. Certain biases can be overcome, certain ones cannot. The bias of people who live in large metropolitan areas toward those in the smaller towns, cities and villages of America will never be overcome. Big city folk honestly believe those in the rural areas live a nineteen-century life of horse drawn carriages, gas lights and doctors with leeches.

"Get dressed," Ian was frantically writing something on a scrap piece of paper. "George's personal physician can see us right away."

"I'm alright, just a head cold," Jaxson struggled to slip into his jeans. He was weak, sick, and wanted to stay home from school.

"Bullshit! Don't make me get my wife! Or you're off the show."

"You wouldn't," but Jaxson could read people and that was one face he didn't want to see how the story ended. He knew. Maggie would drag him by the ear if she had to. He finished getting dressed.

The doctor turned out to have graduated from a real medical school and everything. He had certificates on the wall that appeared genuine and seemed to have some grasp of what he was doing. He gave Jaxson a prescription for an expectorant, Benadryl for his nose and a codeine cough suppressant to help him sleep. He also cautioned there was nothing on this planet that would rid him of the mange before to-night's show. Depression set in.

People knew Jaxson Grahm was the indubitable headliner for the concert. Yes, Josef had closed the last few, special guest and all, but people expected Jaxson Grahm and Jaxson Grahm songs. He couldn't sing with this much phlegm and coughing every second, they'd have to work something out. Though what that might be, Ian had no idea.

He dropped Jaxson back at the hotel with explicit instructions to go back to bed, they'd come get him when they needed to prop him up on stage. He then headed over to the ballpark. Shit! Shit! Shit! Though if this was going to happen, better it happen out here than when they were sitting in NY. The doctor had told them he had high hopes, though he would not be one hundred percent, Jaxson could sing and play at the NY dates, just not all night. They'd work with it.

His head and thoughts flying about ten thousand feet off the ground, Ian was lost in working out this puzzle. This was why he was considered one of the best in the biz, he never gave up, he constantly was seeking a way to make lemonade. He had called the Beacon and they were happier than hell to have this troop in for an extra week. Phones and computers were smoking hot with ticket requests, an extra week would alleviate some but not all of that traffic.

The sound of the grand piano on stage caught his ear, the tune familiar, though he couldn't place it at first. Dimwit! It was his favorite Jaxson song, *'Indigo Sky'*. Damn, who was singing it? The sweetness of the vocal almost made him want to cry, it was Jaxson's song but it was different. He ran to the stage to see who was creating this magnificence out of a magnificent song. Gillian Morse sat all alone on the stage lost in the lyric, accompanying herself on the guitar while one of the road crew—was that Herbie the drum tech? –played the piano. Beautifully, Ian thought, with such a deft touch. If fingers could feel empathy for a song, his did. It was, and here he had to check himself a tad, better than Jaxson. Maybe because they didn't play it all the time, maybe because he wanted it to be. Maybe he had a plan to sooth the savage beast. Maybe because it was Gillian.

A meeting was called of the musicians and singers. If Jaxson couldn't sing, this glorious choir could. Yes, they only had a few hours to work out eight or ten tunes, but these people were the best of the best. Josef even said he would like to sing one, if everyone was amenable. They laughed that he would even think anyone would question his offer. And maybe Jaxson could come out and play piano on *'The Cannons of Peace'* so Gabby could continue his stage time. Which he would've gladly given up in a heartbeat but they were hell bent on him continuing. Maggie gave him a hug and a smile of apology for his discomfort.

The performers came to the show with renewed vigor. If Ian thought they were pumped by the closeness of NYC and the ocean, he had no idea how much more they could give when they were chosen to represent Jaxson. There are performers who are respected by their peers, there are those who are well-liked because they help others, there are those who are revered because of their success over a long period of time, very few are actually beloved. Jaxson, if he hadn't been beloved when they began this romp, he certainly was now. He hadn't done all that much, just gave up a lot of money while giving his time, his energy to help those less fortunate. Not that he hadn't all his life, but now, now he had raised the bar of philanthropy to stratospheric levels. Not for personal promotion or acclaim but because someone had to and he chose to.

Tonight, would be dedicated to the one who dedicated his life to others. He would be celebrated by his contemporaries. They would invite the fans to sing along. Johnny the assistant lighting tech had put together lyric sheets to be projected on the big screens. Yes, this would add to the legend, to the myth of this tour. Lee had been right when he said no one had ever attempted to do what they were doing. They were giving of themselves, of their time, their financial security, their hearts and souls, because other human beings needed them to, and it was working. Or from everything Ian could see, feel from the fans, the throngs of people who not only came for the music but to share knowledge, information, how to help their fellow man, it seemed to be working. Not with drugs and good vibes—though there's always drugs—and empty platitudes but with concrete solutions. And if those solutions didn't exist, they'd invent them. The sixties based on pragmatism, not fantasy and dreams. It was good. Mickey and Judy would approve.

And then the phone rang. The number was unfamiliar and Ian almost didn't answer before he remembered an earlier phone call and who that had turned out to be. He took the call behind the stage where he had a chance to hear whoever was rude enough to call during a show.

Before he could get the hello out the screaming voice made him pull the phone from his ear. While he might not know who this was, he knew someone was pissed. Now to figure out who and why. Maggie walked by on her way to his spot on the stage and silently gave him a questioning glance, then heard the voice, how could she not, and kept walking.

"Hey, hey...heyheyhey!!!!" Screamed Ian right back. "You need to calm down, speak to me like an adult and tell me who you are and what has got you so pissed off!" This was not what Ian needed right now. This guy was snuffing his high. Whatever that meant, he didn't want to be yelled at by anybody.

"Al Campanis with the Jersey Blue Claws, Lakewood. I got almost twenty thousand tickets sold for your show tomorrow night, what the fuck do you mean you are canceling?" This guy was irate and from what he just said had every right to be. The thing was nobody had cancelled nothing.

"What the hell are you talking about?" now there were two irate men on the line.

"I got a call from your office that said you guys were canceling tomorrow night because Grahm is sick and can't sing," Ian's anger seemed to be calming his own. "I mean you got a whole revue going there, I know Jaxson is the big draw and all but, shit, you can't cancel the whole thing now!" Desperation replaced pissed, begging gave anger a vacation.

"Number one, yes I have an office but if I'm not there then there is nobody calling anybody from my office. Number two, nobody cancelled nothing," repeated for emphasis, "We are performing tonight and will be to you by morning to set up for tomorrow night, count on it. Have somebody at the facility early to let us get in and unload, on that you have my promise." Al had calmed, the storm had passed, now was a time for reassurance and civility.

"Well, then, who the hell called me to cancel?" anger crept back in. Though not for Ian but for some unknown person, who if they were smart would make themselves scarce on this continent.

"Do you have caller I.D. on your phone?" Ian asked, hoping.

The call ended with everybody loving everybody, except one unknown person whom Ian had every intention of finding and burying. Yes, his mystical power to accidently save lives was apparently in his DNA though maybe it could also be reversed when necessary. No, he couldn't actually kill anyone, but he sure felt like it right now.

He slowly walked to the back stairs of the stage. He stopped, closed his eyes, and deliberately took ten long, deep, calming breaths. The last thing he wanted to do was bring bad Karma, a pissed vibe onto this stage. Then he heard Gillian's voice, plaintive, perfect, from the mountains of North Carolina, which apparently was in her DNA. *'Indigo Sky'*, everything else from today took wing and flew to the other side of significant. He came up behind Maggie and wrapped her in his arms, this was her favorite as well, and they moved in rhythm to Gillian's strumming, Yogi's fills and Herbie's piano.

Next thing they knew they were dancing on a stage in front of eighteen thousand people yet were all alone. Not even the cheering could break through their love. People in the crowd joined in, musicians and singers took up the dance, if there was a heaven, tonight it was in Trenton.

Talk about an up and down day. Ian was exhausted, emotionally, physically, bankrupt of feeling, for the moment. The bunk on the bus screamed his name. Someone was fucking with him hard, and he didn't need that right now, he was too tired. If he wasn't a month into a tour with all its ups and downs, challenges and finding solutions day after day, he would've gone after whoever or whatever with gusto and glee. Right now, he just wanted to sleep.

He lay down on his bunk on the bus, just for a second, just to rest his eyes while the crew finished tear down and load up. Surely, he could close his eyes for a half hour.

It was the rough road that woke him. He came awake with a start and for a few minutes had no idea where he was before the familiarity of the bus reassured him. How long had he slept and why hadn't anyone woken him so he could do his final check before they left.

"We let you sleep," Maggie said before he could ask or accuse, "you were exhausted and I," she emphasized the syllable, "told them to let you sleep. They are the best in the business, you've told me that many times, they can handle load out without you one time. If they missed anything, it is not needed." Her smile challenged him.

Ian might not be the brightest tool in the drawer but he was smart enough not to cross his wife. He had slept, he needed sleep, she was smarter than him and knew all that. He had to assume she had given specific orders to Ben and Dugan to let sleeping Ian lie. He would have to accept the truth and be grateful. And when he thought about it, he was, and he knew he had to learn to accept the sensation of gratitude.

"Are you sure we have everything and everybody?" Ian will be Ian.

"No, I didn't do a head count but I think we have most of them and whatever equipment wasn't damaged. The rest we left where it fell in battle," nothing says love like a smartass wife.

"Jaxson!" Ian started as if he just remembered his friend and his condition, which he had, "How's Jaxson feeling."

"Like shit, but alive," came from the back of the bus.

"We really wouldn't have left him at the hotel, I did check all the rooms. Everyone is checked out and on the road with us," her tone told him maybe he should trust the one responsible person in their relationship. "Even sick I felt he should probably still come along. I can't believe you think I am not capable of organizing and herding the cats." He wanted to say something but the better angel on his shoulder kicked him in the groin to shut his mouth.

"Did you get any sleep?" Instead, he decided to communicate with the spirit in the back of the bus.

"That's all I've done. I'm singing tonight whether anybody likes it or not!" Ian knew who the anybody was and regretted waking up.

"I'm going back to sleep, wake me when we get near Lakewood. I'm hungry now, I'll be near death by the time we get there," Ian rolled over and closed his eyes.

Maggie kissed the top of his head, "Yes, my love. Sweet dreams."

New Day, New Challenges, New Miracles

It was only a few hours across the state therefore all had decided since they were still up and pumped from the show, they would make the drive and sleep in the hotel parking lot until check in. It was not unusual for a troupe such as this to travel the gypsy way. You weren't going to sleep for a couple hours anyway and as long as you're up, and someone is capable of driving, drive now, sleep when you get in. Most hotels, rather than become upset about touring shows camping in their lot, loved it because the buses usually had the names of the bands on their sides. Advertising of the grooviest sort.

It was around eight a.m. when Ian came awake again, this time easing into the day. He got up, set about making himself a cup of English breakfast tea to help him open his eyes and kick start the day. He needed a shower. Now the choice, bus or wait to check in. Each bus was equipped with a nice shower, though water pressure left something to be desired. It was far better than nothing and he didn't feel like waiting a couple hours to be allowed into a room. The parking lot looked almost full, which meant the hotel would be almost full, which meant they wouldn't be getting into a room until afternoon. Bus it was.

Coming out of the small shower/bathroom he almost whacked Jax with the door. He didn't look like Death, but he had met him and shook his hand recently.

"How's the head and chest," Ian asked his friend.

Bleary eyes met his, a shake of the head and a sniffle, but Ian thought it was an improvement over the last time the two had talked the day before. "I'll live, but I'll wish I hadn't." He made a valiant attempt at a smile.

"Think you want to try and sing or play today?" it had to be asked.

"I won't have a clue until much later on. As it stands now, no, but I'm hoping with love and care, possibly," He took Ian's cup from his hand and drank the hot tea. "Nice."

"Keep it," Ian certainly didn't want it back. "You want I should make you another?"

"You trying to save my life?" Now Jaxson did chuckle followed by a deep chest cough. "Shit. How soon before we can get into our rooms?" He wanted a real bed and a two-hour hot shower, that was only going to come true in a hotel.

"Doesn't look good until much later but I'm just on my way over there now to check. I'll let you know as soon as I find out. Maybe they have a room for you, at least." Ian didn't have much hope; however, some is not none.

He went to the lobby to ask at the front desk for a favor he knew he did not deserve or expect, but all they could do was say no, right? Through the swish of the automatic doors, he caught the sight of a middle to late middle-aged man sitting and reading a small newspaper over in the comfy upholstered chair in the corner. He sipped his coffee while he read.

Businessman, thought Ian, waiting on a meeting. He grinned inwardly satisfied that was not the life he lived. The guy looked business casual with a dark polo, grey slacks and matching sport coat. He had the aura of a man in charge and used to getting his way. He glanced up at the freshly washed, just off the bus newcomer, wasn't impressed, dismissed him and went back to his paper.

Ian waited patiently as people dropped off keys getting an early start on getting wherever their final destination was. He guessed Lakewood, New Jersey in spring was not the hot spot; it was a way station. Summer yes, eighty-five and sunny pulled people to the beaches, sixties and beaches didn't really go together.

He smiled his most gracious and ingenuous smile, baiting the hook and hoping to catch a little kindness. "Hello, I know it's early and it looks like you were pretty full last night," he began.

"Completely sold out," she said in response without humor or a grain of human kindness. She knew what he wanted, they all wanted it, but there was just no room at the inn.

"I get it, but I have a sick entertainer on the bus and... if you could just call me as soon as a room is ready, I would love you forever." Charm thy name is Sperling.

"Give me the number, but it is going to be a while, the house keeping crew isn't due for another half hour," now she attempted sympathy but it was not an emotion that came readily to her features.

Ian handed over his card with his cell number on it and turned to head back to the bus to report in. After that he wanted to head over to the venue. He required motion, though he doubted anyone was there this early. As he turned, he almost ran into the businessman standing, literally, right behind him. Was this how the day was going to go?

"Mr. Sperling, I presume?" The twinkle of humor in his eyes told Ian he would like this fellow.

"Yes," he drew it out as a question of several syllables.

"Al Campanis," he stuck out his hand in greeting, "owner and president of the Jersey Shore Blue Claws. Nice to meet you. I thought after our slight misunderstanding I'd get here early so we could meet and share a cup to get to know each other. Got time?"

"I'm afraid I do. We can't check in until later. Who'd a thunk this place would be sold out this early in the season. Something going on last night?" Ian was always curious what the competition might be.

"Probably people coming down for the concert and then planning on heading home after," Al shrugged his lack of knowledge. "Or it could've been the flower and home show down 't convention center."

"Not sure driving's advisable. Most of the folks at the shows so far probably shouldn't have been and weren't driving after," Ian shrugged his knowledge of the situation. "Let's hope flowers and homes and a new group tonight."

"A little of the whacky tabacky, eh?" He tried to sound hip though extremely out of the era; he shouldn't have. Yet, there was something so genuine about the guy Ian found him endearing because of his normalcy.

"And some wine," Ian laughed, "Al Campanis? Wasn't there a..."

"Yeah, played at Montreal with Jackie, no relation," Ian couldn't tell if he regretted or was pleased, "He is Alexander and I am Alphonso. Different sides of the same tracks. He was good at ball and spotting those who were better. I am good at keeping this little dream alive. The one thing we have in common is a love of the game. We might be a small ballclub on the outskirts of civilization but we're here and have been for twenty years." Now there was great pride pushing the words. Here was a man who had accomplished something he had, obviously, been told was impossible, stupid, a waste of money or all three. Ian loved this guy!

"If you don't mind, can we talk while we go over to the ballpark. I'd like to get a lay of the land. I like to catch any problems early before they have a chance to gum up the show," Ian waved his hand towards the automatic door, "We just have to stop by the buses so I can let someone know where I am."

Attention to detail and curtesy, yeah, Al liked this rock guy as well.

They hopped into Al's car, a late model Cadillac if Ian knew his cars, which he didn't. but he knew what a Cadillac emblem looked like. He also knew what a car with a few miles on it looked like, and he could see both were true here. This guy might have money or might not but if he did, he was not one of the showy types. They swung around the back of the hotel where the buses were parked and Ian quietly slipped into the bus he shared with Jaxson to let him know it would be an hour or two before they could get him into a room, but they were doing their utmost to hurry. Maggie was out like a burned-out bulb, so he made a note, left it on her pillow and went back to join Al.

"All good?" the president and owner asked.

"As good as it can be for now. Jaxson is fighting some kind of bug and could use some time in a real bed that is stable. These buses are fantastic and comfortable, but comfortable for healthy and comfy for sick are two different animals." He winced his concern for the health of a friend.

"I guess being on the road is not the healthiest lifestyle to begin with. Pretty happy in my own little fiefdom." Al laughed and waved his hand at the lovely small town, near to yet not on the ocean, that was home.

As they drove Ian noticed maybe he was exhibiting more than Ian had originally thought he meant to. There was Campanis Motors, and Campanis Hardware, Campanis Fine Foods, which had more the look of a beach town diner. This guy had done alright for himself, but he didn't brag, just showed his pride. Pride in what he had, visibly, accomplished and how his town flourished.

"You know this town it's a wonderful place with really nice people. It's also a good thing you chose to come here rather than Ocean City. That town was founded by Methodists and maintains the morals and temperance of the founders." He grinned over at Ian.

"Wait, what?" Ian turned to look directly at the man. Ian could not imagine a beach town that didn't sell alcohol. Wasn't that part and parcel of going to the beach? He'd been sober for four decades, but he still understood the pull of a cold beer on a hot day at the beach. He had considered the beach front city but they didn't have a facility large enough; and he liked ball parks.

"Can't sell booze in town. Not in a restaurant, not on the beach, no booze," Al glanced over to gauge Ian's reaction. You could almost hear him counting to ten before a huge grin spread across his face. "Don't worry, this is Lakewood, New Jersey, we have beer at the ballpark. We enjoy a cocktail." He laughed. "Ocean City has the name; we got the goods." And again, he laughed for the joy of it.

The ballpark was perfect. Ian knew these small parks would be the exact middle ground between what he had originally wanted and what the tour had grown into. There was a coziness to these parks that was lost in the bigger pro parks, even the new ones that are designed to look like the old ones. Most are too big, too spread out, too impersonal. If you were sitting in the first row behind the dugout you felt like you were watching from a half block away. The best was old Tiger stadium where you could be up in the nose bleeds and feel like you were on top of the action.

As they pulled up to the ballpark, this diamond surrounded by tall trees (Ian had no idea what kind but he liked them) he noted the bus parked off the side of parking lot. Must be the team bus, thought the road dog and then remembered, they're on the road. Al must let folks park on the lot when the team's out of town. Al unlocked to gate leading into the side of the brick building. All ballparks should be made of brick, thought Ian, besides the aesthetic value there was a sense of permanence to brick, a false sense history would show, but a sense none-the-less.

Where the Trenton park had been situated alongside a beautiful river this one had the feel of being out on the plains. The flat land leading to the ocean provided a lovely view of the of the town. Yeah, this would be just fine.

Al gave him the twenty-five-cent tour showing Ian all the improvements they'd made over the last two decades and some ideas for the future. He was a true forward thinker; no grass would grow under the feet of Al Campanis. They had extra stands for beer, wine, and food. They wanted to be prepared for the onslaught coming in just a few hours. The stage showed they had read the rider, though the electrical guys would determine that. Ian felt comfortable as he and Al headed out for the ride back to the hotel to check progress there.

His thought was to send the crews and equipment out here and they could set up early, since they couldn't get into the rooms. He could then send the crews back for quick naps and they'd be ready by the four o'clock gate.

As they walked back to the car, they were approached by a cadre of Hispanic looking gentlemen led by a heavy set, grinning, convivial appearing man.

"You guys work here?" he asked.

"Well, I own the place," said Al tentatively. "This fella is putting on a show, what can we do for you?"

"Not what you can do for us, but what we can do for you," he chuckled and put his hand out to Ian in greeting. Raul Ruiz. We heard that Jaxson has been sick and as we are touring through here, and with a day off, we thought we might offer our services. If needed," here he gestured to the several men standing behind and around him.

Raul Ruiz, thought Ian, fuck yeah.

"The Disidentes! Wow. I don't think we've ever met. You're serious, you guys would like to do a set today? On your night off?" The gesture of giving up a night off on tour to help out another act was not lost on Ian. These guys were the number one Southern Tex/Mex band in the world

"Shit everybody who's within a thousand miles wants on this show, didn't you know? What you cats are doing has never been done. An entire tour dedicated to one cause, one purpose, to not aggrandizing yourselves, but to lifting others. Shit yeah, we want in. Can you use us or is the kettle too full," he wasn't pleading but he was emphatic in asking.

"Yes. Yes, a thousand times yes. It would be fantastic; the people will lose their minds. And it would give Jaxson another easy night before we head to New York." The relief Ian felt was like a thousand-pound weight lifted from his tired body. This, with a day at the beach, could get Jaxson in top form before they hit the city. "Hell, we can give you backup, singers, band, extra drummers, whatever you might need. We have some of the best in the biz and everybody is singing and playing with everybody else. It's kind of a jamboree/revival meeting kind of thang." Ian couldn't contain his joy. Wait until Jaxson and everybody else found this out. Wow.

"One thing, con su permiso, we would all like to meet the Mayan," he kind of shrugged his apology for asking but the band behind him nodded their heads emphatically.

"Yeah, I think that can be arranged," Ian shook Raul's hand, "By the way, we are headed back to the hotel to get the crew and bands moving, have you guys eaten yet?"

Cadillac leading the way, bus following, they headed back to the hotel. Ian tried to call Jaxson and Maggie to give them a heads up but the calls wouldn't go through. His screen told him it was calling yet no connection could be achieved. Bad cell service, he'd run into it before.

When they pulled into the hotel parking lot the buses were a sea of activity. Everyone was either taking travel bags off or loading changes of clothes back on. Ian guessed the hotel staff had busted their asses to get rooms ready and the entire crew was trying to shower, change, and get to the venue. Excellent, they must have gotten his note and Ben and Dugan had the bull by the horns and were leading it down the road.

He saw Maggie standing outside their bus but she was not running, carrying, helping, or much of anything. Not like her. Hmmm, he hoped Jaxson was alright and was sleeping his fever off in a plush hotel bed.

He hopped out of the car and waved at her, though she did not wave back. She stood, arms crossed, frown firmly in place, and foot tapping. The cartoonish depiction of pissed off. What the hell had he done now?

"What's with the pissed off?" he tried to make it sound light and cute, he failed her test.

"Where the hell have you been?" This woman was in no mood for Ian cuteness.

"I left a note for you, I was at the venue with the owner," here he indicated the man who was slowly getting out of the Cadillac, "I left you a note and explained it all to Mr. Grahm." Did no one bother to listen to him at all?

"Well, Jaxson has a fever of a hundred and three, I'm not sure he knows who he is, let alone whatever you may have attempted to impart to him." The steam coming from her ears had deflated the pissed off just a smidge. He thought if he tried to touch her, he would be scalded. He loved his wife but when she was irate it was not irie, it was frightening.

"I left you a note, didn't want to wake you," he mentioned for the third time. His concern for her health and wellbeing should make some difference, shouldn't it?

His batting average right now didn't register. 0 fer the day. "I sent you four texts trying to find you that you ignored, Every. Single. One of them." He opened his phone. Nada. He showed her the phone.

Nada. His eyes plead for mercy but she was the hanging judge and it didn't look good for our hero.

"I think the cell service sucks or something. I tried to call and it wouldn't go through. Ask Al!" He pointed at the man now standing next to him though seeming ready to bolt at the slightest movement from the angry woman.

"He did try to call. I have no idea why it wouldn't go through, who's your provider?" He turned to Ian.

"AT&T. They've always been really good but there are dead spots, but all phone companies have those." He defended the mega corp. as if it were a long-time friend, which in a way it was. He'd had them for twenty-five years.

"Hmm, same as me and I've never had any problem around here. Maybe Google them and see if their having some kind of interference in the region," he shrugged impotence and lack of technological knowledge.

Ian Googled the company to sign in but when the info came up it was in German? Hungarian? Something? All he knew was he couldn't read it and therefore couldn't fix the problem. His phone now had a mind of its own and it wasn't talking to him, at least not in a language he could understand. "You got an Apple store in this one phone town?" Time to get the geeks involved.

"Actually, yes."

"Where's Jaxson?" he asked his now simmering wife.

"They got him into a room so he could take mega doses of his antibiotics and codeine cough syrup. He's out and won't return to the living for a few hours, best thing for him, though I don't think the fans are going to be pleased," now, the real Maggie came out. The one who was mom, health care worker, roadie, wife of the manager, the one who was the support for all his dreams. "You go get your phone worked out, I'll talk to Ben and Dugan and then I'm going to sit with the patient in case he needs anything." Yup, mom was in charge and if you were smart you got out of the way.

"Alright, you do that but I need my phone." Rock and roll is run through the cell towers. Texts, calls, emails, all done by phone. Shit, nobody talked to each other. Nobody knew anybody anymore, just phone to phone. Ian hated it.

The Plot Sickens

The young person behind the counter at the Apple-a-rama appeared to Ian to be around eleven years old, perfect! The last thing he needed was some middle-aged guy just hanging onto a paying gig to pad his social security until he could collect. Ian wanted a child who was born with a phone in hand and texting other new borns in the ward with its teeny fingers like lightning flashing from letter to emoji. This person, to be honest he couldn't tell if it was a boy or girl, but at that age who could, was sent from central casting just to soothe Ian's anxiety.

"May I help you?" it was question and greeting delivered with all the warmth of a dying fish on its last flop.

"This phone is fu....messed up. I am not getting texts, I can't make phone calls, and when I try to Google anything, the answers are garbled or in a language I don't speak," Ian didn't have time for this and wanted immediate gratification.

"Ah, a twelve," said the machine masquerading as a human child as it examined Ian's cell. "These were quite the thing in their day." It smiled.

"Apparently that day is way in the past, like last year or so, because it has ceased to operate properly," Ian was doing his best to maintain civility, but he hated automated phone service and this was it personified.

"Yes, it is quite the antique," came the mechanical reply with the requisite snarky grin.

Ok, now the kid was just fucking with him. Ian might not be the cookie with the most fig filling but he wasn't empty. "Can you fix it?" He hadn't walked in with a boat load of patience and it was rapidly leaking out the hole in his hull.

"I can try, though usually this is caused by malware installed when you downloaded an app or software or certain videos," again the knowing snarky little grin.

Ian would've liked to wipe that smirk off the machine's face but he needed his phone more than he needed this thing's respect or for it to stop insinuating what he was insinuating. He did not watch porn on his phone.

"I have not downloaded anything on this phone. I use it for work and there was already every app I could ever have wanted on it. I don't watch 'movies'," air quotes included for no extra charge, "or anything else on here. I just need the fucking thing to work." In his defense that fuck had been pushing on his tongue for the past fifteen minutes. The fact he had held it at bay was a miracle in and of itself.

"Have you saved all your photos and important contacts, files, whatever to the cloud?" Attitude is everything and this automated child was programmed with an abundance.

"I believe so," Ian tried to remember the last time he had uploaded his stuff to the apple in the sky.

"Then what we are going to do is reset the whole thing. Now it might keep what you have or we might lose it all, which is why I asked. If I have your OK, I will make every attempt not to lose any information but it will depend on what kind of malware has been installed. Do I have your OK?" Thumbs at the ready he waited for Ian to nod, blink, or verbally commit.

"Yeah, It ain't worth shit right now." Ian closed his eyes.

The kid's fingers were a blur. Typing, dancing across the screen, touching this and scrolling that, Ian had never witnessed any human that could move with the speed and dexterity this child was accomplishing. Then it stopped, confusion rolled across its features.

"What is it?" Ian asked quietly not wishing to startle the child.

"Someone has installed a virus on this phone. A nasty one at that. It is a kind of spyware combined with a damaging virus you are dealing with, very clever," there was almost an impressed awe in his tone. "You sure you have everything backed up?"

"I'm guessing, I hope so. Why?" Ian didn't like where this was going.

"I'm going to give you a new iPhone 14 in exchange for this," he held up the cell like it was a diseased pig, "I want to study this." His eyes relayed that he was deep in thought elsewhere. He was impressed with what he had found but also slightly afraid. "First let's see if everything you need is available in the iCloud." He pulled a box out from under the counter, opened up a brand-new iPhone 14, plugged it in to power up while he prayed to the Apple gods this would work. Ian was quite certain if the kid could have sacrificed a digital goat, he would have. He waited to see if Ian's info was in the iCloud and if he could download all of it onto the new 14. The intensity of his excitement caused his slight frame to quiver. This kid was going to cum in anticipation of discovering a new virus. He really wanted to study this spy/malware, never having seen its like.

Luck and automatic save had made all possible. Ian walked out of the store with a new iPhone that worked just like the last one only better, with a better camera and free! He texted Maggie the good news and she texted right back. Happy! Then he called Dugan to see how all fared at the ballpark and he answered the phone. Triple happy! And from what he could remember, all his pictures and files were now on this phone. His 'originals' had been erased from the other, he watched while the kid did as asked.

As they rode back to the hotel to catch up to the rest of the entourage, Ian couldn't help wondering why. Why had his phone, which he'd had for two years and never had any problem with, all of a sudden decided to take a shit. He had to concentrate to try to remember if he had, indeed, downloaded any apps, software, contracts! Wait a minute, he had downloaded contracts for upcoming shows and he'd sent riders and contracts out, had someone inadvertently sent out some virus with their contracts? It didn't sound possible. He'd sent the contract to the person in charge, they signed it with DocuSign, a trusted app, and sent it back. There should be no chance of picking up some kind of virus.

Unless someone had intentionally installed the virus before returning the paperwork. Again, but why? Who would do such a thing?

And if someone had intentionally sent him this virus, Ian needed to know who, why and get a lawyer.

He hated lawyers. But they tended to be a necessary evil. Wasn't that L.A. lawyer still hanging around with Gabby? There was an interesting case. The guy shows up to lawyer them and ends up roadieing alongside Gabby, talk about a Mutt and Jeff combo platter. Gabby was about three times Raj's size, yet Raj did his best to keep up with the larger man. Raj, Ian was pretty sure that was the lawyer's name, was slight of build and had the appearance of a guy who had never done an honest day's work in his life, but he worked his ass off with this crew and had earned their respect. You never knew.

There was a niggling at the back of his head that would not let go. Why, indeed. Why had someone called Al to cancel the show. Why had someone put a shitty roach in his pocket. Why, why, why. None of this would ruin his life or cause the end of the tour, it was just a frustration, an inconvenience. But the more he thought about it the more there was a pattern forming. He didn't like not knowing. If someone was going to fuck with him, he wanted them out in the open. He couldn't strike back at shadows.

"You, OK?" jeez, so lost in his thoughts he'd forgotten Al was driving the car.

"Yeah, just thinking about how to put the show together tonight," Ian lied. No sense bringing Al into a fight he had nothing to do with.

"Gotta stir up the soup when the main ingredient ain't available," he nodded. "These guys, The Disidentes," he mispronounced the name, "they're pretty good, are they? Not really much of a music fan, don't get out of my lane very often." Al had never been adventurous in life. Not in travel, not in women, not in music.

"Are you going to be at the concert tonight?" Ian just assumed Al would be there, he owned the joint.

"Nah, probably just going to sit at home and watch some TV." He winced at the admission.

"No, you are not!" demanded the renter, "You are going to be my guest at the show. Backstage passes, meet the bands, listen from the stage, walk around with me, the whole rock and roll experience." Ian turned to catch Al's eye as they slowed for a red light. "Come on, Al, I'll have ear plugs for the louder ones, most of the others, they won't be needed. Damn! You never heard Gillian Morse, Cinda Wilson, Michelle Ranch, Jess Collins, Josef aka Steven Gatos, The Disidentes, Jaxson and I don't know who else is supposed to be showing up. I think James Nash is going to be meeting back up with us again. You'll love it. You gotta come, it's a payback for all your help today. Come on!"

"I'll see," but he didn't sound convinced.

Ian went to find his room in the hotel. He had to ask the front desk clerk what room he had been assigned and he required his own key in case Mrs. Sperling had decided to go to the ballpark without him. And he would check on Mr. Grahm and keep him up to date on all that had transpired since they had last spoken, which Jaxson apparently didn't remember, and tell him about The Disidentes and how the show had gone last eve. Maggie might have explained all already or she might have let him sleep, it was a coin toss.

Ian hoped he might get a chance to take a quick nap before heading to the park. He was frazzled, his nerve endings were buzzing like an exposed electric line and his head was circling the drain. And he wanted more than anything to know who was fucking with him!

He knocked quietly on Jaxson' door. If he was sleeping, he didn't want to wake him. He required sleep more than information.

"Come in." the voice sounded better, stronger, no raspyness.

"Door's locked," Ian called through the closed portal after giving the door lever a hard push down to no avail.

"Shit! Hang on." Slight frustration added an ounce of annoyance to the tone.

Ian heard him pull off the chain and turn the lock.

"Enter," Jaxson commanded from behind the open door.

He looked like the outer ring of hell which was an improvement over the inner circle. The circles under his eyes were nowhere as deep nor as bruised. The skin on his cheeks did not hang like jowls but had tightened up so he resembled his record covers. He was in a t-shirt, soaked through with sweat—that was good maybe he was sweating whatever this was out—and a cotton blend pair of shorts. He sat back down on the edge of the bed.

"Well, you don't look quite like death anymore," Ian sat on the chair in the corner, "more like death had tried and failed. Congratulations." He smiled.

Jaxson attempted a smile but found it took too much effort and let it die. "How's everything in the land of the living?"

"We're coming along. The ballpark is beautiful. The guy who owns it is great. The crew is on top of everything and my phone is working again," at this point Ian went into detail of the last forty-eight. The show last eve in Trenton, the tribute to his music, which made Jaxson wince as Ian knew it would, though he brightened considerably with the news of the Disidentes.

"Holy shit, this is going to great, but I'm back on the show tonight!" This was one evening he would not miss for health nor death. The Disidentes!

"OK," said his pretend manager, "three tunes and then into the wings with you."

"Shit. Deal." Mr. Grahm was willing to make any deal to get back on the stage.

Showtime and the infield and outfield were packed. People had brought folding chairs, sling chairs, and cushions, they were ready. As were the artists. This was the final tune-up before the Beacon in NY. These people were seasoned professionals. They had played major and minor festivals, venues, and recorded with some of the best in the world. Hell, they were some of the best in the world. Other artists considered it an honor to record with them, but NY was NY was NY. It was its own animal and each time anyone played the Big Apple it seemed to take a bite out of them.

Ian thought it was good for the soul and the ego to be reminded that no matter how good you thought you were, or how good you really were, it was nice to have a few jitters about the big time. He felt nerves for them, so he hoped they felt a little for themselves. They would be bringing their A++ game tonight.

Where in the hell were Maggie and that woman from the Times? They should be backstage keeping an eye on things just in case something happened to him. He had texted her but there had been no reply. What had he done now? She wasn't usually overly sensitive but it had been a long tour for her and when she was tired, she could be slightly irascible. He had best walk on eggshells until he discovered the lay of the land. He texted her again, as he had a couple hours ago.

Walking by the side of the backstage one of the security guys the ballpark had brought in came up to Ian. "There's a guy who wants to talk to somebody in charge," he sheepishly told Ian as if he realized that statement would not move mountains, let alone this man but he was not used to working with these rock and rollers. He sold hot dogs and soda during the games.

"And who might this person be?" Ian needed some Karma right now so he had to be nice.

"Don't know." The guy scratched his clean-shaven face and then itched the back of his short, cropped hair. This could be interesting, he didn't look like a big music fan, just like Al. "Looks like he came down from a mountain and sounds like the mountain is somewhere in Georgia." He shrugged. Great.

"Tell him I'll be out in just a minute I have to talk to Jaxson about something," he didn't but he wanted the security guy to tell this 'mountain man' he was busy without saying those words.

Ian took a quick turn around the backstage to assure himself everything was under control before making his way out to the front.

Yup, he looked like a mountain man, with a cowboy hat, long beard, long hair, and large belly. Standing next to him was a dark black woman who, next to anybody else, would have been intimidating but next to this mountain, she was almost petite. Well, this should be interesting.

"Can I help you?" Ian couldn't help thinking this man looked really familiar though he couldn't quite place him. He was good with faces, but names eluded him quite often.

"Y'all the main man here?" definitely from the south.

Ian nodded in the affirmative.

"Well, an old friend of mine from up the Northeast told me I should pop in here and ask for Jaxson but I thought that might be a bit presumptuous. I ain't never met the man and ain't one for throwing around other folk's names." If this guy was any humbler, he would have thrown in a few 'aw shucks' and 'Gee Whizzes'. There was more here, though, he might be humble but there was a strength, an assurance, a presence that could not be shut down by humility. Damn it! Ian knew who this guy was and he was somebody but the name...

"Christopher," the big man began, holding out his hand to shake Ian's.

"Shackleton," Ian almost shouted. "Damnit, I knew who you were I just couldn't come up with it." He was smacking the side of his head.

"Yeah, I could see the wheels turning, but they wasn't getting no traction. Thought I better throw down some sand before you burnt the transmission." He grinned.

Ian thought he might know what all that meant but he wasn't going to try to interpret at this moment.

"Don't tell me, you want to play?" Hope is a slippery thing, it's there, then it's gone.

"Well, not so much me as this young lady here." He pulled the black woman up next to him. "This here is Joya Olakundo. She's a damn good songwriter and singer and she knows what this tour is about and would love to throw her talent in the ring with y'all." She smiled, but an intimidated smile. "We was doing a show down the road a piece and I told her we ought to bust on up here while y'all was close and ask. All you can do is say no."

Ian might not know much but he knew if someone of Shackleton's talent was recommending another, he would be an idiot not to listen. "I can give her a couple songs right now, if you wouldn't mind backing her up."

It was then Jaxson strolled up, coughed, blew his nose and presented himself.

"Tom Rush said to say hey and thought you might like to hear this brilliant young lady." Mr. Shackleton was not one for wasting other folk's time.

"No time like the present," Jaxson glanced at Ian whom he was pretty sure had already vetted the woman. And he, unlike Mr. Sperling, knew immediately who the cowboy was. "You going to join her?"

Three songs completed she closed with a 'thank you' and tip of her battered baseball cap to thunderous applause and chants of 'more'. She hadn't bothered to introduce her accompanist, though she hadn't needed to. Christopher told her this was her moment not his, she shouldn't diminish her performance by introducing a distraction. He knew they would know who he was, so he tipped his hat in acknowledgement before pointing to the young woman center stage. She'd won them over on her first verse.

Jaxson and Ian met her as she was about to leave the stage. "Don't you hear them?" Jaxson asked through the grandest smile she had ever witnessed on another human being's face.

"You told me three," she replied glancing from him to Ian and back.

"Darling, you just shook the earth. Go play another." Jaxson gently turned her around to face the mass of humanity.

Joya noticed that every other performer and musician was gathered around the stage, each nodding their heads and grinning, pointing to the stage and the awaiting crowd. She didn't think she had ever been around such a group. These people were established, well-known artists. Grammy winners. Each one a headline act on their own and they were encouraging her. If there was ever an illustration of why she loved music this was it; no egos, no one wishing her ill, only love. It truly was about the music.

After her encore, she only did one, you don't overstay your welcome, she once again was met by Jaxson and Ian backstage. "What do your next couple weeks or so look like," Ian took the lead.

"Not much. Christopher is about done with his mini-tour and I really have nothing until about mid-June, from what I remember. I mean, I'd have to look to be sure," she scratched her head trying to remember.

"Would you like to join us in NY? We're doing a two-week residency at the Beacon and I'd love to have you on the show. We all do short sets but jump up and down as needed for each other." Jaxson jumped in.

"I should warn you, I'm kind of a lightning rod for hate groups." She stared at the floor knowing this could cost her something she would dearly love, but truth was truth and honesty had to come first. "I'm black, queer, and a woman." She stated the observable.

"Shit, I hadn't noticed," jibed Jaxson. "Look, we're all of us lightning rods for hate. We fight that with an extra dose of love. It's all we can do. None of us care who you are sleeping with, we care about who we are. Your personal life is your own until it interferes with the music, then it's ours. Fair enough?"

"Yes sir," she grinned.

"Ain't no sirs around here, just folks. I'm Jaxson, this is Ian, the rest will introduce themselves as you meet them." He shook her hand then wrapped her in a warm embrace. "Oh, I'm sorry, I shouldn't have done that!"

"Oh, I don't mind," she said thinking he was apologizing because she was queer.

"No, I've been sick. I don't want to pass that one to you." He held her at arm's length. "Ian will talk to Ben to get you laminates and all the info you need for the upcoming weeks. Buses leave in the morning."

Christopher had turned to walk away when she caught him and wrapped him in a huge Bear hug. "I don't know how to thank you."

"Just doing what's right for all involved." He tipped his hat, "you remember that as you climb that ladder yourself." A quick hug and he was gone.

"He could've stuck around and checked out the show," Ian said.

"Well, he's a big man, with that comes a big heart. I think he was doing what he thought was best for me, but it hurts him that we won't be touring together for a spell." She wiped a spec of dust from her own eye. She had an accent, it wasn't southern, more western Ian thought. It felt soft and warm on the ear.

"For a while," he emphasized, "we all run into each other over and over and it's like we saw each other yesterday. He's good man and it means a lot that he trusts us with you," he gave her shoulder a squeeze and she realized she'd fallen into a loving family. Three, no make that four songs, fifteen minutes and she belonged here. "I don't know if anyone explained to you the money for this tour, how everyone gets paid and such."

"Everybody in the music business knows what you are doing and why. I know what the pay is, as it ain't no secret, and I'm proud to be part of this," she shook his hand, hugged him and Jaxson before, "Thank you for letting me be a part of something that allows the invisible to be seen."

Ian kept searching visually for any sighting of his invisible wife. Time to ask around. He'd texted her something, again, but she had not replied. Someone had to have seen her and where in all hell did that Times woman go? What was her name? Jeanette. She'd been on the singers' bus last night coming over from Trenton, hadn't she? Shit! He had to get a grip on this crew and their whereabouts.

He turned to go grill some of the crew when he almost ran right into Al, again. This was getting to be a habit.

"Al, so glad you came. It's not so loud behind the stage, actually, it's really not that loud out front, once you get away from the fronts." Ian talked to Al while his eyes searched for his wife. They were never more than a phone call and five minutes away from each other. This was creating an anxiety he did not need right now.

"I thought since you're putting this show on in my joint, the least I could do was come down and take a listen. Sounds nice," he grinned clearly pleased with the sounds emanating from the stage.

As well he should, thought Ian, it was Gillian Morse backed by Michelle, Jesse and Bonnie. He'd thought Bonnie was only going to hang for a couple days but she was having too good of a time to leave. Her next tour didn't kick in until mid-summer and though she should be in rehearsals she had told him her band were guys she'd played on and off with for half a century. Practice, they didn't need any stinkin' practice!

He saw Joya sitting on a trap case just off the side smiling like she was in heaven. Cinda was clapping along with the old timey song they were harmonizing on when she noticed Joya singing the words to her own self. Cinda walked over, bent down, seemed to ask Joya a question and then grabbed her by the arm and dragged her to the stage. The crowd's cheers were deafening, although whether from seeing Cinda and Joya or at Joya's obvious discomfort at being hauled on stage to sing with this ensemble didn't matter. Ian couldn't help but laugh, yeah, she was part of the circus now.

Al was saying something, but Ian couldn't hear. He was half deaf and the sound level was drowning out whatever Al wanted to impart. He was smiling, grinning ear to ear. He finally figured out Ian couldn't hear him so he mimed, horribly, the quintet was perfection. Voices intertwining and supporting, caressing each note, each harmony until it was the sweetest sound any ear had the pleasure to be near.

"Let's go out front," Ian spoke loudly in Al's ear. "The mix is much better."

Al gave him a quizzical look. Ian grabbed his arm to tow him out to where the sound man was mixing for the ticket buying public rather than the monitor guy who was not. Monitor mixes are for stage, front mixes are for pleasure.

They quick walked about halfway back through the crowd and Ian handed Al a couple of small wax plugs. Again, Al was befuddled until Ian stuck them in his own ears. They softened the volume with losing very little of the EQ. Al grinned, much better, he mouthed.

Ian pulled out his phone and checked for texts or missed calls, nothing. Damn, where was she? He motioned to Al he needed to make a phone call and he was going into the interior where he could hear. Al nodded and pointed at the exact position he would be when Ian was done. The quintet launched into an original of Gillian's that was just made for these voices. Ian turned to hear just as Gabby ran on stage with a piece of paper for Joya. Lyrics. She didn't know this song, so the crew had hastily written out the chorus for her so she could sing. He loved his road family.

No answer. No answer. Shit, shit, shit! This day was roller coasting from eight miles high to Hiroshima every half hour and he wasn't sure his heart could take another minute. Bonnie was singing solo now with the band backing her. Prine's *'Hello in There'* and he was missing it. He was now almost running through the cavernous interior of the ballpark trying to get one glimpse of either Maggie or Jeanette.

The Disidentes, shit, he wanted to hear them, see them, not be searching for a lost wife. They did a tight set, from what he could ascertain deep in the heart of the Blue Claws, of about half dozen songs. They didn't stretch tunes out so it was a perfect half hour set leading into Jaxson's set.

Jaxson, talking, explaining his flu or whatever it was to the crowd and that he would only be up to singing a couple tunes but he would give them what he had. He launched into four of his best-known hits, then Gillian came out and sang *'Indigo Sky'*. Jaxson picked up the acoustic and began *'The Cannons of Peace'*. Gabby!

Ian knew Maggie would come out to lend her strength to him, yet Gabby stood all alone on the stage. Each member of the crowd now knowing what to do, they thumped their chests in solidarity.

Back to running through the ballpark. She wasn't on the field; she wasn't on the stage. Josef was singing several of his least known recordings yet the crowd sang along. This show was coming to an end and he couldn't find Maggie. He thought he might cry. His heart pounded in his chest. He felt like Brando in Streetcar and he wanted to go to his knees and scream her name.

The crowd erupted in the loudest ovation Ian thought he had ever heard. Something was happening on stage and he was weeping in the bowels of a minor league ballpark. He had to get out there. He stopped at the edge of the infield.

Sir Peadar McCarthy stood on stage waving at the crowd. They stood and were going wild. The band stood; the crew stood. People were actually crying with joy—the feeling, not the singer—though she was in the wings as well, a ringside seat. And there next to her was

Maggie and Jeanette. Maggie seemed distracted as Pete launched into one the Mersea Beats best known hits from 1964 and she searched for a face, a face that should have been standing where she was.

Ian ran, zigzagging through the crowd of fans clapping, and singing and not noticing the elderly man pivoting through them. He was on a mission. After he told her how much he loved her and his terror and 'don't you ever leave me hanging like that again' he would hug her and hold her like he would never let her go.

Her and her fucking surprises! She and Jeanette had evidently run into NY to pick up Pete and, shit, Richie was on drums! And then bring them out here, she would've thought she was pulling off the best surprise of all time.

He ran. His heart in his throat, trying not to step on anyone. There was a woman down on her knees, screaming something but no one could hear her through all the other screaming and cheering. Ian tried to avoid her, did so successfully, but not the man lying on the ground in front of her. He stomped hard on the prone figure, his first foot landing right in the center of the solar plexus. The man rolled in pain and Ian came down hard on his back. He spit out the piece of chicken he was choking on. The last glimpse Ian got was of the woman darting her eyes from where the guy was regaining his breath to where Ian was disappearing into the crowd. Just another day.

He ran up the back steps of the stage and grabbed his wife, his face morphing from joy to pissed, to relief, to love. They could talk about this later. Right now, they were back together. She threw a quizzical glance at Joya and he shook his head as if to say, 'I'll tell you about her later'. He enveloped her in his arms as Pete began to sing his finale.

Ian knew that ticket prices had jumped as news of Josef and guests sets and the quality of the show had spread. He also knew that whatever they had paid was a mere pittance to the show they had received. Jesus, what could New York have that this tour didn't already have. A sense of well-being, satisfaction and unabridged bliss washed over him.

Al was jumping up and down, well his legs were pumping but a man of that size was not about to leave the confines of gravity, like a teenage girl. You could not have sanded the smile from his face. This was a man who had accomplished much in his life. He worked his ass off for his success. What he hadn't done was to enjoy the finer things, music, art, live shows, and here he was bathed in the ecstasy that live music brings. Finally, being immersed in humanity all experiencing the same glorious event. To share something so perfect with people you had never met but now felt connected to on a visceral level, he looked about to come out of his skin. He hugged Ian, then Maggie, then Jaxson, then anyone who walked by. He gushed about the show asking everyone if they had seen, heard, witnessed the most excellent event of all time.

Ian knew it wasn't, but it was damn good. These were brilliant musicians, brilliant singers, and several icons of music and they had given their all. And they were his friends. He didn't know if he had ever felt a pride more acutely, more deeply. The pride one feels when someone you love succeeds, that was true pride.

And then it was gone. New York reared its ugly head. He had made a promise and he meant to keep it. If anyone wanted to leave, they could. And he would make good on that promise, no matter the pain. They might have to start from scratch, and if they did, they did. But the meeting would happen tonight in the lobby of the hotel, after they broke everything down, loaded the trucks, and prepared for the future.

He had asked everyone to meet him in the lobby after they had showered and changed for a late meal. Nothing was open but he had arranged for their caterer to bring fried chicken, pork chops and several vegetarian and vegan dishes so everyone could share what might be their last meal together. It would break his heart. These people had traveled the breadth of the country with him. They had given of themselves physically, financially, and spiritually, he could ask no more. He had promised he wouldn't fault them, there would be no repercussions, and there would be none. Just heartbreak, but que sera sera.

When everyone had assembled—and everyone was here as Al had set it up that Lakewood's finest would monitor the trucks full of equipment in the parking lot—Ian called them to attention. He saw a few fidgeting but forced himself to appear calm and relaxed. Maggie sat with Jeanette; they had become fast friends as he assumed they would. Jeanette had her recorder sitting in her lap. He thought about asking her to turn it off, as this was a private meet, but then thought better of it. There had been no lies, very few secrets, he wiped his brow thinking of his near seizure this afternoon, and he would not hide now.

"Thank you all for coming, though I know you're here for the grub," he smiled, they chuckled, "and I know this will break a few hearts but we will be staying at this fine hotel tonight instead of driving to New York." A few cheers and hands clapping, "Well, we couldn’t get into the rooms anyway." He grinned in faux apology. He looked around the room and his heart filled with love. These were truly his friends. Ben, Dugan, Gabby, Herbie, Regis, the whole damn bunch of them, no, they were family. And there, in the back of the room, standing and hanging with the crew, were Richie and Pete, Josef, Jesse, James, the 'girls' with the new young woman seated with them. Damn this was getting harder. Speak your piece his brain said.

"I cannot thank you enough, each of you has given so much of yourselves on this journey. And I know some of you have suffered some financial hardships because of what was decided. If you came to me, then you know we have helped in any way we could." Rapt silence.

"And I guess that brings me to the crux of this whole thing. As we have discussed, some of you wondered why you had to continue to take a pay cut when so many fans were contributing to, not only our fund, but funds of their own. Tens of thousands have contributed a lot of money, though the most important thing is the light we have shown on the existence and conditions of the Untouchables. You should know that since we began this mission we have raised on your backs and hard work just over ten million dollars. Half a million has gone to feed and clothe the children and families of Pine Ridge Reservation with a good portion going to design a community center/medical center. It won't solve everything but it's a start. It takes millions upon millions to accomplish what you set out to do. We have also channeled medical, food, and educational aid to the villages around where Gabby's family comes from in the western highlands of Guatemala. So far without the reigning junta being the wiser." The crew shook hands to congratulate each other on the good they had accomplished thus far.

"But that is only the beginning. We have at least three more months once we finish our residency in New York and I need to know who's on board and who needs to go home. I'm sorry to push, but if I have to refit this cruise, I need to know. I am aware that some of you might not want to speak up here, in public, so everyone will know, though if you choose not to continue everyone will know anyway. I said there would be no judgement or repercussions and I meant that." Deep, slow breath, "I just need to know," the grief that filled that final statement just about broke every heart within a mile of the hotel.

The silence was numbing. Each person looked to the other, wondering, if this human next to me who had shared so much would be there in the morning when they pulled out for NYC. Then, as if a signal had been given, they all stood and without a word began to file out. Every single one of them. Within a very few minutes all that were left standing in the lobby were Ian, Jaxson, Ben, Dugan, Joya, who wore the countenance of complete bafflement, Pete, Richie, who seemed to find the entire affair hysterical, Maggie and Jeanette. Shit, even Gabby was gone. What the absolute...?

Before Ian could say a word, they all returned, laughing, joking, as each shook Ian's hand. "You didn't really think anyone of us would desert the rest, did you?" Lee was enjoying this far more than Ian thought he should be. "Where's the grub? I heard you were buying dinner." And at that the caterer began to set out all the chaffing dishes, the aroma calling all to a late-night family dinner.

Time To Fold The Tents,

The Gypsy Circus Leaves in The Morning

While the crew ate they gossiped with the lighting techs, and the stagehands bullshitted with the band, the singers wanted to know everything about Joya. Where she was from—Arizona. How long she'd been singing –since she was ten. Church, she told them before they could ask and they nodded approvingly. How long had she been working professionally and writing—a long time. Well, when you took into account she was not thirty yet, a long time is perspective. She had put out her first EP when she was twenty-two and had released several albums since. She happily answered all their questions but there were questions in her eyes she wanted answered as well.

"I thought everyone was on board about this tour," she said to Gillian, who was the den mother as far as she could tell.

"We all are." She answered with certainty, then stopped. "Oh, the Ian thing. Well, someone was stirring up some of the crew and a couple band members. Telling them they should be making more. He could get them on another tour that would take better care of them. Why were they leaving money on the table for someone else when millions were being raised by others for the same cause? Some of the folks started to grumble."

"Really? They didn't realize why this is so important?" Joya was taken aback. She knew. She lived it.

"That's not exactly right," Ian and Maggie had been walking around talking to each performer, crew and band member and had stopped to listen in. ""They knew, they understood. But sometimes people get lost in their own problems and worries. Those that they live with day to day. Other folks, thousands of miles away, can have much larger worries, life and death, literally, issues, great difficulties but they are not knocking at your door. They are thousands of miles away."

"But these horrors are happening here, in this country as well. Certainly, they can see that. How could they let their own minor woes trump the lives, literally, of others?" Joya looked from face to face.

"Because they are human and human beings care about family, then community, then region, then country, then humanity, it's natural." Gillian answered as Jax sat down on the arm of an upholstered chair.

"But didn't it piss you off that they would allow their seemingly minor woes to cause strife in the grander picture? This tour?" She found it reprehensible.

"No, because we know they are good people. That left to their own thoughts and decision they would come to what we felt were the right conclusions. And they did. You cannot condemn someone for having questions, concerns, misunderstandings about other people, to worry about their own, but, given time, most people will see the light. The love." Ian contributed, "You can't force people to accept your concept of right and wrong, you can only explain and hope they see. I'm sure you've run into your own examples of that as a queer woman of color." He shrugged as Joya nodded emphatically.

"Yeah, you can't make people accept, you can only stand as an example of what you want people to see. We are all the same, we are all family," and she shrugged. No need for the soap box around this crew. She grinned inwardly. She was still astounded to have landed here, to have found this other family. Thank you, Christopher!

The food was outstanding, even the meat from what Ian heard. The boys from Mersea Beats mixed with the whole group, chatting, laughing, and just being themselves. They were thankful that Ian had made sure there was veggie fare, but of course he would. He was one of them.

Ian wanted to tell everyone to get a goodnight's rest but he did not have the heart and, what the hell, they had the day off tomorrow with a short bus ride. He made certain Pete and Richie had their own rooms, the best in the house, they had king size beds. They both laughed and reminisced about when they first hit the road fifty some years before. They would share a room with the four of them on two beds. They might be used to better digs now, but they would suffer through one night with the peasants.

Ian wanted to go over some concerns with Jaxson but the look on his friend's face said he'd had enough for this night and he was going to sleep. Maybe even sleep in past sunup. Ian grabbed Maggie and they turned to make their way to their palatial digs themselves; they also had a king. Nobody had more or less than anybody on this tour and he was so grateful that superstars, true superstars, like Josef, Jaxson and the Mersea Beats showed they were not above the rest, even if they might be.

Ben and Dugan were isolated in a corner of the lobby discussing things only road managers understand, Ian knew every detail for the coming residency at The Beacon would be handled. Gabby had found his own corner and was engaged in deep, and if Ian was any judge, Spanish conversation with Raul and several of the Disidentes. Raul grinned the biggest grin when he caught Ian's eye and a silent thank you from his lips. 'Oh no, thank you,' Ian mouthed back. 'New York any time you want it over the next two weeks.'

The day had been long, stress filled, fantastic, fulfilling, horrifying, and he'd made some new friends. It had been perfect. Jeanette caught the two at the elevator.

"Got a minute?" she asked knowing she shouldn't.

"For you? Yes," Ian waved his arm into the opening elevator.

They traded small talk until arriving at their shared floor. "Want to come down to the room?" Ian didn't know what she wanted but guessed she didn't want to talk in the hallway.

"If you wouldn't mind," Jeanette was being quite secretive which only piqued Ian's interest.

As the door closed, she turned to face Ian and Maggie, there was a certain nervousness about her Ian had not seen before.

"Just the three of us?" Ian was slightly taken aback. He would've thought that Jaxson, at least, would have joined them.

"Yeah, I talked to Jaxson for a minute when we got back with Mr. McCarthey, he said just to talk to you," she fidgeted with her purse, as if it was a security blanket. "First off I want to thank you for giving me unfettered access to the crew, the musicians, everybody; most would never do that."

"I told you if we were going to allow you in, we would be open," Ian pointed out, then sat down on the couch.

"Yes, you did, and you were as good as your word. Thank you, again. I must apologize for causing you so much aggravation today. It was my decision not to tell you where we were off to. I'm afraid I suffer from loving to surprise people with great things, and this seemed a great thing. I begged Maggie not to answer your calls out of fear she would give the surprise away. My fault," she bowed her head in supplication.

"She could've answered my texts," he shot, still put out he could not reach his wife for most of the day. He thought he was losing his mind. They were close and always talked, answered, or called right back, it was their way.

"Again, my fault not hers." If she wasn't shamed and repentant, she was an excellent actress. "Now, on to why I asked to speak to you. As you know I have spoken with just about everyone connected with the Untouchable Tour. As I expected there were some that had a few grievances, about pay, workload, lack of sleep, the usual bitches in any organization." She held up a hand to halt his defense. She wanted to say what she had to say without interruption.

"Like I said it wasn't earth shattering or mind blowing, everybody likes to bitch about their workplace. Everybody. But when I asked about the why, the mission, as you call it, each person got quiet. Then they talked about late night rides on bouncing swaying buses with all night conversations about the caste systems throughout the world and especially here at home, with Raj and Gabby, their two experts. Most were shocked and angered by what they found out. Others Googled the information to be certain they weren't being led astray by discontented poor. People too weak or lazy to climb the ladders of success. What they discovered cemented the reason for their sacrifice.

"It was amazing to watch their countenance change. From tired, over worked laborers, to freedom fighters here to set the world straight. There was pride in the doing and shame they hadn't known about all this before. By doing what you're doing you have not only helped to lift those you intended but those who are giving of themselves to do so. I don't know if that was your intention, but it is your result. Your honestly and integrity flows through this group like a strong mountain stream. They trust you, and more importantly they consider you their charm, their protection against harm." She shrugged her lack of belief but acceptance of theirs.

"They might have had doubts, brought on by some outside influence but when the rubber hit the road, they believed more in you. Though speaking of outside forces, and here is the reason I have come to talk to you, someone has been talking to my editor and other reporters at the paper about your financials. They claim that you are siphoning off cash for your own needs. That you are,"

"Stealing!?" Ian felt his blood pressure rise.

"In a word yes. And they want me to delve into your financials and, if I won't, they will get someone from the business section to get your records and go over each and every one of them. Accusations have been made and they have to be investigated. You are a 501c3 and therefore raising money for charity and nonprofit. The people have a right to know." Ian really had no idea black people could blush but she certainly was doing a great job of it. She was embarrassed and ashamed she had to be the one to do this deed, to bring the news. He was now fully pissed. Pissed for her, pissed for him.

He knew his face was flushed and red, he knew he had stood up, he knew this rage. It had been years, decades since he had felt this livid, blind fury. He had sworn he would never feel this nor act on it again in his life. It was the reason he was an avowed pacifist. No one knew about the rage, least not those close to him.

It had been fifty years. He'd been just a kid, eight or so and this neighborhood bully kept at him, poking him, pushing him, tripping him, making him look the fool in front of all the other kids. They laughed and joined the antagonizing of him. Trying to get him to strike back so the bigger kid could kick his ass. That was the whole point. But he'd been brought up not to fight, to reason, to walk away. This kid was pushing him over the edge. He felt his rage rise, his vision clouded by red, a red so deep it was black. He couldn't hear the taunts anymore, couldn't see the other kids, just the bully. That ugly grin, that superior smirk and attitude. And he lost it, lost every single hold on his rage. It took several of the other kids and one of the high school kids to pull him off. They thought he would beat the kid to death. And so had he. That's when the vow was made and it had never been broken, until now.

He wanted his pound and a half of flesh. He wanted revenge on whoever was fucking so hard with his life. He wanted to release all the fear and worry he had built up during the day wondering what had happened to his wife. Yes, it was all good, clean fun, but he thought he was going to lose it several times. They didn't know.

"Are you alright?" it was Maggie's voice cutting through the anger. It was her hand, gentle on his arm. It was her presence that brought him back.

"I am now." He apologized.

He took in the fear on Jeanette's face and the look of horror on Maggie's, what had happened?

"I've never seen you like that before and I hope to never see it again," she whispered, her eyes focused on his hoping to see the man she loved still in there. Avoiding something, but what.

The banging on the door released the tension and their eyes. He looked to where the sound was coming from and saw the hole in the wall. And he thought, what the fuck had happened indeed!

It was Ben and Dugan with a cadre of others behind them, all worried, ready to jump whoever was attacking their captain. All they had heard was the punch and the wall breaking. They had come in force. Gabby pushed his way through. He took in Ian before his eyes settled on the hole.

"You need something, boss?" he was blocking the view of the others, though his voice held a certain admiration as if discovering Ian had a physical strength he never would've believed.

"No, we're good, nothing to see here, folks. Everybody get some rest, we'll get a late check out, say noon," it was the old Ian, the man they trusted and that was all they required. For now. There would be questions at the appropriate time. The posse filed back down the hallway to whatever room had held the party before the destruction.

"Jeanette," he said, "thank you for bringing this to me. And you may tell your editor I am giving you copies of all expenditures, all money taken in, cash, credit, every single penny. You can have your people go over them with a fine-toothed financial comb. If you find anything it's all yours to run with. All receipts, coming in and going out are yours, is that fair?" His rage had run its course, he was laying bare his soul for all to judge. He was just so tired. They had run him through the ringer fourteen ways to nowhere and he just wanted to lay down.

"I'm sure it will satisfy all. I'm sorry to be the one who brought this to you, but I thought better me..." She kissed his check before she left.

"Believe me, better you, than anyone, my friend," he said to the back of the door.

A Tired Mind

As far as Ian's tired, half slumbering mind could remember, he had fallen asleep before the door closed completely. He had to assume that Maggie had picked him up as if he were a child and carried him to the bed, as he did not recall making the journey. A tired, sleeping mind can create acts of might and pith heretofore considered impossible except when aided by love; the woman lifting a car off her child; telling the beautiful, young, scantily clad woman no, he was a happily married man; the same man telling his wife of the adventure, even though, yeah, even though he knew what her reaction would be. Humans are capable of unbelievable courage, strength, and stupidity all in the name of love.

He didn't know if Maggie had undressed him, though when he turned to lay on his side and got tangled in the comforter, he realized he was still fully dressed and on top of the sheets, oh well. Reaching over to touch his loving wife he found the space empty. A moment of panic until he raised his head and saw her snoring softly on the couch. He should retrieve her, she looked uncomfortable. He fell back into a deep, deep sleep.

He awoke to the scent of tea and warm pastry; it was a lovely way to meet the new day. His wife looked tired, circles under her eyes, not deep but noticeable, and when she smiled at him there were some creases he had not noticed previously. And he knew every inch of the woman's face. He should've gone over, woke her, and made her come to bed, no one is comfortable sleeping on a hotel couch. He knew, he'd done it many times while coaching certain acts into sobriety.

Ian had fought the battle himself and knew only the alcoholic or drug addicted person could quit, but to have someone who truly cared about you by your side was a huge support. So, his payback for all the years sober was to be that support. It was a position he cherished.

"Why didn't you come into bed?" he asked softly, "There's plenty of room and you know I sleep better when you're by my side."

"I started off there but you began thrashing and mumbling something I couldn't understand, it was driving me a little batty. So, I took the couch, it's not bad, though not the bed." Her eyes lit with love for him.

"Have you heard anything from any of the others?" Ian yawned.

"I ran into Ben and Gabby in the breakfast room. They told me they wanted to sleep in but woke up early anyway. Both appeared rested and ready to hit the big city. I think everyone is excited to be in New York and to have a spot to lay their heads for a couple weeks," she chucked, "Though I dare say that within about ten days they'll be itching to get backout on the road. Gypsies are gypsies, they never change. You can't chain them or make them sit in one spot too long, they get itchy feet."

"Are you referring to any gypsy in particular?" he furrowed his brow daring her.

"Well, let's say I've known some gypsies and you can't tie them down, even ones that love you. They love the road more. I'm not complaining, I've gotten to travel most of the world because of that wanderlust. I would never demand you plant your ass in one place to prove your love for me. I would never demand you make the choice. I think I would hate losing to blacktop." She kissed him deeply to show there was no accusation, no regrets, just facts.

"Well, then, my gypsy girl, leave us shower and see what the day holds for us. I hope less stress and worry than yesterday. I need to talk to Raj, our beloved roadie/lawyer, to see if he can put together all the receipts for Jeanette. And I want to discover who is spreading rumors and vitriol." He kipped out of bed, threw off his clothes, and hopped into the shower.

People had gathered at the breakfast bar, most had eaten and were now engaged in conversation, cups of coffee and tea. They were in good moods, and he was not going to be the one to stifle their morning.

"Ben," he called the road manager over, "do you have a list of rooms and occupants?"

Ben gave him a glare that asked if he was insane, of course he did, but instead, "Yeah, I got one." He grinned.

"Could you ask our Mr. Bharadwaj, if he could come down here for a few minutes. I have something to discuss with him and I would like all of our caravan present when I do." There was something in his tone that sent the crew to quickly gather those not assembled.

The breakfast room was filled to overflowing, everyone thinking that some explanation for last night might be in the offing. Ian asked Jeanette and Raj to come to the corner of the room where he stood.

Once the group had settled in and quieted down, he began the meet. "There have been some accusations leveled at me from an unknown source. I am doing my best to find that person and though I have no proof, I think I know who the person is." That's the way to start off a meeting, with total confusion and a roundabout of words. "Anyway," he said to the confused faces, "someone has insinuated that I am absconding with a large portion of the funds from this tour and your work." Now there was much mumbling and discontent, tempers were beginning to rise. "So, whatever access Ms. Serling had before," he waited, "has been increased to total and complete. I want every one of you to be as honest as your conscience and what you've told your significant other at home, will allow. She has free reign to ask you anything about your money, what you know about my money or anything else. Honesty, openness, truth are the only weapons we have. Raj, I need to get all the paperwork on the 501c3. Every nickel that has come in and gone out and to whom and where. No secrets. Jeanette is to have full access. If you are not sure if you should tell her something, tell her. If that puts me in a bad light or as an asshole, then that's my problem." Now the tension eased and all laughed, but they understood.

The boss had been smeared and the only thing that would take the stink away was the pure white light of truth. The question they all wanted answered was, by whom and why? It seemed to be the question of the tour.

As Ian turned to leave the breakfast area, he saw the two former members of the Mersea Beats sitting in a corner all alone. No one was bothering them for autographs or asking questions. The tour was not the only group of humans residing at the hotel, there were normal people as well, yet no one seemed to notice them. He had to assume it was Pete's theory of not appearing to hide. Just be normal and normal ye shall be. He had wanted to speak to them before everyone hit the road anyway, so this was the perfect opportunity.

"Morning, boys," he pulled out a chair to sit at their table.

"I don't remember asking the thief to join us, do you?" the percussionist asked, dry as the Sahara.

"I think you're right. Here we are sitting all alone, in this five-star hotel, minding our own, do you think they have security?" the guitarist munched on a piece of buttered toast. Though probably margarined was more like it, Ian thought. "Stealing from himself, ought to be ashamed, I tell you."

"Have we had our fun?" asked Ian with a pained and sorrowful expression.

"Not yet, but there's plenty of time," Richie laughed.

"I assume you two will be riding the limo back to New York?" he glanced from face to face.

"Not we," announced the drummer, "we have decided to join this band of gypsies and ride along with our adopted tribe. It is our fervent wish that we passed the audition last eve," he feigned hope as he spoke the words of a young aspirant passing his first test. He did not do it well. "It is our dream to live the hard tack life of road musicians living off the land on the very meager earnings this tour pays."

Ian sat stunned, were they serious? "Are you serious?"

"Absolutely!" They said in unison. "It's been a while since we rode the hound and we thought this late in our careers it might do us well to remember how the other half lives." For a couple of boys from the other side of the tracks of Liverpool they could put on airs. "We'll be riding the dog with you." Pete informed him. "We shall suffer the calamities of the road with our brethren and sisteren!"

"Number one, we don't exactly ride the hound," Ian stated in reference to Greyhound Bus, "Number two it's only about two hours to the city."

"Yes, we did the Google," said Mr. Stainesby, "we're not stupid, you know. We shall suffer the slings and arrows of the road dog for two hours and have many stories to tell our contemporaries back in civilization of our harrowing adventures," He assumed the posture of the sad, hard worn, road musician, not easy for one of the most successful musicians in history, but he was an actor.

Ian clapped his hands in delight, "This will be wonderful. Maybe we can have a flat tire and you two can help change it!"

They shook hands on the deal before the megastars went to retrieve their meager belongings. Ian shook his head in gratitude of these wonderful friends. Once word got out, holy shit. He headed upstairs to collect his own meager belongings.

Ben began banging on doors and announcing, "Ten minutes", he didn't have to, it was a courtesy he always provided for the best crews.

Dugan was waiting for him outside the bus they shared with Ian, Jaxson, and Maggie. And now, it would appear, with two legendary stars. Even in the hierarchy of Rock there are stars and then there are the Mersea Beats.

"All set?" Dugan asked his co-manager.

"Yeah," but there was something in the way Ben said it that said more than a thousand words could.

"What is it?" If there was a problem, Dugan wanted to have at it before the wheels started turning.

"Nothing probably." He hesitated, "You know Jake, the electrician?"

Dugan nodded, "The curmudgeon?" Jake was a lifer, literally. He had become a roadie when he was young and fit, but when most moved on to other jobs he stuck with the bands, changing jobs within the crew as his age and physical condition dictated. He was their chief electrical engineer. The one who almost fried a few weeks back but didn't thanks to their secret weapon. "What about him?"

"I don't know." Ben shook his head with a quizzical expression and laughed. "He's in a good mood." normally this would not arouse comment, but with Jake a good mood meant he had probably poisoned his mother.

"I'll check it out. Ask around, I think these folks trust me," Dugan smiled. Ah, the life of the road manager. He 'liked' Jake, he knew his business, never caused a problem, but he was cranky all the time.

Ben had worked with him on a dozen crews and had never known the man to be in a good mood, hence the concern. Jeez, what a world when somebody's good mood was cause for concern. Ben thought if he ever began to truly understand humanity, he would go off to live a hermit's life in a cave in the mountains.

There would always be people who were ill tempered. No reason, no rhyme, just sour. Jake was that guy. A sour disposition since Ben had met him twenty years ago on a crew with Bad Company. Nothing made the guy smile. And this was the guy who would've died without Ian tripping in. You would think that would make him thankful. Nope, just more ornery. People.

He saw Jake walking toward the bus. He was smiling and whistling. Maybe the electrical shock had finally caused a stroke. They should take him to a doctor but why fuck up a good thing.

"Hey Jake, how's it going," Ben shot.

"Going so well, I could shit!" Eloquent. "You know Ben, life is a wheel, it goes round and round and Karma will catch you every time! Something done a lifetime ago, someone steals your dream, ruins your life, and then there is a comeuppance. And we're on our way to NY, the perfect city for that. I can't wait to get there. I'm going to take that pound of flesh I've been owed and have it bronzed." He was about to bust buttons on that shirt.

Whatever he was talking about, whoever had done him wrong, was in NYC and Jake couldn't wait to get there and have the scales even out. Ben had to wonder what had been done to this guy and by whom. Why had it taken so long for him to get his revenge? Maybe the other guy hit the road, sailed overseas, and had finally come home to roost. Whatever, Ben could not imagine anyone doing anything that would make him hold such hate, such vengeance in his heart for a lifetime. That had to be one hell of a grudge to carry for, what, fifty years? More?

It's funny, one would think that being as close to Ian, Jaxson, Maggie as Jake had for so many years, some of their decency would rub off.

"Going to meet an old friend?" Ben thought he should play along, "Someone you haven't seen in a while?"

"Yeah, It's been a long time since we were in school together, he probably won't remember me. He was always the arrogant one, Mr. Popular. Not me. Even if he remembered me and what he did, he certainly wouldn't recognize me. I ain't the same guy I was in middle school." He grinned.

Jake was built like a wrestler or dockworker and Ben had to assume he had been all his life. He felt a twinge of pain for whoever Jake was going after. Senseless, that's what this was. No matter what had happened in the past, it was the past, leave it lie. "Well, don't do anything I gotta bail you out for. I will, but Rikers is a bitch. Keep me up to date."

They boarded their respective buses. Ben had an itch he couldn't scratch, something felt wrong, but he couldn't put his finger on it. Jake was surly but he'd never been the violent type, never gone after another crew member. He wasn't angry, or a bully, he was the first one to help when someone asked. To be this happy about possibly harming another was just not in his character. Ah well, Ben had enough to worry about. He'd inform Ian and he could worry about Jake! They might be seeking a new electrician.

"Hey, tell Ian thanks for me," Jake waved before disappearing into the interior of the crew hooptie.

All loaded, wheels rolling they headed north towards the Big Apple. Maggie and Jeanette shared one couch, Pete, Josef, and Richie the opposite, James Nash on the arm, Ben, Dugan, Jaxson, Ian, and Raul—how had he sneaked aboard, Ian chuckled silently but his joy at seeing the man could not be contained—scattered about on chairs, countertops and the floor. It was time for the big meeting about how the two weeks in NY would go.

"First I have to tell you about my run in with Jake," Ben began.

"Our electrician?" Jaxson was taken aback; this was not where he thought their discussion would begin.

"Yeah, just a quick note and Duge will back me up," and he told of the curmudgeon's change of attitude, his glee at finally settling some score from a hundred years ago that would be brought to a head when they arrived or sometime during the next two weeks. Ben's concern was evident in his every word.

"You think he is actually going to cause physical harm to somebody?" asked Maggie.

"If he gets the chance, I have no doubt," Ben confirmed. "Anybody that can hang on to a grudge for, I don't know, forty, fifty years, yeah, I think they're capable of anything." He shook his head in wonder.

"I could use a guy like that. There's a fellow I wouldn't mind taking a few whacks at right now," Ian said it softly, but not softly enough. The shocked expressions told him he was heard. "Come on now, somebody's been fucking with me since Buffalo and the roach over the border incident. That and canceling dates and now this bullshit of accusing me of stealing from my own tour. Wouldn't you want a little piece of someone's heart?" He half-heartedly defended his thoughts, though knew in his own soul they were not him. Not anymore. Not since the incident fifty years ago. Funny how childhood could rear its ugly head so many years later. Time to grow up.

Though when he took his eyes from his shame, he noticed not every eye condemned him. There were some on this bus who got it, though would never act on it. That they understood was good enough, he could rest with that.

"Alright, so by the end of two weeks we might be seeking another electrical guy, so everybody put on your thinking caps and see who comes to mind. Not sure I want a guy around with that much hate and anger boiling just below the surface. Until then, let's focus on what we are going to do with this show," Jaxson had concerns he had not heretofore voiced, he would give them weight now. "It has been fantastic that so many artists have wanted to jump onboard as we've traveled. But the traveling kept them spread out so we weren't overwhelmed with fifty people wanting to play on any certain night. Now, here we are sitting ducks. Sitting for two weeks, and in New York City. Two very powerful magnets for everybody and anybody wanting to jump on the crazy train. We have to control this."

He had focused them on something they had not considered. The word was out and artists being who they were would want to be part of it. Number one, because they believed in the mission of the Untouchables, and number two, because it would be fun to hang with this retinue, and C, because it wouldn't hurt to be seen and heard with this circus. No one took the stage for purely artistic and altruistic reasons; ego was always the driving force. Most could control the impulses, some could not, but all marched to the beat.

And to be honest there were some Jaxson, and he assumed others, would not welcome to the stage. People in the music business sometimes needed to be seen doing something for others to temper their image. Maybe they'd had some bad press and wanted to show their fans they weren't the asshole portrayed, kind of like community service. The problem was, the intent was not always from the heart. He didn't want their purpose to be sullied by others. They didn't need the buzz or the bump, they had plenty sitting on this bus. And at the heart of it, these shows were supposed to be fun events shared with people they loved and respected, not names.

"We would like to be part of this, if you'll have us, but we don't need to be main stage every night," as usual there was Pete understanding the problem and willing to pull back. Selflessness and generosity seemed part of his DNA. "Maybe some nights we," he pointed at his drummer and himself, "could act as background singers or wave from the wings, kind of thing. That way we are not taking up space on the stage." A quick lift of the shoulders and nod of the head said anything else he might've thought.

"Thank you, of all people, it's always the greats who understand," Jaxson was humbled by their consideration. Why couldn't everyone in this business be them?

"Also, take into consideration that we are doing fourteen nights in a row, some of our people might like a night or two off. Or hang back with Mr. McCarthy and Mr. Stainesby. We should talk to all the artists and see if they would like to do a rotating order kind of thing." Ian's brain was kicking into full gear and away from wanting revenge.

"Aren't some of the female singers already kind of doing that?" Jeanette threw in her two cents.

"Yeah, that little ensemble they put together last night, then had Joya join in on, was magnificent," Dugan's excitement and appreciation for what he had heard was contagious. He was a man who had roadied for some of the top acts in history, it took a lot to impress him. Joya had impressed, the six women singing had impressed even more. "Maybe they could choose a couple of each other's most well-known tunes and join forces. It could be one of the most powerful moments in the show."

"You should continue to sell this as what you began. Those people who were on the show that grew into this movement. These Untouchables. Those who have sacrificed all along the way. Their names should be on the posters and promoted. 'With Special Guests each Night' kind of thing, so you are not saying we'll be there every show, or Josef will be there every show or anyone. Let people assume what they will but the show should always be about those who committed originally. And a few extra stars in the sky." Pete was one hundred percent onboard and from the expression Richie wore, so was he.

"Keep an extra set of drums on stage in case someone wants to join in on some songs without taking up time for himself," Richie was thoughtful as if wondering who that wonderful person might be.

The rest of the time was taken up by Ben and Dugan figuring out logistics of the stage set up so they weren't moving amplifiers and keyboards every other tune. While the rest talked music, touring, bad gigs and hard times, disasters on the road. It was funny, Ian thought, that when musicians got together, especially those who had spent the better part of their lives performing all over the world and had achieved great success, they never talked about their success. They always enjoyed sharing the worst times, the hardest days. It was like a competition to see who could tell the most horrifying story of the worst gig, the most devastating accident, the time they played while throwing up in a bucket or while their mother lay in hospital dying or stroking out, yet they played. Musicians, performers, were a unique and odd genre of humanity.

The trucks took the stage equipment over to the Beacon while the buses took the crews, musicians, and artists to the hotel a block away. Ben took over check in and Dugan took over load-in. Jaxson herded all the musicians and artists into an empty conference room to go over the ideas they had been discussing on the ride up. Everyone started talking at once. Some wanted to be on stage every night, some wanted a few nights to hang with friends in the Apple. Some wanted to know if there were going to be any promotional appearances on the late-night shows and if so, who was going to perform. They had their ideas of who probably would, who they thought should and what some thought would be representative of the whole. Who would explain it all and why anyone should care? Egos were checked, no feelings hurt, and Jaxson had decided the workload should be spread around.

Yes, there would be appearances on late-night shows. He would do the talking about the show, Gabby would explain the why, and the artists could determine who should come on and sing. Most loved the idea of combining efforts to showcase all.

Gillian raised her hand as if in school, Jaxson laughed and called on her. "I get the why, and love that we are all sharing in the bounty, as it were, but, hmm, well, have you asked Gabby about this? I mean it is one thing to get his nervous ass up on a stage, but we're all there for support. This is TV you're talking about. I'm just trying to say maybe he could tell one of us the pertinent parts and we could tell the story," heads were bobbing and silent yeses were being passed. They all loved Gabby, he had become part of the family, the last thing any of them wanted was of him to come off as a buffoon or some hick from Guatemala who barely spoke the language.

Jaxson got it, but he knew in his heart he was right, it had to be Gabor. "You'll all be there for him. We will have most of the front rows reserved for us. If you're not performing on the show, we are asking you show up in support." Now the smiles were shared with hugs, they would not let their brother down. Those most glad were the ones that didn't have to break the news to the big Mayan. "We have a taping Wednesday," Jax threw the tidbit as a pleasant surprise, "on the David Stevens Show." The number one late night show in America, why not start big? "Dugan or Ben will arrange transport. Thank you all for being so understanding. We are not taking anyone off any show unless you want a night off, but we are going to try and make room for special guests and friends. So, if some can rotate from front to back, I would greatly appreciate it. I love each and every one of you more than words can express."

"How are people going to know who the special guest each night will be?" Asked Bonnie, always the show woman.

"They won't. The only names they will know for sure who will be on the show are you all. It was Pete's idea. He figured since you are the ones who have been on the show since the beginning and have sacrificed the most, this is still YOUR show, no one else's. Nobody's fame will top what you have accomplished so far. People will know there are special guests every night, they just won't know who. They are not the draw, you are. You and the rest of the Untouchables," here they all beat on their chests in solidarity and support. It had become their sign.

Wednesday would come soon enough, now it was up to Ian—the glories of being the manager, you get to do all the shitty assignments no one else wanted—and he hoped, Maggie, to explain to Gabby why he was the only one who could pull this off. Gabby trusted Maggie more than any other person besides his mother, and he would see her sitting right in front of him while he sat at the desk. That was one good thing, he didn't have to stand alone on a stage and do his speech. He would sit next to Jaxson, look down and see his friends, his family, he would talk to them, not the four hundred others.

"Where have you been?" Fame's petulant tone cut across the top of the mountain.

"Putting things in motion. Unlike your loves mine do not require constant monitoring. I put destiny in motion and it flows as life intends." Fate's arrogance rubbed the other goddess's nerves raw.

"Maybe because mine accomplish so much due to their love for me I consider it an honor to reciprocate." She could not hide her peevishness.

"Is that why you keep pushing the big Mayan, who also does not seem to want your ministrations." She sipped wine from a goblet that had appeared out of thin air. "It would appear you've lost your main project. Mr. Sperling has shown himself immune to your allure."

"There are many faces to notoriety, not just adoration." Her smug reply told Fate all she needed to know.

"You have set up the thievery to make him seem a criminal. To be famous for being a louse, a criminal." Fate was shocked, though she didn't know why. She knew Fame would do anything to anyone to fulfill her need.

"I set up nothing, I just allowed humans to act in accordance with their humanity. People will always revert to type."

Fate had to wonder exactly what Fame was talking about, Ian had never been despicable or a louse. How was he reverting to type? She would have to keep a closer eye on the proceedings.

Late Night is Where Angels Come To Die or Fly

Wednesday came on the dying wings of promise that Tuesday would keep it at bay. Gabby sat on the edge of his bed wishing Tuesday had pulled Wednesday with it. And praying the calendar was wrong that it was actually Monday again and all he had to do was get ready to go over to the Beacon to prepare for the opening night. How he let these people talk him into doing things he would rather crawl under a rock and hide than do, he had no idea. Jaxson Grahm was a brilliant songwriter, maybe that was the answer. He had the silver tongue to make thousands of people swoon with his words, Gabby didn't stand a chance.

He had promised the three of them he would sacrifice himself before the television gods and he resigned himself to lay prostrate and give up his dignity and his anonymity. His mother would be watching him! She had called to tell him how proud she was. How could he tell her how terrified he was? He would represent their people. That was what he would hold on to. That and the fact that his 'family' would occupy the first row of the theater, they would be there for him. Maggie said she would sit right in front of the chair where he would sit. She promised, and he trusted her more than anyone he knew except his own mother.

He would sit quietly next to Jaxson, who would talk to David Stephens, the host. He just had to say the things they had practiced. Short, sweet, and don't make it sound like it was memorized, which it was. They had all helped him try to sound natural. And now it was Wednesday, judgement day.

He should get dressed but he was sweating so profusely he didn't want to soak his TV clothes. He would just take them with him and put them on there. Shit, shit, shit! The soft knock on the door almost made him jump out of his skin.

"Hang on," he said to the wood as he slipped into his jeans and a T.

The crack revealed Maggie's smile. He opened the door all the way. She was in a jovial mood or pretended well. "What do you think? Ready?" She encouraged.

"Never," sullen, he sat back on the bed, as if that would negate the day and what it meant. She shook her head and he resigned himself to fate. He raised his large frame from the bed. Maggie thought she heard creaking but decided it was her imagination.

"Come on," she tugged at his arm, "It's not like going to the gallows or chopping block. Well, not exactly." Humor was supposed to ease the tension, humor lied. She grabbed his freshly pressed black button-down shirt and new jeans that were hanging on the rack by the door.

They appeared as nothing more than a mom with her recalcitrant child walking down the hall as Ian and Jaxson stepped out of their respective rooms. They both smiled and patted Gabby reassuringly while pushing him towards the waiting limo. It was TV, you traveled in style for TV.

Their whispered conversation reverberated in the well-upholstered motorcar, at least it did in Gabby's ears. He shut them out trying to remember his speech. Two minutes, that was all he had to retain. They had condensed his message down to two minutes. The most agonizing two minutes in history. He would do it for his mother and his people and for these people who had become his family.

They walked into chaos. Anyone who has ever done an interview on national television knows that the hours before taping are chaos. The script is being constantly changed, especially on late night shows where so much of the monologue depends on the news of the day. The band was running over their contributions to the show. Make-up—Gabby became even more horrified at this torture—was to be worn by all. The stage manager was telling them what was about to take place while running and bumping through the technicians, camera people, grips and the other hundred people it took to put on a show like this. None of which helped to settle Gabby's nerves.

They finally settled into the dressing room to await their appearance. They would be the first guests of the night before an actor neither he nor Jaxson had heard of—not out of the ordinary, if the person wasn't on one of the DVDs on the bus, they had no idea who they might be—would come out to promote her new movie and then Jesse Collins supported by the Untouchables Choir—Gillian, Bonnie, Cinda, Michele, and, now, Joya—for back-up would close the show. It would be simple, almost a Capella with just Jesse's guitar. It would be beautiful. They would get approximately fifteen to eighteen minutes. A large amount of TV time, but the affable host loved Jaxson and what this tour represented.

David Stevens had been warned about Gabby's nervousness and lack of experience, though he agreed Gabby was the one who should speak his piece. Monologue, short comedy skit from the desk, and then it was time to intro Jaxson and Gabby. David and Jaxson talked for several minutes about the tour, the constant revolving door of special guests—had Pete and Richie really shown up and played? Josef? You know David had worked with him years ago. He loved the whole thing.

Two commercial breaks into the show and Gabby would speak next. Jaxson had told the story of the tour, mentioning those who began and would come back like James Nash, another favorite of Mr. Stephens, The Disidentes, Joya, all the regular cast, most of whom, he pointed out, were here tonight. Gabby sat quietly next to him as still as a statue. His hands clasped on his knees, his black hair pulled back into as tight a ponytail as his nerves, muscles, and marrow. He could swear he was soaked in sweat, his black button-down shirt feeling extraordinarily tight, he could hardly breathe, brand new jeans chafing at the waist, sweat pouring down into his well-worn work boots. Their one concession to his wardrobe. He was a mess.

David looked at the big Mayan with concern on his face, this could go south in a hurry. He hoped Gabby could pull it all together. Commercial break over David introduced Gabby by his given name and spoke about his heritage, his reason for being here tonight—to explain the why of the tour, its mission and the Untouchables.

Gabby stared at the crowd, trying to focus on his friends and family in the front row. Silence. It might have lasted two seconds, an eternity in television or it might have lasted an actual eternity. Gabby had no idea. David looked at Jaxson, Jaxson shook his head.

Then David without a word began to pat his heart, first with an open hand before immediately shifting to a fist. In rhythm to his heartbeat, he knew, this was the signal, From The Heart. Jaxson took up the beat, then the first row. Support. Love. Family. The band took up the sound, bass drum booming, hands hit hearts. The audience joined in. Life returned to the big man.

Gabby began his recitation, quietly, but as he spoke, he felt the love in this studio, the first studio that had hosted the Mersea Beats, and glanced over to see the two Mersea Beat stars beating in rhythm on their hearts, and he spoke not from rote but from the heart.

At the two-minute mark he told of his mother and her people. Proud, strong, rulers of their own destiny until another civilization came along and subdued them and then spent a millennium trying to exterminate them. But they lived. At the three-minute mark he told of his new friend, Raj Bharadwaj, who was born into the highest caste in India but had come to America to learn a new way. A way to live together not in castes but in harmony. Only to find that America had the same caste system. Not recognizing their own red, brown, black brothers and sisters as human for centuries. They had all become what in India were known as the Untouchables. People so below any caste of humanity one would have to wash in pure water if the shadow of one of these fell on them. That black people could be tortured and mutilated for the crime of speaking to a white person in the wrong tone or not getting out of the way fast enough. Of the indigenous peoples who had been hunted for their skin and ears. It had to stop.

At the five-minute mark he told of what this tour had done to raise money to feed, educate, and lift these invisible people, these human beings into the sight of those who refused to see. Building hope and jobs, new schools to teach knowledge and skills, to give them, the forgotten of the world, worth. Worth in their own minds as well as to others. To show the world they mattered. At the seven-minute mark the stage manager was frantically signaling for him to stop. He was way, way over his time, he had to stop. The Stage manager was almost yelling for David to cut him off, they had another guest.

David glanced over to the spot where the next guest could be seen waiting her entrance, to talk about her first chance as an actor to star in a new movie. Instead, he saw the young woman beating on her heart, tears flowing down her cheeks and she shook her head 'no', she didn't want him to stop. She'd come back another day and then she smiled. This was so much fucking cooler.

Gabby stopped as if realizing where he was and what he had just done. Silence. "That was for my mother," he said and noticed he was standing on the stage. He didn't remember getting up. But he was out near the front of the stage. He turned to look for the chair.

Ian didn't remember jumping up on the stage and holding Gabby with all his might. Maggie holding him from the other side. Soon the road crew was up and surrounding him with their love, the band of gypsies next to them. It was a scrum of love. Jaxson joined in. Those waiting in the wings to come out and sing ran over and piled on, David jumped over his desk to add his love as well. The audience was dead silent. Before one man began to clap, slow, in rhythm to life, to love, to his heart. Soon everyone in the audience took up the clap before exploding in a raucous cacophony of joy. Commercial break.

Once order had been restored David went over to apologize to the young actor, as he knew they no longer had time to have her on. She laughed and hugged him. This was so worth every second of her time. She would come back, but was it OK if she stuck around to hear the song?

The stagehands set up Jesse and the Choir of Untouchables with microphones. It was all they would need. Louis asked if it would be alright if the Late Nite Band could join in near the end. Jesse smiled acquiescence. They would be singing *'Love Now',* his anthem from the late sixties. Naturally.

David introduced Jesse and the Choir of Untouchables. The song was perfect, the voices, weaving, knitting together each word and harmony. Joya walked off during one of the band's solos and grabbed the young actor who hadn't gotten her time and brought her out on stage to sing with them. As if on cue a woman walked up to the stage and stood until Bonnie walked over to help Brandi Carlyle up on the stage. She had come to the taping to listen but found herself overwhelmed and in need of song. More of the crew and band members from the tour came up and sang. Jaxson and David joined in for the last chorus. This would be one for the books.

As they wrapped up the show and the lights dimmed, David thanked the audience for being so patient, so kind, and they stood to give him and everyone on the stage a five-minute ovation.

"Well," he said turning to Ian, Maggie, Gabby, and Jaxson, "that is something that has never happened in the history of late night as far as I know. You have done something truly magical tonight." He was grinning from ear to ear.

"I'm sorry, I don't know," Gabby whispered but all could hear.

"Don't," David and Jaxson said in unison. "It was perfect. Magnificent. That will be the greatest show on late night forever. Thank you. And I am going to contribute a hundred thousand dollars to the cause and if you all would like to come back again while you're in New York..." he couldn't say any more, he was now in tears.

The party spirit began as soon as the buses pulled up to the hotel. Those who hadn't been able to go wanted to hear every single thing that happened. Those who did not perform on the television show, as Late Nite recorded in the early evening, still had a show to put on. Those who had participated would come along to be part of that audience and then return to watch the television show on the TVs in the lobby as a family.

It was a quarter to one in the east when Gabby's phone rang. Who the hell would be calling him at this time? He answered. It was his mother. He never would've known by talking to her, she couldn't get a word out, she was so filled with pride and joy she was about to burst. Hence the massive leakage of fluid from her eyes, she explained. He could hear dozens of people in the background cheering, yelling their love. It was his whole family back home. His tears mixed with those three thousand miles away and helped wash away much.

Ian couldn't sleep, overwhelmed as he was by the events on the taping and the watch party following. Maybe he shouldn't have smoked that last half joint, maybe he was filled with the love of all things possible and good.

Raj had reported that within the hour after the show aired on the east coast and Midwest, contributions to their Untouchable non-profit had jumped by forty-five percent. People could not give fast enough or enough. Villages, first nations, poverty-stricken neighborhoods, and towns from all over the country were asking what they could do to help. Not asking for help but what they could contribute as far as knowledge, teachers, volunteers, anything they could do for their own cause. It would seem they were not looking for a handout as had been previously reported but a hand up, and they would do the rest.

Yes, Ian was filled with the love and hope of humanity. Shit, he thought if he ran across someone who was dying, he might even help them on purpose. He laughed out loud, the concept so foreign to this former self. He needed to walk, to think, to wonder what they might have kicked off. And what it might morph into. He explained to Maggie he needed a little Ian time. She knew because she knew him.

The streets of New York during the day are a madhouse of movement, everyone has somewhere they have to get to right now and they will run you down to get there. At night they relaxed their grip on humanity and gave a man or woman room to stretch the leg and think. Two completely different towns.

Of course, at night the danger level reared its ugly head, but Ian had traveled these streets many times at every time of the day and night over the past several decades, he felt if not confident, then cognizant of his surroundings. Stupid and oblivious got you mugged, beaten, or killed. He had no desire for any of the above.

So, he was paying particular attention to his surroundings as he made his way back to the hotel and saw the horrendous outfit covering the slimy, sleaze making its way towards the same entrance Ian headed toward. Sonofabitch, he almost yelled but decided to wait until he had closed the gap and the slimeball could not ooze away.

The lobby was vacant, so Ian could see Vilhelm walking directly towards the bank of elevators. He quick stepped as soundlessly as his sneakers would allow and caught the man just as he was about to press the 'up' button.

"Wilhelm!" He whispered threateningly. "Finally."

"It's Vilhelm!" Insistent and surly, came the reply as he turned to see who he had corrected.

Ian couldn't tell if the expression on the man's face was one of surprise, guilt, or cornered rat, but he felt a sense of gratification. He would get his pound of fresh meat.

"I was referring to your last name, if that truly is your last name." Ian's grin was not pleasant. "What is your name, really? And why are you fucking with me?"

"I told you, my name is Vilhelm Wilhelm and I haven't a clue as to what you are talking about. I am not fucking with you in any manner. Why would I?" He honestly seemed confused, completely baffled by the accusation.

"Well, for one you said you were a record rep yet not one of the artists on this tour knew who you were or had any connection to you, so you lied!" Ian began to lay out his case before the non-existent jury.

"I never said I represented any of the acts on your tour, I said I was a record company A&R man, which I am," he reached into his back pocket, slowly, so as not too upset Ian any more than he was and pulled out his wallet. Chained, of course, to his belt. Jeez, central casting was working overtime on this one. He pulled out a card and handed it to Ian.

Ian took the card between thumb and forefinger so as not to get his hands greasy. Avetriel Records, Cleveland, Ohio. Vilhelm Wilhelm, A&R. "Never heard of them," he said handing the card back to the supposed record rep. Vilhelm waved off the card with a 'keep it' vibe.

"We are a very small Classical label. Innovative, always seeking new ways to get the music to the people. Our artists really are the driving force," he began his pitch and then stopped when he saw Ian's expression.

"We don't have any 'classical artists' on the show," Ian's temper was not improving, "So, again, why are you fucking with me and this tour?" He wanted answers and he wanted right answers. "You said you were checking to make certain the artists were being treated well. Why would you do that if you didn't rep any of them?" He had the sleaze now.

"First of, again, I am not fucking with anybody," Vilhelm began. "Second, I wanted to know how the artists were treated to see if I wanted any of mine to join with you."

"You didn't slip a half joint in my pocket in Buffalo? Didn't call and try to cancel the show in Lakewood? Didn't call the Times and tell them I was stealing money from my own non-profit?" His voice rose with each accusation booming and echoing off the walls of the barren lobby.

"Now why would I do such things when I came here to ask you for a huge favor?" his features contorted into a combo platter of wounded, indignant, disbelief, and panic.

"When did you come here?" Ian was going to get to the bottom of whatever was happening just like Sherlock would.

"Three days ago, to wait for you. I didn't know when you would arrive, as I noted you were adding dates as you made your way across the states. And I knew I wanted to talk to you before your stint at The Beacon began. I almost caught you a couple times but you had so much going on, I thought it wiser to wait until you had a moment. Looks like this is the moment." This was making too much sense for Ian's liking.

"I just find it interesting that none of this started until you showed up and then abruptly left," he was clinging to his dislike of the man when he knew intellectually that this might not be the best course of action.

"I will tell you this, if I was going to come after you, for whatever supposed reason that might be, you would know it was me. I don't hide, I would face you and let you know why," though his appearance shouted this to be false, Ian could not deny the sincerity of his words. He wasn't pissed, he was steadfast in his defense. Ian was wrong, but then who?

"So, what did you want of me?" Might as well ask and get this elephant out of the room.

"I represent some of the finest, least known, classical artists in the country. You represent some of the finest and best-known acoustic artists in the world. You are sitting in The Beacon, now, for another twelve days. How would you like some opening music while people are entering and being sat, getting comfortable, kind of thing. It would take no time away from the show, people would get to hear something different they might dig, and these artists would get to contribute to a cause they would dearly love to be part of. The label pays the hotel and other expenses, it's a win-win for all involved." He shrugged and smiled.

Ian hated to admit it to himself but the greasy bastard was growing on him. "Let me talk to Jaxson in the morning."

They rode up in the elevator each lost in their own thoughts, dreams and wants until they came to Vilhelm's floor, Ian shook his hand as he got off. "See you in the morning." Something was definitely wrong here, more wrong than Ian had imagined. If it wasn't this guy then who? An apology looked imminent.

The elevator stopped on Ian's floor, the doors whooshed open and he stepped out into the vacant hallway. He sat on one of the upholstered chairs across the small hallway from the elevators and took a glance at his watch. Three a.m. He needed a few minutes to think and he didn't want to wake Maggie, this seemed as good a place as any to let his mind wander.

He had been so certain that this Vilhelm guy was the culprit he hadn't considered the implications if he wasn't. He was the outsider, the sleazy record company rep. No skin in the game. If he threw in a monkey wrench, he was the one it wouldn't affect, yet he had no reason to do so. Ian had picked him because he didn't like the look of the guy. It was that simple. And yet, he liked the idea of exposing their crowd to a classical quartet or string ensemble before the show and he thought their fans would dig it as well. How could he have been so wrong? And now he had to seriously reconsider who it must be.

He slunk down the hall and as quietly as he could, opened the door to their room. He sat on the couch to take his shoes off when he saw her lift her head from the pillow and rest it on her right hand, elbow bent for comfort.

"You OK?" she asked.

A single bedside table lamp illuminated the room enough he could get undressed and slide in beside his wife. He was so tired and he'd smoked a third of joint while he walked. It usually helped the thought process, tonight it just made him tired.

"No, I don't think I am," he sighed before telling of his meeting with Vilhelm and what he had discovered. He had been horribly wrong which meant he was horribly wrong about someone else. Someone close to him on the crew, the band, the singers, the artists, someone with an ax to grind that Ian didn't know existed. Someone he trusted was fucking with him and throwing accusations from a blind spot. That was the worst part of it all.

"Any Idea who?" She knew before she asked but she had to ask anyway.

"Not a clue," he tipped his head back and rested it on the pillow. "I feel betrayed and haven't got a clue who would do such a thing. I mean, before, when I thought it was that slimeball—and he really isn't, he just dresses the part—it was easy to be pissed and want my revenge but now, I just don't know." He leaned forward, head in hands and shook all over. He wasn't crying he was shaken.

"Well, hold me and try to sleep; it's been a long, emotional day. Maybe tomorrow we can shine some light on the whole thing. We have to look at it from a new perspective anyway." She lay her head back down and held out her hand for him to come and hold her. She knew if he held her, she would actually be holding him, he ached for something solid to hang onto. She would be his rock once again.

Morning arrived on an undertaker's carriage. Ian felt like death. He hadn't slept, as he knew he wouldn't, and had deep purple trenches under his eyes. This was not what he wished for today. It was the mid-week mark of the first week at The Beacon and there was work to be done, he required a clear mind.

As he walked through the lobby on the way to grab coffee—yes, he needed coffee, strong, black coffee—everyone was in a chipper mood. The appearance on The David Stevens Show and the ensuing show at the Beacon had lifted this tired troop out of its doldrums and they were chomping to get back on stage. Ian tried his best to reflect their optimism, their excellent mood, but one of them was betraying him and he couldn't shake that turd off his shoe.

He found an empty table and sat down hoping to be left with his thoughts, an excited Jaxson was oblivious to Ian's mood.

"Did you see the morning paper?" He asked obviously excited, "it's all they're talking about."

"What?" Groggy would have been generous.

"Last night's appearance. Gabby. Jesse's song. The troop coming up on stage and sharing in the moment. It's never been done before. Usually, New York would tear something like that apart, but they're not. The mood is one of rejoicing in what took place last night. Well, except the Post, but fuck 'em, right?" He laughed. The man who had been camped on death's doorstep for the past week now had been miraculously healed.

Ian should feel the bliss. He didn't.

"What's the matter?" Jaxson asked, finally picking up the negative vibe, and it was battering his buzz.

Just then Vilhelm strolled up and sat down at their table. Jaxson glanced over at his friend and nodded, now he knew. Ian shook his head in a negative fashion before explaining Vilhelm's idea about the classical ensemble while people were coming in and being seated. Mr. Grahm warmed to the idea, though he could tell there was more, much more, that Ian had to say.

"I was wrong and I owe Mr. Wilhelm an apology for thinking what I thought, when what I thought was something I shouldn't have been thinking. I'm sorry Vilhelm." He bowed from the waist in his seated position.

"Nothing to be sorry about, I would have thought it was me as well. It's the outfit, isn't it? Everyone tells me I should tone it down, guess they're right." He reached over to shake Ian's hand, who was nodding in agreement wondering why they guy didn't tone it down a bit. Vilhelm turned his attention back to Jaxson. "What do you think of the musical intro to the show?"

"I like the idea and I think the fans would dig it as well," He grinned and then it hit him. "Could you excuse us for a few minutes?" He turned toward Ian as Vilhelm left the table with phone in hand setting up the quartet for this evening and looking for either Ben or Dugan to discuss logistics.

"It has to be someone else." Jaxson said in shocked, hushed tones, "Someone you trust, someone close, someone who might be able to fudge some numbers or I don't know what!" The horror of the realization came on full fury. Who could they trust? He would've said every single person on this crew up until a minute ago. Shit now he didn't know.

"That's the thing, isn't it? Between us we have known every single person on this crew for decades, that's the reason they were picked for this, because of the comfort factor. Now, I feel like I have to be looking over my shoulder every time I turn around. It's nuts," Ian was as bummed as Jaxson had ever seen him. You could steal money or time from this man but don't ever mess with trust. Ian's stock in trade was his name and reputation, now someone, and it had to be someone close, was dragging that through some very disgusting mud and muck.

"What about that Raj guy?" Jaxson knew he was pulling straws from a very large pile to find the short one, but the guy was the one wild card. He had come in late, up in Montana, and had hung around long.

"Too obvious. And if he wanted to fuck with the money or my name, he didn't have to come out here and work himself half to death to do it. He could've sat in a nice, air-conditioned office in L.A. and played with the numbers. No. Besides, Gabby trusts him, and Gabby might be a bit on the innocent side of people but I trust his instincts." Ian was shaken up and not sure he trusted his own instincts right now. He had always trusted his gut, but his gut was turned upside down and churning. "We got a show to put on, that is all I know. I'm just going to have to keep an eye on everyone and see if someone gives themselves away." He rubbed his face with both hands as if he could wash this away. "God, I hate not trusting people, especially people who I know I should be able to trust." Fucking circles!

Jake stood off to the side of the table, just enough he wouldn't seem to be eavesdropping but close enough to garner attention. Ian noticed. "Hey Jake, what's going on?" No matter how many times Ian asked someone that same question it always came out in Marvin Gaye's voice in his head, he smiled. It was just what he needed.

"I'm going to head over a little early to check the power and stage. I know they do this all the time and have had the best at The Beacon, but it's an old room and things happen in old rooms," he lifted a shoulder as if to say, 'you never know and I'd rather be on top of it.'

"Thanks, man," this was why Ian had selected these people. They were the best and they were loyal. Nope, if he was going to find the culprit he would have to look outside this box. He couldn't live with thinking one of these friends had betrayed him.

"I can't believe the change that has come over him, speaking of people, like Raj, changing. Maybe it's just getting here and off the actual road for a minute but that guy definitely has a lilt in his step these last few days. Always been the biggest sourpuss on the road. Damn good at what he does but a pain in the ass to try and be around. Now he's like little Mary sunshine." Jaxson shook his head as he grinned, "I'm not complaining, it's a beautiful resurrection of spirit. Just unexpected. I'm going to go change some strings and run through a few tunes in the room, haven't been playing much lately." He excused himself from the table.

Ian had to smile, the last thing Jaxson Grahm needed to do was practice and he had a guy who took care of the guitars, but old habits die very hard. It was like guys who ironed their own shirts before a show, it was the routine. Take that away and the show would suffer. Jaxson was right about one thing, Jake sure had changed his attitude and it was certainly welcome. It would appear this tour was having some impact not just on the fans who came to experience it, but also those who were giving of themselves.

To The bottom of The Well

Raj was bone weary tired. He had never done any physical labor in his life, he and his family had people for that. Untouchables, his shame colored his face and ran rampant through his body. He had been brought up to believe something that was a terrible fallacy. A deceit that had survived thousands of years, that not all humans were people, some were far lesser beings. Chattel, no, worse, below chattel. Worth less than a farm animal. Farm animals had worth; untouchables had none. You used them then threw them away. He thought he had moved well beyond those beliefs but what has been ingrained in the soul, buried deep in the loam of the heart would take many more generations to dig out. So, he worked his ass off with his Mayan friend to prove his worth. The worth of the lower castes.

He also had a responsibility to this troop of musicians, roadies, sound, and light technicians. To the artists who brought such magnificent talent to the aid of others. He could do no less than to give his strength, physical and mental, to their cause. Hence why he was sitting here after that brilliant performance just past the midpoint of their first week at this wonderful hall. He sighed and rubbed his left arm. He'd pulled something while moving one of the amplifiers during the show. Now he was backstage separating and counting the large piles of cash the audience had collected. Who knew a Thursday night concert could be packed and filled with such love, just as the first three nights had been, it amazed the small man.

He forced his eyes to focus though they only had thoughts of sleep, do the accounting first, then rest. The numbers balanced, the piles consistent with the generosity. His back was stiff and sore, bent over as he was, it was time to stand, stretch out tired muscles before putting it all in the heavy safe the club was allowing them to use. A quick walk around the backstage and some yoga should help ease the tightness. Then come back and wrap up the night and hop the last band bus to the hotel. It would only take a few minutes to loosen up.

He closed the door and touched his toes, straightening he quick stepped several laps behind the stage before several minutes of rudimentary yoga. Yes, that was just what the doctor had prescribed.

He failed to notice the dark figure stealthily moving from speaker to amp to the closed door. Nor did he notice the same figure slip into his 'counting' room. With just the glow from a cell phone the almost invisible figure took bills from each pile, not enough to be noticed without a careful counting but enough to be noticed when that counting came. Shoving them into his pocket he peered out the cracked door to be certain Raj would not notice his taking leave and he was gone.

Raj knew he was overly tired when he came back to the room and found the door not closed tightly. He must have been careless and not closed it completely. Damn, he would need to be more cautious in the future. He locked his numbers and the money in the safe before closing the door once more, this time making certain the door was, indeed, closed tight and locked. A tired mind makes foolish mistakes, his grandmother's voice reminded him. He ran to catch the last band bus.

The lobby had been awash in chaotic activity since the first of the gypsy caravan popped their little pumpkin heads down at the breakfast bar around nine-thirty this morning. By eleven it was a hive of activity with musicians, singers, road crew, technicians, buzzing here and there scarfing up every scrap of food available. The breakfast was supposed to shut down at ten, but Ian had convinced the staff earlier in the week to hold it until eleven for this late moving group. They were a large percentage of the total occupancy of the place so the hotel was happy to comply. They were getting used to the comings and goings of the troop.

Then, just as quickly, the troop cleaned up after themselves and were gone. It was as if they had never occupied the lobby. They ate, they bussed, they fled the confines and hopped on their transport or walked over to The Beacon for rehearsals of new tunes and arrangements. One thing Mr. Grahm and his associates wanted to do was to keep the show fresh. They would rearrange order, harmonies, songs, backgrounds with different artists and keep everyone, including themselves guessing who and what was happening next.

There was fresh buzz that a new guest spot was being put in place tonight. Though it would be hard to outdo Sir Peadar, Richie Stainesby, Josef and the gang over the last few nights. Everyone sang and backed up everyone else, the stage was full of the finest talent on the planet. But there was always room for one more, Ian grinned. He knew who, but he remained tight lipped. He would tell the band when he handed out sketchy scores, but not until.

The entire crew would be on hand every night for the rest of the week so all would know the ins and outs of linking up superstars with the regular suspects. The first couple nights had been with the known superstars, tonight would be different. Though it was the superstars that would provide the least hitches. They wanted to be part of this and they would take their egos and shove them into their back pockets for the opportunity to perform with such a brilliant group of artists. If you weren't excited to be part of this, you had no pulse.

A lone man came down the stairs from his room and approached the front desk. The clerk recognized him as one of the troop, she ought to after the last few days, obviously one who had slept in late. He was tired and distracted as he approached and nodded his hello. He wasn't the friendliest, but he wasn't an ass. She smiled and asked what he needed.

"I got a call from Ian that he needs some papers, union stuff, and his address and phone book out of his room," his attitude was one of a man being put to the test, being asked to perform a duty well below his station but like a good soldier he would do his duty. "I just need a key and I'll bring it right back down," he huffed.

She felt for the guy. As someone who was constantly asked to do menial chores that had nothing to do with her job she related to his predicament. They weren't supposed to give out keys to other rooms but she knew he was with the band, and she also knew she wasn't going to make him grovel for the damn thing.

Several minutes later he returned the key with his thanks and a handful of papers and a leather-bound phone book. All was well in the world. He grinned as he walked out the door and in the direction of the concert hall, whistling.

The buzz backstage was electric, everyone knew there would be a special guest tonight but they didn't know who. Though how whoever could be more special than their first few nights was hard to fathom, though they didn't have to be more special just different. Different special guests brought different energy and different energy brought a completely different show.

There wasn't a whole lot for the road crew to do except check the equipment, make sure everything was working properly. That all turned on and made noise! Raj excused himself to go finish the banking from this half-week. Usually when sitting in one place for a few days they would hold on to the cash until the end of the week, but people had been very generous and he wanted to get it into a more secured location, like an actual bank.

After several minutes the door to the office flew open and Raj appeared, like a man awakening from a nightmare. His hair was akimbo, his eyes showed the fire of panic glowing like a pumpkin on Halloween. The grimace on his face told the story of a man in intense pain and discomfort. Ben jumped up from where he had taken a few minutes refuge backstage to check on the little lawyer.

"What the hell is wrong?" His harsh whisper rasped against Raj's ear.

Raj whipped his head around and stared hard into Ben's eyes as if he didn't recognize him. Terror filled each breath, "Some of the money is missing." He searched Ben's face to see if he comprehended. Ben's shocked expression showed he understood completely.

"What the hell are you talking about? That can't have happened you locked it in there, right?" He grabbed Raj by the shoulders as if to steady him in a violent storm. "How much is missing?"

"It's not the amount that is staggering it is the distribution. I mean, there is a little more than a couple thousand dollars missing, but whoever took it, didn't take a pile of money and run. They were very careful to take bills from each pile, tens, twenties, fifties and hundreds so you wouldn't notice right away, only when it was counted again." Ben couldn't tell if Raj was flipping out because the money was gone or because someone, and it had to be someone connected with the tour or they wouldn't have known about the cash, stole money from the mission. The Untouchable Fund was, well, untouchable, sacred.

"We need to find Ian and Jaxson, now!" Ben called on the two-way radio and told Ian and Jaxson to meet them at the office.

When all had been explained Jaxson was shocked and disappointed, Ian seemed distracted as if unconcerned. "You guys look into this, I have to stay here and make sure we are set for tonight." And with that he was gone.

"What do you want us to do?" Ben looked to Jaxson for leadership.

"I'm not sure, but I know I don't want everyone running around accusing each other of theft. I certainly am not going to start searching rooms or people. No amount of money is worth that! We are not turning this tour into one of suspicion." Jaxson was despondent. "Just keep an eye out for anything weird or suspicious without acting like we're the fucking cops."

Ben radioed Dugan to fill him in on the state of affairs. A quick meeting between the two behind the monitor board and they established they would not enlist any others to act as undercover detectives, it would be up to the two of them. They didn't like sneaking around checking and spying on friends but there was no other recourse.

"Hey guys!" They almost came out of their skin as Jeanette snuck up behind and surprised them. "Planning a party or something?" She chortled at her little funny and then stopped. "OK, what's going on?"

Ben and Dugan's guilty expressions gave them away. They were not good undercover cops. They spilled the beans and their concerns. Jeanette went from perturbed to angry to pissed in three point two seconds. "Who would be so low?" She was disgusted. Here she thought she had found this island of misfit humans who actually believed and lived by their credo, only to find rot in the heart of paradise.

"We don't know, but it apparently falls on us to find out," Dugan was crestfallen. The last thing he wanted in this world was the duty of narcing out a friend for theft. Shit!

"This has something to do with the accusations against Ian. I can almost taste it. Why else would anyone be so cautious about the distribution of bills to conceal the theft until the money was counted again." She was good at her job, Ben and Dugan nodded appreciatively at her reasoning.

"Shit! That only makes it worse. Not only is someone taking the cash but doing so to frame Ian is despicable," Ben's disappointment was only diminished by his anger.

Raj had returned to the office to count the cash a few more times just in case the impossible had happened and he had miscounted. He hadn't. A figure in the shadows smiled before turning away.

As Paul Simon took the stage he nodded to the band, by now they were as ready as any band could be to play with a legend never having practiced with him. Ian stood to the side of the stage, the wings, and watched. He knew he should be concerned with the theft but he just couldn't. It was money, money that was needed to help others, but money. Replaceable, finite. What was happening on stage was irreplaceable, infinite and would continue to reverberate throughout the universe forever. That's how it felt. It was as if Paul's energy, the electrical impulses of his life flowed through the notes, the vibrations of the strings, the vibration of the sound. And the people could feel it as well.

They cheered until they were almost hoarse. This was his town. He had created some of his greatest works here in this vibrant city and now he was giving back to benefit not himself but others. People all over the planet would benefit from his largesse, not just financially but emotionally, spiritually, from the heart. And Paul was having fun, jumping from hits to ancient songs he had recorded in the late fifties.

And that's when the pain began. It started as a small ping in the center of Ian's chest, like a muscle cramp which grew into a crippling, twisting knife between several ribs. Not enough to kill just enough to torture. Why? The question burned into his mind. Why would someone hate him so much they would tear down this perfect musical odyssey of love and healing? For what? To get back at him for something he couldn't remember. How much had he harmed another human being that they had waited, who knew how many years, to destroy the one really great thing he had done in life? The pain threatened to explode from his chest. He couldn't breathe. No one noticed. He slipped down onto a folding chair. He closed his eyes and searched for one deep, calming, lifesaving breath. One breath to sustain him until someone noticed.

All eyes were focused on Paul Simon, on the choir of angels weaving their harmonies with his perfect music. The band was caught up in the sound, the songs, the love. The crowd of just over two thousand six hundred, with standing room sang along with their youth. Reliving adolescence, young love, marriage, children, growth, all of which Paul Simon had carefully scripted in lyric and melody for almost sixty years. They rode memory until it almost hurt.

If Ian had to die, this was it. There would be no last-minute miracle as he had accidently done so many times, there was no one close who could help him. His diet cola slipped from his fingers as he slipped from the chair. Laying prone on the side of the stage, in his wings where he belonged, he closed his eyes as the diet cola reached the reserve electrical snake two feet away. The electrical charge shot through the liquid and into Ian's body. He jumped once, twice before the cable shorted out. But it was enough. Sparks flew, though since nothing else was connected no one else lost power.

Ian saw a great blinding light as the shock shot through his body. He took a deep, life affirming breath as air filled his lungs and his heart skipped a beat, tried to revive, skipped, and sputtered a second time like a sixty-four Econoline trying to gulp down a spit of gasoline into a two-barrel carburetor. Before finally catching and igniting the engine. He hiccupped three times, felt his body jump, jolt and jerk and he knew he would live. He laughed, laughed as hard as he had ever laughed in his life.

When Maggie found him laying on the stage in a pool of his own urine and laughing, she thought maybe he had fallen off the wagon after all these years. Then she saw the diet cola, the burn mark on the floor and the condition of his body. She screamed for Ben to come now and call an ambulance.

"Really?" Fame tapped her toe in annoyance.

"What?" Goddesses can be anything they wish, even innocent.

"The diet cola and electric boogie? If he isn't going to be famous in life why not in death?" Fame's words were cold as her heart. She'd wanted this one and he had refused her. Let him die.

"Wasn't his time. I should know. This play isn't over yet, there is at least one more act and maybe a sequel." Fate gazed at her perfect fingernails and wiped her prints from the page in front of her.

"Well, you can have him, then, I have no use of him anymore," And Fame stomped off into the clouds.

Wrap It Up and Tie It With a Bow

When Ian awoke in the hospital, he was surrounded by wife, scrubbing and pulling at the short locks of dyed hair in worry and helplessness, a nurse and no friends. They were seated away from him out in the corridor. She would not let anyone near him except this head nurse. All others were to stay in their chairs and wait, quietly. His eyelids had to weigh at least five pounds each, he could barely lift them but her voice called to him and he had to answer. One did not ignore the call of Maggie. She wanted to know if he lived and if he did, she wanted to kill him.

Why hadn't he called out to someone on the stage when the pain began? Why hadn't he tried to get the attention of the monitor tech? Or the guitar tech? Or god, fer chrissakes? Instead, he had sat down and waited to die or so it appeared to her. He was NOT getting out of this marriage that easy. Dumb bastard!

She wept as his unfocused gaze found her eyes communicating, he lived. Ben ran down to give the good news to the full waiting room. Musicians, roadies, techs, stars, and superstars filled the horrible plastic chairs awaiting news. He would live. The party would move from the waiting room to the hotel and beyond. Drinks and pipes for everyone. Well, almost everyone.

Jaxson stayed behind at the hospital to keep Maggie company. There was nothing worse than being in the hospital with no idea why something went haywire, waiting for results from a hundred tests and being alone. Jaxson was a friend; he would keep her and Ian company.

Relief washed over the hotel lobby like a warm breeze after a frigid winter as the gypsy caravan returned. Ben and Dugan sat off to the side where they wouldn't be bosses keeping an eye on the proletariat, just a couple guys sitting and talking while the party ensued. Jake caught their attention as he sat off by himself apparently having found his dour mood once again.

"There has never been a more surly human being on the planet," Dugan said just loud enough Ben could hear him, as he gestured to where the morose Jake sat staring off into the blackness of the universe.

"I thought we'd turned a corner, finally, with that guy, but a rock can't change its perception without a quake big enough to move it," Ben thought he remembered something like that being said when he was a kid. "And that rock has been sitting in a mud hole since I've known him. If he wasn't so damn good at his job..." he let the thought trail off into the sunset. "It's just, well, his attitude had flipped over the last week or so since we got here. I thought maybe we'd turned a corner but I guess it was just a slight bend in the road." Ben shook his head.

"Actually, I thought he'd had an epiphany just before we got here." Dugan's thoughts were now considering order of occurrences as to the state of Jake's mood swings. Now Dugan was lost in reflection and timelines. There was something weird going on and he wanted to know what it might be. Shit, there was nothing but weird going on, weirder than normal. "Excuse me," he said to Ben as he got up, "I need to consult the great oracle Google for a bit. Meet me for dinner if you would. There's a great little joint around the corner from the Beacon where we can grab a bite right after sound check tomorrow. This may take a little digging." And he was gone.

Ben watched as his co-manager cut across the lobby to the elevators and, he assumed, his floor and room. Dugan had his teeth in something and Ben knew the man would not let go until he had found what he sought or discovered it was a mirage.

Meanwhile, back at the hospital.

"What happened?" Ian remembered feeling the pain, the weakness but most of the rest of the evening was lost to electrical shock, unconsciousness, and death. It was good to find one of those had not stuck.

"You might have had a heart attack, though the doctors seem to be leaning away from that possibility. Maybe stress, maybe an arrhythmia, maybe exhaustion. The thing to concentrate on now is getting your strength back." She hugged him close and for a long moment.

"How long was I out?" If memory served, and God knew it didn't, he was out for a few decades maybe a century as he wandered lost in the blackness of space.

"Nobody really knows and we don't know when it began. We were all caught up in Paul's performance. It was so perfect, no one could take their ears or eyes from the show. Except you, of course, you were busy having a seizure or something. We're hoping to have some word on all the tests pretty soon and that will give us some idea what went wrong in the old wiring," she pointed at his head and chest.

"Something came to me, right before it happened, a memory from a hundred years ago, but I can't get it back," frustration filled each word. "I think it's important, and its right there, right on the tip of my brain, but I can't get my fingernail on it."

"Relax, sleep, take some time out. Maybe it will come, if you stop concentrating so hard, think of something else. Paul and the two from the Mersea Beats have promised they will stick around for the show tomorrow night." She smiled just as the head of Mr. Grahm came through the doorway.

"Everything good?" Jaxson's grin filled the room.

"He's alive and breathing," Maggie reported.

"Good, I wanted to see for myself so I can go get some rest. It's been a long night for all and we still have shows to do. I'm guessing you have been informed that Paul, Pete, and Richie will be sticking around as they had so much fun last night and there's a rumor," here he smiled so Ian wasn't sure if it was a rumor Jaxson had ignited or one born of truth, "Bruce might pop in for a few tunes this week as well."

"Then I have to get well in a hurry. Any movement on the other front?" For any and all health concerns Ian might have, his concern for his reputation far outweighed all. He had never had great gobs of financial success, oh, he'd been comfortable, and, until his affliction kicked in, he had never had fame and was quite happy to have avoided it. So, all he had was his name, his standing in the musical and entertainment community. He hoped between Jeanette, Raj, and the others, they could figure out who was behind trying to destroy what he'd built over a lifetime.

"Nothing yet," Jaxson shook his head. He wanted to report good news but he was no Sherlock Holmes. Like Ian he was relying on the investigative skills of the newspaper reporter, the inquiring minds of the road managers and luck. Mostly luck. "I know they are still digging and if anyone can find anything it is that woman!" Jaxson was a true believer. "If you need anything I am only a phone call away," Jaxson told Maggie to reassure, "They should have results in the morning or early afternoon, I'll be back here when that happens. Try to get some rest."

As Jaxson arrived back at the hotel the party had subsided and most had trundled off to bed. There were still a few hangers on in the lobby but it was mostly crew. Artists needed their sleep. He stopped by the front desk to let them know that Ian would be back in a few days and the hotel clerk pointed to the squat woman sitting quietly in the overstuffed chair by the elevators.

"She's been waiting for a few hours for either you or Mr. Sperling." He nodded his thanks.

"Marie!" Jaxson was truly happy to see the great granddaughter of Marie Laveau sitting patiently with her needlepoint. "What brings you to New York?" Either she had wonderful news for Ian or him or devastation, that was the way it went with voodoo. You didn't come all the way across the country just to say hello and remind your clients to stay away from herbs that caused rashes.

"How is Mr. Sperling?" she cut to the chase.

"Well, we had a bit of a scare tonight but it seems he will be alright," Jaxson answered cautiously. The woman had something on her mind, he wanted to know what that might be.

"I got here as quickly as I could, but air travel is a nightmare." She closed her eyes and collected her thoughts, "His health might be improving but I have received word from my sources that there is some malevolent spirit or delusional soul that means him harm. I am not certain what shape, human or other manifestation it might take, but something means him ill. I thought I should come personally to check." She nodded as if agreeing with her own wisdom. "I hoped I was not too late."

"To be honest," Jaxson took a quick glance to his left, right and behind, "there is someone, though we don't know who, that is making life difficult for Ian." And he told her about the roach, the cancellations, the accusations of theft and the missing money.

"I may be just in time. Is there someone close who Ian may have done wrong at some point in their life or who perceives he might have?" She thought it best to seek the obvious first. That was the problem with fate, it was the future she affected but she could see little of the past.

"Not that we can find. No one from his far past works for us or with us, and everyone here has known him for decades and loves him. He has helped most everyone out. Hell, he even saved a couple of their lives in the last few months, what more could someone want?" He sat down in the chair opposite her. He wanted nothing more than to go lay on a nice hard bed and close his eyes, but Marie thought this important, and Ian was his friend.

"Hmmm, how many has he saved? And who?" she was holding the end of a very fine thread and wanted to see if it would lead anywhere.

"With Ian, who knows? I mean it seems to be just an everyday occurrence to him anymore. Even the crew and security ignores it when these miraculous accidents happen. You don't think someone is pissed because he saved their lives, do you?" The whole idea was ludicrous. Someone pissed because you saved them?

"You never know with people. There are some here who have a fog around their past that I cannot break through. It is very strange." There was more she was not saying and Jaxson couldn't pry for fear of upsetting the voodoo. "We have to find a way to dig deep into the past of those who hide the past for any connection to Mr. Sperling, maybe from as far back as childhood." And she realized she would need the humans and their contraptions to do the digging. Gods and Goddesses could do great things but computers could dig into the deepest, shrouded pasts of any human life. It would require her using her influence on humans to go beyond what they thought themselves capable.

"You think someone could be holding some kind of blood grudge since childhood?" Jaxson was incredulous.

"The human soul can suffer torment for decades waiting for retribution," she considered something he could not imagine.

Jeanette's eyes had slowly drooped until bottom eyelid met top eyelid in the middle and they both surrendered. Sleep, sweet, sweet, RING. The phone next to the bed's shrill call to action caused her to sit straight up in bed. Her first reaction was to take said phone, throw it across the room, and smash it against the wall. She was dog-tired and drained from searching through files and records fifty years old. There had to be something in Ian's past that would cause another human being to cling to a moment, a hatred so acute, they could not let go. She had discovered nothing.

She answered the phone, why not she was awake anyway.

"Jeanette," she heard Dugan's insistent invocation of her name. "Did I wake you?"

"No, I was up knitting doilies for my great aunt Velma," sarcasm was usually a strong suit in her family but fatigue had dulled the edge.

"Why would you be up knitting doilies at this time of night?" either that or Dugan was not the freshest apple in the drawer at this hour.

"Nevermind." Sheesh, "What do you need?"

"Another pair of eyes and a working brain," he sounded as exhausted as she felt.

"Do I come to you or are you heading this way with whatever you are playing with?" She got out of bed to slip into PJs and a robe, either way she required covering.

The soft knock on her door announced the arrival of Mr. Dugan. She opened the door and he slid in with a laptop and a ream of paper spilling out from under his arm.

"I don't know what I've found, if anything, but I need another set of eyes and thoughts to see. I was going to wake up Ben but thought he needed his sleep," he said without thinking and she reacted without him noticing. Yeah, don't wake up Ben but Jeanette, sure, she isn't doing anything but sleeping.

Jeanette, against every fiber of her being said nothing. She sighed and then, "What have you found or not found?"

He opened his laptop, sarcasm still missing its mark, and showed her a tree he had created with each name of every person associated with the tour and how they related to Ian. None went back further than a branch of a few decades, the trunk remained unsullied.

"So, none of these people have interacted with Ian until, what's that, thirty years ago. But this grudge, this vendetta goes back further, or would seem to. Someone has carried hate a long way and it hasn't worn off the rough edges." She sighed again, "But we know that, why have you disturbed what should be a lovely night's sleep?"

"The broken line! The broken line!" he shouted pointing to one name that hung on thin air. There was no connection to the tree, yet there was a distinct possible dotted line that could connect if you looked at it a certain way to another name attached to the tree trunk. It was a name neither recognized.

"But he has no connection to anyone on the tour!" She wanted to shout!

That was when the second soft knock came on her door. Now, who the fuck could that be? Though she didn't voice the question. Instead, she cracked the door to find Ben in his shorts and a T, bleary eyed, leaning against the doorframe.

"What are you two doing up in the middle of the night? And why are you making so much noise?" She pulled him into the room.

Dugan sat him down and showed him what he had found. "Nothing!" Ben wanted to shriek, but there was not nothing there was something. You just needed to connect the dots.

Jeanette could see the pattern but they needed more than a pattern. They needed facts. "There is something very odd here," she said, gazing from Dugan to Ben and back, "and we are going to need some help putting this puzzle together."

"What do you have in mind?" Ben asked.

"We need deeper investigative research than we can do ourselves. We need a cop with access to criminal records or hidden files." She sat on the edge of the bed, thinking.

"And I suppose you just happened to have a cop who would do that? Like in a movie? He will just step up and solve the mystery?" The quick bark of a laugh showed what Dugan thought of that idea.

"Well, she," and she emphasized the word, "actually is a good friend, we went to college together, just like in a movie, and I think she'd be willing to do some digging." She shot a grin back at him. "Give me this stuff and let's find out. You guys go to work on your end and I'll go to work on mine!"

Morning came far earlier than Ian was used to. Morning in the music biz came just before noon, morning in a hospital came with the first glint of sunlight peeking over the eastern horizon. Testing began as they cleared the bowls of Jell-O and oatmeal, the breakfast of champines! Heart, lungs, brain scans, EKGs, MRIs, stress, and ultrasounds. Pins and needles and blood work, lunch, and more testing. All for naught. No heart damage, lung abnormalities, brain function as normal as Ian would ever get. Must have been the stress of the road and the accusations. The missing funds and worry.

He should spend another night in the ward but that was not going to happen. He had a show to put on. Though the others were capable. If they didn't want him to have another episode, they had best let him out and in the wings. They'd bring him a comfy chair.

Paul and the two remaining members of the Mersea Beats would be there, The Disidentes were coming in for a few tunes, Josef, James, and Jaxson, The choir of greatest singers ever assembled with Joya as part of and solo. Ian had missed most of Paul Simon's performance the night before, he would not be absent tonight. It was Friday and the buzz of excitement was beyond electric. The weekend promised to blow the doors off anything anyone had ever witnessed in New York, and that was saying something.

Shit! David Grisman was in town doing a solo club gig, across town were Jerry Douglas, Sam Bush, and Bela Fleck. New York was bursting at the seams musically. But The Beacon was where everyone wanted to be. Ian would put his worries in an old kit bag for the evening. Though he really didn't know what a kit bag was, old or new, it didn't matter. They would walk over to the venue just to show his commitment to a healthier lifestyle.

There was a niggling at the base of Ian's skull as they walked over to the show. Something had triggered the massive stress response, but what? Paul Simon was singing one of his oldest songs, a regional hit, 'Hey, Schoolgirl'. He'd been having a bit of fun with the band and backup singers and threw that one into the mix. It was the last thing Ian remembered from the evening.

Which was odd, it was a song he barely remembered from his youth. It was a song so far down memory lane Ian couldn't have found the path if it was marked in iridescent pink and orange ribbons. But there it was. The question remained, why? And why would it have such a profound effect on his psyche sixty years on? He'd probably never know and for now he pushed it to the base of his brain stem. He was in too good a mood to worry. Tonight, was for celebration of life, music, lifting human souls and knowledge.

A padded chair had been set at the exact spot Ian usually stood listening to his friends wow the multitudes. A trap case set on its side served as a small table with a diet cola and some healthy snacks, vegies and cheese. It was his oasis to enjoy the show in comfort.

Sir Peadar stood at the back of the stage and gazed admiringly at the set-up. Richie stood next to him making crude remarks on aging, senility, and the frailty of the human form. Pete found his remarks humorous on a different level than Mr. Stainesby may have meant them, as Richie was at least a decade older than the patient.

As the string ensemble wrapped up a Mozart string quartet in G minor people applauded with enthusiasm. Yes, this had been a wonderful addition to the show. Now, it was Showtime! Joya had offered to open the show, warm up the audience, as she was the youngest member of the troop and the one with the least credits at this point. Bonnie Welch interceded saying she would do the job, followed by the other singers jumping in to demand equal time. So, the 'Choir' came out onto the barren stage, devoid of band or accompaniment. They, Bonnie, Lucinda, Michele, Joya, Gillian, and now, Brandi, stood around a single mic without introduction. Joya began to sing a Capello a song she had written in the afternoon.

She didn't know where it had come from, but she had feverishly written it down, though quite certain she would remember it in its entirety. As she sang it the others could feel the pulse, the pulse of the lyric, the beat in their hearts. They felt the audience pick up on the fact it was brand new and when Joy came to the chorus she pointed up and they all just knew. *'Look Up'* they sang in unison to the thrill of the packed house. It was the perfect introduction to the show. Bass, guitar, percussion, and keys slowly made their way out onto the stage to accompany the round robin of artists and their songs. Each singer choosing from a lifetime of music and the others adding their voices.

Ian stood for about twenty minutes before Maggie pushed him down in his chair, seeming to indicate, 'they brought this out for you, now use it'.

Jesse joined the 'Choir' with renditions of songs he hadn't performed with full band and backing for more than forty years. The crowd lost their minds as they returned to a youth long forgotten. A thing of beauty.

James Nash stuck his head out from the left side of the wings and joined Jaxson for several songs, before Jaxson was joined by Gabby and their new rendition of *'The Cannons of Peace'*. Now the audience knew what was to follow and they sang with hearts on full until Gabby began to speak. A hush wrapped in quiet background music filled the hall. His voice quiet yet strong, his words plucked from the vines of truth and laid before the masses. He had said the words so many times he knew them by rote. The audience had seen them a thousand times on phone video, on YouTube, and Facebook, some mouthed the words as Gabby spoke. A connection as solid as steel ran from person to person, wrapped in each other's arms they swayed with the rhythm of words spoken from the soul.

Ian sat mesmerized by the whole scene. Maggie stood behind him, hands on his shoulders. Gabby no longer needed her reassurance, though his furtive glances in her direction showed he still relied on her steadfast presence. People passed the hat and a bucket along with a joint accompanying, to loosen pockets.

Josef walked on stage to share a tight set of eight tunes at two and half to three minutes each and the handoff was made to Paul Simon who introduced, though unnecessarily, Pete and Richie. They took over the stage backed by the brilliance of the Untouchable Band. It was good Ian was sitting or he would've fallen over. Paul Simon started jibing back and forth with Sir Peadar and the next thing you knew they were trading sixty-year-old love songs. Big hits and small, they laughed as they re-membered a verse here and a chorus there until Mr. Simon began *'Hey Schoolgirl'* to the delight of the elderly in the audience.

And, to the consternation of Ian's subconscious. What was it about a barely remembered song that ignited such passion in the mind of the sixty some year-old Ian? It brought back a memory, the one memory he thought eradicated from his conscience until a week back. He felt the fury building from down in his groin. The kid had kicked him hard in the balls and the pain was intense. The other kids were laughing and pointing, mocking him, and the big kid was circling. Ian felt helpless as he was outnumbered, outmuscled, and about to take a beating he hadn't done anything to deserve. His temper rose, the injustice of this stupidity stoked a fire in his soul, the pressure in his head was about to give way. He couldn't see or hear the other kids anymore, just red and silence.

That was when he tackled the bully and started pounding him mercilessly. His little eight-year-old fists punching and punching, as if of their own volition. The kid screaming for him to stop. The other kids screaming for him to stop. Finally, they pulled him off and he lay on his back panting. His rage spent. He was empty. He could feel nothing. He wept and swore no one would ever push him to that limit ever again. It was the last time he ever struck another human being.

As he returned to the present he couldn't move. He was seated in the chair, but he couldn't move his arms or legs. He opened his eyes and saw Maggie sitting on top of him, her arms encompassing him. Ben held his thrashing legs and Dugan hugged him from behind. He'd had another episode. Luckily with the volume of the band and the intensity of the performance no one else seemed to have noticed. He went limp. Gazing into Maggie's eyes he nodded that he was alright, maybe more alright than he had been in decades.

He thanked the three who had come to his rescue with a promise to explain back at the hotel. Concern filled the visages of his wife and friends, more concern than was warranted by this fit. Their concern suggested he was not the only one with truths to expose.

The buses pulled up late in front of the hotel and the weary but elated performers schlepped into the lobby. All had come back to the hotel for a nightcap and to decompress. The stars mingled with the roadies who mingled with the merch folks who were just happy to be included. They had two more shows this week. The Saturday show and an early show Sunday. Ian had told them there would be some switch ups, as far as guest sets were concerned. They would not be better, just different.

James Nash was sticking around for a few more nights, Paul Simon had to get back to preparing for his own tour, though thought he might stick his head in for one. Sir Peadar and Sir Richie would hang around as long as they could. Josef had business in NY so he wanted to cling to the fun, as well. That was the attraction, getting to play and hang with people you never got to play and all for a good cause. Fun! This was the best of all worlds and the reason most of them had started to play music in the first place. Well, that and a way to meet girls!

Ian was surrounded by friends, family, people he respected above all else. He was in his glory. Raj was the last person to make it to the gathering in the lobby and he did not look happy at all. He had noticeably come down the elevator, he must have beaten them back to the hotel. He was accompanied by two police officers and someone who central casting had picked to portray the detective. All of them bore the weight of the world on their shoulders. They bore some errand that was distasteful but had to be carried out.

Just as they approached Ian, Jaxson, and Maggie, Jeanette walked through the door streetside with two more police officers and a nattily dressed Asian woman. They did not appear in any better humor. The police all greeted each other before the detective turned to Ian.

Raj looked like he was about to come out of his skin. If he could've transported himself anywhere but here, he would've, but he was stuck in the middle of this and he would see whatever it was through to the end.

"Mr. Sperling?" The detective looking guy tried to sound official but came across as reading his lines. "It would appear there are some discrepancies in your accounting. Thousands have gone missing from cash collected under the pretense it would go to a nonprofit, tax exempt fund but it would seem," and here he took in the assembled of which he recognized at least half, they were famous, after all, and swallowed hard. "the exact number of which has been found nestled away in your hotel room." The murmur and shouts of liar filled the lobby.

Ian turned to shush those behind him. He loved their support, but he didn't need it right now.

"Raj?" Ian said softly so the man could speak without recourse.

"What he says is exactly true. The money is missing, the exact sum was found squirreled away in your room, including bills I had personally marked after some cash had gone missing initially." He nodded to Ian in apology.

Ian thought he heard a familiar muffled bark of a laugh from out near the front of the lobby. The jingle of handcuffs filled the accompanying silence.

"Surely, there is some other explanation," Ian plead. He scanned the throng of faces hoping for someone to see he was telling the truth, but the police, Raj, and evidence pointed another direction. The snap of wrist cuffs seemed to end the discussion.

"Excuse me," the nattily dressed woman said to the detective, who backed down to the apparent superior officer. "You may take Mr. Sperling in just a few minutes, but a moment if you don't mind waiting. I just want to clear up a few loose ends here." She walked over to the front desk where a lone clerk stood, eyes quivering and darting side to side as if seeking an avenue of escape. "May I ask you a few questions?" The Captain, Ian finally noticed the badge, asked sweetly.

"Yes, ma'am," the clerk, head down and contrite.

"Has anyone had access to Mr. Sperling's room over the last week?" She faced the clerk, back to her audience.

"Ma'am?" the clerk dodged.

"Did anyone ask for and receive a key or to be let into Mr. Sperling's room over the past week." Now everyone leaned in to hear the answer.

The squeak of the lobby door brought their attention around to where the flamboyant Coke dealer/eightiesescapee/classical record rep squeezed himself into the lobby. This looked interesting, he thought, I believe I have walked into the big reveal. He wished he'd listened to his inner child and stopped for popcorn.

As everyone settled back into rapt attention the captain repeated the question, "Did anyone ask for and receive access to Mr. Sperling's room? And I would mention we have CCTV digital recordings."

The clerk's eye's searched everywhere except the captain's face. She was seeking salvation but finding no redemption only blank stares. Could someone, anyone, save her, save her job, her career, her, "I have two kids and my husband is out of work, I can't afford to lose this job. He said Mr. Sperling told him he forgot something in his room and he was to bring it. I knew he was with these folks; I'd seen him every day, he was one of them. And a troop's a troop, right? They're all the same, they work together, friends, they wouldn't do something to harm one or the other, would they?" The words spilled from her lips in rapid succession.

She didn't have to say who, the scuffle near the door told everyone who the who was. He was being constrained between Dugan, Ben, and, Ian was pleasantly surprised to note, Al from Lakewood—who was holding up his cell phone and smiling at Ian indicating they had used his phone to tie this together—they had been informed ahead of time and were ready. Sometimes the trail leads true. The nice policemen that had entered with their natty captain were happy to take over for the road managers.

"I don't understand, it was Jake?" Ian asked. "Jake? Why?"

"Simple," Jeanette said as she opened her laptop and powered it up and held it so Ian could see. "Jake isn't Jake. He changed his name when he got out of Juvey hall. He served three years for whacking some kid with a baseball bat. Cold cocked him. Came out of the blue, kid never saw it coming. They say the kid was never the same, like something got rattled in his brain, maybe a short circuit. What do you think?" She grinned at Ian; realization slipping across his features.

"It's what I came to warn you about, though I must admit it was not exactly what I'd thought." Marie said out of the side of her mouth to Jaxson." But I had a feeling, a feeling deep inside," Marie appeared serious but Richie's reaction spoke another sentiment as he mouthed, 'oh yeah'.

"Are you talking about me?" Ian was still confused, sometimes it takes a few turns of the globe to get the light to shine. "I mean, I know I did something horrible when I was just a kid, but you would think I would remember being whacked with a baseball bat. As I assume you are referring to me." He stared from face to face. The entire troop was aghast in the lobby. No one had ever heard even a rumor of Ian being harmed as a kid. And some had known him since he was in his late teens and on the radio. He was the child prodigy of the new format. He could feel if a song was going to be huge. He knew music better than anyone alive.

"You're saying Jake is Doug who I beat up in elementary school," his shamed expression taking in his friends and fellow peaceniks. They just couldn't imagine Ian being violent and neither could he, but he knew, he remembered. It was the most shameful event in his life. But whacked with a baseball bat? That would stick in a man's mind.

"It's true," came a familiar voice and face walking towards him from the streetside door.

"Michael?" It was his older brother, older by three years, his big brother, his protector when Ian would refuse to fight back.

"Well, I figured you were just too busy to come visit family so I came to visit you. A week in NY and not a call, a note, a text for a favored older brother. And it looks like my timing couldn't be better," he hugged his little brother and his wife. "This is weird, I just came by to say hello, not reveal ancient family secrets and save your skin, especially in front of this audience. But, if we're going to play 'This Is Your Life, Ian Sperling', then let me get the party started.

"First off, I'm sorry. I should've been there when this guy took a swing at your pumpkin. I was trying to get this pretty girl to go out with me, I should have been there." Remorse fifty some years in the past was fresh again. "You were knocked out and taken to the hospital. To be honest we didn't think you would live. Mom sat by your bed every single day and dad slept in a chair next to you each night. I brought food and stuff from home and gave them breaks. I even brought in the portable record player so Dad could play music for you. If you were going to die, you would die with family," a tear saved for almost sixty years trailed down his cheek. "But you were pigheaded and refused to quit. When you regained consciousness three months later you didn't remember a thing. Just the music. Dad and I would bring in every record we could find, every new release, every single, and album from every corner of the country. And we played them for you. When the staff complained about the noise we brought in headphones. You were a radio receiver for every piece of music we could buy, borrow or steal. We thought it might stimulate your brain. And I guess it did."

He shrugged as realization continued its trek across Ian's features. "I guess it all seeped into that damaged head of yours. I don't know, I do know that when you came out of the coma you knew production, lyrics, arraignments, what makes a song seep into a soul and what balanced with what else." He grabbed Ian by the shoulder, "Maybe we made you a genius by accident." He laughed.

"Mom thought we should tell you about almost dying and the recovery but since you didn't remember a single thing about it, Dad thought it best to let sleeping memories lie," Michael gave the impression he was somewhere in the middle. Too late now.

"God, there is just so much to sort out. Three fucking months? I don't know if I want to remember that or the whacking. And what do we do with Jake?" He knew now it wasn't Jake, it was Doug, but he'd known him too long as the one to change to the other. He pointed where Jake sat, now almost comatose, between the two police officers.

His eyes vacant, his features slack, staring at the ceiling, insensate, he'd snapped.

"We'll take him down to the station book him for theft, blackmail, whatever we can think up," said the nice nattily dressed captain.

"Do you have to?" Ian couldn't believe the words came out of his mouth. This man had tried to kill him when they were teens, then tried to frame him for drugs at the border, cancel several shows, and then tried to frame him again for theft. He should want his head on a platter. But he felt sorry for him. Jake/Doug had carried this feeling of victimhood for sixty years. What had that done to his soul? Shouldn't they try and help the guy? "It doesn't seem right to leave him hanging out in the wind like this. We are supposed to be on this quest to help others, to see to those left behind, to lift the forgotten and the untouchables and now, because of money we're just going to fry Jake?"

"Speaking of which, didn't you save his ass when he was being fried?" Ben wanted to get a few cents of reality in here, "Don't you think saving the man's life should be payback enough? Why in the hell would he turn on you like this?"

"Guilt," said Marie Laveau the fourth. "When Ian saved him, it was the worst thing he could imagine. He'd tried to kill Ian when they were kids, ruin him as an adult, yet here comes the 'good, decent guy' and saves him instead. That had to play havoc with his equilibrium. He had to take Ian out so he wouldn't have to be reminded."

"I vote we adopt him and take care of him. Get him some mental health care and see if he can't turn around the rest of the years he has," Maggie was all in. Ian hugged her.

"We still have to account for all this mess," said the detective.

"Well, it would seem all the cash has been recovered, yes?" Ian glanced over to Raj to be certain, who shrugged and nodded in the affirmative. "If we can keep Jake/Doug's name out of the papers that would give him a clean record to begin his healing. Jeanette, can we cleanse some of this as a misunderstanding?" Ian was grabbing for short straws and favors from new friends. "And if no one is going to press charges..." Ian shrugged, his eyes pleading his case to the Captain.

"If cash is still missing, we'll chip in to balance the books," leave it to Sir Peadar and Sir Richie to step up.

"That won't be necessary," Raj reassured.

"Then let some healing begin, both for him and me." Ian was so tired; he hadn't slept a wink in days.

Everyone agreed it was the best solution to a horrible situation. This would be their mojo for Saturday. This was what the tour was supposed to be about, helping others. You cannot be magnanimous to some but bring the hammer for others. Especially someone who had suffered for so long due to a short in the wiring.

Saturday night felt as though there had been a cleansing. The air was crisp and clean, a sweetness permeated the hall, serenity, and perfection. Al confessed to Ian he couldn't stay away after what he'd witnessed in his ballpark. Ian beamed as he handed Al an All-Access Laminate. Showtime!

After the string quartet allowed their final note to ring out, and they stole from the stage, a rhythm from the soul of Africa began soft and steady. The lights flickered and a woman dressed in formal Daishiki slowly, in time to the drums danced her way to the center of the stage. A dozen singers and dancers in African regalia pounded their feet on the wood stage creating organic music. Brenda Fassie's voice filled the auditorium without the help of amplification, supported by the singer's droning chants and stomping. They were in the depths of the jungle as she sang a healing song. A healing for all here and her home as well. She had come to participate and represent her people.

Bruce had shown up and stood next to Maggie. Pete and Richie danced with Joya, Bonnie, Michele, Gillian, and Cinda. Jaxson and James grinned in bliss filled wonder. Gabby stood off to the side next to a small brown man. Yeah, it looked like the ending of a syrupy, Hallmark made for TV movie, but sometimes life imitates shitty art.

Ian came running from the back of the theater, late, up the right-hand aisle. His coat was ripped, there was a tear in the back of his pants and he was hell-bent-for-leather. Two of the roadies picked him up under his arms as he closed on the stage and set him on his side of that stage.

Maggie looked him over and reluctantly asked, "What?"

"There were a couple kids and a kitten, two big dogs came at them just as I was..." she stopped listening to him and turned towards the music on stage.

Ian glanced over at Bruce who had a quizzical look on his face. Ian shrugged, waved off any explanation and turned his attention to the stage as well.

Somewhere in the mist covered heights of the tallest mountain on Earth, as Fate would have it, Fame sat staring into the pool of life, watching several young people of moderate talent who wanted more than anything to be famous singing her praises. She covered her ears, moderate was generous. They stopped and prayed to her, she smiled. Sometimes you just had to work with what you were given. Besides, humans had invented Auto-tune.

Ben Friedman and Kevin Dugan sat just off-stage where they could observe all that was happening while going over the logistics for the southern swing of this tour with an atlas and laptop. The work and planning for some is continual.

Author's Bio

∞

Mr. Zonneville has spent the last forty-five years as a professional comedian, singer, songwriter and has written eight books previous, five novels, American Stories, Carey Come To Me Smiling, Great Things, A Novel, To Dance Among The Stars, and To Sail The Barren Sea; a biography of his father, Z; a rock and roll meoir of David Spero, A Life in The Wings, and a children's book about one of their rescue dogs, Greta. Harper's is in the works. He has performed throughout the United States, Canada, Ireland, and Holland. He loves his two adult daughters, to travel, write, read, and be married to his most beloved.

www.ingramcontent.com/pod-product-compliance
Lightning Source LLC
Chambersburg PA
CBHW060602310726
48982CB00008B/1208/J
* 9 7 8 1 7 3 4 4 3 3 2 7 2 *